CELLAR DOOR

Words of Beauty, Tales of Terror
Volume One

READ ORDER

28 → 62

71	107	145	241
111	234 (7)	157	204
125	76	178	219
130	116	280 (12)	85
199 (5)	169		255
65	271 (9)		
	135		
	189 (10)		

90000
NEW

CELLAR DOOR

Words of Beauty, Tales of Terror
Volume One

Edited by Shawna L. Bernard

Copyright James Ward Kirk Publishing 2013
Web: jwkfiction.com
Twitter: @jwkirk
Facebook: James-Ward-Kirk-Fiction

Cellar Door on Facebook:
https://www.facebook.com/beautifulWORDSterribleTALES

Cover art by Tais Teng
Editing, cover concept, and design by Shawna L. Bernard
Book design and composition by Shawna L. Bernard
Illustrations & Vector Art courtesy of Shutterstock (Tribal Raven Tattoo Stock Vector © Kaetana), clker.com, 123rf.com, clipartpal.com, wallgc.com, and clipart.ws (Tattoo Spider)

ISBN-13: 978-0615874975 (James Ward Kirk Publishing)
ISBN-10: 0615874975

All rights reserved. No part of this book may be reproduced in any form or by any electronic or mechanical means, including information storage and retrieval systems, without written permission from the publisher or author, except in the case of a reviewer, who may quote brief passages embodied in critical articles or in a review.

"Look at how a single candle can both defy

and define the darkness."

— Anne Frank

This book is dedicated to you, the reader; and the love of literature, language, and all the things that led you here...

CONTENTS

PART I: POETRY

PART II: FLASH FICTION

PART III: SHORT STORIES

PART IV: ARTWORK & PHOTOGRAPHY

Introduction

It is rare for the ears of many to hear a single sound all at once. Most often, we hearken to a tune for which we alone may be listening.

You will find, however, that this anthology is a collective murmur. Voices from all over the world have come together to sing in unison through artwork, poetry, and fiction in a vast array of creative displays.

Once you lift the cover of this book, you are opening the cellar door wide enough to cast a sliver of light upon the imaginations of visionary minds from every corner of a once-darkened, quiet room.

Listen for the beauty of the language. In it, you will find the loneliness and longing of characters; the haunting sounds of anguish echoing against walls; love, loss, and things to be afraid of all in one place; a doorway to a universe you never knew existed.

Using the common thread of what linguists call the most beautiful sounding phrase in the English language, we bring you a tapestry of work woven to ensure you all discover something that will move you. Sweep away the cobwebs and blow off the dust with each new tale within these pages...

...and find what's behind your cellar door.

Shawna L. Bernard
August, 2013

PART I: POETRY

Hide and Seek

By Stephanie M. Wytovich

There's a cellar door in my head—
an empty room filled with cobwebs
and lost souls—one that I try to visit
when I climb into bed at night,
scare myself to sleep.

A montage of pictures flash behind
sleepy eyes as old faces and forgotten places—
dog-eared memories, yellowed and frayed—
crawl out of the darkness and into the dusty
musk that floods my head.

I see behind the closed doors,
collect monsters and nightmares
in mason jars, and when the cold
embraces me—wraps me in its secrets—
I smile at the whispers from the voices
that can't stay buried, laugh in the dark
at the handprints on the walls,
and when I follow the footsteps…
I hear them behind me.

They live in the forgotten, the grey area
where baptism fails, where they thrive
in the impossible—floating on broken
legs with cut heels, their necks snapped
and limp on their shoulders—and when I open that
cellar door in my head, the bad dreams
become real, the things that lurk underneath
wooden floorboards surface,
and madness comes out to play for one more
round of Hide and Seek.

Lullaby
By Simon Critchell

Each night I lay here, wondering,
truly, terrifyingly pondering,
about the awful noises
that are coming from below.

The banging and the scratching,
the muffled moans and knocking;
the source of which I'm surely
altogether dread to know.

Is a monster down there, hiding?
Waiting, in its time, abiding?
Preparing to grab and steal me
from the safety of my bed?

As it lurks beneath my feet,
I'm vexed by what fate I will meet,
and all the ways in which
my awful death might lie ahead.

Behind the dreadful cellar door,
a nightmare dwells; of that I'm sure.
To sleep is near impossible,
knowing evil lies in wait.

And on this night, another sound,
a desperate plea from underground:
"Will someone please come save me?
Come and save me from this crate!"

As she begs, I get cold chills—
a frightening reality builds;
a much worse beast becomes the source
of all my nightly dread...

Tonight the monster proves to be
the man who reads and sings to me
Before cradling and tucking me
into the safety of my bed.

Penumbra by John Stanton

(Caged) Floral Motif (Madness)
By David S. Pointer

Imaginary monsters wearing
twin cellar-door-snowshoes
atop white evermore underbelly
searching for decorative iron
ankle bracelets for guest rooms
with hard dirt headboard fights
usually appreciated decades out
by architectural salvage buccaneers
unaccustomed to old wholesome
house arrest, or reupholstered
wall mounted alumni association
of the post-modern happy family

Olive Branch
By Theresa Newbill

Behind the cellar door,
the sounds of an electric
train haunt the house;
clicking and clacking
as if wheels still rolled
on the tracks.

A toy train flickers
in the shadows with golden
blinking lights and whistle
blaring, passing through
a tunnel on its way to
hell.

On the wall, a gentle
curvature, like the wings
of a bird, embellish it
with reckoning time; an
olive branch bearing fruit,
not to be trusted.

By the entrance, a noble
woman from an ancient
family knots together
her noose; a residual effect
from where she hung
suspended.

The cellar door itself
holds antiquity, and is
another channel where
purple blood flows, cleaved
open in the chasm of an
orchid.

Its peeling paint is a
gentle reminder of many
years gone by, where hope,
routine and mechanization
have burned off just a little
of its energy.

There is a lesson in the fine
art of its ripples, way beneath
the scratching, thumping and
awful cries, heavy with the
sounds of giggling and
expectant breathing.

Harbinger by Beth Murphy

Last Lament

By Matthew Wilson

Darling Mother, have no fear,
I know Father's bones lie near.
He hurt you, so you hurt him,
I know this since the walls are thin.

Hear him shuffling up the stair?
A dead man in a cellar's snare?
With just a need to take a life;
to climb the stairs and find his wife.

Groaning, slipping, he does walk
further up with garbled talk.
The rats have chewed away his tongue
His last lament, long since been sung.

So Mother, dear, be not afraid
now midnight's here, my plans are made.
He spits out hate with every breath,
But I have his gun to welcome death.

Beneath Yellow Roses

By Rose Blackthorn

Past the lilac hedge, it squats
hump-backed, rounded with age
long grass, uncut and untrained
fills the cracks between water-curved stones
The earthen roof is hidden
a raised bed for the thorny canes
they arch and descend, clustered with blossoms
the color of butter, or gold
Bees drift and drone through the leaves
murmuring amongst prosaic beauty
unaware of the darkness that crouches
beneath wild yellow roses
The door is old and weathered
unassuming, silvered and roughened
planks hand-hewn and bound with iron
hung on hinges dark with rust
Opened, the stairs revealed
are stones swiftly descending
into dark and musty shadows
and whispers, hidden behind closed hands
If you listen, there are riddles
like spiders spinning secrets
through the hair-fine roots of roses
into the dark that has no end.

Labyrinthine Dream
By Mathias Jansson

Doors, doors, doors;
my father's fortune gone,
invested in old cellar doors
from around the world.

The fool had them all installed
in the basement of his mansion;
a gigantic labyrinth
of doors.

I read a quote from Dante
before I entered the first door,
and door after door led me deeper
into the darkest places of my mind.

I started to hallucinate,
hearing screaming and pounding
from behind every door.
I was lost in a world of evil.
Doors were opening and closing.
The horror was approaching.

I understood what my father had done.
These doors were built to keep a secret,
to conceal the most terrible places
of the darkest side of human nature;
of hell, cruelty and torture.

My father collected them all
with the ambition to create
the ultimate door of evil,
a passageway leading
to the ninth circle
of Dante's hell.

Immortal Serenade

By Larissa Blaze

Such a handsome lad, he once was—
knowing not from vain glory, but from distant vivid memories...
Ladies swooned, unashamed of their lust-filled cravings;
unrestrained sweet tongues, soft lips enticed his desires.
How could he resist, as trembling delicate hands clamored,
exposed and caressed him where he ached?
Cries of ecstasy echoed in the dark—
The unspeakable delight of his hard flesh, thrusting like mad
as their bodies gyrated, insane with carnal bliss.
They could not get enough...
Insatiable wrecks!

Ah, but he was blinded by his own pride,
enslaved by his growing lust
Unstoppable stallion, thrusting as if his life depended
on keeping each lover sated.
Until the day, a jealous and enraged femme fatale hurtled acid.
Burned, his distorted, malodorous form
turned into a horrifying sight.

Disgusted at his own squalid reflection,
he crept to the cellar below
Its darkness became his blanket, until death's sweet mercy
relieved his bane
His once flawless form putrefied,
becoming a sumptuous feast for maggots and worms.
Though flesh had turned to dust, his soul lingered—
lascivious longings finding no release, he wailed incessantly.

Entrapped and forgotten by man as eons passed....
'til the day she came through the ancient cellar door—
Fumbling, stumbling, crawling.
she whimpered as an injured lamb, wet and shivering.
Her wraith- like form naked and marred by jagged slashes,

blood and bowels spilled upon the filthy, icy ground...
Titillated by the sight, he hovered over this wounded waif,
wondering,
Maid, from whose hands did you suffer such dreadful fate?
She turned around, her hazel eyes widened with apprehension.
Fear not, sweet lamb!
He leaned closer, hoping to bring her comfort,
Instead she quivered with the freezing gust
"Oh merciful death, come take me now!"

He stared at every inch of her body as she writhed in agony;
deep gashes could not disguise her beautiful, lithe frame.
Guilt flooded his soul as his pleasure heightened, watching this
spectacle.
Centuries had not tempered his desires!
He burned, only too aware of her impending demise.
A sonorous cry filled the air, as twisted desires
danced within his core.

Our tragic fates unite in death
Upon your passing, my solitude ends
Till then, these intoned pleas are none but distant whispers
of the cold wind upon your form.
But soon, the barriers between our worlds shall break.
Listen, as the inevitable draws near ...
Succumb to my beckoning
as I welcome you into my realm
with my haunting, immortal serenade!

Revelations

By Michael Randolph

Riddled by guilt, devoured in sin,
I stand upon a threshold of the damned.
Voices in the air conspire to send me
downward into the cellar of despair.

Hidden glyphs saturate my vision;
I hesitate, unsure of this decision.
What shall become of me?
The world above bemoans this life of evil.

Ghosts, friends of old, float behind,
reminiscing over all the evil I've done.
How many souls have I sent to Hell?
I've lost count in my depraved existence.

Yet unchartered lands wait beyond
this cellar door, homestead of the insane.
Eternal fate, destiny tied to this wooden door.
A life unfettered by morality lies just beyond.

Decisiveness speeds my hand. Reaching forward,
I pull open the door to the creature's lair.
Somewhere deep in this abyss sits the master
of the demented Belroth Meiltonour.

Warmth invades my spirit as I pass through the portal.
I've dreamt of this day for years.
Passing through to the immortal realms,
I rejoice in impure revelations.

A guide of sorts has been sent to light the way.
Follow my footsteps into the domain of
hidden horrors and tales of terror from ghastly origins.
Once chosen, this path cannot be reversed.

Obliging my condemnation of the world overhead,
I follow this monster to his master's lair.
Treading on the spirits consumed by hatred,
we stand before his greatness on a carpet of red.

Silken skin, putrid vindication of the evil within,
the master of the cellar devours my soul;
owns my existence, reinvents my squalid condition.
Drawn to heights above the rest, I cannot resist this demise.

Gliding in exaltation over the pools of ichor,
a chair is set beside the master of this domain;
a just reward for this life deemed shameful.
Consenting to his wishes, I sit upon my throne.

Come forth, child of mine. Listen to my words...
Grace only comes to those strong enough
to rip it from the hands of God.

Divinity by Natalie Sirois

Behind the Cellar Door

By Esther M. Leiper-Estabrooks

My folks bought an odd old house
With fifteen rooms or more
But what I find most scary—
I can't get past the cellar door.

I mean I ***could*** but feel so weird
'Cause I hear odd sounds below!
Might an animal be kept there?
Sounds silly, yes, I know—

My Mama says it's surely rats
So we'll need an exterminator
But she has lied to me before
So at times I almost hate her,

While Daddy kind of snickers
When I tell him I am scared
But he says that as a big girl
I'd go down there if I dared!

Mama wants to store sealed jars
Which she puts up every year
On wide shelves in that cellar,
But what I find is queer:

Daddy never digs a garden;
---No rows of beans or beets—
So what is Mama canning,
And just what sort of eats?

She plans on growing mushrooms
Since a cellar's good for that,
But I sense a stench of musty
And worry of mice and rats.

Worse: Now my parents scare me
For seeming weirdly changed,
While I sense secrets hiding here,
So might they be deranged?

Why is it they chose ***this*** house
Far off the beaten path?
I s'pose that it sold cheap enough
Yet I sense some hidden wrath....

....

Today Mama told me at noon,
"We'll have French Fries tonight.
Your Daddy will be hungry—
I'll turn on the basement light.

"You fetch those taters up here;
They're stored in a burlap sack.
Don't be silly, getting willies,
And girl, you come straight back!

She almost shoved me downward
Sniffing, "Fear's a stupid thing,
Go, kid, you'd best get over it;
No use to whine and cling."

"I don't do steps like I used to;
Old Arthur's got me bad!
Yes, my mistake to birth you late
Plus the only kid I've had."

--Well, I took a pot down cellar
Being scared as I could be,
Where a bare bulb cast shadows
So the walls were hard to see.

From the sack I grabbed potatoes
That seemed immense in size
But, shuddering, I filled my pan,
Then I saw their blinking eyes!

Those shapes were busy sprouting
Spiky tendrils reaching out
Which ended in round eyeballs
So I fled with a dreadful shout,

While after me came mutterings
Thus I dared not look behind
Where horrid sounds re-echoed
All forbidding and unkind!

But Mom snapped I was foolish
Plus my Daddy laughed at me,
But then ***he*** came from up-cellar
Turned green as he could be!

"There is ***something*** down there!
Don't ask; I can't explain.
I'll find a padlock for the door;
Jeez, all this seems insane!

"Perhaps some poisonous fungus
Has took to growing here
Our girly sensed before us;
Stuff plainly wrong and queer.

"We could try a priest or exorcist;
Apply for Welfare; sneak away?
Better yet, we've ***fire insurance,***
We'll burn this place; ***they'll*** pay."

....

This drama happened long ago
And I'm alone, grown now;
Living safe up in a high-rise
With no basement anyhow;

At least not one I'd dare to set
My footsteps in at all.
I crave fair and upper air
Plus these days I walk tall—

Yet still can't shed the tragedy
Which long ago befell:
A flaring fire so swift and dire
It sent my folks to Hell.

The fire marshal ruled "accident"
What happened long ago,
And my memories stay jumbled
Though I recall torrid glow,

Plus there were horrid voices
In the midst of roaring fire;
Taunting—or in agony?—
An uncanny, eerie choir!

--I sleep here with a nightlight
And shun all darkened places
Fearing dreams of spiky eyeballs
Mixed with my parents' faces!"

For You, the Universe

By Max Booth III

Dirt from under the tire swing caked into my fingernails;
so raw, they're beginning to hurt like hell,
layers crusted upon layers until they're busted.
You can smell the smell and I can tell
you're disgusted.

You shoot me down
with that knowing tone,
as if you're too good,
as if I'm just scum
with dirty fingernails,
with that ass that shakes in your stride
as you walk away from me,
as you shoot me down.

I'll shoot you down.

You leave me trembling
in my wake,
in my sleep,
as I shake,
as I weep.

Soon you will tremble,
and I will win,
and after you've realized
why we're perfect,
you will also win.

We will tremble.
We will win.
We will love.

Perfume savored,

I return to my sanctuary,
my four walls;
walls stripped of character,
walls strangling my mind,
a mind running out of time,

and the cellar door
leading to my dirt floor,
where I can collapse
on my knees
and scream pretty please,
and pound my fists
into my skull
until I bleed
enough sin to succeed
in my goal of filling
a paradoxical hole
eating my stomach
to shriveled bits.

Crimson tears forming puddles
to drown my fears of failure,
I continue to formulate your ideal man,
so you will be my ideal girl,
and together we shall rule the world.

I pry at magazines with cutout eyes,
I dine with your hologram,
but it's never the same.
I need the real thing,
I need you here,
underneath me,
on my dirt floor,
where you are mine,
evermore.

When I am through,

flowers will grow differently,
and the moon's glow
will never glow quite right again.

Music will sound completely new,
histories forever tainted,
our love will stay true.

When I am finished,
nothing will ever be the same.
They will say nasty little things
that you'll never hear.

They will say I'm crazy,
and they're right:

I am.

I am insane, but at least I know
I am the rain and I am the snow,
I am the cloud destined to guard you
until the sky falls down.

I am the hand that comforts,
the lips sewn into your own,
the bleeding heart dying
beside your bleeding heart.

I am the creator,
and you are my prize.

Claim thee I shall.

My fingers bury themselves
in my cellar floor,
underneath my cellar door,
as I try to grasp

how to make you happy,
how to please you,
how to complete you,
how to have you,
got to have you,
need to have you.

Must have you.

Fingers so dirty, it's sickening.
Maybe one day I'll cut them.
Maybe one day, a lot of things will happen.
When I'm finished with my project,
maybe that day will come.
When I'm done building your present,
maybe you will have me.

When I've built your man,
maybe I'll build you.
With a toolkit like mine,
there are no exceptions.
I can reject your rejections,
and accept my paradise.

Madman's fingernails
claiming handfuls of hair,
so stressed, so pressed,
trembling on my workbench,
striving to at last add
the finishing touches
on our present,

the one I've built
just for you;

my magnum opus.

I hope you like it.

Halcyon Days by Shawna L. Bernard

PART II: FLASH FICTION

The Blossoming Bride

By Aaron Besson

A body could get lonely up here if it wasn't for Miss Kelsie. Miss Kelsie's reared me since I could remember. Her n' her daughter, Aileen. Miss Kelsie's kin have been takin' care of me n' mine since before we all came over from Scootlin. Miss Kelsie's Gramma reared my Ma, n' her Great Gramma reared my gramma before that, goin' like that way back. Miss Kelsie said Aileen will take care of my child when it comes to it, too. I liked the idea some, but asked why I couldn't take care of my own baby. Miss Kelsie just shook her head n' said that ain't the Unnerster way. "Not the Unnerster way." I've heard that enough in my twelve years to know not to argue it none.

Never knew my Ma n' Pa, they went away before I could remember. When I asked Miss Kelsie why, she just said it was the Unnerster way. Miss Kelsie says they all will be at my weddin', n' that my husband-to-be owns more land than there is in all of Calhoun County, n' is held in great regard, even for an Unnerster. When I asked her when I get to meet him, she just said "In due time." Whenever I asked her what she's goin' to wear to my weddin', she gave me that smile that looks sad n' tired at the same time, then started singin'.

Miss Kelsie knows more songs than a head should hold. She said they all come from Scootlin, where they have more songs than stars in the sky. I could listen to her for hours. She's got the prettiest voice. My favorite is "Doon in the Wee Room". I don't know how it all goes, n' a lot of it don't make much sense to me, but I do love the chorus:

Doon in the wee room underneath the stair
Everybody's happy n' everybody's there
We're a' makin' merry, each in his chair
Doon in the wee room underneath the stair

When I found out that Aileen was going to be comin' around to help more, I was fiercely excited. I remember playin' with her when I was wee. Then Miss Kelsie stopped havin' her around. Miss Kelsie said it ain't been the proper time for her to be around so much, but that she'd be there when needed, word as bond. I missed Aileen somethin' fierce, but if Miss Kelsie says it weren't a good time, there weren't no quarrelin' about it. Aileen comin' back made the days a mite better.

Aileen was my best n' only friend on the mountain, near as I had to a sister. She loved to braid my hair, sayin' it was like white gold. She'd tell me about how all the boys in Holderby's Landing were all tryin' to court her, n' we'd laugh about them. When I asked Miss Kelsie if we could go to Holderby's Landing for a day, just to see the sights, she got all stern n' such, n' firmly said the folks in Holderby's don't take kindly to Unnersters at all. When I asked her why, she'd just change the subject or start singin' again. Aileen didn't talk much about goin' to town much after that, either.

One day after me n' Aileen spent the better part of the day pickin' berries, my fingertips started achin'. I reckoned I had got stung by a nettle or somethin', so I didn't think much about it n' went to bed. When I woke up in the mornin', I saw that the skin on my fingertips were peeled back like petals, showin' purple skin underneath that smelled like cinnamon n' somethin' else weird. 'Course I screamed like a banshee. Miss Kelsie came runnin' into my room with Aileen close behind her, both of them with eyes real wide when I held my hands out to them, all in a fear. Aileen' looked like she was goin' to faint, but Miss Kelsie just held her hands up her mouth and went on over and over 'bout how I was all growin' up.

She calmed me down with hugs n' kisses, tellin' me that everythin' was just fine. She told me she'd be right back with somethin' that'd help. She ran into the other room, leavin' Aileen to stand in the doorway, not comin' an inch further into the room. She smiled at me n' asked how I was fairin', but I could tell she wanted nothin' more than run out of the house. Miss Kelsie came rushin' back in, glarin' at Aileen somethin' fierce as she stuck to the doorway. Miss Kelsie handed me a cup of tea that smelled bad. "Drink that all, now," she said. "That'll clear you right up." The cup was hot n' smelled like rotten mushrooms and dirt, but I was so scared just then that I'd drink a cup of lightnin' right there n' then if you told me it'd make things better. I drank it all down while Miss Kelsie hugged me n' sang me songs. I watched Aileen starin' at me all fearful from the doorway until I fell asleep.

When I woke up, I thought it was still night time 'cause I couldn't see a blessed thing. I then felt it was because my hair was coverin' my face. I tried movin' it aside, but it was stuck in place like it was glued there. Nothin' felt right at all. I could feel that the petals weren't just on my fingertips no more, but all over my hands. My legs weren't right no more either. I had too many, n' they were more like snakes than anythin' else.

I started cryin' n' screamin' for Miss Kelsie, my voice soundin' all weird n' gurgly through my hair. I heard n' smelled her n' Aileen runnin' to my room. Aileen screamed when she saw me, but Miss Kelsie just sighed n' said "You look just like your mother on her weddin' day."

So now I'm standin' at the top of the staircase to the root cellar where Miss Kelsie never let me go. They're all waitin' for me: Ma and Pa, my husband, n' all the other Unnersters. I got my bouquet n' veil, n' I smell music startin' up down there. It's goin' to be a beautiful weddin'.

Doon in the wee room underneath the stair
Everybody's happy n' everybody's there
We're a' makin' merry, each in his chair
Doon in the wee room underneath the stair

A Polished Poem

By Morgan Griffith

Abandoned buildings often smolder with absorbed emotional trauma that defies time. In extreme cases they shed light on man's inhumanity—penitentiary's and asylums reverberating with silent screams until their deterioration reaches dangerous levels and demands razing. In the case of Canker House, called so in part because it had stood empty so long no one remembered the name of its original owner, residual fear consumed its entire neighborhood.

Such neglected areas can be found in older cities. In time disrepair spirals down into squalor and avoidance until even the rats and roaches can find no sustenance. Canker House combined that with disturbed souls and unresolved horror. The eeriness of the House could be compared to one of those abandoned, Japanese amusements parks. Broken windows and boarded up doors slashed with grotesque drawings and graffiti leered over the top of sprawling weeds like the hungry eyes of a rusted merry-go -round. The block of empty houses surrounding it seemed more like forsaken cabins on a resort whose appeal has been forever tainted.

As a member of the city's team to clear the area for authorized demolishing, I was one of the first to experience its dark nature. The work leads one to see depressing things as a rule. This, however, was even beyond the scope of the evil men do to one another.

It's true that a transient was discovered in a semi-petrified state in an adjacent home. Skeletal remains were also found of dogs and cats in an upstairs bedroom. Working our way into the heart of the area we came to Canker House, and I formally admit to an increased heart rate and lump in my throat as we approached from its back yard, chopping down weeds as thick as had we been exploring a jungle. A headless doll was found during that clearing, as well as a pile of age-stained, black and white photographs.

Not one of us was unaffected by the unnatural quiet and oppressive sense of foreboding. You could see it in everyone's eyes. As machetes hacked brittle weeds away from the cellar door a sinister poem was revealed. The easy assumption was that it had been written in blood, but in truth the childish handwriting had been penned in a god awful shade of red nail polish. Below the last line on the concrete walkway was a used, hypodermic syringe.

In the cellar there lives a monster
That feeds off of hopes and dreams.
There's no place to hide once it lures you inside,
And no one can hear your screams.

Our team leader bashed that door into rotten splinters, along with the beaming happy face alongside the poem. From that point on I am not allowed under a disclosure provision to discuss what we found in that house. Demolition was immediate and thorough.

The irony came when we learned that we had endured witnessing the aftermath of madness and some unnamed, more horrific threat in order for a large, popular retail chain to be built on the property.

City Council members called it "cleansing the area" and "bringing life back to a historic section of the city". Yet our team knew the truth. Even the brightest colors cannot paint over frantic scratches on a door from an abduction victim. Fluorescent lighting can't hold supernatural shadows at bay or ward off the whispers and chilling touch of a creature that has never walked this earth in human form.

Smiling door greeters can't stop it from following you home.

It was only a matter of time before disquieting reports would start coming in.

An Epiphany by Greg McWhorter

Incarnadine
By Lisa Landreth

It was a pinkish flesh color—incarnadine. That was what first attracted Jesse Sears to his wife, Lucie, her flawless skin, creamy peach with a reddish underbelly. So beautiful. Their love was one at first sight. However, the new wedding bliss soon died. With the addition of not one, not two, but three rowdy boys, marriage wasn't what he expected.

To come home to a house filled with noise. Always noise. Dinner was never ready. The children never listened. His headaches grew with every child's sticky fingerprint or lazy smirk from his wife. Their pure existence grew to irritating new heights.

That was when the knocking began. A gentle rap echoed from downstairs, but loud enough to wake Jesse. He pushed at his sleeping wife, but she never lifted an eyelid.
Armed with a baseball bat, he crept down the stairs and into the hallway. The house sat quiet except for the ticking of his wife's grandfather clock, a wedding present from her mother. He turned to go back to bed.

Knock, knock, knock.

The sound pieced his ears. It was coming from the cellar, Jesse was sure of it. Slowly, he opened the door that lead to the underground room and turned on the light. There, at the bottom of the stairs, was the old wooden door. It sat as quiet as ever. He stood there for moment, waiting.

"Dad?" The innocent voice of Oliver, his youngest, broke the trance. The boy stood in the hallway, with teddy bear in hand.

"What are you doing?"

Jesse shook his head. "Nothing." He turned off the light and closed the door. After getting his son some water, he tucked him in bed, and returned to his own, snuggling against his wife for the rest of the night.

The next morning, Lucie and the boys were already at the breakfast table. He came into the kitchen still wearing his robe and slippers.

"Want some pancakes, hon?"

With a nod, Jesse moved Lucie's blonde hair back, readying his kiss, but he froze mid-pucker. Her skin, once a beautiful pearl with red undertones, was no longer. Red veins pulsed beneath a parchment of flaky skin. He reeled back.

"What's wrong?" she asked.

His brow furrowed. "Have you been in the sun too long?"

"No...why?"

He glanced at the boys' faces. Their skin suffered the same fate, reddish veins running throughout. "It must be me," he mumbled, reaching past Lucie to grab the coffee pot.

The following night was no different. After an evening of burnt roast and temper tantrums, Jesse checked the cellar for anything out of the ordinary. He turned up empty-handed, and laid his head down to sleep, free from worry. However, the rapping sound returned. Again, it came from downstairs, and he found himself standing in the hallway of the first floor, his wife still in bed.

He opened the side door and turned on the lights, hoping the noise would end. That was not the case. The knocking actually grew louder, more like banging, and the locked handle rattled. Someone or something was trying to get out.

Jesse swallowed hard. He knew it wasn't a burglar. The cellar had no windows or outside doors. Nevertheless, something was in there and it wanted its freedom.

"Hey, I don't know who you are or what you're trying to do, but you better go back where you came from before I smash your face!" he yelled down the stairs. As if on cue, the cellar door fell quiet. Jesse breathed a sigh of relief. Perhaps now he could sleep. The lack of rest was making him feel crazed. He didn't know how much more he could take. But just as he turned to go, the door began rattling, even harder. The force behind it, even stronger.

Jesse made up his mind. He'd leave the house with Lucie and the boys. They'd spend the night at a motel until morning. Yet, as he flicked off the light switch, the shaking and pounding stopped. He waited there until his feet grew tired. Nothing.

Slowly, he climbed up the stairs and crawled back into bed...this time, with the bat.

The next morning, his headache returned before he even hit the kitchen. There was his wife and three boys, just as always. He cringed at the monotony.

"Good morning," Lucie said cheerfully. Jesse's jaw tightened.

He thought of telling her about the noise but stopped, figuring she wouldn't listen. She never did. They never did. He sat down at the table, and stared at his boys with wide eyes, his mouth agape. To his horror, their faces were blood red. His wife, too, sported a face painted in crimson.

Jesse jumped up from the table and ran down the hall. He reached the bathroom in just enough time for his stomach acids to fill the toilet.

"Honey, what's wrong?" Lucie asked as he flushed, then washed his hands. He couldn't stand to look at her. Her pretty face, now just a mass of bloody meat. He raced up the stairs and locked their bedroom door. No sooner did his head touch the pillow than was he asleep. How long he slept, he didn't know. But for the final time, the strange knocking woke him.

Darkness encompassed the house. Jesse called for his family. No one answered. Same as before, he followed the rapping to the cellar. However, the old wooden entrance was no longer. In its place was a door made of raw flesh—the insidious color of incarnadine.

Jesse didn't have his bat, but he knew he didn't need it. The axe in the cellar would do just fine. A smile spread across his lips. Methodically, he moved down each step until he stood inches from the flesh door. With an off-pitch laugh, he pulled the bolt back. The door opened and Jesse stepped willingly into his madness.

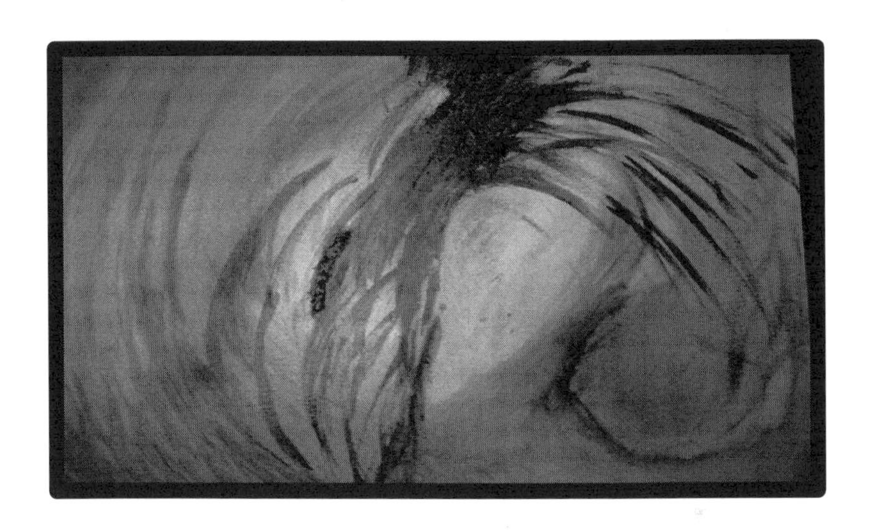

Serenity by Beth Murphy

The Draft

By Matthew Wilson

I heard a scream that final morning, and mother came at me with anger in her eyes.

No, I hadn't been down the cellar, nor knew we had one. The damn thing was hidden behind a curtain like a dirty secret.
No, I didn't know how the door opened.

Just a crack.

"There's a draft in this house," mother moaned, and said I was never to go down there. How foolish I was to think she had my Christmas presents down there, but I was naive and quite caught up in the excitement.

A new room I had no knowledge, and best of all BANNED! I would be Mr. Popular when word got out I had been the explorer, and going against mom's tyranny.

I'd be cool. But when mom went to the store and I stood at the top of the stair, a terrible fear overcame me. The door was dark and smelled of mold.

Mom was right. There was a draft coming from it, a terrible coldness that chilled me. This gust of wind carried sound like a chain rattling. Someone called my name.

"Dad?" I asked.

I knew dad was long gone for there had been a terrible argument that last evening and at dawn, mom said dad was gone like a spirit in the night. He would never be back.

But someone called me to me, asked me to take the chains off.

The cellar door opened and hungry eyes stared at me, tiny pools of hate the likes of which I had never known before pierced through me. A stench of rot near overpowered me and before I had a chance to fall, someone had me by my collar. Mom was angry, dragged me back into the kitchen with one hand and dropped the bag of shopping with the other. I was grounded, banned from video games and playing with friends. Mom had always been mean to me, I had to admit to myself after my beating that things had been better with dad here for he had never hit me. It took two hours to find the key hidden at the base of the sugar bowl, though I didn't have the courage to take it down to the hateful eyes. Crossing my fingers, I threw the key down the cellar and ran to my room.

There is a shuffling as I write this. Maybe it is a confession, my part in a coming murder for someone is coming up the stairs.

Their chains rattling, their breath heavy and hacking as their feet pound the stairs.

What's that?

Mom screamed. I think she was a liar like dad said, for she called the thing by name. Dad's name. There was such a little struggle. I think things are going to be what they were once like round here.

But I still have to go down to the cellar from time to time. And make sure mom is well fed. Those chains must be real uncomfortable for her.

Little Drummer Boy
By Tom Johnstone

"He's not going to like it, Mary."

"That's easy for you to say. You're out at work all day. You don't have to put up with the racket, not to mention the neighbours complaining."

They think I'm so dumb that I can't hear them talking about me. But I'm outside the door listening. Better be ready to make myself scarce before they come out though. Don't want them to know that I know they're talking about me.

"I know that, love. It's just, well, he's been improving since coming out of Seaview, hasn't he?"

"Well, yes, Howard, I suppose so."

Seaview. That anti-septic hell-hole. With the sign outside that reads: *Promoting mental health, challenging stigma.*

"Well, Mary, I think a lot of it's down to him letting off a little steam, taking out his aggression on his drum kit."

"Maybe. Or maybe it's down to the new medication they've put him on."

Good. They think I'm taking the happy pills. My dumb act must work, as if I'm a happy sheep who swallows all their bullshit. But I don't, any more than I swallow the pills, which fog up my mind and prevent me seeing the Truth. My skin's stretched tight as a drum as I listen out. It seems like they're lowering their voices now. Maybe they sense that I'm outside.

"So how about a compromise, Mary?"

"A compromise. What do you mean, Howard?"

Compromise. Always the old man's watchword. Well, it is nowadays. I don't remember his belt compromising much when I was a kid.

"Well, the way I see it, playing the drums is good therapy for him. We need them if we're to keep him on side with the care plan."

"Howard, you're starting to sound like one of the shrinks!"

Yeah, keep Johnny boy drumming, shut him up and let him bang his heart out on those skins. What would they say if they knew that I imagine it's them I'm beating on when I pound away? But if the old man wants to think I'm following the care plan when I bash out a rhythm on his skull, good for him.

"Maybe, Mary, but they only want what's best for Johnny—and us. So what I suggest is, we move the drum kit into the cellar. There's plenty of room for it down there, and it's sound-proofed."

"No, Howard, I say we get rid of it. It can't be healthy, a lad of his age shut away playing the drums all the time. He should be getting out, getting a job, a girlfriend."

Yeah, right. As if any employer would touch me with a bargepole, as if any girl would look at me.

"Mary, if we're going to make a go of taking care of him at home, we've got to face facts. Those things just aren't going to happen overnight."

"Yes. I suppose."

So what's this leading up to then? What are they planning now?

"But this way, if it seems like he's going to have an episode, we can suggest he goes and plays with his drum kit."

"Howard, you're a genius! That cellar door's got a lock on it."

These new drum skins are really something.

I wasn't sure if they'd work, but now they're on nice and tight, they give off a really good sound. I don't know if it's the acoustics down here, but they give off a kind of echo.

Of course, I had to treat them to keep them taut. The only problem's the smell, which keeps coming back, even when I douse them with formaldehyde.

And then there's that echo.

Sometimes it disturbs me a little. Especially when it starts to sound like voices. Their voices.

I shouldn't have done it. I know that now. But I heard them talking again. They'd found out I hadn't been taking my meds. They were going to lock me in the cellar until I took them, just like they used to when I was little and I wouldn't eat my greens. It was the only way to stop them, the only way to shut them up. Still, the cellar's not all bad. It was down there I first started discovered drumming as a kid: the battered little tin drum I found lying in the dirt I bashed hell out of until my hands bled, to try and get them to let me out. It never got their attention though. Nothing did. What I did more recently: that got their attention, if the screams were anything to go by.

Whenever I play the drums, I hear their screams again. And though I stretched them so smooth and taut over the frames, now the skins are beginning to warp into the shapes of their twisted old faces.

Wait a second...the cellar door's locked. How can that be?

I can hear their muttering, scheming voices getting closer, their dragging footsteps creaking on the floorboards leading to the cellar door. Imagining what their flayed corpses must look like, I'm glad the door's locked now.

Until I remember that the cellar door locks from the outside.

Latent Light by Natalie Sirois

Natural Selection
By Tony Thorne

It had been an accident waiting to happen, and finally it did. Elsa had been teasing the cellar door lock with a safety pin for almost ten minutes, but it didn't show any signs of opening. It always looked so easy on the television! It was a moderately windy day, and the ocean surf pounding in the background drowned out any clicks that she thought she was supposed to be hearing.

She felt she was beginning to panic. Then suddenly the door flew open. She fell forward with gasp, and there confronting her, unbelievably...was a large black seal, very wet and with one flipper resting on the now lowered door handle. Elsa gaped at it in astonishment as it waved the other flipper at her and then began to communicate.

"You…happy now?" Its head was raised and the big brown eyes were looking directly at her, but its lips were not moving. The voice must have been coming from inside her head. She nodded and forced a smile. The voice came again, softly, "Me… heard you…calling."

Astounded, she realized that must have been well over half an hour ago, when she'd slipped, on the top of the steps, and the cellar door handle had snapped on the inside. Somehow this wonderful, but incredibly impossible, creature had picked up her cry of anguish. It must have understood her plight and, after swimming ashore, had crawled all the way up to the beach house to help her.

"What are…er, I mean, how can I ever thank you?" That was all she could think of to say. The bland expression on the seal's face seemed to change, and she wondered, could it be trying to smile at her?

"Me…happy…help you," it communicated, then paused for a moment. "But…was chasing good fish…hear you call…think all gone now."

The creature regarded her expectantly. Into Elsa's mind suddenly came a picture of her kitchen table and the fat salmon she'd put out to defrost that morning, ready for the evening meal. She knew exactly what to do.

The seal followed her out to the kitchen, its feet slapping, and making a series of wet patches on the newly tiled floor. Elsa picked up the salmon and handed it over. The seal's facial expression seemed to change again as it grasped the fish in both of its flippers. Squatting back on its haunches it began to crunch into the almost defrosted flesh. In just a few minutes the whole fish had vanished. The seal looked around, then bent over and licked up the few, perhaps imaginary, scraps from the floor. "Good fish!" the voice came again, as the seal stretched up and looked straight into her eyes. "Can be…more?"

Elsa was still feeling very grateful, and after all, there were plenty more large fish in the big freezer in the cellar. She patted the seal's head and replied. "Just a moment, wait here and I'll get you another one."

The creature regarded her for a few moments, as though listening for something, then nodded slowly.Elsa felt sure it had understood everything she'd said. She went back through the cellar door and descended the steps. She was about to open the big freezer when she heard a sudden sloshing sound and the door slamming shut. She turned and dashed back up the steps in alarm. It was clear to her what must have happened. The over eager seal had followed her and accidently pushed against the door.

"Open the door again please!" she called firmly, and waited, but there was no answering voice in her head. She tried again, but it was no use, something must have caused the friendly seal to leave and head back into the sea. Perhaps it was already too far away. She sighed and began to feel around the edge of her apron.

It always did look so easy on the television! Elsa tried teasing the door lock again with another safety pin but it didn't show any signs of opening. The ocean surf was still pounding in the background, drowning out any clicks that she thought she was supposed to be hearing. She began to panic again. Her husband wouldn't be home for at least another three hours.

Then suddenly, the door flew open and she fell forward with gasp of alarm. There before her this time stood, unbelievably...a very much larger seal, very wet and with one big flipper resting on the door handle. Elsa gaped at it in astonishment. Then it spoke, aggressively, inside her head, "Want fish…like little sister!"

Elsa reeled back in dismay. There were several other big seals in a queue behind it, and lurching ominously past the kitchen window she was horrified to see something else…a great deal larger.

The Door in the Floor

By Ken MacGregor

Nate took another swig of beer. It was room temperature, but he didn't mind. The first few were cold anyway. Nate thought for a minute and picked up where he'd left off.

"Okay," Nate said. "How about kicking a puppy?" Nate asked.

"Nothing is beneath me; I keep telling you that," Bob said. Bob shrugged.

"Jesus, man," Nate said. "A puppy? All right. Hang on. Let me think." Nate polished off the beer and set the bottle in the 12-pack holder. Six left. Nate pulled a fresh one and offered it to Bob, who took it. Nate got another beer for himself, too, and both men drank.

"Would you," Nate started, formulating the question as he went, "sleep with another man's wife?"

"Really," Bob said, "nothing is beneath me. Why is that so hard for you believe?"

"Everyone's got their limits," Nate said. "I'm just trying to figure out where yours might be."

"Okay," Bob said. "But you're wasting your time. No matter what you ask me, no matter how horrible or impossible it might seem, the fact remains: nothing is beneath me."

"You'd kill a man?" Nate asked. He was sure Bob wouldn't.

"Yes."

"That's fucked up, Bob." Nate shook his head. He didn't want to talk about this anymore. Nate looked around the room. Bob's place was spartan; the wooden chairs on which they sat, a coatrack by the front door and a cot against the wall. The other door led to the kitchenette-bedroom combo. The accordion door next to it separated them from the tiny bathroom with the stand-up shower, toilet and sink huddled together. There wasn't much to talk about. Bob set his half-empty beer on the floor and Nate's gaze was drawn to the trap door in the floor.

"What is that?" he asked. "Root cellar or something?"

"Used to be a root cellar," Bob said.

"What is it now?" Nate asked. There was a metal ring set in a round metal indentation.

"Nothing," Bob said. His lips evolved into a smile.

"Heh," Nate said, grinning. "Nothing is beneath you. I get it now. Funny." Bob grinned back, nodding.

"You want to see?" Bob said. He stood up. Nate knocked the rest of his beer back in several loud swallows. He belched.

"'Scuse me," Nate said, patting his belly. "Sure." Bob stood and spun his chair around on one leg so it was off the cellar door. He waited until Nate was hunkered down before grabbing the handle. Nate shot Bob a look, like come on already and looked down at the door. Bob lifted it. There seemed to be a slight breeze and Nate could hear wind whistling somewhere far away. Nate looked down into blackness.

"I can't see anything," he said.

"I know," Bob said. "That's because there's nothing there. I told you..." Bob put one hand on Nate's shoulder and grabbed Nate's belt with the other. Bob tossed Nate through the door in the floor. "...nothing is beneath me."

Nate fell screaming into the abyss and never stopped.

Bob closed the door in the floor and sat down to finish his beer. He opened the app on his phone to see if any of his other high school buddies were around.

Ray Guns and Rocket Ships

By Todd Nelsen

Do you believe in ghosts? Do you believe in monsters? I do. Because I've seen one a time or two.

Once upon a time, in an ordinary place, in an ordinary neighborhood, in an ordinary house, just like your own, there was a small child…

The child slept, resting his tired eyes. Dim moonlight shone in through drawn curtains, casting thin shadows throughout the interior of his room. As the child slept, he dreamed. He dreamed of cowboys and wagon trains, of baseball and Willie Mays, of ray guns and rocket ships on the bright, bright surface of a round, white moon. Beside the child, nestled in his arms, was a stuffed toy bear. Its fur was soft and brown, its nose a black button on the end of its snout, its beady eyes, black, too, set apart between two tiny ears.

But this was no ordinary bear, mind you. It was a special kind of teddy bear. And this bear, if you didn't already know, was me.

The old grandfather clock slid its gears together with a metallic click. The brassy bell struck one, bringing in the new hour. The child's eyes opened, as many children do during the night.

With a yawn, he stretched his small arms in his warm pajamas.

"Mamma?"

Then, just as quickly as it came, he squeezed me once, and drew in a long breath, letting it all out ever so slowly. Then his eyes drifted half closed again, then closed entirely, and he returned to his sleep and dreams.

I watched, and I waited.

Every night, I watched, and I waited.

See, most think we're only toys, made in shops and factories, cut and turned, stuffed and stitched, with loving care, wrapped in colorful paper, tied with ribbons and bows, placed beneath trees when the winter is cold and bright and the snow is falling. And we are this, but we're so much more. This isn't to say all bears are alive, of course, but some of us are. The special ones are. The ones gifted with magic and thought and heart…most certainly are. We're protectors, you see. We guard them—your little, sleeping bundles of soft innocence and light—from the things that remain hidden from their eyes. Because there are things in this world that are not so nice. Terrible things. Dreadful things. Things best left under the covers or kept under the—

The cellar door opened.

* * *

It was morning, a new day, and his mother was drawing the curtains.

"Mamma?" he asked.

"Yes, dear?"

"Where do we go when we sleep?"

His questions delighted her, though they were strange to her, at times, as if they came from a place only he could understand. "You go to the land of dreams," she replied.

The child yawned and considered this. He glanced to the cellar door. It frightened him.

"Is it a good place?" he asked, rubbing his eyes.

His mother paused. "I don't know," she said. "I'd like to think so. What do you think?"

"I guess so. But I don't always remember. Sometimes I think it's bad. Do you dream?" The question suddenly seemed important to him. He squeezed his teddy bear tight. Though he didn't know why, he loved this stuffed toy bear. Teddy, as fluffy as the clouds. Teddy, who'd come to him one early Christmas morning and seldom left his side.

The bear loved him, too, he thought, but he didn't know why this was either.

"Yes," she said, "I dream." But in truth, she couldn't remember if she dreamed or not, so she told him a half-truth and quickly changed the subject. "I dream mostly of you."

The child smiled at this, and it gladdened her heart to see him do so. She bent down to him and rubbed his head affectionately. He was a good boy.

"Now get dressed," his mother said. "It's time for school."

"Okay," he replied, bringing his legs to the edge of his bed. His pajamas rumpled up about his legs and arms like elephant ears.

"Can I bring Teddy to school today?"

"No," she said with a small laugh. "Teddy will be here for you when you return. Will that be okay?" She sat down on the edge of the bed beside him and took the bear from his hands and asked him, too. "What do you think, Teddy? Will that do?"

"Are you sure he'll be here when I get back?" He squinted up at her in concern. Again, he looked to the cellar door, and the question seemed very important to him.

"Of course," she said. "Now get dressed. We have a whole new day ahead of us. The first things are always the best things, you know. Remember what we talked about?"

"I like first things," he said, agreeing, though he wasn't quite sure about this just yet either. "I remember."

* * *

I smiled my own smile as she gently placed me back on the bed.

He was a good boy. A very good boy.

We're protectors, you see. We guard them—your little, sleeping bundles of soft innocence and light. Because there are things in this world that are not so nice. Terrible things. Dreadful things. Things best left under the covers or kept under the—

Not this night. Not yet. Be a child.

Luna

By Vada Katherine

Luna, nude, stands before her mirror. She smiles.

Thunder cracks outside my house, vibrating the yellow porcelain vases holding crimson flowers; lightning fissures the spectral night sky, inevitable forces of nature holding sway over all. Clear water roils in white ceramic wash basins placed around and within me. But this storm moves hastily: damage done, like the residue of a nightmare upon awakening.

Luna pads down the hallway and pauses, caresses me, glowing in the murkiness like an unsolved mystery, and then moves on. She has people to love, to hate. She is pregnant with emotion cinnabar and emerald, contemplations competing like identical twins for mother's love.

From my vantage point, there are no mysteries; no part of this house is secret. Movement may be strident or secretive, voices loud or whispered, emotions scented like soap or decay—nothing escapes me. This house is mine.

Luna pads to the front door, the chiming expected, her guests beginning to arrive.

She opens the door and says, "Hello, Robin and Richard. Please come in!" Flickering electricity in the sky is farther away now, not malevolent. More like the glow of a firefly.

The Concupiscences, childhood friends themselves, are old friends to Luna since her twelfth birthday, when their families moved from Italy. Robin is blond, her heritage the north of Italy. Richard's hair dark, as his heritage lay in the south.

Luna closes the door and turns into Robin's embrace. She moistens. "It's nice to see you again," Robin says. Luna accepts a hug from Richard. Feeling his thickness grow from her touch, she hesitates.

Robin reaches for Luna's hand. "Come. Let's enjoy some of your wine." Robin leads the three of them with a familiar knowledge, like fingers moving across piano keys fluent with perfect melody, the music of familiarity as old as their connections, into the bright kitchen.

Animal hunger tresses them like vapor. The storm returns. Luna senses Richard's taught gaze as she pours the claret, one hand firmly gripping the neck of the bottle as if her hand were wrapped firmly around his length; she traces the tip of the bottle with one finger. Luna embraces Robin's ruddiness as she fills her chalice, as if she is delicately cupping Robin's breast with the same familiarity. Robin stands on one side of Luna, Richard on the other, both sides of the same argument. She hovers between light and shadow, spring rain and soot, divinity and depravity. A faint glow begins to throb between her legs, aching in symphony with her heart.

Luna hands each of them their generous goblets and they smile to one another, bringing their glasses together in a toast to the unsaid.

A shriek of thunder laughs across the sky. The windows rattle in their panes. I open one just a crack, but it is enough. The three of them drink, but Luna finds her eyes straying over the glass to the chiaroscuro circus outside. A peal of thunder shakes the house to its very foundation, to the dark and damp place, to the cellar below me, where she stirs from slumber.

"Let's move to the sitting room." Luna says, pulling her guests from the bright kitchen.

The sitting room is illuminated with candle light. There are two sofas, two chairs, and a round oak table with four nutmeg leather-padded chairs positioned on each side. Four perfect books lie about the top of the table. Robin and Richard each lift a book to read the title.

"This book is *William Wilson,*" Robin says.

"This book is *The Fall of the House of Usher,*" Richard says.

Luna says, "I love Poe. I can't seem to get them to the library upstairs. They seem more at home here, where I spend the most time."

The front door bell chimes. No one is surprised. Other guests are expected.

Luna excuses herself, finishing her glass of wine on the way to the door. She licks her lips.

Luna opens the front door. The Doctors Obsidere, Mary and Jack, have arrived. Luna believes they teach cognitive behavioral therapy because they cannot perform alone in an office with another human being—Luna has never seen them apart. She puts their bags near the door, as the Obsideres bring books and wine with them no matter their destination. Luna leads them to the kitchen, passing me by, forgotten for the moment but ever present. Luna may have me no other way. The physics of her passing opens me wider, just a few more feet, and the human detriment and debris below me stands as one. What is left of Luna presses, her number two, and we join like Orpheus and Eurydice. Luna's guests drink wine, and Luna is their match. Her friends do not question Luna's solitariness as they understand why, as do I, and celebrate Luna, as do I.

The Obsideres bring Luna gifts, a bottle of wine and a book.

Mary says, "Its French." The bottle is labeled *Deux Esprits*. I'm sure you'll find it absolutely amazing." Mary laughs; proud of herself, as if she has presented perfection.

Jack says, "The book is entitled *The Number Two*. The author explores the work of Poe as it speaks of the universe and the magic of the number two."

Luna takes the book from Jack. Luna's eyes fill with tears, moved by the gifts. "Please take the wine to the cellar and shelve it where you believe the bottle best fits. I'll take the book to my library."

"Of course," Jack says. He and Mary pass by me and descend into the cellar and are forever lost, devoured and absorbed into a single golem—Robin and Richard, separate but identical.

Luna enters the sitting room. The incense of sex ebbs and flows; both opaque and murky in form, enveloping Richard and Mary as they copulate upon the divan.

Luna stands, nude, before her mirror, her smile reflecting.

Last Reign by Natalie Sirois

Cellular Door

By Aaron Gudmunson

Murdoch Police Department Case Report 776780, marked "Confidential." Faxed to a wrong number in error and intercepted. Partial narrative transcribed here.

Hello any1 there
:::SHY GURL:::
10:51pm 10/21/12

Who is this?
:::DAVID:::
10:52pm 10/21/12

Michelle. i might need help
:::SHY GURL:::
10:52pm 10/21/12

Do i know you?
:::DAVID:::
10:53pm 10/21/12

No ☹
:::SHY GURL:::
10:53pm 10/21/12

How did u get this number?
:::DAVID:::
10:53pm 10/21/12

On a scrap of paper
:::SHY GURL:::
10:54pm 10/21/12

Where did u get the paper?
:::DAVID:::
11:54pm 10/21/12

Found it here... Can u help me
:::SHY GURL:::
10:55pm 10/21/12

Lol help u how
:::DAVID:::
10:56pm 10/21/12

Do u still need help
:::DAVID:::
11:07pm 10/21/12

U there??
:::DAVID:::
11:15pm 10/21/12

O god i hear them
:::SHY GURL:::
11:21pm 10/21/12

Hear who?
:::DAVID:::
11:21pm 10/21/12

Not who
:::SHY GURL:::
11:22pm 10/21/12

What do u mean?
:::DAVID:::
11:23pm 10/21/12

They want 2 kill me
:::SHY GURL:::
11:24pm 10/21/12

Is this a joke??
:::DAVID:::
11:25pm 10/21/12

Hflp md pls dauid
:::SHY GURL:::
11:26pm 10/21/12

How can i help i don't know whats wrong
:::DAVID:::
11:27pm 10/21/12

They got claws
:::SHY GURL:::
11:29pm 10/21/12

R u drunk lol
:::DAVID:::
11:30pm 10/21/12

Ther at the door i hear em scratchin
:::SHY GURL:::
11:33pm10/21/12

WHO???
:::DAVID:::
11:33pm 10/21/12

The ♣♦♥•◘!
:::SHY GURL:::
11:34pm 10/21/12

If ur in trouble call police dont text me again plz
:::DAVID:::
11:35pm 10/21/12

Cant phones broke text only
:::SHY GURL:::
11:36pm 10/21/12

R u really in trouble?
:::DAVID:::
11:42pm 10/21/12

Hello? Michelle?
:::DAVID:::
11:44pm 10/21/12

They got in send help
:::SHY GURL:::
11:47pm 10/21/12

Hurry im in cellar
:::SHY GURL:::
11:47pm 10/21/12

I'm callin cops
:::DAVID:::
11:48pm 10/21/12

I called cops & gave em ur cell #
:::DAVID:::
11:52pm 10/21/12

U still there?
:::DAVID:::
11:53pm 10/21/12

Michelle u ok
:::DAVID:::
11:54pm 10/21/12

MICHELLE??
:::DAVID:::
11:55pm 10/21/12

Omg i smell em like burnt hair
:::SHY GURL:::
11:56pm 10/21/12

Smell WHAT
:::DAVID:::
11:57pm 10/21/12

The ◘♥♦♠•♠
:::SHY GURL:::
11:58pm 10/21/12

WTF??
:::DAVID:::
11:59pm 10/21/12

Pls hdlp!!
:::SHY GURL:::
12:01am 10/22/12

Send me ur adress
:::DAVID:::
12:02am 10/22/12

40654 W Red Pointe hurry
:::SHY GURL:::
12:03am 10/22/12

K i'm here where r u
:::DAVID:::
12:27am 10/22/12

This house is empty
:::DAVID:::
12:32am 10/22/12

Fukin dumb cant believe i came out here
:::DAVID:::
12:34am 10/22/12

HELP ME!!!!
:::SHY GURL:::
12:35am 10/22/12

WHERE R U!?
:::DAVID:::
12:35am 10/22/12

In cellar!
:::SHY GURL:::
12:37am 10/22/12

Liar. Outta here
:::DAVID:::
12:38am 10/22/12

No please!
:::SHY GURL:::
12:39am 10/22/12

Funny joke
:::DAVID:::
12:39am 10/22/12

HELP!!! Theyre down here!
:::SHY GURL:::
12:40am 10/22/12

K if I come down there n ur not there,
im gonna be pissed
:::DAVID:::
12:41am 10/22/12

HURRY!!!!
:::SHY GURL:::
12:41am 10/22/12

Im comin down
:::DAVID:::
12:43am 10/22/12

Im at door..call my name
so i know where ur at
:::DAVID:::
12:44am 10/22/12

I heard scratchin. that u michelle?
:::DAVID:::
12:45am 10/22/12

Watch out it's the □♣☻♥♦• !
:::SHY GURL:::
12:46am 10/22/12

The WHAT
:::DAVID:::
12:46am 10/22/12

The ☻♠◘•♦♥!!!
:::SHY GURL:::
12:46am 10/22/12

The messages stop here. According to the police report, both cell phones were discovered at the address noted in the correspondence, one behind a heavy oak cellar door covered in deep gashes, the other on the stairs outside the door. The casings of each bore deep scorch marks.

The house on West Red Pointe Road in rural Murdoch had stood abandoned for several years, but local teens occasionally held parties there. The only other evidence discovered at the scene was the scrap of paper containing David McNamara's cell phone number. How it happened to be at the scene has yet to be determined.

Similarly, the inexplicable symbols in Michelle's messages as she tries to warn David about her assailants have a federal code-breaking team and experts in cellular technology at a loss, but all agree her texts were somehow scrambled to avoid revealing the identity of her assailants.

David McNamara and Michelle Randall, who friends and relatives confirmed did not know one another, are still missing.

End Report

PART III: SHORT STORIES

Stray Cat

By Gregory L. Norris

The stray cat Funderson heard yowling around what passed for the apartment house's yard got into the main hallway. It tested doors, made noise, and screwed deeper with his head. Without cable—that had gone dark two months and what felt like centuries earlier—the minor but insidious commotion invaded his filthy little first floor living space whose paint, slapped on haphazardly over the years like globs of cake frosting, had absorbed untold decades of sweat and misery.

Out there. In the hallway. Making human baby noises.

Before the end of television due to Erik Rance Funderson's failure to pay the bill on time—the age of rabbit ears now gone thanks to the greedy cable companies and greedier government officials, he could still play his limited though tired collection of DVDs, porn mostly, until the electricity, too, got switched off—he saw a program on cats. One of those How and Why Things Work documentaries, which theorized that after cats were domesticated, they evolved a sneaky tactic: the ability to mimic human babies in order to tug upon our most basic sympathies and heart strings and bend us to their will. Crafty little fuckers. Funderson hated cats, the smelly, miserable creatures.

The stray cat in the hallway galloped over the dirty carpet. Funderson raked his fingers through his hair, desperately in need of a cut; more, some shampoo. He lit a cigarette. Funderson didn't have money for cable. Hell, he was two months behind on the rent and the next threatening letter, he knew, would require his signature, would arrive in the hand of the sheriff. The cigarette trembled between two dirty fingers. He sucked a desperate hit. Somehow, he always found money for his smokes. Not as often but with regularity, the same held true for drink. Half a dozen longnecks had survived the recent weekend bender.

Funderson drew a beer out of the fridge and knocked back half the bottle. The rush of suds dulled the building pulse in his skull, but the relief was short-lived. Without television, other peoples' TVs, radios, conversations, shouting matches, footsteps, and fuckings wandered through the walls and into his ears. The stray cat mewled, scratched at the length of dirty paneling outside, and the sound traveled inside the apartment, into him.

He finished the bottle in two angry chugs, belched. Another full drag off his cancer stick left Funderson pacing, pulling at his hair. It was in the hallway. Inside his skull.

The building's main front door was a joke. Banged by so many hands over the years, it no longer fit flush in the frame and didn't lock. An endless stream of low-life visitors wandered into the place, along with one stray cat. It was out there, scrawling on the walls, mewling. His insides tightened. The contours of the room phased out of focus, and everything dimmed to shades of sepia and charcoal.

Funderson exhaled his bottled breath. The room emerged from the filter of grayness. Bald yellow daylight illuminated the apartment's sallow details. For a terrible second, Funderson grew intimate with the lightning bolt crack in the ceiling's ancient plaster, the greasy cobwebs above the stove, the punch hole in the drywall from a fist he'd thrown in anger, uncounted days behind.

His eyes zeroed in on the scratchy old blanket on the sofa. Funderson grabbed it and hurried to the apartment's front door.

"Here kitty-kitty," he said in a voice even he found scary.

The ground floor apartment was one of four, all connected by a long hallway. Two additional doors offered escape from the wet dog stinking press of the pitted walls, which bore numerous tattoos in scars and scribbles.

For a good time call—

Bésame, Mami—

Nat loves dick—

For the umpteenth time, Funderson wondered whether Nat was a 'Natalie' or 'Nathaniel' on his way toward one of those deceptive escape hatches. The window of the door at his left peered over the weedy strip of pavement leading to the parking lot. The other descended into the basement's darkness. Thirteen dirty white stairs. More graffiti. A pair of coin-operated washers that never really cleaned your clothes. A matching number of dryers that barely dried, and left your wash loads smelling like other people's odors.

Beyond the laundry area, the basement stretched out in one direction. The oblong windows had been kicked in long ago, replaced with lumber instead of glass. In that realm of shadows lurked gas meters, the electrical panels, and a utility closet where an ancient, barely-used mop bucket on wheels was stored.

The stray cat screamed, kicked.

His anger fueled, Funderson's grip tightened. He felt something snap. The kinetic mass in his hands went limp. The utility closet door hung ajar. Nothing in this shitty place was plumb anymore, not one single element, in any corner. He shoved it the rest of the way open with the toe of his boot and tossed the shroud into the blackness. Dead weight clattered into old plastic.

Funderson snorted through his nostrils, smiled, and turned back in the direction of the stairs, aware of his sudden erection and a strange buzzing emotion, something that felt like happiness, only not quite. Happiness's dark twin.

He wasn't flipping burgers, no way. Funderson had applied to every convenience store and gas-and-go within walking distance, figuring he'd find a way to evade the security cameras and swipe a generous discount on smokes and beer. Hell, he'd lift money meant for the pump from customers who paid cash. There were plenty of eyes squinting down from the ceiling, sure, but Funderson knew how to make things disappear. Like stray cats.

Only he hadn't gotten any calls on jobs.

Later that afternoon, a knock sounded at the door, one more fingernail than knuckle. It shattered the last of Funderson's dark joy.

He grumbled a swear beneath his breath, dragged on his cigarette, and barked, "Just a minute." Zipping up, he answered the door.

One of the neighbors stood on the other side, announced by her cloying scent a fraction of a second before Funderson recognized her red nails, which matched lipstick, and the bleached platinum hair piled and pinned over darker roots. Her denim shorts were too small for her hips; her cans were too big for her top. Too cheap even for him, he thought, disgusted.

"What?" he snapped.

The woman flashed a smile. "Hi, Eric. It's Eric, right?"

Funderson didn't answer.

"You seen my kid?"

"Kid?" Funderson parroted.

"Yeah, my youngest. The boy. I haven't seen him in—"

"I haven't, neither," he said, and slammed the door.

She scrabbled her nails on the other side. "Hey, my kid—his name's Leo, like the sign. I'm starting to get worried."

At that moment, so was Funderson.

He paced, smoked. One cancer stick after another.

Little Leo.

A stray cat had gotten into the building, that was all. Desiccation eroded his tongue and worked into Funderson's throat.

Foot traffic in the hallway multiplied. Then numerous voices from the endless parade of skanks that lived in the building and concerned others began a chorus in the alleys and parking lot, all howling the same off-key name, a pride of cats in heat.

"Leo! Leo!"

Sobs and shrieks crescendoed. Flashing blue lights soon followed. By that point, not even the last of the beer in the fridge could dodge Funderson's thirst.

It was only a cat. A stray fucking cat!

He gathered up a handful of clothes—jeans, a few tee-shirts, socks, whatever his shaking hands retrieved from the pile on the floor. His own stale sweat assailed Funderson's shallow sips of air. His breaths came with growing difficulty.

The ruse worked. Clothes in hand, he slinked down the hallway, to the cellar door, business as usual. In his panic, the stairs stretched from thirteen to twenty-six in distance. When he reached the laundry area, Funderson tossed the clothes on the grimy cement floor and scurried into the region of darkness, wherein the utility closet lurked.

Opening the door washed the foul litter box smell of stale urine into his face. Disgusting creatures, they'd manipulated humans into feeding them, changing their piss and their shit, seduced our heart strings by speaking in the same tongue as human babies.

Funderson rolled the old mop bucket out of the utility closet and into the gloomy gray illumination oozing from the laundry room's lights. One of the stray cat's skinny legs jutted out of the blanket and hung over the side of the bucket.

The stray cat, Funderson saw, wore a powder blue sock and, higher up its thigh, a diaper.

Redolence by Greg McWhorter

Belladonna

By C.L. Hesser

January, 1933
Raven Cove, Massachusetts

From a lone expanse of black, storm-shattered shore, a pale cliff rose like a sentinel out of the rain, shell-white and phantasmal. Lightning splintered the midnight sky—across the nighttime landscape, shuddering swarms of dark-winged nocturnal beings undulated against the black trees.

In a tall, rickety house clinging to the cliff side, a small family crouched about the crackling fire, cold and solemn in the rotting ballroom. A girl with crinkly yellow curls jabbed the iron poker into the blackened logs, casting sparks about the fireplace. Her mother shivered and drew the ratty horse blanket around her daughter's shoulders. "Quiet, Emelie."

The girl held a rag doll to her chest, its red yarn hair encrusted with mud. The doll's black button eyes glinted in the firelight. The girl disentangled her left hand from the blanket and petted the little doll's white forehead. "Mama, I'm cold," she whispered.

"Hush, Emelie."

"But I'm hungry."

The young woman with sorrowful brown eyes kissed her daughter's cold little hands. The fingers were pale and bony -- a dolls' hands. A rat scurried over her foot, its tiny sharp claws scratching her naked skin. Her hand shot out and grabbed the tiny mammal about the middle; she could feel the beast's heart jabbing violently against its brittle ribcage. The rat let out a plaintive squeak, its ruby eyes skittered about the dusky room, its heartbeat fluttering.

"Mama..."

Her mother's pearl teeth flashed, her round yellow eyes glinting in the dusty light, and she dug her eyeteeth into the rat's furry grey coat, tearing open its throat in a jagged gash. Hot blood slicked her long fingers in a coat of sparkling red. She pressed her lips to the ruddy gush, then tore into the flesh of the still creature. When she put the little body to her daughter's hungry mouth, strings of pale flesh and gore clung to her teeth, sticking to her sleek lips. Her mouth had gone slack, her chin stained crimson.

The young girl snarled as the corpse of the rat brushed her lips. She feasted voraciously on the willing flesh, nostrils flaring, feeding with abandon.

When the rat had been reduced to bone and gristle, the girl sat picking bits from her teeth. Sleepiness softened her dark eyes and as the mother lay the girl down among the animal bones, her head resting on a rolled up knapsack for a pillow. Her mother lied down beside the little girl, wrapped her skinny arms about the tiny body, and shut her tired eyes, listening to the wind and rain howl and rage against the boarded-up windows. The two waifs of the world drifted into unconsciousness while the house softly settled about them, the rotted floor heaving under their crumpled forms as the sticky residue dried on their chins.

Shadows crept beneath them and kissed their sleeping faces, drifting across the stained floorboards like pools of black water, and with them - a figure draped in gauzy mists. Her twig-like fingers brushed a curl from the girl's brow, blackened, muck-encrusted nails rustling the girl's potato-sack dress. A shuddering sigh went out from the child's quivering lips, and the form above her quivered.

The child's eyes opened slowly, and she raised herself from the floor as in a trance. Her feet seemed to skim across the floor as the undulating figure took her little hands in its own phantasmagorical paws. Pearly tears splattered the child's feet as the ghost woman's eyes melted within their sockets, then reformed themselves. As the girl watched, enchanted by demonic presences, the figure seemed to lose control of its physical body; her face transformed from a countenance of saint-like mercy to one of terror, then wrath played with her features in turn. Her bones convulsed and she grew and shrank in height rapidly. Her hair shuddered and climbed the walls, pooling out about her on the ballroom floor or sticking to the ceiling like cobwebs.

She gradually regained control of her appearance, clasping close to her breast the child's warm fists.

The ghastly visitor's train of silvery hair trailed to her dainty feet, her now steady form slender and graceful in the moonlight.

Outside, the storm continued to rage, and one might hear the wailing of spirits on the cliff.

She was a creature of haunting, peculiar beauty, with skin white to the point of transparency. Her face was one both refined and delicate, her expression poignant and pleading, her soft gaze compelling.

The small child looked up wonderingly into the phantom's pale eyes and let herself be taken up in ghastly arms and spirited away in a whorl of dust, leaving a deathly cold chill in the dark ballroom. Mama slept on in a dreamless sleep, her breath coming in low, even strides.

Emelie awoke to a rhythmic clicking in her ear and the feel of a nearby fire on her skin. The child opened her eyes and beheld a small, dark, warm room, comforting and old-fashioned, decorated with rustic charm and old-world particularity. Dried lemon peels hung from pegs in the exposed wooden ceiling beams, diffusing a light citrus scent throughout the room. Emelie sensed the nearness of the ocean, the waves pounding on the shore. Indeed, despite the definite warmth and cabin-like interior, the walls of the room were interspersed with areas of exposed rock, as if the snug dwelling were carved out of a cliff-side.

The child lay with her slim arms folded over a patchwork quilt; between cream-colored sheets, she rested her yellow head on a pile of thick down pillows. Firelight and an oil lamp softly lit the area about her—shelves of odd artifacts, jars of glistening, undulating specimens, and colored glass bottles.

Two bookshelves faced each other from opposite sides of the room, each bogged down with double-stacked, leather-bound editions—titles obscured or detailed in gold filigree.

Across from her bed, Emelie could see a figure at a spinning wheel, its figure obscured by a woolen shawl, its face turned to the dancing flames. The fireplace had been inlaid with storm-tossed shells and water-smoothed rock, looming up to the low ceiling. Apart from the fire, to the left of it, a cellar had been dug into the ground; the cellar door had been closed and a bolt thrown across it, but Emelie could smell even through the wood the rich aroma of cookies and seed cake, baked potato and honeyed ham. She rose quietly from among the bedding, stuck her little feet out from beneath the blanket, and plopped down ungraciously to the floor, where a thick carpet swallowed them up like comfits.

The figure at the spinning-wheel stood, smoothed her calico skirt, and turned about to look at Emelie. The woman had silvery-blond hair, bound up in a knot at the back of her slim neck. Her eyes were soft and her manner maternal; she treaded the few steps across the room and squatted down beside Emelie.

"Did you sleep well, darling? Mummy's gotten a nice breakfast all prepared for you."

Emelie blinked and tried to clear her groggy mind. "You are not my mama. Where is my mama?"

"Of course I'm your mama." The woman took Emelie in her arms, smelling of lavender and lemon." And you are my Emelie, and I love you very much." She pressed her soft lips to Emelie's feverish brow.

Emelie smiled gently as a flood of memories seemed to rush into her mind from the point where the woman's lips met her skin. "Oh, mama!" she cried out, and flung herself into the woman's embrace.

The face before her lit up with redoubled happiness as Emelie pulled herself away and danced about, her feet tripping gaily across the carpet. "Mama, where is my breakfast?"

"In the cellar, love-of-mine. On the shelf."

Emelie grinned mischievously and went to the cellar door, where the woman helped her to slide away the bar - the door easily lifted, and Emelie slipped inside, beaming up at her mama from the opening in the floor. "Mama, I—her words cut off in a silent scream as her body was plucked from below, her little throat slit and gurgling.

As a spray of virgin blood spattered the opposite wall, the cellar door swung shut with such force that it sent a tremor across the yellow boards. The woman sighed and rasped, her facial muscles shifting into something...something else.

Intricate Restraint

By Robert J. Santa

Cindy didn't expect to find a metal box behind the loose wallboard. And she certainly didn't expect to find the pictures inside.

The top picture was the least disturbing. The black and white image was of a woman intricately restrained, leather cuffs around her wrists with her arms pulled back to the wall by ropes. A belt around her waist had a metal ring in the front, and a short chain connected the belt to a point off camera. There was a wide collar on her neck, and through another ring in the front there was a chain that held her upright, connected to a point on the ceiling that was also off camera. A ball of rubber was stuffed into her mouth, held in place with what looked like a silk scarf. A wider scarf was tied around the rest of her head, concealing her face as it blindfolded her. The painful position in which she was imprisoned was much more graphic than her nudity, fully displayed as something held her legs apart, as the way her arms were pinned thrust her breasts forward.

There were other pictures, and Cindy flipped through them slowly, captivated by each image for its obscenity. When she encountered the last picture, the one with the woman in segments still tied with ropes and leather, she dropped the box and fled up the stairs, thanking God the photograph was in black and white so she could be spared the vision of all that red.

Cindy held the mug in her hands and tried to take just a small sip, but she was trembling so much she spilled more of the fresh coffee into her mouth than she wanted to. The liquid burned, stripping away the top layer of the meat of her throat as she reflexively swallowed it. The pain helped her focus the honeybee activity of the thoughts inside her skull. After the last drop of coffee had sluiced into her belly, she stood up and went downstairs. Then she gathered all the photos—the last being mercifully face down —and put them back inside the little, metal box. The box went back inside the space behind the wallboard.

She picked up the phone and listened to it drone on while she tried to think of someone to call. Margaret was out of the question. Despite their closeness, she didn't want the whole office to know about this. Her brother was in Disneyworld with Abbey and the kids. And she didn't want to call her husband because the little person that lived in her head and occasionally fed her advice was screaming something Cindy didn't want to believe. The phone began to wail for her attention in intermittent bursts of mechanical rage, so she simply hung it back on the receiver and poured herself another cup of coffee.

An hour later she was staring at the Queen Anne four posted bed. It was a beautiful piece, its dark wood covered in the bright blue and yellow comforter set, the edges of the pillows poking out from underneath. Last night Mark had tied her hands to the headboard. Right up until she saw the pictures in the basement, she had thought it a thrilling experience.

Her vomit tasted like coffee. Cindy tried to lie down after she cleaned the bathroom. She didn't hear Mark come home, and when he walked in the room she imagined it was someone with a carving knife.

"Sorry," he said, "didn't mean to startle you." Mark had a plastic bag in one hand, and he went into the bathroom to put away the deodorant and shaving cream. A moment later he bent over her. He gave her a quick kiss, and she tried not to recoil, but it was obvious he noticed.

"What's the matter?" asked Mark. He smelled of fresh Old Spice.

"Nothing," she said. "You just caught me off guard."

"Did you eat yet?"

"No." The idea of food made Cindy's innards do somersaults.

"Good. I bought some stuff for a brunch. Give me about half an hour." He left the room, and Cindy felt a relief she would be ashamed to admit.

How long had she known him? Barely eight years. Mark and Cindy had met in college, sophomore year. Cindy had gone on to get her marketing degree, to climb the ladder until she had bulls eyed with a dopey ad for a two-unit rug warehouse. Who would have figured three grown men—warehouse employees, not even actors —dressed as cowboys and calling themselves "rugboys" would become a fulltime fixture, even in primetime? Everyone knew she and Mark would get married, and the bonus and following steady work gave them the income to do it. Even though Mark had never graduated, he had found corporate success with a toy chain, becoming their management poster boy to prove that a cashier can become area manager with enough hard work.

He'd never tied her up before, never even suggested it. Their bedroom time was hardly straight-laced and was very rarely boring. She didn't know he wanted to tie her up until afterwards; lying there together, he told her he had been wanting to do that for "a while now." What else didn't she know about his fantasies? Did he like to take pictures?

Did he like to hide them? This was his house, after all, bought with the meticulously invested paychecks of his youth. There were probably dozens of nooks and crannies she'd never investigated.

"Breakfast is ready," Mark said, and this time Cindy restrained herself from jumping only in the instant before he spoke, when she saw his shadow in the doorway.

He'd made some potatoes with onion and paprika, sliced some melon, and grilled petite tenderloins with a little hollandaise on top. Cindy wasn't hungry but didn't want him to be suspicious. When she put the forkful of filet in her mouth it didn't taste like his usual superb cooking. It only tasted like dead flesh.

It wasn't easy to steer clear of Mark all day. She needed some time and some distance, and they usually spent the one day of the week they both didn't have to work together. But they each had a small list of projects to get done around the house. Cindy did a lousy job putting touch up paint on the stair rail while Mark aerated the lawn. She avoided lunch by saying she was still working on such a big breakfast, even though she had hardly touched it. Dinner was harder to dodge. She pushed chicken Caesar salad around her plate until Mark asked her if she was done. He did the dishes while she folded some laundry downstairs. She'd only folded one towel, yet she had looked at the corner twenty times. Behind the wallboard, inside a metal box, there were pictures of someone she feared her husband had known.

Cindy tried to stay awake until Mark had gone to bed, but she was so tired. Mark said he was going to watch a movie, so she went upstairs and hoped that her mind would slow down enough for her to be asleep when he joined her. She wasn't even warm under the covers when he came into the room.

He had a husband's kind of look in his eyes.

"Please," Cindy said, and she was startled at the desperation in her voice.

"What?" Mark said. "I haven't even asked." Cindy said nothing, and after a few seconds Mark must have realized she wasn't kidding. He went to his side of the bed and slipped under the covers. His hand found her butt cheek for a quick goodnight pat, and despite his desires, Mark was asleep in ten minutes. Cindy watched the clock numbers change. The last one she remembered was 4:48.

Downstairs on the laundry table was a basket of unfolded towels. Cindy stared at the one she had done yesterday until she had to shake her head. Then she stared at the wall beside the dryer.

She had the radio to blame. Cindy had been listening to a talk program about house fires and the preventative steps everyone can take. One of the routine maintenance ideas was about cleaning the dryer hoses. As she was unclamping the hose, she noticed the very neat slice in the wall, what turned out to be the hinged side of a well-concealed panel.

Cindy was kneeling next to the dryer again without realizing she had done so. She pushed against the panel, and it pivoted open to reveal the simple, metal box that so neatly fit the space within.

That same photograph was on the top of the stack. The woman was still bound, her body pulled in several directions at once. The way in which she was tied at the arms and waist reminded Cindy of a particularly brutal image from the Vietnam war, of a prisoner whose arms were chained at the wrist and pulled cruelly back. The photo of the woman differed for its nudity and for its eroticism, which had nothing to do with the lack of clothing.

She must have been cold. Her skin was covered in gooseflesh, and her nipples were so hard they must have been painful. Cindy wondered what it was that held the woman's legs apart, for the picture ended at mid-calf. Perhaps there were cuffs connected to the floor. Or maybe it was a wooden bar with cuffs attached to either end. As Cindy shifted a little, her tee shirt brushed against her bare nipple, and she felt it swell.

Cindy slammed the lid down on the box and took the stairs two at a time.

"Tell me again about the first time you opened the space."

"We've been over this so many times," Cindy said, not bothering to hide the weariness in her voice.

"I know," replied Detective Robillard. "I understand you're tired. This will be the last time."

The detective was an attentive listener, and Cindy told him for the fourth time about the box full of photographs. She spoke freely and without interruption. Detective Robillard waited for her to pause before he asked his specific questions about some small detail she hadn't even thought about. When they had met in her kitchen, she thought he was too young to be a homicide detective, a college student's head perched atop a massive frame as big as a doorway. She led him and a woman who had the mannequin eyes of someone who had seen too much downstairs where they poked around with flashlights and brushes of powder for half an hour. Cindy had ridden in their car back to the police station where they took her fingerprints on a machine that photocopied them without ink. Then they had talked, over and over about the same things. It wasn't until Detective Robillard asked the third of his penetrating questions that she realized he was much better at his job than his boyish face filled with laugh lines admitted.

She sat in her kitchen again, another cup of coffee fading away to tepid death on the table. Cindy had his card in her hand, and she flipped at the corner and listened to the sound it made as it snapped back into place. A simple question ricocheted off the walls of her skull without losing momentum and without gaining any, a screensaver thought that refused to disappear. The phone rang, and she was startled not so much by the sound of it but by the fact that two hours had passed in a blink at the kitchen table.

"It's me," Mark said. He paused, an ugly silence. Cindy knew where he had been and whose penetrating questions he had been answering.

"Hi." It was easier to say than "I should have called you."

"I'm going to stay at a hotel tonight."

"Okay," said Cindy. It was a hollow word that held no meaning, simply took up space in the conversation because a void needed to be filled.

"I just thought I should call you." He hung up without saying anything else, and Cindy felt the slap of his hand across her cheek.

Dinner was a package of Pop Tarts, cold from the pantry, and four Tanqueray and tonics. Her stomach rebelled in only fifteen minutes, and her vomit tasted predictably like lime juice and chocolate frosting. The mouthwash did little to make her feel better. She went straight from the sink to the bed, stripping down to tank top and panties. The bed was cold, and after an hour of sleeplessness Cindy realized that half of the mattress had not yet warmed up.

She was dreaming. The world was such an awful place, filled with gooseflesh and leather. There were manacles and handcuffs, rings of soulless metal that had lost their ability to glitter. And it was all in black and white.

Cindy awoke when Mark put his arm around her. The room was very dark.

"I couldn't sleep," he said into her hair.

"I'm sorry. I should have called you."

His arm hugged her tighter. His cheek nuzzled the back of her head. Mark sighed once and fell asleep. Cindy stayed awake long enough to realize they were breathing in rhythm.

Another weekend came, interrupted by days of work and nights of foot massages, vanilla candles, and sauvignon blanc. Cindy was in the kitchen cleaning up after Mark's famous eggs Florentine when the telephone rang.

"Mrs. Sandberg?" said a woman's weary voice, aged, with the life drawn out of it by too much talking.

"Yes?" said Cindy. She almost said "can I take a message, please," a defense mechanism for telemarketers.

"This is Detective Adams," said the woman, whose voice suddenly brightened. "Detective Robillard passed along your case to me."

"Yes?" Cindy said again, this time with more emphasis on the question.

"I just wanted to call you and thank you. We lifted some prints and matched them to a suspect already incarcerated for a variety of sex crimes. He confessed to the murder of the woman in the photograph. He used to live in your house, many years ago."

"Oh, that's terrific," she said, though it hardly felt like it was.

"I was the original investigator on that case. I always thought I knew who the killer was, but he never admitted any wrongdoing, and we had no evidence. It's something that's bothered me now for almost thirty years."

"I'm glad I could help."

"Anyway," said Detective Adams, her voice more energetic still, "thanks again. And if you need anything, remember my name. I owe you one."

"Okay." The receiver clicked before Cindy could say "goodbye."

Mark was mowing the lawn. Cindy would tell him the good news when he was done. The dryer buzzed, and she headed downstairs.

As she bent down to open the machine she glanced to the left. The seam for the little door was difficult to see, and she wondered how she ever saw it in the first place. Cindy bent down and ran her hand over the wall, her fingers caressing the door. She pushed on it. The space was empty behind it. Somehow, deep in the recesses of her mind, she expected to find something.

Mark opened the door and headed down the stairs. Cindy stayed crouched down and readied herself to playfully pounce on him. But instead of coming near, he walked to the far side of the basement. He turned the light on over his workbench and leaned, his body straining with the effort of listening. Cindy remained low to the ground and wished for herself to be smaller.

Mark turned his back and reached under the workbench for a toolbox she had never seen. He opened it and took out a photo album. Even from ten feet away she could see too-young, pink flesh and cheerleader skirts. Mark flipped a few pages and ran a finger over one of them, lingering on legs split in mid-air. The pigtails were bright blonde and held in place with baby blue ribbon.

He closed the book and put it back in the toolbox. Mark then straightened his clothes with his eyes shut, deep breaths filling his lungs. He was pointed directly towards the dryer, and when he opened his eyes he would know that she knew.

Mark walked forward and turned his head. Cindy could see the profile of his eye as he turned again and climbed the stairs. He reached the top without seeing her in the shadows, without changing his stride at all.

She heard him call her name. Footsteps above her moved around the living room, then into the dining room and back into the kitchen. Cindy wished for one of those farmhouse exits from the basement, but hers was a raised ranch built fifty years ago on land that had never been a farm. She stood, wondering what she could do until his shadow filled the doorway at the top of the stairs.

"Cindy?" he called, his voice nervous. "Are you down here?"

Mark's eyes found hers. He stood there, a silhouette of anticipation that crumbled in seconds as he passed through stages of denial and anger and ultimately acceptance. It was a short journey, and when he was done he turned away and walked out the door. Cindy heard his car engine start then get softer as his Taurus pulled away.

Cindy stood next to the dryer and trembled. When her legs stopped quivering, she walked over to the toolbox on the bottom shelf of the workbench. She carried it upstairs and felt the objects inside it move around. She identified the photo album, and there was something metallic and something else that sounded like solid rubber. Cindy walked out into the sunlight of the front yard and stared at the empty driveway.

Then she tossed the unopened toolbox into the trashcan and went back in the house to wait for Mark's phone call.

Narcissa by Beth Murphy

Visions of a New York Loft

By Tracy L. Carbone

Timmy cried in his cranberry juice as he listened to "The End of the World" for the twentieth time. It was one of his wife's favorite shower tunes. He'd taped her beautiful voice singing the sad ballad as she shampooed her long, thick, dark hair.

But now Amy was on the way to gone. She claimed it was a weeklong trip away with her girlfriend to think, but he was no fool. The marriage was over. He looked around the great room with dismay. She had hated this house, a million-dollar brick Tudor in Andover, Massachusetts. Any other woman would be thrilled to live here, grateful to be married to an ophthalmologist. Timmy was handsome, to boot. Worked out, avoided caffeine, red meat, sugar...he was a catch.

But Amy wasn't happy. All these years later, and she was still pining for her first husband—the demented, tortured artist who had died of a drug overdose. Timmy had been forced to listen to her carry on ad nauseum about the spacious loft they'd had in Greenwich Village across from an all-night diner.

But it wasn't too late for him to give her that loft in the city.

He looked down and gasped. A spot of burgundy liquid soiled his crisp white shirt. Damn. He rose from the imported leather couch and walked to the laundry closet to get the Tide pen.

He dabbed the tip of the pen on his chest. Better. He took the shirt off and frowned. The stain had bled through to his white t-shirt. He disrobed and hurried to their bedroom.

The room was splendid: cathedral ceilings, skylights, and an entire wall of glass overlooking two acres of lush lawn. Breathtaking.

But not to Amy. She wanted a brick wall and a pink neon doughnut blaring through the window.

He pulled a perfectly folded t-shirt from the stack of a dozen others just like it. As he put it over his head, he glanced at her side of the closet and winced. Shirts haphazardly tossed into what she called piles. He started to straighten them but caught himself. *No. Stop it, Timmy. You've got work to do.*

He headed down to the basement, grabbed the sledgehammer, and walked up to the wall of their great room. Before he struck the wall, he thought angrily of the waste of Ralph Lauren Suede paint and all the time he'd spent getting the brush strokes just right. Well, he'd just have to repaint it. He had a marriage to save.

"You're what?" Carole said.

"Leaving him. I can't handle it anymore," Amy said, sipping her third Jack and Coke.

"Are you nuts? He'll never let you keep the house," Amy's best friend Carole said.

"I don't care about the house."

Amy had hoped Carole would understand, but how could she? Her whole life was her house and kids. She viewed her loving breadwinner husband as a necessarily evil to maintain a life of luxury. At the best of times, Roger was a task to be completed.

"Are you going to stay in Andover?"

"No. Going back to New York, cashing in my retirement, and writing a novel. After Eli died I thought I wanted order. I looked for someone settled, safe, and controlled. But you know what," she drained her glass and gestured to the bartender for another. "I can't handle that level of order. I don't like choosing all my meals for the week on Sunday or laying out my clothes days in advance."

Carole observed her, like a bug under a glass.

"I'm sick of Tim following me around, straightening up after me, telling me what to eat, or what time to go to bed. And I'm tired of the suburbs."

"You've got too much time on your hands is all."

"No, Carole. I have an OCD control freak for a husband and I'm losing myself a little more each day. I want me back. I haven't written anything decent since I moved into that monstrosity of a house."

Carole smirked. "Come on, Amy. When you were in New York with Eli, living hand-to-mouth in that roach-infested apartment—that was not living."

"Yes it was," Amy said, as dizziness set in. "That was living. This is dying."

After that tirade, Amy chewed the ice in the bottom of the empty glass. "No one is going to take away my dream of making it as a writer and living in a New York loft. I have to pee. I'll be back."

The next clear memory she had was waking up, sitting on a couch. It was a month later and she was blind.

"Where am I?" Amy asked in a timid voice. Her world was shrouded in utter darkness. Foreign smells overwhelmed her.

"It's okay, Sweetie. I'm here," Tim said. He held her hands and for a moment she felt safe, relieved by his presence. "We're in the new house. I've told you ten times. But the doctor said it's natural that your short-term memory would be affected."

"You didn't tell me that. I would have remembered."

"You wouldn't. That's why they call it memory loss. What matters is that you're alive."

"But I'm blind." She reached for her eyes. No scars on the lids or sides. Normal from the outside. This wasn't still a shock. It had been, and she'd screamed, cried, and fought. Vague memories skittered through her mind like roaches. Why was it she could remember discovering her blindness and working through it, but not where she was?

"Wait a minute. You bought a new house?" Amy asked.

"When you disappeared I went out of my head," Tim said. His voice sounded sad, weak. Not traits she'd even known in her husband. "When they found you in that alley in Miami two weeks later, like this, I knew I had to make things right. I sold the house in Andover and bought you a loft in Greenwich Village."

"I'm in New York?" The thought brought bittersweet joy.

"It's one huge room, open concept like you wanted. The bed is over there." He picked up her hand and pointed for her. "The kitchen area is over there. And the bathroom, there."

She pulled her cardigan around her shoulders. "I was found in an alley?" He'd probably told her that story before too, but she couldn't remember. Just disconnected feelings with no pictures.

"You were kidnapped and blinded. Left there to die."

"Did they catch him?"

"No. I'm sorry. That's another reason we moved," Tim explained. A chill went up her spine.

"But I'm safe now? Here in New York, I'll be safe?"

"I'll take care of you." He squeezed her hand tight.

Amy rubbed the leather of the couch. At least something was familiar. "I don't recall anything from before a few minutes ago. How long have I been walking around confused like this?"

"What happened to you was traumatic. It's better you don't remember." His hands held fast.

"But how long have I been back here? Awake?"

"It doesn't matter. We're in New York and you can start writing again."

"How can I do that when I can't see?"

"Come here." He stood her up and she walked across the room, each step an exposé in anxiety. Would the ground disappear beneath her? Were there stairs? If she fell, would he catch her? Amy wanted walls to lean against, the familiarity of the house in Andover she had hated so much. She appreciated that Timmy had moved them to a loft. Maybe he did love her after all, in his way—but maneuvering around a place utterly devoid of light was horrifying.

"Here, sit." Gently Tim coaxed her to a chair. The woven fabric of the seat comforted her. *My old office chair.* She felt the grooves in the ridge along the front of the desk. Her desk. She moved her fingers along the top. A mug with pens. Red pens, she knew.

"What good does all this do me? I can't see the screen."

"I bought you voice recognition software. You read into this microphone." He placed her hand around a metal tube. "And it will transcribe it for you. The computer can read it back to you. Or you can print it out. I'll read everything you write and help you edit it. Type in your changes."

Amy cringed. She couldn't think of a worse scenario. Well, yes she could. She could be dead. But this was a close second.

She took a deep breath, feeling selfish. Here was Timmy trying to help her, and once again, she was fighting him.

"What did he do to my eyes? The man who kidnapped me. There isn't anything you can do to fix them?"

Timmy had been one of the top ophthalmologists in Boston. She didn't know how he'd rank in Manhattan. "I tried. Called in consults from everywhere but there was too much damage. I'm sorry."

"What about your practice? Don't you need to get a license to practice medicine in New York?"

"Don't worry your pretty head about that. I'll take care of the business end of things. Just work on learning to use this software. It will take some adjusting to but you'll get it." Next thing she felt his lips on hers. And his tongue. She had never liked kissing him, but who else would ever want her now? Her instinct to push him away lessened and she returned his kiss.

After an endless few seconds, he pulled away. She put her hand back on the mouse and rubbed it like a worry stone. How did he expect her to remember how to use the program when she couldn't recall things from an hour ago? His voice droned on and she struggled to focus. She was trapped here with him. Forever in the dark, in a loveless marriage. No freedom ever again.

Maybe together they could make this work. If she could write again, that would be something. A start. A way of eking out her identity, reclaiming herself. He'd relocated for her, given up his practice in Massachusetts. The least she could do was try a little harder to tolerate him. With her left hand, she reached out until she found his arm. "Thank you, Timmy, for doing all this."

"You can't make it alone, Amy. I wouldn't even want you to try. I'm here to help you every step of the way. No thanks, necessary."

Later that night, Timmy agreed to walk to a local deli to get Amy a pastrami on rye with a pickle. A blast from her past, she had said. An authentic New York deli sandwich.

It was reassuring to him that she was adopting a New York mindset. Silly Amy. So trusting. He smiled as he walked out the door of the loft and, not through the streets of Greenwich Village, but into the great room of their Andover house to prepare her dinner.

She believed it. All of it. Actually accepted—hook, line, and sinker—that he had sold the Massachusetts abode and moved them to a New York loft. Had no idea she was residing in the very same house she had always hated, smack in the middle of an Andover cul de sac, surrounded by housewives and soccer moms.

It had cost him a small fortune to renovate the place while she was sedated, awaiting him to awaken her like the prince in Snow White. She never heard the ruckus of the power tools and the workmen who knocked down and reconfigured walls. Oblivious to the crash as the contractors popped through the old ceilings to give the "loft" echoes so she'd envision the space properly.

He'd had someone brick over the interior walls of the new inner sanctum, the newly constructed part of the house. The New York loft within a brick Tudor. He'd had floor-to-ceiling windows installed in the walls of the loft. They opened not to the city, but to drywall, a four-inch barrier to the inside of the old house. But they were permanently closed. No need to worry. Timmy had even had lights and heaters installed behind the faux windows so Amy would think there was sunlight pouring through. She couldn't actually see anything, thanks to his handiwork with a laser, but she might be able to tell the difference between a light and dark room.

The construction took so much longer than Timmy had planned, but Amy was none the wiser.

If his precious Amy ever walked out the front door of her loft, dared to venture outside—which she couldn't because he locked it from the outside—she wouldn't actually find herself in the hallway of a building in Greenwich village, but in the fringes of her old great room. Beyond that, the front lobby with the imported crystal chandelier and the sprawling stairway to the spacious second floor...

Soon after, she'd enter the farmer's kitchen he had built her two years ago. The one she detested. A "tangible symbol of her sellout to domesticity." The same kitchen where, right now, he prepared a straight-from-the-deli pastrami sandwich, and folded it into a wax wrapper. He added a half pickle and impaled the bread with a toothpick, making a snap as the point punctured the paper. He shoved it into a paper bag from the package of them he'd created at the printers. Amy's sense of touch would only grow more sensitive over time and he'd made sure to get raised printing on the bag. "Harvey's Deli" in smooth blue letters, replete with a street address in Greenwich Village. One more bit of proof for the life he had created. Another concrete bit of evidence for Amy to cling to.

Timmy had thought of everything, he reflected, as he walked back to the "loft." He'd taken his shoes off to walk through the Andover house. Socks only on his Brazilian Cherry hardwood floors. Now he had to slip the shoes back on so he could pretend he'd been outside. Just a small bit of aggravation to keep his wife eternally blind and helpless, and trapped on the set of a brick loft.

Amy heard Timmy leave for work a couple of hours ago, to wherever he commuted. So long as he left her alone most of each day she didn't care where he went.

Since the other night when she suddenly found herself sitting on the couch, she'd remembered everything. Mind was sharp as a tack. But before that, nothing: a blank slate from Miami until she awoke in New York, a visual cripple. There were snippets of conversation with Timmy, when he'd told her about what had happened; but it was all out of sequence.

Denouement by Natalie Sirois

Well, this was what she had always wanted, right? Frustration filled her and she clenched her fists. Finally living in her New York loft with nothing but time to write, and someone to support her while she sat home and poured out the creativity. Except she couldn't see a single word. Ever again. Could feel her fingers type the keys but couldn't witness the transformation, the transubstantiation, as she created life on the screen. Turning words into people, the energy flowing through her fingers, striking the keys, hammering characters from clay to human...

That process, her lifeblood, had been stolen from her.

She buried her head in her hands. Just the thought of a lifetime of this was too much. Amy had come so close to leaving Timmy. So close to breaking free. This wasn't how it was supposed to work out.

She faced the warmth filtering through the massive windows, then stood up and walked toward the sunlight. Her world was completely black. Couldn't tell day from night, sunlight from pitch dark. But the heat emanating from the panes told her there was sun streaming through, and that gave her hope. She carefully maneuvered twenty steps to her right to the window. Nothing in the way. No doubt, Mr. Careful had made their whole living space blind-lady-safe.

She touched the panes and yanked her fingers back from the shock of the temperature. Warm. She had expected cold. This was March. The panes should have been icy.

Even in summer, glass was cold. She tried to open the frame but it was stuck. Thick paint covered the grooves. Sealed shut. The prior owner must have slopped paint down and left it to dry. Amy pushed her shoulder against it, used all her strength to heave it open, but it was no use. She'd have to get a knife and come back to break the seal.

Amy rested her face against the window. She wanted to be outside in the city so badly she could taste it. All day and all night long, the sounds of traffic and an occasional shouting taxi driver filled the loft. A world bustling with people, artists and writers—hell, she'd welcome the company of homeless beggars at this point. But it was completely beyond her reach, just like the sunlight

She called out. "Hello!" Louder. "Hello! Can anyone hear me?" There was an echo because of the fifteen-foot ceilings and hardwood floors. Timmy had ensured it was a replica of the place she'd lived in with Eli.

But what if the ceilings were eight feet? Nine feet? Timmy could lie about a lot and she couldn't prove it either way.

Yes, she could. There must be a broom somewhere. If she stood on the couch and held the broom up as high as it would go that would be about eleven feet. Maybe more.

Amy ran her hand along the walls in the kitchen area. Where was the broom closet? Damn. No closets anywhere.

She walked the whole area of the loft again, touching every inch of space she could. Counting her steps, trying to memorize locations. No closets. Where were all their things? It wasn't right.

Amy sank into the couch. Of course, it wasn't right. She was blind now. Nothing would ever be right again. She closed her eyes and curled into the fetal position. This is what her life had been reduced to: worrying about why the windows were warm or why there were no brooms or closets. Aching to find a way to measure the ceiling height.

Amy wanted her life back. She sobbed so hard she couldn't catch her breath, and it was only the lulling sound of the constant traffic, the honking of horns, a swearing cabbie, that gave her any comfort. The unobtainable universe a few floors below soothed her.

At least she was no longer tortured by the silence of the suburbs. The rush of cars pulled her from her misery so she could nap until Timmy came home. He'd go to the deli for her again, get her a fresh pastrami sandwich. Eventually he'd take her out when he felt she was strong enough. She'd pay attention and learn the way out of the building. Commit to memory the number of footsteps from one block to the next. Get used to the feel of utter darkness in a visual world.

Amy would learn Braille and get a Seeing Eye dog. Then she wouldn't be so dependent on Timmy.

And then, thank God, she could leave him. Again.

"Why don't we have a broom?"

"What?" Timmy asked as he handed her the fat laden pastrami sandwich. It repulsed him to watch her eat it. Made his stomach heave. But he had resolved to give her the semblance of freedom.

"Today, I was looking for a broom and noticed there weren't any closets. Where are all our coats?"

"On the coat rack."

"But where's the rest of our stuff? We had a lot of belongings in Andover. And there isn't a broom or a mop. I know how much you like to clean."

"All our things are in storage in the attic. The residents of this building are allocated sections. When we need things, I go up there and get them. And no, I don't enjoy cleaning. It's tedious and never-ending. I just prefer a clean house so have to keep tidying up so it stays that way."

"I'm sorry." Amy faced him but he knew the expression in her eyes meant nothing. They weren't windows into her soul anymore. They were only as telling as the glass eyes of a mannequin.

But Timmy didn't care. Amy needed him. For everything. And he'd provide it all: Food, shelter, love. His heart pounded with excitement as he looked at her shiny, blank stare. She'd love him whether she liked it or not. What choice did she have?

"I'm sorry. Honestly, we haven't been here long enough to do any heavy duty cleaning." He patted her head. That was a lie.

All his cleaning supplies were in the Andover house. Until a few days ago, he'd kept the door that joined the two homes open and had cleaned religiously and constantly, as was his habit. But since he'd let her wake up, he hadn't resumed his routine. He'd have to buy duplicate provisions for here so she wouldn't grow suspicious.

"As far as the broom, my mother always said you need to make a clean sweep when you move. It's bad luck to bring one from an old house. Color me sloppy, but I haven't gotten around to buying a new one yet. All I've been thinking about is your healing, and getting settled in."

"It's okay. Let's just eat and forget about it."

He put his hand on her arm and she moved closer to him.

"Want me to run to the liquor store and get you a bottle of Jack Daniels?"

"You're not going to give me a hard time about it?"

"No. It's your body." He rolled his eyes but she was none the wiser.

"Thank you. I could use it. I'll help clean once I get acclimated."

"Don't be silly. I'll do everything for you from now on."

She cringed. "I don't need you to. I can do things for myself." A tear ran down her cheek.

He smiled broadly, and then he put on his saddest voice and reached for her hand. "No, Amy. You can't. Not anymore."

Another week went by and Amy was still ensnared in the loft without human contact, except for Timmy. The phone wasn't hooked up yet, though he promised the technicians would be there any day. She had a cell phone, but the battery was dead and Timmy hadn't gotten her a charger yet. She hadn't turned on her computer since the second day she'd awoken from her fog. What was the point? How the hell was she supposed to even position the mouse to get the software running?

Amy was helpless and trapped. Not a conducive environment for creativity.

Doubts kept her up at night. Things that didn't make sense.

So far, she had managed to avoid having sex with him. Avoided kissing him too for the most part. But she didn't know how long he'd put up with that. She needed to get away. Now that he was her whole world, her only gateway to the life outside her four walls, he was intolerable.

Timmy left for his job—wherever he worked, he was painfully vague—and as she did every day, continued plotting and planning her escape. Once the phone was connected, she'd make calls. Carole would help her. And if not her, one of her old coworkers. She couldn't believe none of them had sent letters or fruit baskets.

She swallowed hard. Or maybe they had tried to contact her.

Where was the mail? Why hadn't Timmy mentioned receiving any?

In the old house, he had routinely set it all on the island. Amy carefully walked to the kitchen area here and felt all the counter tops. Nothing. She opened the trash under the sink and sifted through it wishing she could glance at the contents instead of digging her fingers in refuse. Her hands were good at recognizing things though. She was surprised at how quickly her other senses had compensated. A few minutes of rifling in the bag yielded coffee filters, an empty cream container, eggshells, paper towels, plus a few things she just couldn't identify without sight. But no envelopes. No mail. Not even sales flyers.

There should be mail. Was Timmy keeping it from her? Had her friends tried to reach her in New York?

The city and its noises bustled on below but she still couldn't get to them. It wasn't safe out there for a blind woman, he'd said. Until she got her bearings she had to agree.

Filled with despair, she walked to her warm window. There was something about that oddity that she couldn't accept. She rested her cheek against it, still unsettled by the room-temperature panes.

She pressed her ear hard to the window. Nothing but a hum.

She raised her head up to the ceiling. Cars and muffled voices. A horn. The rush of traffic was unmistakable. Amy put her ear back to the window, the one that was supposed to lead to the streets of Greenwich Village.

Warm glass and a hum.

Sounds should get louder by the window.

"Hey asshole!" The distant cabbie voice yelled in the distance, not from the outside, but from somewhere in the room.

Amy gasped. *Hey asshole.* She'd heard it before. Over and over. That voice yelling the same phrase.

Amy counted her steps and ran to get the broom and mop. Timmy had finally bought cleaning supplies. Yesterday she had stood on the couch and verified for herself that the ceilings were at least twelve feet high.

But it had another purpose now.

She tilted her head up again. The sounds of the street weren't coming from the window, so where? A recording? She took the mop and broom and tied them together with a dishtowel.

Slowly, Amy moved the long probe to where the wall and ceiling met. And shifted it along. Inch by inch. The mop/broom snagged something. A speaker? She heaved the tool and swung as if she was aiming at a piñata and the payout wasn't candy, but her life. Direct hit.

Suddenly the city sounds were different. They were still there but there was hole. A gap. An area of the room that didn't supply the noise.

Amy didn't need to find the rest of the speakers. One was enough to know nothing was as it seemed. Need to get out! Now!

She walked to the door, undid the three locks and turned the knob. But it wouldn't open. She tugged and pulled, her hand sweated and slipped. Locked from the outside.

My God, what did you do?

Screw it. Blind or not, she was out of here.

She picked up a kitchen chair, teetered to one of the big windows and smashed it.

Crack! Thud.

She stepped back. The glass shattered but the wooden legs banged against something hard.

Amy set the chair down and moved closer.

Her fingers carefully touched the frame. Broken glass. But there was no outside breeze flying in. She pressed her hand carefully around and past the jagged glass. A wall. A warm wall behind the window, with forced hot air streaming from above.

The heat I felt was never from the sun.

She picked the chair back up and used the legs to strike the partition. It was an exterior wall and surely brick, but she had to try. Expected to hear the gritty dead sound of wood hitting mortar, a useless attempt at escape.

Thwack!

The legs were stuck. *What the hell?*

She reached out and let her fingers follow the wood to the wall. It had pierced through. Through brick?

She pulled it out and set it down, then felt the hole. It was about an inch thick. Then hollow, then another inch on the other side. Drywall. Behind a window? She picked the chair back up and stabbed the barrier of her prison again and again, wishing it was Timmy's chest.

When she stopped, the hole was big enough for her to crawl through. She popped her head out and listened—silence.

Where are the sounds of the city?

She pulled her head back and rocked herself, feet first, through the hole. Then jumped. If this was the city, and she fell a bunch of stories to her death, that was all right. It would be better than a life of darkness and domination with Timmy.

But she only fell about two feet.

In her stocking feet, she hit a hardwood floor. She moved her head back and forth, listening and sniffing. Where the hell am I?

It was soundless here. She tottered, one foot in front of the other; afraid the next pace might drop her from a cliff, or the ledge of a building. Blindness was so much more terrifying that anyone could ever relay, especially after so many years of sight.

Finally, she found an interior wall. She cried out in relief.

Amy staggered ahead with hope of escape but also dreadful realization. Her loft had been nothing more a set within another place. But what was this other place? A warehouse maybe?

Suddenly the texture of the paint on the wall changed beneath her newly sensitive fingertips. It was course and dry. Textured. I know this paint. Timmy had used the suede paint in their great room. All the walls were—what was the color? Arrow Wood. Timmy had spent a whole day with the roller and then the paintbrush, making exact strokes, eschewing the random exes the video suggested.

I'm still in Andover.

Never went to New York at all, never left my house. Her whole body started shaking and the hair on her neck stood up as she fathomed that Timmy had built her a loft in the middle of the Tudor.

She gulped and cocked her head, hoping to sense something. Was Timmy home? Right here, inches away, watching as she made her discovery? Plotting a new way to trap her?

At least now she knew the way out. She turned and stepped forward to the front door.

Uhn! Why is there a wall here?

She put her head down. Of course, the loft was in the middle of the great room and who knew how far it extended? Amy began to walk the perimeter of the new addition to gauge its size. But she knew already. The interior was forty-six Amy footsteps by thirty. She'd walked it repeatedly, paced it like a lion in a cage. Knew the inside of the loft by heart. Its outside was just a tower of drywall.

This kind of construction, the elaborate kind Timmy had orchestrated took planning. Nothing that could be thrown together in a handful of weeks. How many weeks or months had really passed? How long had he kept her asleep while he built her crypt? It explained the confused memories, the snatches of conversation. She stiffened when she realized he must have bathed her, probably made her wear a diaper.

Rage filled her. He'd had sex with her. She'd had nightmares, vivid horrific dreams since she had awoken. But they weren't nightmares; they were memories. He had violated her repeatedly when she was semi-conscious.

She touched her eyes. Timmy had done this to her! Drugged her in Miami, fabricated her abduction. Blinded her with his ophthalmologic expertise and then built her a cage smack in the middle of the suburban prison where she had spent the previous five years.

Have to get out. Now!

Amy followed the wall to the front door—

The familiar grinding hum as the garage door opened stopped her before she could feel her way to the knob.

No time now.

The door that connected the garage to the house swished open. Shit. Her heart pounded hard in her chest.

The only way back into the loft was that shattered wall, but she was not going back in. She'd die first. Amy hurried frantically up the stairs she knew so well, to the second floor. As long as Timmy didn't go into the loft he wouldn't know she'd escaped.

She arrived at the landing and entered the closet of the spare room.

Amy felt around inside for a weapon. Anything sharp or heavy would do. She silently opened boxes and fished through their contents: Armfuls of audio books on self-improvement he'd bought her. Stress balls for when boredom struck. Hand weights to keep her toned for him. An afghan hook. Timmy had bought the hook, a how-to video, and some skeins of expensive yarn one year in hopes she'd pick up a domestic hobby. She hadn't, but it seemed she'd finally get some use out of the long metal skewer.

Timmy's footsteps creaked as he walked past the room and into their bedroom. His after-work debriding ritual. He hadn't been taking early evening showers since they'd moved to the loft and she thought he was weaning off his need to constantly bathe. No such luck, he had been scouring his body here instead.

The water ran but Amy knew he'd make a foray into the closet and pick out his evening outfit first, then toss the clothes he'd soiled during the day in the hamper.

She hovered by the entrance of the spare room to listen. There it was: The sound of the shower door being wrenched open. And closed.

Any knew she could safely call 911 now, then run downstairs, and out to the front lawn. She could go to the neighbor's house and tell them everything, and Timmy would be arrested. Then he'd spend his life in jail for a variety of charges: rape, kidnapping, maiming/ blindness, and probably insurance fraud if he'd told people she was dead.

But that wasn't enough.

She tiptoed on the thick lush carpeting and walked into the master suite, and to its windowless bathroom.

And shut the door behind her. Flicked the light off.

"What the hell?" he shouted.

In the darkness, she had full advantage. She opened the glass shower door. Amy felt the heat of Timmy's body come toward her. Hot water splashed over the two of them, splattered his precious peach marble floor. The thud of his wet feet stopped a foot before her as she imagined him fiddling for the light switch.

She jabbed the hook hard into his mid-section, right through his six-pack abs. He doubled over, slumped down. "Who are you? What do you want?" The words escaped his mouth in a wet hiss.

"Who the hell do you think I am?"

"Amy?" Then his tone turned helpless, but still condescending. "Listen, I'm sorry for what I did to you. I can explain. You need to call an—"

She cradled his face in her hands, and in two deft strokes stabbed his eyes, one after the other.

She dropped the hook, stepped out of the bathroom, and dialed 911, ignoring his pitiful sounds.

Amy knew she wouldn't get in trouble for wounding him. Self-defense. Plus a plethora of psychiatric excuses any good lawyer could come up with. Once she walked out the door, she'd be free. Blind, but free. And who knew, maybe someone could reverse what he'd done to her.

Not so for Timmy. He'd survive the injuries, but would never see out of those eyes again. The sound of the sirens reminded her of New York, bringing a smile to her face.

Timmy would spend his life in a dirty cage.

She walked toward and opened the windows and imagined that the warm sunlight streaming through them came from the downtown Village.

She was free.

Third Crow by Tais Teng

The Sun Sets Too Soon in November

By Gregory L. Norris

"There's someone in the basement," Nora said.

The maintenance man, a scruffster in his young thirties with a chain of barbed wire around one arm visible in the summer when he mowed the lawn sans shirt, fixed her with a look from behind dark sunglasses. "In the basement?"

It was late autumn now. The trees had shed their clothes, while Christopher the Maintenance Man at 102 Height Street took to wearing layers—a long-sleeved shirt, powder-blue, under a gray tee, a vest over that. He pulled a cooler and clipboard out of his car. She'd cornered him in the parking lot of the big, brooding house after he turned through the gray granite obelisks at the mouth of the drive and sped to the rear, space enough for the cars of the six tenants who lived in the once-grand lady who'd been savaged and ravaged over time, chopped up from one residence to half a dozen.

He grunted something under his breath in dismissal and straightened. Christopher was an okay maintenance man who cared for the building's needs and repairs after putting in hours at a day job. He mowed the lawn in summer, shoveled the front veranda and walkways in winter, though his heart clearly wasn't in the title beyond what Nora assumed was a generous discount on his monthly rent. So if the shelf in the laundry room toppled down or her sink refused to drain, Nora knew to factor in days, sometimes weeks, before he fixed what was broken.

"The basement's off limits," he grumbled. "There's nobody down there."

He breezed around Nora and started toward his private entrance, past the lockbox where she dropped off her rent on the third of every month, toward the staircase to his apartment on the second floor of the house's east wing, the largest of the six units. She'd mostly been on time except for a snafu with her disability check two years earlier that had gotten her a late fee and a threatening letter from the building's owner, who liked the rent paid when it was due. But she kept her one-bedroom on the ground floor of the west wing tidy and didn't play her TV too loud, and so she pursued.

"There is," Nora said, doing her best to match the long strides made by Christopher's construction boots across the red and charcoal brick pavers sunk into the patch of dead lawn. "At night, I hear him down there, moving things around and banging on the pipes."

Christopher fumbled his house key into the lock. "I'll check it out, Nora."

His voice contained just enough of a note of condescension that she recognized it.

"Would you kindly check it out this century? After all, you're the maintenance man. It's your job."

Christopher shook his head, exhaled through his nostrils, said something about what a fool he was living someone else's dream. More shit than the job was worth, she heard through the door after it closed behind him and he tromped up the stairs.

* * *

Nora Thomasine O'Roarke suffered from a bi-polar diagnosis. The disease rarely energized her anymore, keeping her up for days cleaning and organizing and being proactive before, inevitably, swinging in the opposite direction, those dark times during which she never left the bed. Expensive, cutting edge medicine carried her to a meeting place somewhere in the middle, a state that wasn't necessarily happy but one in which she functioned well.

No, she wasn't crazy. And no, she hadn't imagined the scuffles and clangs emanating up through the vents and floorboards at late hours of the night and early morning when the other residents at 102 Height Street slept.

She returned to her front door, located off the big front veranda whose balustrades were overdue for a fresh lick of paint by several years. The cold chased her into the kitchen, crouched low among the cabinets, and attempted to nibble at her marrow by entering through any and all exposed skin. She closed the door. The heat kicked on. Its normally comforting sighs of hot, dry breath lacked reassurance.

You aren't hallucinating, she told herself at the coffee pot while pouring another cup, black. The coffee had sat on the burner long enough to grow bitter. Still, she sipped. There is someone down there at night, in the basement!

The sun set early, too early, as was inevitable in November. Nora turned on the news, only to quickly switch over to a rerun of a sitcom she had little more interest in. Her dinner consisted of leftovers that she barely touched, preferring instead to move the microwaved pieces around on the plate with her fork, going through the motions instead of eating.

It got dark earlier and earlier, and the world had turned frigid. The weather was hungry for her bones. Lately, Nora had taken to turning on lights inside the apartment until it positively blazed, and to drawing the drapes tight against the early night beyond her 600-square feet of living space.

Sleep these past few nights had been elusive and, in addition to her greatest concern, Nora worried she was developing new and dubious bad habits, ones that would establish a shift in her patterns and lead to a serious downward spiral out of the middle and toward a deeper form of darkness at one extreme or the other.

On Sunday night, Nora's bladder had roused her at eleven minutes past three in the morning. She wandered into her boxy little bathroom with its vent perched above the section of basement that contained her propane boiler and water heater and heard the clank and clatter of someone down there, moving about.

A sound jarred Nora out of the spell of thoughts she'd fallen prey to; thoughts that centered around the cold weather, the death of one season, specters and dark spirits that clanked chains of dead leaves outside the apartment's windows and shackles made from metal beneath its floorboards, in the basement.

Nora pushed the tray table away but remained frozen on the recliner set before the television, managing only the strength to hit the mute button on the remote. Strangulating silence blanketed the room. Something invisible fluttered its wings near her ears. She realized the flaps owed to her own heartbeat, now launched into a full gallop.

And then the sound came again, a metallic clank bookended by dusty footsteps over the ancient cement floor laid long ago atop sour earth, down there. Waking from the palsy took conscious effort. Making her way to the basement door, which hovered in the last shadowy corner left in the entire place, at the end of the hallway linking bedroom and bath together, demanded herculean focus. Eventually, she made it, slid back the deadbolt, and turned the antique cut glass knob. Nora's pulse raced at the image framed by dark walls on two sides and ceiling on top, thirteen wooden steps leading down to dusty cement lit by the bald glow cast by a network of bare bulbs at the bottom.

She tried to speak, but no words emerged. Coughing, Nora eventually said, "Hello? Is someone down there?"

A shadow slinked across the cellar floor. Nora's flesh crawled. Her next attempt at breath failed. Somebody was down there—Christopher, who'd arrived on the job weeks ahead of schedule.

"Just me, Nora," he said, his words projecting frustration, exhaustion.

Nora covered her heart and exhaled. "Thank God it's you. I thought—"

"You haven't been down here, have you?" he asked.

"In that mess?"

He glanced around, hands tucked into pockets, and grunted a base yet telling, "Hmmm."

Her relief at seeing him instead of phantoms evaporated. "What? Did you find something? Does it look like somebody's been down there, like I said?"

Christopher's eyes continued their sweep to places offstage and mostly out of view. "I've got a heavy padlock out in the shed. I'll slap it on the bulkhead door. Let me know if you hear anything else."

"I will," she promised, and closed the basement door.

Long minutes later, she heard the bulkhead slam down, its metal gong ricocheting across Height Street and high into the frigid night sky.

Nora crawled into bed and drew the covers to her neck. A terrible image formed in the darkness above her eyes: that of her body, robbed of its bones by the hungry cold, only an aching puddle of soft, old flesh left behind. A bag of ancient skin, liquefied, lost. So this was what old age really felt like.

Pops and snaps reminded her that she was mostly intact, solid at the center. Sleeping with the lights off wasn't far different from trying to sleep with them on. She rolled over and was serenaded by a chorus of crackles from joints and bones. Untold minutes that felt like hours later, she turned onto her other side. Neither position helped Nora attain more than a fugue state of limbo halfway between waking and slumber.

At a quarter past three, according to the alarm clock's bleary green numbers, a clap of thunder shook the west wing of the house. Nora jolted up in the darkness, convinced her heart would jump out of her chest and into her throat.

Thunder, in November—!

In that strange clarity that comes quickly after a person is shocked awake, Nora identified the cannonade for what it truly was.

The basement's bulkhead door.

Someone's down there, she thought, and reached for her cell phone. In the darkness, the place on the nightstand beside the alarm clock could have been a hundred miles away. Maddening moments later, she found the phone, flipped open its cover, and dialed the first 'C' saved to her directory. On the second ring, the maintenance man picked up.

"Christopher, it's Nora O'Roarke. You told me to call if—"

"Hi, you've reached Christopher. Leave a message."

Choking down a heavy swallow, Nora killed the call.

And listened.

The vent in the bathroom drew her to the spindles of pale light drifting up from the basement through the tiniest of gaps in either the heating conduit or around the vent itself, not flush with the oblong hole carved out of the linoleum.

Nora hunched down and held her breath. Her pulse hammered a frenzied tattoo into her ears. A sharp metal clank rose up from the catacombs that tunneled beneath sections of the old house, in whose dark corners the plumbing, gas pipes, and electrical guts were tucked. Another thunderclap clawed at her ears, and another after that. In her mind's eye, her imagination translated the sounds into whole stories.

There was someone in the basement, and he was angry at being locked out. Perhaps he was beating on the pipes, the furnace, with the same bolt cutters he'd used to slice off the maintenance man's padlock. Banging, swinging, scuffling around down there like a madman!

The light from below cut out as someone maneuvered between the bulb casting the glow and the vent. Nora gasped and instantly regretted the telltale noise. Whoever was down there tracked it and gazed up. The light surged back at half strength. An eyeball took form in the gap, wide and white.

Whoever he was laughed and said, "It'll take more than that to keep me out."

Nora recoiled and screamed. She dropped the phone in the darkness while scrambling back to her feet. She found the light switch, then the phone. The clock on its screen read: 3:27. Twice, she misdialed 911.

As the call went through, the banging and clanging on the pipes in the cellar resumed.

At 3:29, as the dispatcher attempted to calm Nora down, imploring her to speak slower, to make sense, 102 Height Street exploded in a monstrous fireball of flames and debris. Fueled by propane, the mushroom cloud rose high into the sky above the conflagration where a house once stood, and people had lived until a minute before, and a deafening thunderclap echoed across the town before the night again fell mostly dark and silent.

Druid by Morgan Griffith

Heavy Heart

By Dave Dormer

"Have you gotten any response to our ad for a tenant yet?" Steve asked, hauling bags of debris up the stairs.

"I got a call this morning from a lady named Omorose. She seemed anxious to see the apartment. I told her that we'd be finished the renovation by tomorrow and she could come by on Friday to check it out. Hopefully we'll be finished by then," Natasha replied.

"Yeah, we should have it done on time." Steve said. Natasha and Steve exhausted transforming the old cellar into a livable apartment. Steve knew he'd complete the project with two days remaining of his holidays. Natasha, seven-months pregnant waddled down the stone steps to the cellar door, "What else can I do to help?"

"Go and rest Nat. I'll take care of the clean-up," he insisted. The couple moved into the old farmhouse two years earlier from Boston and in the last few days Natasha had spent most of her time down in the cellar. It gave her chills, she couldn't explain why. Neither one of them had reason to visit the cellar before now other than the occasional blown electrical fuse or to clean the furnace filter, but when they did go down into the musty bowels of their home, they did what they had to do and got out, looking over their shoulder as they went.

The couple admired the purple-flowered field of alfalfa from the dining room window when a car pulled into their driveway.

"She's here," Nat said and quickly cleared the table. Steve went to greet their guest at the door; she was tall, tanned skin and lean. Steve's face felt warm, his attraction to their prospective tenant was obvious and his pregnant wife was closing behind him. After an uncomfortable introduction, Steve and Natasha led their would-be tenant to the cellar. The slender stranger seemed intent on the alfalfa field. Omorose walked through the newly transformed cellar, admiring the obvious work involved, "I love it. If it's alright with you, I'll move in this weekend."

"We're glad you like it. Welcome to our home Omorose," Nat replied. Omorose handed her an envelope of cash, first and last month's rent, "Thank you for inviting me into your home. I'll be back tomorrow with my things."

Nat cradled her abdomen; stabbing pain buckled her forward. She struggled to climb into a dining room chair preventing her from crashing to the floor. This was her first pregnancy, but she didn't think it would hurt this bad. She looked to the field of purple flowers for comfort attempting to slow her breathing. The purple field was gone. In its place sprawled a field of reeds tended to by a dozen dark-skinned workers, men in linen loincloths. The image was serene. They appeared content. Nat rubbed her eyes in disbelief. She strained to focus on each man's face, all were clean-shaven and wore short hair, but she didn't recognize any of them. One worker shimmered and vanished from the field.

Terrible shrieks reverberated inside her home from somewhere below. Nat struggled to her feet, searching her house for the source. Tears filled her eyes from the anguished cries. She hobbled nearby a heating register, the sounds carried through the duct. She looked to the field filled with strange workers but they were gone. The field was as it should be a sea of purple flowers. The screams diminished to silence. Exhausted and confused, Nat lay on the couch and slept.

Nat refused to burden Steve with her strange episode, chalk it up to pregnancy, she determined. He was busier than ever, it seemed to Steve that his fellow co-workers saved the lion share for him when he returned. He wasn't bitter he'd rather stay busy anyway, he reasoned. Every afternoon Steve worked and Nat had one of her episodes. The screams and accompanying pain continued and with each vision, one worker vanished from the field of reeds. Within two weeks, Nat's health deteriorated visibly. She looked exhausted, continual dark circles around her eyes and dehydrated. She worried she might miscarry. She had to let Steve know what was happening at their home.

Nat explained the encounters to Steve, "Are you sure this has nothing to do with being pregnant and overtired? Maybe I should be taking you to the hospital to get checked out?" Steve asked her.

"I know what I saw and heard Steve. I'm not losing it!" she barked.

"Okay, Nat. I'll stay home tomorrow and check this out myself. Why don't you go and rest. I'll call you when supper is ready," Steve insisted.

Steve and Nat sat patiently waiting at the dining room table for anything to happen. Hours passed and doubt crept in. Steve grew impatient, thinking of the work he should be doing right now, then it began. The field of reeds appeared and in it stood one solitary worker. They watched in disbelief and awe. It was if they peered into another time or realm, they agreed to one another. The sole form began to shimmer. "Let's go," Steve ordered.

They raced outside and down to the cellar door. Steve slowed his pace to help his wife waddle down the stone steps.

"Omorose…is everything alright?" Steve beckoned through the closed door. He heard movement inside, but no response. He shouldered the door, shattering the latch into splinters. They peered into the cellar and the room flickered with golden torch light. Peculiar pictographs festooned stone walls. Atop a raised dais sat, the small wooden box Nat discovered renovating the cellar. She had no idea what it was or its origin, but thought it would make a unique centerpiece. Its lid propped opened and several miniature figurines lay scattered around the ornate box. Looming above the box stood a grotesque figure that held a dripping mass in its claws. The beast's head resembled a crocodile; it had a torso of a lion, and the under-carriage of a female hippo. Saliva dripped from its maw. Steve and Nat stood rigid, paralyzed. They didn't make a sound, their eyes widened in horror. Another figure stood on the dais, a humanoid with dark-skin. It adjusted a large, golden scale. It turned, revealing its jackal head and placed a feather on one side of the scale. There was no sign of Omorose.

On the stone floor beside the dais sprawled the lone worker, a gaping wound in his chest and blood puddled around him. The monstrous creature placed the still-beating heart it held in its claw on the alternate side of the scale and waited impatient. Steve and Nat grasped one another attempting to retain their sanity. The scale tipped in the heart's favour. The jackal creature lowered its head. The monstrosity screeched its delight. It leapt forth with incredible reflex and began to gnash and maul the unworthy worker, denying the afterlife.

Shiva by Ashley Scarlet

Raison d'être

By J. T. Seate

It was a door to a cellar that held Edmond's secret, a lynchpin between the sane and the insane. The room behind the portal had become both home and sanctuary. From within the smoke blackened walls, he could hear the bells ring from the towers many levels above the cellar door. The muted tones sounded a clear reminder of the distance between him and the world for which they rang, a distance equal to that between heaven and hell.

When first condemned to the cold and wet stone walls and earthen floor behind the door, he feared the exit, for it represented imprisonment, an entombment from the society that shunned him, little better than a dungeon. The church had once again moved him. He had been cast out of one sanctuary when a nun awakened to find Edmond at the foot of her bed fondling her toes. The look of revulsion on her face made him feel more inhuman than he already did. He thought of the cloistered women every time he heard the clang of an iron bell calling the faithful to worship. The church deemed there was nowhere else for him other than this monastery, sequestered within the privacy of a cellar and its protective door with nothing but the silent order of monks without.

As time went on, however, the door became Edmond's friend, for it was through a smaller opening in the door that provided meager nourishment. And it was protection against prying eyes that might discover his secret.

Before Edmond was transferred to the monastery's cellar, the tumult of the Paris streets had changed with the beginning of the insurrection. He knew something about the lives of both those inside marble palaces and those inside small hovels, but the toil and sweat and suffering of the masses, or the sudden downfall of the aristocracy were not his concern. As long as he was in this new place, he didn't care how long the chaos and destruction and the cries of Vive la France continued. He'd been given shelter and another chance, and was happy for the opportunity to service the dead before returning to his private place behind the door.

Before his move, he had witnessed some of the executions from the back edges of the roaring crowds. Too near the entertainment might be cause to offer him up as an undesirable sight fit to be shuffled toward the executioner. Like wild rivers, treacherous undercurrents ran through the country. Anyone could find themselves in dank prisons awaiting his or her turn to climb steps to their deaths. The executioners, covered in black robes and clustering like crows, stood in solemn judgment on the unfortunates as cheers went up each time the blade of the Guillotine descended, or a platform dropped out from underneath a pair of feet.

The lure of revolution and liquor made the populace lusty and indiscriminate. The degeneration into depravity hadn't produced a living human to comfort Edmond; yet, his latest internment provided what he needed. Deformed and misshapen since birth, he was ugly in a way that attracted second looks, but seldom pity. Slow and hunchbacked, it was only in the safety of his current surroundings where there were no disdainful, repugnant glances to ogle his genetic misfortune.

The monastery had agreed to receive the bodies from the gallows and prepare them for Christian burials. Reluctant at first to leave his dank abode, Edmond was guided to an anteroom just beyond his private chamber. He was instructed to cover arriving bodies with lime, use a knife to cut lengths of canvas, and sow the cadavers into the wrappings. When done, the corpses were removed to graves beyond the cloistered walls. The monk charged with instructing Edmond seemed grateful for his aptitude at completing the simple task, saving his having to do it himself. Edmond soon looked forward to the job for he was never beyond sight of his cellar door, and he was able to indulge in a certain proclivity of which he'd dreamed.

He was provided with two types of corpses. Hanged bodies exhibited purple faces and protruding tongues, but heads severed by the guillotine were spared such unnaturalness. The males were no more than stilled husks of clay to be prepared and dispatched quickly, but Edmond did not think of the female victims in the same manner. Rather, they were silent companions to which he now had access, non-resistant women finally quieted before their time due the current state of affairs. In his youth, Edmond heard a tale of a beautiful woman who took pride in her delicate feet above all else. She soaked them in warm oils. Then Lanolin was applied to the soles, arches, and ankles. The result was feet of perfection without calluses or blemishes. They were powdered and perfumed to smell as fetching as they appeared. It was no wonder the woman took such pride in her tantalizing feet, for she had no arms. Edmond liked the story. It spoke to both attraction and the lack thereof to which he could relate, for there was something specific to the female corpses that captured his interest. He never explored above the ankles. He was not interested in knobby knees or the biological functions of the torso, or the stretched necks or severed heads. None of these did he find provocative. It was the lower extremities, the dainty feet with their miraculous toes as vulnerable as Robins' eggs that provided enticement. He could not have approached living women given his beastly appearance. They would have shared whispers like murmurs of the pious as if something unholy was passing among them. With the rampant imprisonments and hasty trials, however, those once fine ladies who might have tossed him a coin in the street now stood atop a gallows or kneeled at the altar of a guillotine. Now many were brought to him providing heretofore unimaginable access to his fetish.

An Asian woman, somehow caught in the crossfire of revolt, a servant to one of the nobles hung along with her master, had found her way to Edmond's anteroom. He marveled at the smallness of her feet, not much larger than a child's. He adored them perhaps even more than those which belonged to Antoinette herself. He treated the dead feet of women with more delicacy and intimacy than they could possibly have known in life.

Another nice specimen had arrived on this particular day—a woman whose bare feet had seldom touched ground, one whose fancy jeweled slippers had been replaced by rough-hewn cloth slip-ons for the final hours of her life. Edmond's eyes grew large when he slipped off the foot covers to inspect the pampered feet on the wrong side of current politics. There was something the gendarmes had missed—a band of silver around the second toe of the right foot. Edmond's loins stirred as he twisted the ring and slowly removed it. He knew the article was worth more than he could earn in a year, but there was little to do except consider it a keepsake from a contributor he would only know through the well-tended, terminal part of the vertebrate upon which she once stood.

He placed the band on the tip of his smallest finger and admired the craftsmanship. It remained perched there precariously as he explored the owner's feet. He ran his hands over their surfaces starting at the ankles and moving down to the toes. He toyed with each digit tracing each cuticle with the tip of his forefinger while the ring glinted in the dim light of the room. He ran his thumbnail on the underside from the heel to the ball of one foot as if the corpse might respond to his tease. Edmond was about to place his mouth over the toes when the door of the room banged opened. The monk who provided the bodies entered. The two men were comically mismatched. Brother Maurice was gaunt and angular whereas Edmond was husky and stooped due to his affliction. The monk's face possessed beady eyes and a hawk-like nose. The face tapered severely down to an almost non-existent chin. Edmond was wary of him, especially when he made unscheduled appearances. At this moment he wanted nothing more than to retreat behind the refuge of his cellar door.

Edmond stepped away from the body on the wooden slab and bowed slightly. With a profile as sharp as a hatchet, Brother Maurice took inventory, looking around the room and at the corpse before his gaze shifted to Edmond. His small rodent-like eyes glittered like the black beads of a stuffed toy as they burned into Edmond's large ones.

"What have you there?" Edmond reluctantly held out the hand that wore the ring.

"Are you stealing from the dead, Edmond? Give that to me." Edmond pulled the find from his finger and placed it in Maurice's palm.

"What else have you taken," he demanded.

"Nothing, Sir. Nothing at all." The monk's features turned harder, the skin growing taut across the bones in his face, his distaste clear.

"I've given you the opportunity to leave the confines of the cellar out of the goodness of my heart and you repay me by taking property." The ring disappeared inside the monk's robes. "Starting tomorrow, bodies will be delivered elsewhere. You will be confined to the cellar once again to pray for your indiscretions. Do you understand?"

"Begging your pardon, but I'm happy to do this duty for the good of the church and am good at what I do." The man snorted scornfully.

"Don't trifle with me, Edmond. A trained monkey could accomplish these tasks. Now that I know you to be a thief, my decision seems well-founded. I've allowed you beyond the cellar door long enough." He spoke in a tone that was without remorse or pity. "This body will be the last for you to prepare. Consider it an act of kindness that you have been allowed to perform such an activity for this long."

"Oui," Edmond mumbled, and hung his head shamefully. His stomach churned and his hump ached more than usual. Agony sliced through him like a scythe with the realization he was soon to be deprived of his latest passion.

The monk harrumphed and turned for the doorway. Edmond cast him a glance of anguish. His fear of losing access to what he craved was no longer abstract. It now had weight and substance. A knot of despair twisted inside him. He was easily defeated for he had been controlled his entire life. He could not let this happen. The prizes squirreled away behind the cellar door had made the place his secret kingdom. The bodies were his subjects. Every nerve ending flexed. His wariness of Maurice turned into something more demonstrative, from desolation, to anger, to action in less than a heartbeat. The thud of the monk's sandals made the pulse in Edmond's temples throb. A red haze of rage clouded his mind. He picked up an iron rod used to position corpses into a box and approached his tormentor. Edmond swung the instrument at the back of Maurice's head with all his might.

Swackk!

His former protector yowled from the impact like a child who had been pinched, but he didn't fall. His hand quickly covered the injured side of his head. Blood leaked between his fingers. As he staggered unsteadily toward the anteroom's door, Edmond struck again, harder.

Whack!

The monk fell to his knees as if in prayer, crumpled from the second blow.

Some men were hard to kill. A third swing ensued.

Crack!

Maurice toppled sideways onto the floor, the weapon following him down, lodged in his skull. The tip of the iron rod had caught on brains and bone. Edmond had difficulty extracting the weapon, but this man could no longer threaten to take away his raison-d'être.

Edmond wrapped a cloth rag around the man's bloody head then lifted the fresh deadweight over his shoulder. He dropped the body on a second wooden slab. He was breathing hard and his hump was on fire, but he had to act quickly. Edmond's treasonous act would not be complete until he committed this final defilement. The monk's head tilted back and his dead eyes stared accusingly at the ceiling. Edmond took the knife meant for cutting the yards of woven fabric and sawed back and forth on the victim's neck. Using all his might, he finally managed to sever the head from the body. It wasn't nearly the clean cut the guillotine provided, but good enough for the burial wagon. He then wrapped the cadaver in the customary burlap long-cloth and secured the bundle with knotted rope at chest and ankles with the head inside like he'd done many times. He planned to leave the body to be removed as if the monk was but one more victim of the revolution.

Then he began to panic. Others would wonder why Maurice had not returned. There was no one to lock Edmond's cellar door with him safely inside. He was intelligent enough to realize he'd killed the hand that fed him. Eventually, men in fancy red, white, and blue uniforms with the word *Liberté* embroidered on a patch would come and take him away, as resolute as the nuns and the monks before them.

There would be no liberty for him, or mercy. He had cracked open the skull of a holy man belonging to a monastic order that served the cause. Edmond thought he would rather be taken to the gallows himself than be parted from the cellar behind the door, and the lovely feet he worshipped so. There would be but a few precious hours before his guardian was missed. He could at least make the best of it. The feet of the most recent female arrival still rested uncovered at the foot of the other slab. The sight of them smoothed the bubbly waters of Edmond's fears. He returned to the cadaver and performed his ritual of covetous delight.

* * *

Edmond returned to the cellar, pulling the heavy door closed behind him, hoping it would appear to be locked. There, he went to the darkest corner and looked at the piece of canvas that served as his headrest. He pulled it back for a final indulgence, for more than likely, he would be making his own trip to the gallows sooner rather than later. What the removal of the canvas revealed was Edmond's collection—sets of half-feet severed at the point where they flatten out above the ball of the foot. They sat in three rows on the earthen floor, just enough of the feet taken to go unnoticed inside the heavy woven material tied around the entire corpse prior to burial.

Satiated from his ritual with the latest pair, Edmond gently laid them next to others. He pondered the ultimate escape from justice—laying open his wrists with the same instrument that had severed his treasures from their lifeless owners. That would leave two dead men for the monks to find. Could he bring himself to abandon the feet in the cellar to unsympathetic hands? He shuttered at the thought as his ears attuned to a rustling sound. His eye caught movement as a rat skittered along the dirt and disappeared into a crevice of a dark and dank inner wall where vermin waited to conduct their business around the conveniences of humans. Perhaps he should leave his precious collection unwrapped for the rodent and his friends to get what nourishment it could provide. He couldn't allow the authorities to toss his treasures into a bag to be delivered to a pig stall or onto a bonfire. The cache of women's toes was his legacy.

A better idea came to Edmond, a profound idea whereby he would not lose his inventory. He picked up one pair of the Asian woman's toes. He made a gurgling sound that passed for a chuckle, the laughter of the damned. "Come, my little friends," he said to the vermin lurking in dark places. "You've wanted access to my treasures all along, so come and feast with me."

The toes he admired had turned greenish-blue and were decaying rapidly. Edmond took hold of the dainty nails and pulled each one out of the rotting flesh. Then he began to nibble. He wiggled the toes of his left foot and admired the band he had taken first from its owner then from the pocket of the would-be usurper, now displayed on his own pinky toe. All that stood between him and his prizes, and the reality of the outside world, was the exquisite portal where he had found solace, a place to hide the spoils of his fetish, the bloated and discolored toes of those even more unfortunate than he.

Perhaps the authorities would not find the ring he wore when they took him. Perhaps he could wear it for eternity in the pit where his body would be placed, hopefully near the women who had given him so much.

Antique Languor by Natalie Sirois

The Light of the Fifth Stair

By K. Trap Jones

There is a certain beauty in death—an unexplainable idealism that surrounds a person when their time has come to an end. The moment when pain is no longer a factor and when fear ceases to exist. It is an aura of calmness, as if the journey has ended within a beautiful garden created solely by the mind of the person. Strolling upon that darkened road of death and seeing the peaceful tranquility of the lighted garden up ahead...The feeling of freedom that spills from the mind and coats the body must feel like heaven to those who were, just moments ago, afraid of death's approach. To step from the darkness into the light would be cleansing for the soul—a reassurance that everything would be alright.

I became fascinated with that crossroad—the exact moment when the traveler's foot breaks the threshold between dark and light. I was curious as to the hesitation that occurs when standing on that crossroad. Was there a moment of thought? A choice that the mind and body must agree upon in order to proceed?

A cellar door served as my introduction to the concept of death's crossroads. As a young child, I despised the cellar. It was always dark, and the lone light bulb hanging from the ceiling never worked. When prompted by my mother to fetch something from the cellar, I always stood at the top of the stairs, staring down into the darkness. There was a clear line between the light and dark that appeared halfway down the steps. The darkness tormented me like a luring beast in the shadows. It knew I needed to enter its domain, so it howled at me through the plumbing pipes and furnace.

Each step I went down seemed to anger the darkness as it shifted like the currents of a troubled sea. Standing on the last step, still within the reach of light, always plagued my mind with horrific intentions and mind-altering visions that would later disrupt my sleep. Reminiscent of a cliff's ledge, the separation between light and dark struck my nerves with brutal consequences. But my mother was waiting for me to deliver the sacred mop that was hidden within the depths of madness...so my foot sank into the darkness as I continued to dive deeper into the abyss. Suffocation gripped my throat and held it tightly as my eyes drained uncontrollably. Grabbing the mop felt as if I had located the Holy Grail. Sprinting back up, I breached the surface of the darkness and inhaled a deep breath of light.

Through the years, I constantly found myself on that ledge of darkness; that last step within the reach of the light. For some reason, my mother always needed something in the cellar, and I was always the one she chose for the adventure. It became mundane and annoying, but all of my anger turned to fear once I stood on those steps.

I remember the turning point well—a dust pan that I was tasked to retrieve—and again, I found myself on that fifth step; the last remaining one within the light. Crossing over into the darkness was a choice I had to make. Even though I was afraid, I still continued.

Why? Why not just stay within the light and never venture down there again? Sure, my mother would be upset. But I was not afraid of getting into trouble. I was afraid of going back down into that dreaded cellar. I had a choice; a crossroads of my own creation displayed upon a wooden step that separated light and dark. Knowing that I had a choice, I felt the fear slowly vanish as if it were being evicted from my skull by the thoughts in my mind. There was a feeling of power instilled in me; a sense of control over the fear. Each step down offered me additional acceptance that I gratefully inhaled deep into my lungs. From that moment on, I was not afraid of the darkness.

Something odd occurred next, though. I began to ponder how others would react to the same crossroad. Would they overcome their fear? Or scamper to stay within the safety of the light? It was a sadistic question constantly luring within my mind that proved unavoidable. To feed my curiosity, I started small by throwing my dog's ball down the steps. He always stopped at the edge of darkness, but his mind was not like a human's. I needed another test subject, so I took my little sister's favorite doll and tossed it into the darkened sea of the cellar. Angered, she walked down the steps with ease until her foot sank beneath the darkness. All of the anger that she once had towards me vanished in an instant. Fear climbed upon her back and twirled her ponytail. Her head snapped around, and her swollen eyes stared up at me as if I was forcing her down into the darkness. She loved that doll so much. I had even seen her wrestle it away from a possum once, but the darkened crossroad tested her loyalty. She knew the doll was only a few steps away—and yet she couldn't overcome the fear, the choice of giving in to the unknown. I eventually retrieved the doll for her, but only after my mother made me.

The fascination with the choice of others when standing on the crossroads controlled my every waking hour and appeased me within my slumber. Even with my mother's passing and my sister moving away to college, I found myself still enamored by the line of darkness upon that fifth step. I would spend hours standing on that particular step, pondering the idealism of the crossroads. I stood on it so much that the wood was beginning to warp. There was a wonderful concave bend that creaked whenever I stepped from it into the darkness. That three-foot-long plank of rotted wood became the basis behind my studies and the backbone of my curiosity.

My mind wouldn't stop racing with more questions regarding the choices of others. I desired more evidence in order to come to peace with myself. The whole idea took hold of my reins and guided me towards a place into which I never intended to venture. During dinner with my girlfriend, my appetite was suppressed. She had no idea of the burden buried within me. As I watched her eating a plate of pasta, I couldn't help but wonder what her choice would be. I imagined her standing of the ledge of darkness, but could not predict what she would do. I told her I had forgotten the bread in the oven, and asked if she would go down to the cellar for more wine.

Peeking around the door from the hallway, I saw the back of her head. She was motionless, standing upon that fifth step. I became frustrated with her because she didn't even attempt to try to subdue the fear. I saw her as a weak person; one that had no self-worth in my eyes. Her hair twirled as she turned around, allowing our eyes to meet. There was fear within her eyes and a pulsating vein protruding from her neck. She was pathetic. She did not know what true fear was—she would never know unless I showed her. I slammed the door with a vengeance and held the knob tightly as she screamed, trying to open it with every ounce of her strength. I could sense the darkness creeping up the steps, consuming her very essence and swallowing her soul. My lip curled in a grin every time her fist hit the door. She would know fear. She would embrace the darkness.

The pounding subsided and her cries diminished. Within my mind, she had welcomed the darkness within her—much like I had done. Turning the knob, I believed that I had helped her face the fear and provided a means to overcome it—but her hand slapping against my face proved otherwise. I tried to explain that I was only trying to help, but she quickly grabbed her belongings and left.

Alone in the house and needing more wine, I stood at the top of the cellar steps with a smile. I greeted the darkness like a long lost friend. I appreciated what the shadows of the cellar had to offer me. The bond that we had created over the years was unlike any relationship that I will ever find again. It was a mutual respect that we provided one another. No one else would be able to understand...so why force a fictitious relationship?

Fully satisfied and still seeking wine, I stepped onto the fifth step like I had done so many times before. The rotten wood splintered and gave way, allowing my foot to break through. Losing my balance, I tried desperately to grasp ahold of the railing—but I was already falling backwards into the darkness.

For a brief moment, I could see the light at the top of the steps but could not feel the lower half of my body. With my eyes fading, I saw the door slowly closing, stealing the light away with every inch.

There is a certain beauty in death; an unexplainable idealism that surrounds a person when his time has come to an end. Through the darkened forest I walk, surrounded by the shadows of death and the tormented souls of those who lingered past their welcome. The damned souls swirl around, following me as I venture towards the light up ahead. The rotted bark of the trees moan in agony with every step I take. My eyes swell with fear within the darkness as I long to reach the light. I am no longer curious about the darkness; I no longer admire it. I want only to cross the threshold into the light. But the crossroad I seek seems so far away. My mind torments me and begs me to stop, but I will not give in to the temptations of the shadows -- even as the ground trembles beneath me. The fog tries to fade the light, but my eyes remain focused on the horizon. With my heart beating uncontrollably and my eyes almost swelled shut, my legs blindly lead me forward, breaking through the outreached limbs of demented trees. Just like my sister, who gave up her most prized possession in order to return to the light, I too had to make a choice.

All these years, I had thought that the darkness was my friend, but I was wrong. Mislead and confused, the shadows of the cellar exploited the weakness within my mind and contorted everything that constructed me as a man. As my legs pull from the tightened roots which protrude from the ground, I struggle forward by keeping the light within my sights. I do not wish to die within the darkness; I do not wish for it to consume my soul. I will fight along the path to reach the crossroad and when I finally arrive at the threshold between light and dark, I will answer the question that started it all...

While standing at the crossroads of death, is there a hesitation to cross the threshold?

For me, the answer will be no.

Reminiscent of the Rain

By Carmen Tudor

"Damned rain hasn't let up all evening."

"What?"

"I said the blasted rain won't stop. And turn that prelude off, won't you."

"Madam, 'tis true. 'Tis true, 'tis pity. Er...I know this part..."

"Come again?"

"Pity? Oh, I said you're quite right. Look how it falls, as if a spiteful hand dashes it at us from above. *Raindrop,* it's called, though not by Chopin himself. Von Bülow, it was."

"I don't know about that. Damned nuisance to be sure, but it's just rain after all. Do you think they've gone?"

"You might always go and check. It's your house, you know. They were quite lovely before I left them. Old Liszt's son-in-law, you know."

"No. I'm happier here by the fire. I'll wait it out. It would be nicer if one had the option of seeing out the window. Shame about the steam. Adds to the place's mystique and such, I suppose. Don't you think?"

"Shame? 'Tis *'tis* true. You're right. Mystique. And all that. But then she was carrying on with Wagner. Wagner!"

"Are you even listening to me? Sometimes I can't be sure."

"Mm. No art. I'm listening. But you might just go and check. They might be gone. Have you thought of that? Eh? They might be gone now."

"Ha! I can hear them writhing around from here. Squirming, writhing—"

"They don't squirm. And I've never seen one writhe. To be sure, the incubation period's the pits. So I've heard. But your guests are hardly in the throes of agonizing...incubation."

"It's enough to see them eat, to watch them gorge themselves in that grotesque manner. Have you seen it? Have you?"

"Yes. It's nothing once you get used to it. No art, really. Nothing at all."

"Don't mangle the language. They say the language skills are the first to go. I couldn't bear it if you started blathering like they do. You've got your wits; use them."

"Mm. My wits. My brains. Mother always said I possessed brains."

"Forgive my sleeves a moment, won't you. I really must...see out the window. There. That's something."

"And it is reminiscent of the rain, the prelude. Much of a view?"

"Nothing."

"You really don't need to stay hidden here. Why, they might have gone. He might have seen them all out by now. It's your house, anyway. You're free to come and go as you choose."

"No. I really do prefer it down here. As I said, I like the fire. Cosy, excepting that blasted music of yours."

"It's quite mad to hide away. Best to accept the change, my dear. Go on up. They're likely gone. If not, pop your head in, say a cheery hullo and adieu, and either way you'll have your answer."

"Many words have been hurled my way, but never *mad*. Oh. Moon's rather large. Nice, isn't it? Can you see from there?"

"I see it, though just barely. Silly little cellar windows. I know they're there primarily as an escape means, but really. One would think the cellar door a much more prudent resource. In any case, wouldn't you like to peek in? Even if they haven't left, dinner's surely over; they won't be eating. It's not as if they'd be eating, I say."

"No, I won't do it. I prefer it down here."

"It can't be changed, you know. Altogether too late for that."

"That's the shame of it. It's too late."

"And they can't help it any more than you can the flu."

"That's the shame of it."

"Pity."

"Yes. Pity."

"Mm. The cause...the cause of the defect. Hold on, I know the line..."

"Come look at the moon. It's rather like a large face peering down—a crying one. Even through the rain and steamed glass it's something to look at. Will you take a look?"

"We could go up together if you'd like?"

"No. But the moon—come see the moon tonight. Rather like a large face. I knew a gell in school who looked like that."

"What was the cause of her defect?"

"Eh? Defect? No, just a large head, I should think."

"Was that the front door opening? They must be leaving. Go on. Go up. You can wish them goodbye and such. It'd mean a lot to him, to support his friends. Huh, *Raindrop*. More like drowning, this bit, this little interlude."

"No. It's cosy down here. I prefer it, anyway."

"They're leaving. You'll see them from the window. Oh, stay. You might even wave to them."

"I won't wave to them. That's absurd. Why, they might feel the surge of hunger welling up in their squirming, wri—"

"They don't squirm. The cause of their defect...or is it the effect of their decomp...I know this line..."

"Don't blather, really. Must you? It's so distasteful. What would Mother say?"

"Taste is a funny thing, isn't it?"

"Not if you're one of those creatures. I shudder at the thought."

"Are they leaving? Go back and look. Come on. Just a quick wave."

"You look. Better yet, you go up and see for yourself, if you like. I won't stop you."

"It's your house. They're your guests."

"No. They're his. Not mine. Never mine."

"It's a pity you can't accept things for what they are. The world is what it is now. They won't harm you. These silly notions will have to stop eventually. A waking-up must occur, such as the prelude's little interlude—the storm before the calm."

"Winning advice. I thank you. And I'll thank you to leave it alone now and go back to your book."

"And you your *Country Life?*"

"Yes."

"Mm. I see how thoroughly intrigued you are. So much so that you've read that frontispiece eleventy times since sitting down. There's the window. Just a peek. Just a quick flash of your hand. Barely a wave at all."

"No. I declare I can't abide them."

"Good. Ah, *good, madam*. Yes. Then...why, then you'll be confined to this cellar. He'll have them over frequently. Best to acquaint yourself sooner rather than later."

"Do stop this...this aphasic nonsense. One is never too old or too tired for semantics."

"You mean pragmatics, dear—"

"They say the speech is affected first. I can't abide your blathering like one of those. I won't have it."

"'Tis pity, 'tis true."

"Eh?"

"I said you're quite right. They've all gone."

"I didn't say that."

"No? My mistake. Put the magazine down now, won't you? Go. He'll be awaiting you. See them off."

"More likely they'll see me off."

"That's in terrible taste."

"They'd know."

"Perhaps...perhaps it's not so bad. Once you get used to it. Like drowning."

"You're out of your mind. I'll pretend for both our sakes that you didn't just say that. However, if this nonsense persists you should go up and see if there are any scraps left under the table. Flung there, no doubt, in their gorging frenzy."

"You're right. I said, you're right; they have gone. And the drops weren't flung, dear; supposedly they splashed down upon the chest of a drowned man. Von Bülow, perhaps, after he found out about Wagner."

"What are you talking about? I didn't say that. You're not listening again. Just go back to your Shakespeare. And turn that prelude off."

"Oh. 'Tis pity, I say."

"Eh? What door was that? Not the front..."

"*Urp.* 'Tis true, Madam, that all things must wake. I swear I use no art. No art at all. 'Tis *'tis* true."

Raptura Sub Rosa by Colleen Keough

Luminescence

By Michael Randolph

Grace only comes to those strong enough
to rip it from the hands of God.
~ Belroth Meiltonour

Alive, yet dead for eons, phantasms have existed between the realms of man and Gods. The few that have triumphed stand in the soup of mirages of the human soul pursuing life's long quest of dominion over others.

The human travesty of it began not years or centuries ago, but in the cold depths of myths and legends passed down from the beginning of time. The true battle for eternal life was not waged in the rules and commandments inscribed on parchment or carved in stone, but in the internal working of the soul invested in the creatures called humanity.

Hellish pits have come and gone in history. Yet, at times, one comes along that is truly the abyss. These are doorways to an abyss so dark that history buries the secrets in man's ashes.

Edinburgh, Scotland 1296

Cultures languishing in turmoil and remorse warrant the infernal Hell they have wrought. Murderous thoughts raged in a torrential downpour at the monument of humanity standing before him. Two stout granite barriers aged to a deep black stood resolute, a somber reminder of times past.

Auras flashed along the carved runes decorating the doors as Belroth traced their outlines. Battles tempered by loss of countless kindred weighed on his solitary existence—long years pass in this prison. Soft rhythmic beats rolled through the deep roots of the castle's foundation. Belroth's senses tickled as other's thoughts were bent toward his resting place deep below the city.

Spreading his fingers, gently caressing the hard stone, the intricate carvings blazed with heat. Focusing on the souls above as the heat intensified, he willed them to make haste. "Fulfill your destiny," he intoned to the nameless abyss imprisoning his spirit.

Guttering torches flickered within a substantial draft moving along the tunnel. Cloying in the confined space, Eric trembled with each dull boom cascading through the rock. Engines of war beset the besieged city that night. Edinburgh rocked under the onslaught as the southern hordes tightened their stranglehold on the already impoverished city.

Dust filtered down from the cracks forming in the roof.

"Come my lass, the tunnels below are the way for us." Searching the soot covered walls, he motioned to an opening. The dim light revealed his wife and children huddled together a few feet away. Hidden by Ellen's skirt, his youngest peeked out—a face awash with tears strangled his weary heart. "We must hurry past the refuse below."

"Husband, what ilk abides down here?"

"Hush my love. Better to brave the lower levels than face the English hordes. Keep Isabella and Robert close." Approaching the opening, he coughed as rotting garbage alongside the overwhelming stench of sewage poured toward him. Stagnant puddles of urine and human castoffs threatened to beat them into submission.

"Cover the--" a low moan issued from the dark. Struggling against his desire to run, Eric stepped forward, intent on finding the source of pain.

"We wish to pass friend, tell me where you lie. We can help." Frigid metal slithered along the cold stone, sending sparks skittering into the pitch dark.

"Friend? Above worlders do not belong here. Go back before we gut you." He pulled a torch from the nearest sconce, the burning oil trailing over the stone as he waved it into the dark.

"Allow us passage—Edwards's army takes the upper city. This is the only way beyond their reach!"

"City scum! Only death will greet you inside these warrens. No escape exists here. Go back and face your King."

Pushed back, Eric hefted his iron mace out front as the jarring voice solidified within the circle of flaring light.

"I brook no trouble between us. An escape below leads out of the city."

A deluge of blood flowed away from the half beheaded corpse lying on the floor. Raising his blade, the man howled. From the edge of yellow light a face smeared with gore leered at Eric. Mottled flesh rippled with worms wriggling under the surface. "Only death or worse await you here, there is no escape."

"I am the city cartographer. A doorway—a bolt hole—was hewn into the roots of the mountain centuries ago." Pulling his family close, Eric edged around the room, keeping his mace trained on the fiend.

The air reverberated with laughter as they hurried through a doorway. Rushing along the small corridor, he led his family deeper into the tunnels. A rumbling staccato built into a deafening roar.

"The tower has fallen," he cried. Pieces of granite dropped from the ceiling as cracks shoot across the weakened stone. Breaking from the tunnel, they skidded to a stop at the top of a large staircase leading down. Shrieks and moans floated upward from the depths. "I can't go on, Eric," Ellen whimpered.

"We can't go back, they'll kill us."

Splashing through the fetid waters cascading down the steps, Eric steered his family down the stairs and halted at the bottom as bodies strewn across the wide floor came into view. Prostrated in unnatural poses, the unfortunate cried out as others sat astride them, tearing chunks of flesh away. Growls punctuated the steady booms from above and their intrusion went unnoticed.

Roughhewn blocks encircled a yawning pit in the middle of the room.

"Fresh meat comes to us on two legs," one wailed.

Searching the room, columns rose up out of view into the darkness above. Slick with blood, the floor was canvassed with the leftovers from meals. A dull thumping from the stairs drew their attention.

Each gripping a leg between them, two ragged clothed figures drug a body behind them. Retched filth hid the pale skin beneath, except for the yellow eyes reflected in the torch light. They might have been beggars from the row; unfortunate souls Eric would have passed in the street.

"We have unexpected company!" one cackled. Moving to intercept them, a taller man edged around a column.

"Do give us one of the little ones." Salivating at the prospect of tender meat, he pulled the rags from his chest, barring the only way out as he edged around a column. Pulling himself to full height, he pantomimed brushing his hair with his hand. Encrusted blood fell away in crumbs. He wetted his hand with spittle before cleaning the gore from his cheeks. "Do stay for dinner. It's been sometime since we've had a lady of prestige among us lowly creatures."

"Stay back. We only want to pass," Eric uttered.

"Castle man you be; keep one of your rats and the rest stay." Seeing no way out, Eric huddled Ellen and his children behind him, bringing the heavy mace to bear. Sensing movement, he swung around in an arc feeling the jarring impact as bone crunched from the force of the iron top.

A heavy weight fell across Eric, and he tumbled to the ground with Ellen's screams in his ears. He twisted around. Fetid breath filled his mouth; within inches of his face, the larger man crushed him to the floor.

Pinned down, the ball of his weapon digging into his throat, Eric strained to move. "You could've left when I gave you the chance. Now we eat you!" Blood stained yellow teeth filled his vision as the gaping maw moved closer. Eric turned his head to the side to avoid snapping teeth before a shudder ran along the man's body. Fluid gushed down his neck as the weight was suddenly lifted from his chest.

Shifting to the side, he saw a knife sticking from the man's neck and Ellen standing over them.

Grim determination urged Eric on as he vaulted to his feet, pulling his mace from the floor. Motioning to Ellen, he picked Robert up before flanking the squalid display about them. Trailing him, she whispered, terror edging into her faint voice.

"What have you brought us into?"

Gripping her hand, Eric shook his head. Adrenaline surged into him as a face shone in the pale light cast from the torches. Ragged strips of flesh disappeared into its mouth. Scuttling off the corpse, its yellowed skin undulated with muscles in the faint light. Thin claws raked across the stone, cutting furrows into the granite. Eric heaved his mace in an overhand blow as the creature vaulted across the room, springing like a spider jumping on its prey. Crunching bones awakened the others as he struck the beast to the floor; howls of rage erupted from all corners of the room.

"Run!"

Pelting across the floor, Eric slowed in an attempt to untangle himself from Ellen before dashing through an unblocked door, the raging beasts a step behind. Laughter erupted behind them. Dollops of flesh slapped against the tunnel walls, frenzied howls echoed in the dark tunnel as they sprinted further into the catacombs.

Darting into a doorway, Eric sat Robert down and prepared to face the menace. Pushing them to the side, he propelled them into an adjoining room and silently pulled the door closed.

Pounding feet disappeared into the distance as Eric stood against the door with his head bowed. Torch gone, he moved by hearing alone.

"Ellen," he whispered into the pitch black.

"Here." Reaching out toward her voice, he counted them by touch.

"Keep hold of my shirt." Following the wall, they moved around the room, stopping as a cold draft moved up from a set of stairs through an opening on the opposite wall.

Running his hand along the wall of the staircase, rough carvings appeared a few feet down. "What are those?"

"What, Eric?"

"Nothing, love. We must make haste." Descending the stairs, he noticed a faint glow surrounding them, becoming brighter as they moved lower. Scraping over the stone, their feet sounded loud in the close confines of the stairwell. Slowing, Eric studied the runes. Intricate glyphs decorated the walls halfway up to the ceiling.

Reaching out, he jerked back at the sight of his skin radiating under the sleeve of his leather jerkin. Shocked, he turned and stood mute. Ellen leaned against the wall a few steps higher, her skin radiating in the darkness.

"Hurry, we need to get out of here!" He grabbed Robert and headed down, intent on the reaching tunnel near the bottom. Ending up ahead, the ceiling turned into open air as they approached the bottom. Diffused light emanated from every part of their skin not covered by clothing.

"What is the meaning of this? Have the Fey taken the castle?" Shaking his head, Eric led them across a vast hall that ended in a set of double doors set into the face of a massive wall.

"We have reached the bolt hole, Ellen. Help me open the doors." Striding up to the face, he studied the runes, which were carved in an ancient language. No handle was evident.

"Eric, no! Can't you feel it?"

"Hush, we have to get through." Touching a glyph, it flared in response. The oppressive weight of the room threatened to bury them.

Fulfill your destiny...

Reaching out, he touched a second rune on the other door. Brilliant flashes of light cascaded up and down his arms. He cried out from the numbing pain which rooted him to the spot. Grinding resonated across the room as the doors grated open. In a flash, the light was extinguished. Stepping back, Eric grabbed Ellen.

"Stay close. Just a little while longer and we will be safe."

He froze as he turned toward the opening. A few feet away, a man—if he could be called that—stared back. He was surrounded by an eerie yellow glow, and eyes darker than the abyss of Hell pinned him to the floor.

His wide grin was pronounced by rows of jagged teeth. A long narrow chin ran up to wide, dark cheeks. Black hair flowed down his shoulders over a robe of richly sewn silk.

"Welcome to my home. You have fulfilled the destiny you were born to." Stepping forward, the creature glided across the floor to the center of the room. Raising his arms skyward, he intoned in a long dead language, cruel yet musical in its quality. Lights flowed across the roof.

"You have released me from my prison. Join me." Stunned, they stood mute, unable to respond to the Fey creature. "You have no escape; your souls belonged to me the moment you opened the doors." Jarred from his daze, Eric hefted his mace.

"Let us alone, beast. We wish only to pass!" The creature turned his gaze upon the smaller human, a laugh forming along his lips.

"You jest! Come...feel the power of Belroth Meiltonour." He closed the distance in blinding speed and ripped the mace from Eric's hand. Slamming him to the floor, Eric's ribcage shattered under the powerful onslaught of the demon's attack. Pale as a ghost, long fangs splayed out from his jaw while a blackened tongue flickered out to test the air. This nightmare image from the foulest depths of imagination confronted them as his long, razor sharp claws ripped the man open from navel to sternum.

Heaving him into the air, Belroth spun the frail human around, gripping his neck with one hand while forcing his head onto his chest and popping his spinal cord out.

Darkness flowed from his eyes as he bit into the cartilage and neck bones seeking the soft juice inside. Blood spurted from the gaping wound. Biting deeper, Belroth's mouth elongated, engulfing the man's neck in one bite. Clear fluid began filling his mouth as he triumphed against the human. Darkness overcame his mind as he sought the fleeing soul drifting upwards toward its eternal home.

Wetted from the inflow of blood, his organs crackled as the fluid poured down his throat. He began reverting to a state of life as the infusion of new plasma and nutrients rushed through his body. Convulsions from the absolute pain tormented him. Blood was his way to extend life, but if he waited too long the process became one of horrific proportions. Unable to feed in any other way, his journey back to life was fraught with pain. The essence brought a new and overwhelming desire to him. The need for the conquest of a human's soul subjugated his inner core. A place of well-being enjoyed by humans, the journey to overcome that walled off place of peace was a dreadful, violating attack unlike any other he had experienced in his long years of existence. Blood lust succumbed to the need to possess a soul. Rage flowed through his limbs at the treatment he had endured for a thousand years, bereft of contact, left to languish in a prison until the end of time. Near the edge of his vision, he spied the soul dancing away. A faint glow steadily built around it as he reached out and pulled the spirit back.

Immaculate terror pleased Belroth, knowing he was the reason for the ultimate damnation of the human creature. A small fragment of humanity within that spirit reminded him of the life he led centuries before. He raged at the violation of his mind as the soul's energy coursed into him. He pushed his humanity deep into the abysmal depth of his core. Belroth crushed the last remnants of the soul. He devoured any chance the man had at a blissful existence beyond that shimmering portal of death.

Turning, he advanced on Ellen, intent on taking her soul. Smashing her to the ground, he bit deep into her neck. Memories of his early days carried his mind away as he drained the woman of her fluid. Once finished, Belroth threw her body to the floor. He raised his head and cried into the darkness. Screams of rage penetrated the gloom under the castle. The ancient call chilled anyone that was unfortunate enough to hear it; though they felt foolish afterwards, thinking it was just the sound of the wind.

For his victim lying dead under him, it was the end of life. Having savagely ripped into her neck, he left the flesh a mangled mass of tattered skin and muscles. His teeth had crushed the bones of her neck.

Huddled on the floor gripping one another, Robert and Isabella clawed at each other. Walking close, Belroth knelt down, taking each child's hand in his.

"Do not worry little ones. I will take care of you now. In time, you will learn the doors to the soul are the way to grace."

Moonlight Sonata by Shawna L. Bernard

Face of an Angel
By Lisamarie Lamb

Elsa sat on her tiny single bed, all squeaks and creaks and moans, and seethed at the unfairness of it all. It seemed that no matter what she did, no matter how bad she was, how late she stayed out, what she destroyed, who she hurt, it was still not enough to make her parents punish her as she wanted to be punished. The anger of not getting what she wanted made her head pound and her hands sweat. It made her think very bad thoughts that should not have been thought. It made her imagine blood and brains and broken bones that wept and wailed into the air as they died.

It made her think of the door in the floor and the cellar that lay beneath it, dank and rank with mildew and potatoes growing eyes that would never see.

It made her think of the other thing that was in the cellar that could most certainly see and was even now watching her. At least she suspected as much. It always seemed to know everything, every little thing.

And that made her smile her thin lipped, crowded tooth smile.

At least that knew she deserved to be punished.

Elsa bit her tongue and swallowed the bright red saltiness that came from it, feeling halfway sated. There would be more, a lot more, a river of it that would burst its banks and leave her drenched and drowning, but that was for another time. A time when she was finally dragged into the darkness and left, supposedly alone. For now she closed her eyes, squinted them shut, and lay back, her head making the slightest of dents in her pillow, her dark blonde hair fanning out across the stark white cotton. Lights danced behind her eyelids as she pressed her fingers into them, hard, harder than she should have done, and then whipped them away to blink into the glooming day. It got dark fast now, as though the day couldn't wait to get away from her.

A knock at the door had Elsa sitting up, straight, feet on the floor, silent and waiting for the familiar keening of the hinges. She knew them so well, just as she knew the sound of the cellar door as it rasped open. Just as she knew the sounds that came from the cellar too, the ones that echoed through the house in the dead of night and bounced from room to room, searching for prey. The ones that were shiny and sharp.

"Elsa?" The voice was hesitant even if the man behind it entered the room with no faltering at all, as if privacy was not something that Elsa might ever want to enjoy, as if the thought had never occurred to him, or her. "Elsa? Your mother and I want to know what the problem is." Strong, clear words, but Elsa's father was not strong, and he was not clear, and he bent a little, stooping as he stood next to his daughter, hoping she would give him an answer he would be able to compute. He cocked his head and looked at her in an understanding way from beneath long lashes that would have looked perfect on a woman but that made him seem fragile and forgotten.

Elsa tipped her head to one side, mimicking her father, a subtle movement that he noticed but ignored. As he always did. About everything.

"Where's Mum?" Elsa asked, and she was surprised to find that she cared about the answer. Where was her mother? Why wasn't she here, asking the questions, doing the prying? Why had she sent this timid little man to do the hard work? Or had she, in fact, sent him? Perhaps she wasn't even aware he had trudged up the stairs and was even now blinking in the greyness of the coming night as he tried to be patient and loving.

Elsa's father sighed and slumped down onto the bed next to his daughter, blushing lightly as the springs cried out in protest.

"She's upset. We're both upset, but she's… You hurt her, Elsa. The things you said. You're breaking her heart."

There was one moment, just then, right there, in which Elsa almost confessed everything. But then the last decade of pain came tumbling back in on her and she shrugged instead, giving away the chance for redemption. "Good," she said, licking her lips to hide the trembling one. "I'm glad."

"No you're not," her father told her.

Elsa flashed him a vicious look, venomous in its ferocity, and he stood up, backed away to the door and eased halfway out.

"Just..." He tried to say something poetic and poignant, but he faded away into himself and shut the door behind him.

Damn it.

The mother should have come.

Elsa would be in the cellar by now if she had.

Which is exactly where she wanted to be.

Which is exactly where she had to be, and soon, otherwise that thing, that big, glass ghost of a monstrosity down there was going to take its revenge on her after all, after it said it wouldn't, and that wasn't fair. Life wasn't fair, she had often heard said, but she'd rather have an unfair life than an unfair death. She had to survive, no matter what it took. No matter what the cost.

Elsa stripped and slipped under the covers, not caring about her teeth, her hair, her skin, for one night. She was too angry and frustrated for that. She knew she would have to redouble her efforts at being punished tomorrow, and the thought of it was weighing down on her. It was tiring. She was tired. What was next? What else could she do?

A thought began to form, but it was incomplete and it lacked something. Something important. Something that should have been clear but that was hiding in the shadows that the dark left behind.

It was too hot too cold too late too early too much to think. The girl could feel her eyes closing, stinging and burning, and she flicked them open, her breath catching. She'd almost forgotten her prayers. Dear God, no, that would have been the end, the actual end, and she didn't dare breathe as she fell from beneath her too thick duvet and knelt on the floor, the carpet doing nothing to protect her knees from the floorboards beneath. She had knelt in the same spot at the same time for ten years now, since she was six years old, and despite the pain it brought, there was a certain comfort too. A sort of calm. She could feel it through the scars and creases on her legs.

"I'm sorry," Elsa began as she always began. The words were the same every night -- had been for a decade -- and they had to be said, no matter what. "I'm sorry for destroying you. I'm eternally sorry. I'm sorry for breaking you. I'm eternally sorry. I'm sorry for killing you. I'm eternally sorry. Please forgive me." When the words were spoken and the incantation over, Elsa stayed kneeling, listening, hoping to hear the acknowledgement that she craved. It hadn't come for many years, and when it finally did it took the girl a long time to recognise it. But now she knew it, and she wanted it. A scraping, aching cry of anguish that started low and became high. It sounded as though it was in her head, but it couldn't be.

Could it?

Because it was coming from the basement where the thing was.

Nothing else made sense.

And there it was. A noise that cracked against itself and pricked at her skin.

Elsa crawled back beneath the covers when she finally heard it, smiling to herself. It was okay now. It was all right. She was forgiven for her past sins.

The thing in the cellar had pardoned her completely now. Apart from one little thing, one minor thing. Her payment. Elsa slept. But she dreamed bad dreams. One bad dream. The same dreamed she had dreamed since she had been excused. And it wasn't even a real dream since it was a memory and no one had ever denied it had happened.

Elsa was six years old once more, and the thing was whole and standing in the corner of the hallway, a massive glass figurine that seemed to tower above the little girl's head, shimmering where the sunlight dared to stumble across it. In reality it was not that big at all, not in the least, but memories have a way of melding into parodies of themselves, and this was no exception.

So the glass figurine was enormous, and Elsa was teeny tiny small.

It was her mother's favourite thing in the house, loved more than her daughter, even, or so it seemed. A gift from her parents on her wedding day, it was a hideous, monstrous glass statue of an angel, massive wings curved forever upwards in an attempt at flight, waves of icy hair cascading down, covering the creature's nudity. In its hands it was holding something, some poor, trapped beast. Elsa was never quite sure what it was meant to be; bird, butterfly, cherubic baby...It was a blob of clearness held in inexpertly sculpted claws. The angel's face was narrow and pointed, grinning wickedly, it showed shards of teeth that were sharper than an angel's had any real right to be. Its eyes were hollow, deep, and dark.

But, despite all this, Elsa's mother adored it.

And, despite all this, Elsa was fascinated by it, even though her mother had warned her, ever since she could remember, ever since she could understand, not to go near it. Not to touch it. She hadn't meant to do it, of course. Only...she heard it. A voice trapped within glass, muffled and small. "Help me. Let me out." It was strange, really, because it had never spoken before (although it hadn't seemed to be silent since), and what it was about that particular day and time and moment Elsa never did find out. Not that it mattered. It happened. That's what mattered.

It spoke, beseeching the child for help.

What else could a six year old do but do as she was told? Elsa's chubby hands grabbed at an umbrella resting unneeded in a coat stand by the front door and with a whack that smashed its way through the house, she tried to free whoever was caught inside the giant glass coffin.

But no one rushed to freedom.

Her mother rushed to find out what the sound was and made an even louder sound of grief, a shriek that the neighbours still talk about, even now, although they bring it up with a laugh, so funny, that time you went crazy and scared us all shitless, ha ha ha. What was it you said again?

But there were no words. No real words. Just sounds, and actions, and the worst action of all was to open the cellar door and push Elsa down the steps to stay there, in the dark, until she was suitably sorry.

Elsa was sorry immediately. She felt betrayed, tricked by the wicked angel, as evil a demon that ever lied, and as her mother threw the remains of the glass statuette down upon her, raining beads of shattered face and hands and bird or butterfly or baby, she was already on her knees, praying for forgiveness.

The glass was sharp and the little girl soon learned not to move from where she had fallen. So she stayed still until her father rescued her. It was the only strong thing he had done in his life, and it wasn't enough because he had let it happen. He could have saved her, but he left her to rot for an hour.

That was his crime.

Her mother always treated her differently after that, as though she was tainted, a broken child who could never be whole again and was to be shunned because of it.

And as for the glass angel…

It took ten years for it to forgive Elsa, but it was not completely satisfied. There was still one more thing to do. Which is why the dreams reminded her of what had happened (as though she could ever really forget), and of what should happen now.

Which is why she had to be punished, and taken down into the cellar again. Her punishment would lead to their punishment in a nice, neat circle. And perhaps, finally, when it was done, she wouldn't have to beg anymore. She wouldn't have to pray.

"Tomorrow," Elsa whispered, wanting desperately to sleep, needing more time than she was being offered. She had to get it right; the idea of failing the angel was sick making.

"Tonight." There was no mistaking the order in that once trapped voice, that tricking, trickling tickle of power. "Tonight." It wasn't that Elsa was against the idea. If anything, the thought of the blood and jagged ripping cuts and the revenge excited her. It was just that she didn't know what to do to precipitate the whole ordeal. It was taking too long as it was, and now, when it was late and time was ticking and the air was hungry with desperation...

"But—"

"Now." There was a growl behind that single word, something unearthly cold and dripping with a burning, oozing drool.

Without any more thought, Elsa swung her legs over the side of her tiny, child's bed and tapped her feet on the moonlit floor. She swallowed hard, but the lump caught in her throat wouldn't shift, and instead of relief her actions only brought her a fit of coughing, made worse by her trying to keep it quiet, stifling the sound before it could be born.

Her lungs burned and her ribs ached, but the glass angel's insistence was not to be ignored, and so she stood, wincing at the whines her mattress made. But no one heard. The house was as still as a statue and twice as silent.

Elsa's heart pounded in her chest, begging to be let out. No. Not now. There was still too much to do. And at the thought of it, of all that was about to happen and the angel's grating voice and the peace that would follow the blissful screaming, Elsa woke up a little. She smiled a little. She felt as though she might even know what she was supposed to do. Just a little.

Her parents' bedroom was across the hall and a nightlight, left over from when she had needed it (which was never because a light would not scare a demon away, especially a barely lit orange seashell shaped one) showed her the way. Elsa pushed open the door and heard a snuffling-shuffling, the sound of a disturbed sleeper. It was her father, who snored gently and then turned over, not caring enough in his unconsciousness to bother opening his eyes. Her mother didn't move. Her mouth was open and her breathing was heavy. It matched Elsa's.

"Help me."

The voice was a tiny one, and it was a surprising one. It came from the wall above her parents' enormous bed, so large that no one had to touch anyone else at any time, which was perfect for them. It came from a picture that had been hanging in the same place for as long as Elsa could remember. Longer. It had been there since her parents' wedding, and, in all that time, Elsa had never noticed the little lone figure within it, caught behind the glass, pleading to be set free.

It was not just a landscape. Not just a pretty picture of poppy fields and an azure sky, clouds tumbling across it. No. There was a girl in it. A lovely girl. An angel.

"Help me. Just break the glass and I'll be free."

Elsa had no choice. Any thoughts of being bad flew away, shattered as she tiptoed and wavered and reached up to grab at the painting. With a flourish that twisted her insides, she whipped it away from the wall and flung it down against the bedpost, smashing the glass into a thousand shining diamonds so that they rained down on her parents' faces as they slept. On her mother's mainly. Mostly. And where it landed it shredded deep.

The angel in the painting was immediately silent.

She wasn't even visible, the canvas itself had torn and burst and was no longer recognisable.

With a cry of absolute animal fear, her mother flew from her bed, her face a mass of cuts, her eyes wide, her hands shaking as they fluttered uselessly, trying to stem the torrent of blood that was weeping from her eye where a stray sliver of glass had landed and been rubbed in, probably by her own thick fingers. Elsa's father, calmer although not by much, flicked on the main light, flooding the room with brightness that stung and clawed. Elsa gasped at the carnage, at the glinting, sparkling beauty of it as the remains of a once loved possession lay in pieces on her parents' bed, on her parents' night clothes, on her parents. She hadn't intended to do anything more than free the angel (the second angel, she corrected herself), but whether that had happened or not, whether the angel had been there or not, it hardly mattered now. What mattered was her mother's bright red, round, slavering face with its wide blood pooled eyes that blinked and choked in an effort to see, and its snarling, snapping teeth that were as white as moonlight against the scarlet rivers that ran through them and over then and dripped out the other side.

Elsa's mother tried to speak, but fury, a hot and painful and violent anger that took away words and replaced them with squeaks and squalls so similar to those the woman had uttered ten years before – the ones the neighbours still laugh about. Only no one was laughing now, and if the neighbours could hear the screeching they were having no fun with it.

Slower than treacle and bitter as dirt, the mother moved. Elsa could have run away; she had the time, she was right by the door, her father was silently wishing she would make a break for it, but instead she stood her ground, waited, wanting to be caught and dragged and dropped.

"Hang on, girls," said the man, his voice small against the hugeness of the moment. "Let's talk about this. I'm sure Elsa had her reasons, maybe she was sleepwalking, where you sleepwalking? Were you? Sweetheart? Sleepwalking? Were you?"

"No, Dad," whispered Elsa. She didn't look at him, but kept her eyes firmly fixed on her mother's torn face. "I'm not sleepwalking. I did it on purpose. And I'm not sorry this time." Elsa didn't have a chance to register her father's reaction, although she was quite sure it was sad and disappointed and ineffectual. Her mother's massive arm, make thick from too many cream cakes and not enough care was wrapped around her throat, and she was moving, her head snapping back and forth as the bones in her neck crunched painfully, her feet barely touching the worn out carpet on the landing, bumping down each stair, burning across the beigeness.

"Jim! Get the door!"

Elsa heard the words, muffled beneath flab. She closed her eyes and relaxed. It was happening. Finally, she had done what she had been asked to do.

Elsa's father leapt down the stairs, and Elsa noted that he'd taken the time to put his slippers on. Wouldn't want to get cold feet, Daddy dear. Can't have you backing out now. Open the damn cellar door.

"Jesus, Jim, you're so Christing slow! Open the damn cellar door!" It was this scream from his wife that finally sped the man up, and he huffed over, not looking anywhere but down. With an effort that cracked his back and made his wince for so many reasons, he flung open the door in the floor and kicked away the rug that covered it. Done.

Without waiting for words, for an apology, for any begging, without, even, waiting for a light, Elsa's mother threw her daughter into the cold darkness where the broken thing laid waiting. The girl bounced, once, and lay still, breathing in dust and mould.

"Shut the door, Jim," ordered the mother, glancing down, not wanting to see anything and having her wish granted. It was too dark down there. It was a thick, soupy dark that ate away at itself at night.

Jim, face ashen, lips trembling, blinked at his wife. "I don't think I will, Sue. I don't think I can." With that, he dipped himself into that swirling darkness. And Sue lost him.

"Jim?" she asked, voice quavering as she peered down and down and down into nothing. "Jim, what are you playing at? Leave her down there, she'll know better than to break my things by morning, and that's for sure."

But no reply came to her. Not even a simpering whimper. "Shit, Jim, I'll leave you down there with her if you don't get up here this instant." But Sue was not so sure that she would do that. She couldn't quite make her hands reach out for the door, couldn't quite grasp it. She stood at the top of the steps and argued with herself about going down there.

"Almost forgiven," came a voice from behind her, leaking into her ear, a hot whisper of fetid breath. With a shriek, Elsa's mother toppled into the cellar, the thud of her landing echoing around the basement room.

The glass angel was almost whole. It sat, resplendent, holding its pet in its claws, smiling its fanged smile. There was a hole here and there, a spot where the glass hadn't quite mended. Yet. But it was so close to being whole. So close to forgiveness.

Elsa, her neck aching and possibly broken, sat with it, giggling to herself. Laughing. The sound bouncing from the dirty dark walls, tripping over old Christmas decorations and boxes of discarded toys and baby clothes.

And there was Jim, bent as always, hobbling, trying to move but not able to get too far. Well, who could when they were trying to walk across broken glass? Shards and slivers, potsherds and crystals of slicing diamond clarity.

"Walk." The angel had few words, but the ones it did have were commanding.

Sue, stunned, in love with the thing again after forgetting how much she had adored it, did as she was told. She looked down at her feet, but only once. Once was enough. Once was too much. Skin was torn away, flesh ripped off, until the very bones of her were all that were left. Jim fared no better. When his feet gave way, he fell forward, landing on his belly. Ordered to keep moving, he did so, until his guts spilled out. He was still after that.

Sue, just about breathing, offered up one last apology. Whether it was to her daughter or to the angel, no one could tell, but it hardly mattered. "Sorry." It meant nothing now. And when she tipped forward and glass sliced her throat, Elsa was glad. Her mother couldn't speak any more.

The glass angel became silent after Jim and Sue had expired. Perhaps it was happy. Perhaps it was tired.

Elsa wondered what she should do, now that she had been absolved and her parents were so plainly dead and the angel was, she now noticed, completely whole again.

What was left?

And it was just as these thoughts began to rattle around her brain, and the pain in her neck became a screaming, churning monster, that she heard it. Quiet at first, but growing louder, insisting on being noticed. A voice. The voice. The trapped one.

Again.

Elsa rolled her eyes towards the glass angel. But no, it wasn't that. It was silent and empty now.

But a glimmer of light in her mother's clotted hair made her think. Made her remember.

The angel in the picture.

It was angry, wasn't it? Just that like glass angel before it. With a sob at the unfairness of it all, Elsa jolted to her knees, her head hanging too low to one side. She could ask. It wouldn't hurt. It couldn't hurt.

"I'm sorry for destroying you. I'm eternally sorry. I'm sorry for breaking you. I'm eternally sorry. I'm sorry for killing you. I'm eternally sorry. Please forgive me."

Dark Hearth by Shawna L. Bernard

Stone Butterfly

By David North-Martino

Vanessa Petros awoke on a lumpy cot in a finished basement apartment with no windows. Her head pounded, and her eyes squinted from the harsh light of a solitary bulb. Had someone slipped something in her drink last night?

Her mouth dry, she felt more thirsty than afraid—although some part of her, deep inside, knew that terror resided just below the surface, waiting for its opportunity to escape.

Mortified, she discovered that someone had removed her clothing and squeezed her into a charcoal gray sports bra and a matching pair of shorts. She flushed with anger and embarrassment from the thought of a stranger seeing her body.

She had been overweight since childhood and had suffered the mocking and teasing of children, and the disapproval of adults. Now, as an adult herself, she also dealt with a prejudice that affected her daily life.

Her abductor meant to humiliate her. She couldn't stand the thought. The passivity with which she had approached life was suddenly replaced with a desire to act...perhaps kill.

By sheer force of will, she held back the threat of tears. Steadying her breathing, she tried to relax and slow her racing heart to stave off a growing headache, the pain in her head increasing with each beat of her heart.

Now a bit calmer, she needed to take in her new environment. Figure out where and why she was here and plan her escape.

She slowly stood up from the cot. The springs squealed as they expanded to their normal size. In front of her, an old wooden staircase ran along the far wall.

She walked over and peered up the darkened stairway at the metal door that stood as a barrier between her and escape. She felt a sudden fear that the door would open, and her abductor would descend upon her like a spider with eight hairy legs and beady predatory eyes.

She walked away to dispel the thought and explore the small kitchen. Her captor had thought of everything. She had all she needed to live there: a stove with hood vent, a microwave oven, a sink, a small bathroom, even a refrigerator. But upon opening it, she discovered he had forgotten one very important provision—food. Then, with a growing panic, she remembered a television news report and knew at once who the spider was that had ensnared her.

The door at the top of the stairs creaked open. Vanessa ran back to the cot as if she could somehow find protection there.

Her abductor descended the stairs and came into view. He wore a white robe with hood pulled over his head, framing the frozen expression of an ancient Greek tragedy mask that obscured his identity.

"My stone butterfly," the voice behind the mask said. "That's what you are, and that's what I'm going to call you."

"What do you want from me?" Vanessa screamed. She hugged herself in a halfhearted attempt to hide her rolls of fat.

"I think you know what I want from you." Vanessa imagined that the man behind the mask smiled when he said this.

"You're going to starve me to death, aren't you?" Vanessa asked.

"I'm going to make you into my finest creation," he said.

"The last woman you abducted died," Vanessa said. "I remember the news reports."

"True. But she wasn't as strong as you. You're a heavier piece of marble." Vanessa winced. Her heart sank from the pain of the insult more than the prospect of not getting out of this situation alive.

"I'm going to chisel you down, metaphorically, to perfection. I think you have the will to live. Even your name suggests that."

"What are you talking about?" Vanessa asked.

"Vanessa means butterfly, and Petros means stone. You are the Stone Butterfly... my transformation rock."

"You're crazy," Vanessa said, standing up, tensing her whole body. "You can't keep me here!"

The robe hid much of his body, but he couldn't have been taller than five feet, six inches. She might just have a chance to fight him off and escape.

"I can and I will," the man said. He pulled a cattle prod out from under his robe.

Vanessa slumped back onto the cot, heard the springs squeal under her weight and suddenly felt exhausted. She just wanted to go home.

"I go by the name Andrias. If you need anything—anything besides food, that is -- feel free to call my name. I have a camera and a microphone hidden down here, and I will provide you with whatever will make you most comfortable."

"You're watching me?"

"Of course. I need to watch my creation as it develops."

"What about some clothes? Or a sheet?" Vanessa felt very exposed. She longed for some form of comfort.

"I'm afraid you can't have those either. I can't watch the process of sculpting the new you if you're covered up. I suggest you don't move around too much. You'll expend your calories too quickly and get sick. I'll leave you to it."

"Wait!" Vanessa screamed as Andrias returned up the steps. He didn't turn back or say anything, just opened the door and closed it behind him. She heard a locking mechanism clicking into place, and then, once again, she was alone.

Vanessa wept freely and hated that she couldn't hold back her tears. She wanted to say so many things to family and friends before she died, wanted to do so many things. She mourned for words left unsaid and dreams unfulfilled... especially her desire to get married one day and have a child. She thought of her parents. What a terrible blow to lose their only daughter, their only child. A full branch of the family tree sheared off as though it had never existed.

Andrias wanted the impossible, and his desires would lead to her death. The greatest irony was that she had wanted to lose weight, had fought the battle of the bulge and lost so many times. Maybe in some way, God had answered her prayers. She would accomplish this elusive goal, but in the end it would be the death of her. God had more than a sense of humor. He had a sense of irony.

* * *

Even if she did manage somehow to survive and escape, in the weakened state she knew was to come, her metabolism would be shot. She'd gain all her weight back and more. Perhaps her body would be incapable of weight loss after that. What a funny thing to worry about when death lay only weeks away. A terrible death, filled with nothing but regrets and hunger pangs.

Snot plugged her nose and she squinted with tear-swollen eyes. She prayed then, prayed for a way to escape, a way to survive, a bit of comfort. She didn't know how long she had prayed, as the sun rose and set obscured by her prison walls, but an idea finally connected, and she knew what she needed to do.

"Andrias!" she screamed, sitting up straight, looking at the ceiling as if invoking a dethroned Greek god. "Andrias!"

She heard him open the door and knew her time had arrived.

* * *

Andrias stood on the stairs staring at her, his eyes shimmering behind the stony expression of the mask.

"I want to be perfect," Vanessa said.

"And you shall be. Allow for the transformation process, Butterfly."

"I know a way I can survive the transformation process," Vanessa said.

"Go on," Andrias said.

"You need to let me eat. Not just anything. The right things."

"Out of the question," Andrias said, he turned to walk back up the stairs.

"The ancient Greeks created perfect form by exaggerating muscle," she said, speaking quicker, knowing she was losing him. He stopped and turned back to her.

"Among other things," Andrias said. She could tell he was intrigued.

"You could do the same with me. With the right equipment, the right foods, the correct amounts of protein and carbohydrates I could..." she quickly corrected herself. "You could sculpt me into the perfect specimen. You could turn me into a female bodybuilder. Imagine it, even the Greeks would marvel at your creation. From an obese woman to a masterpiece."

Her words sounded ridiculous now to her ears. Perhaps she should have waited, should have thought of a better plan.

Andrias stood silently for a moment as if pondering her offer, her revelation.

"I'll think about it," he said and returned up the stairs.

* * *

Vanessa awoke to a rumbling in her stomach. She hadn't remembered falling asleep.

The waiting was the hardest part. Here, alone in the small apartment, there wasn't much to do besides loop in her mind how she might escape and concentrate on her growing hunger. She tried not to think of her family or her impending death. There had to be a way to survive. If only Andrias would allow her to eat and exercise it would buy her time to figure out how to escape him.

She heard the bolts unlatch and his footfalls on the stairs. She felt fear all the way to her bones. What would be his verdict?

He stood before her, a terrible visage of insanity, an ancient gargoyle come alive inside while its stony exterior waited and watched throughout the centuries.

"I knew you were the one, my Butterfly," Andrias said. "I spent some time researching and considering if I should change my plan."

"What did you decide?" Vanessa asked, her throat tight.

"Weight loss is a confusing subject, so many varying opinions, so much money to be made by keeping people ignorant. But you are right. The bodybuilders understand how to take weight off and sculpt their bodies to near perfection. But you must know, my Butterfly, that there are many female bodybuilders. Why would the world marvel at one more?"

The churning in Vanessa's stomach grew louder until she felt that, even across the room, he could hear it.

"You said near perfect. You could make me perfect."

Vanessa imagined that she heard Andrias's eyebrows rise and his lips pucker in thought behind his mask.

"That's what I thought, as well. The training will be harsh on you. What if you fail?"

"You win either way," Vanessa said quickly. "If I fail you go back to starving me."

"I guess I can't argue with that," Andrias said, a smile creeping into his voice. "Wait here."

Where else am I going to go, asshole, she thought.

He returned carrying a box that looked heavy.

"Don't think I won't be able to drop this box and punish you if you try to escape," Andrias said as he walked slowly to the middle of the room. He put the box down with a thud. Three magazines lay stacked on the box.

"What's in the box?"

"Those are your dumbbells," Andrias said. "I've also provided you with some women's muscle magazines. You are a bright girl, reading them will keep you from too much boredom. If you study hard enough you might even become a co-creator."

He tossed the magazines on her cot.

Co-creator? She didn't like the sound of that. She had hoped he would leave her to her own devices, but could she do it alone? She didn't think she could. She got off the bed and onto her knees, onto the scratchy area carpet and looked at the box.

"This is just a cheap weight set you can buy in a department store. How am I going to build my body to perfection with vinyl weights? I need real iron."

Andrias looked at her suspiciously. "I'll see what I can do. For now you will use these and keep to the plan. If not, it's back to starving the weight off of you."

* * *

Vanessa poured her attention into the magazines, reading and digesting every nuance over and over again. Even articles in the same magazine contradicted each other and she knew she would have to figure out what worked for her.

The regimen was deceptively simple: she needed to keep her calories at a ratio of 50% protein, 30% carbs, and 20% fat while increasing her activity. She would use low weights and calisthenics at high reps and perform the exercises in intervals to keep up her heart rate. In this way she would begin to tone her body and shed the pounds. Then, in stage two, she would crawl into a metaphorical cocoon of low reps and heavy weights to emerge a butterfly—Andrias's Stone Butterfly. Andrias sat in a folding chair counting out the reps as she began with kneeling pushups.

She found the exercise difficult, and her arms soon felt like lead. Her face grew flush from the exertion and the embarrassment of not being able to perform such a simple exercise. She would need to get a lot stronger if she thought to overpower and disarm him and then escape.

"Do one more," Andrias ordered.

"I can't. It's too difficult," Vanessa said, feeling defeated. She could already feel the sweat glistening on her forehead.

Andrias pulled out the cattle prod and punched it into her arm.

The jolt shot pain up and down her limb as it branched into her body. She screamed and rolled into the fetal position.

"One more," Andrias commanded.

Fighting the residual pain, she crawled back in place and gave him one more pushup, on shaky arms, before dropping back to the floor.

"Very good. I knew you could do it. Now onto the weights."

He had bought her a set of cast iron dumbbells that went up to fifty pounds. She figured that would be plenty enough weight for a long time... she didn't want to think about how long.

Andrias called out the exercise routine and Vanessa gave him the reps. When he asked for one more, she did her best, knowing that if she didn't he would provide her plenty of incentive.

When he was finished with her the sweat slickened her skin and her sportswear. Her breathing came in short rasps and droplets of sweat tickled her scalp.

"Your arms and shoulders will be sore," Andrias said. "Tomorrow we will work your legs. Have your protein shake now before you lose any muscle you may have gained."

She nodded and went to the refrigerator and he in turn climbed the stairs. She would do what he told her to do. Her arm still smarted from the punishment.

* * *

As the days progressed and her body adapted to the exercise, he increased the reps or the weight. And when she became used to one setting on the cattle prod he would dial one higher. He had created the perfect carrot and stick: the pain of electricity and the pleasure of food. She spent hours every day submitting to his demands. The workouts turned so grueling and the shock punishment so painful that more than once she begged him just to kill her. But she knew he could not stop now, and neither could she. Slowly, she watched her own body transform from soft weakness to fleshy steel.

After the workouts her arms and legs had a hard time responding to the simple demands of cooking. Grilling a piece of chicken or mixing a protein shake felt like a monumental task. But the minutiae kept her from thinking and exhaustion helped her to sleep. And in that sleep her dreams were filled with the sorrows and longings that she repressed during the day.

* * *

How long she remained under his tutelage she did not know. Months? Years? Each day seemed to spill into the next with only one goal: total transformation.

She looked into a mirror he had installed on the outside of the bathroom door. Every muscle was perfectly sculpted by his method and her work. She didn't recognize her own reflection. Stone Butterfly remained, but Vanessa Petros was gone.

The door opened upstairs, the same as it always had, but now she didn't dread his visits. She longed for them.

He descended the stairs, looked at her, and rubbed his hands together.

She walked over to her weights, picked up a set of 50-pound dumbbells and placed them on either side of her. She felt ready.

"No exercise today. Flex for me," Andrias said. And she did, feeling the bulging muscles push and expand her skin. He clapped, giddy as a child on Christmas morning.

Moving beside her, he lovingly ran his finger over her flexed bicep, tracing the perfect lines in her arm. The fine hairs on her body stood on end. She felt both ecstasy and revulsion at his touch.

He traced his index finger over her trapezius muscle. With his attention elsewhere, and seizing the moment, she slowly bent her legs until her right hand could reach the iron dumbbell. Her fingers tightened around the bar. Her body tensed. Adrenaline surged.

Then she released her grip and let her hand slacken. She couldn't do it. She couldn't kill him, couldn't bludgeon him with the cast iron even though a part of her cried out for it. She could no longer do any of this alone, and she couldn't imagine going back to the way things had been, the big chunk of marble she used to be.

"What do we do with you now?" Andrias asked. "Now that I have created perfection."

Would he kill her now? Or would she be subject to living out her life in the small apartment, a masterpiece hidden away in his private collection?

"I want to show you something."

Her words woke him from his trance. She turned away from him, his finger still out, dangling in the air where her muscles used to be. She held an open magazine in front of him.

"This is what I want to do. I want to show off your creation to the world." He looked at the advertisement and cocked his head.

"You wouldn't be using this as a way to escape from me?" Vanessa's throat went dry but she forced herself to speak.

"That was my original plan."

"What changed your mind?"

"I realized I couldn't do this without you."

* * *

"The time has arrived, Butterfly," Andrias said. Vanessa hadn't heard him open the door or walk down the stairs, but she wasn't startled by his silent arrival. She turned from the mirror to face him. "Are you ready?"

"I am," Vanessa said.

"Then take my hand," Andrias said, extending it toward her.

Vanessa reached out tentatively, and then placed her hand in his. He turned and led her up the stairs. She no longer felt afraid; only a rising exhilaration and expectancy at the chance of a new life. Andrias reached the top of the stairs and slowly turned the handle. He looked back at her and nodded, and she returned his gesture. He opened the door and the bright daylight saturated everything beyond the threshold. Vanessa squinted, wondering, after so long in the dimness of the cellar, if her eyes would ever adjust. She hesitated for just one heartbeat, took a deep breath, and then followed him through the doorway to meet her destiny.

"Well, Frank, this competitor's story is as crazy as I've ever heard. She was just an ordinary overweight woman working a day job when she decided to disappear. She went into seclusion with a very eccentric trainer, and he put her through the paces, let me tell you. She was gone so long that everyone thought she'd been abducted by a serial killer who starves fat women to death. I mean, you can't make this stuff up! Then one day, she reemerges as a professional level bodybuilder and starts winning competitions. And here's the best part. This guy, this trainer, wears a Greek tragedy mask. I mean, nobody knows who this guy is or where he came from. Wait until you see him. This is stuff right out of Big Time Wrestling."

"That's very true, Vince. But Vanessa Petros, the woman known as the Stone Butterfly, and her eccentric coach, only known as Andrias, have put woman's bodybuilding on the map. I see a long career ahead for both of them…"

A knock at the door took his mind away from the broadcast.

"Mr. Andrias? Five minutes," a voice called from behind the dressing-room door.

Andrias shut off the television, thankful not to have to hear any more babbling from talking head sportscaster idiots. Still, he had finally received the recognition he deserved. He had spent so much time carving his Stone Butterfly to perfection, and it continued to take a great deal of work to keep her that way. Entropy was constant, and he had to make sure she stuck to the plan and provide consequences if she did not.

He affixed his mask, one that had been created by the great mask maker Zeph Alardo; a man who never asked questions of his clients.

Andrias stood up from his chair in the dressing room, opened the door, and walked into the underground hallway. He watched the Stone Butterfly exit her dressing room in what he could only believe was a beautiful synchronicity that connected the artist to his work.

She smiled at him before walking steadily down the hall. He followed her, watching her perfect form from behind. Neither of them spoke. They didn't have to speak. Over the years they had become like one person, so hard now to separate the creator from the creation.

A stagehand stopped them from entering the stadium, and by some soundless cue a group of bodyguards surrounded them. The announcer heralded their entrance and the stagehand pointed, letting them know it was time.

Entering the arena, the crowd roared. The fanfare filled him with pride. If they had thrown roses, as was done in gladiatorial times, he might not have been able to contain himself.

A group of larger women waited by an iron barrier which kept them at a safe distance from the athletes. They held out glossy photos of both his Butterfly and himself. He walked toward them, the bodyguards following, as his Butterfly, a few feet ahead, met the crowd for autographs.

One large woman screamed, "Train me!" He could hear her shrill voice perfectly over the din.

Another plus-sized would-be marble slab pushed into the shrill sounding women. She held out a pen and photograph and screamed: "No! Train me!"

Andrias took the pen and picture and signed his autograph. The women continued to beg for him to train them.

Andrias handed the marble slab back her pen, along with the newly autographed photo, and smiled behind his mask.

Fallen Angel by Ashley Scarlet

Solitude

By Guy Burtenshaw

Mary stared at the old oak door set in the wall beneath the stairs. It led down to the cellar, where she knew her brother would be sitting in the dim light thrown from the old hurricane lamp he kept by the foot of the stairs. It had been five long years since they had first arrived with their mother at the old house in the centre of the town. Mary had been eleven, Thomas three.

Their mother was running away from someone in the city. Mary didn't know whom from, just that she was running—and the only person her mother knew outside the city was her half-brother, David. She had taken Mary and Thomas there and, one morning less than a year later, disappeared. Mary's last memory of her mother was of her kissing them goodnight. She had been wearing a red dress, and said they would soon be going home.

Mary stood in the centre of the hall listening as Uncle David walked across the landing to his room. She was about to call down to Thomas when she heard Uncle David coming down the stairs. Somehow she could tell that he was in a foul temper, likely worse than normal due to his inebriated state.

"You've been in my room!" he shouted as he descended the stairs.

"I haven't," she lied. She never believed that her mother had abandoned them, especially not with a drunk like Uncle David.

"The window is open," Uncle David shouted. "I think I would remember if I'd opened it myself."

"I thought I would make it cooler for you, to let some fresh air in." That was the truth. She had waited for him to leave the house earlier and searched through the draws in his old dresser. She knew there must be a clue to where her mother had gone somewhere in the house. She had already looked everywhere else, but there was not even a trace that her mother had ever existed. The air in the room had been overbearing, and she had meant to close the window again—but was distracted by her thoughts.

For a moment, she thought he was going to hit her. She could smell a mixture of alcohol and tobacco on his breath, and she knew it meant trouble—real trouble. He walked past her into the lounge, and she wasn't sure whether he wanted her to follow or not. So she stayed where she was in the centre of the hall.

"Come here," he shouted from the lounge. She walked towards the door.

As she entered the room, a glass narrowly missed her head and smashed against the doorframe to her left.

"Stay where you are!" he shouted.

He staggered across the room towards her. She wished he would trip and break his neck, but he didn't. He grabbed hold of her hair and pulled her head forward until her face almost touched his; and as he spoke, she was hit by the foul stench of the day's debauchery.

"You're a sick old man," Mary told him, and immediately wished she had remained quiet.

He pressed his thumb into her throat and she tried to pull away, but couldn't. He dragged her by her hair out of the lounge and across the hall to the cellar door, which he swung open.

"You speak to me like that ever again, and I'll kill you," he threatened through clenched teeth. She glared into his eyes with as much hatred as she could manage. He struck her across the face before pushing her through the open door, and then slammed it shut behind her.

She felt herself falling. She desperately tried to grab the handrail, and watched the door closing above her as she fell. As her back struck the hard wooden edges of the top steps, the pain was intense—but by the time she reached the bottom, she was unconscious.

When she opened her eyes, the pain rushed back to greet her. She was sore and aching all over. The lamplight was flickering on the ceiling and spread grotesque shadows moving in all directions from the cobwebs that dangled and trailed from the old wooden beams.

She sat up and looked for Thomas, but could not see him. As she stood, the floorboards creaked, and something moved in a dark corner of the cellar. She picked up the hurricane lamp and held it out towards the darkness. She could see the dark outline of someone kneeling with their back to her, and knew there was only one person it could be.

The cellar had been the place Uncle David had banished them to as punishment, but it had become the only place either of them could feel safe. Uncle David never set foot in the cellar, and while Mary would never have chosen to surround herself with the old brick walls, Thomas often sat alone in the cellar as though he found comfort in the solitude.

She walked towards him slowly, her whole body sore from the fall. As she reached him, he turned his head to look up at her, the shadows drawing dark holes in place of his eyes, the light making him much older than his eight years. She shivered as a cold draft brushed past her.

"She's been calling us," Thomas said.

"What are you doing?" Mary asked. Her skin crawled and the hairs on the back of her neck stood on end

"She's frightened for us."

Mary saw that Thomas had pulled up some of the floorboards and rested them against a wall. The shallow space below was cloaked in darkness and hid whatever he was looking at from her.

She lowered the lamp into the hole and dispelled the darkness. A chill shot straight through her like a cold bolt of lightning as she saw what lay beneath the floor...what must have been there for all the years they had been left alone. Her mother's skin was dry and brittle as though she had been mummified, but her dress was just as red as the day Mary had last seen her.

Mary couldn't move. She could scarcely believe what she was seeing, but slowly began to understand why her mother had never returned...she had never even left. For all those years, Uncle David had been lying to her. For all those years he had been sending them down into the darkness, letting them believe their mother had abandoned them…while all the while, she lay buried beneath their feet.

"She's been so lonely," Thomas cried.

Mary turned, filling with rage, and went to the stairs. She stood staring up at the cellar door and tried to control her anger, but it only intensified. She felt a hatred that she never knew was possible.

Ignoring her pain, she climbed the stairs and tried the handle of the door. She was surprised to find it unlocked, and burst through it so hard that it banged against the wall. She didn't care how much noise she made—Mary was not scared of him anymore.

She crossed the hall to the lounge and saw the glow from the reading lamp. The door was slightly ajar, and she pushed it all the way open. An old black and white film she did not recognise was on the television.

Uncle David was slumped over in a chair by the window. His eyes were closed, mouth agape, arms hanging limply by his sides. For a moment Mary thought he must be dead, but he let out a wheeze. By his feet there was an empty bottle of Johnny Walker that he had apparently used to drink himself into unconsciousness.

The more she watched the vile drunk slouched in the chair, the more she wanted to cause him harm, to make him suffer. She walked towards him, holding the lamp out in front. The lamplight cast a sinister orange light across his chubby face. All he needed was a couple of horns and he would have looked just like the devil.

Mary leaned down and picked up the empty bottle by its neck. She had read in the newspaper how women had killed their abusive husbands and got away with it. One had even poured petrol over her husband and burnt him to death. 'Battered Wives Syndrome' was the term they had used. She doubted whether they would accept that as her defence, but she was willing to find out.

She raised the bottle over his head—but as much as she hated him, she could not do it. She lowered the bottle. Perhaps she was not as strong as she thought she was.

Mary placed the bottle down on the small table next to her uncle, and he grabbed her wrist. His eyes were open wide and glaring at her with a madness she had never seen. He looked wild. She had been wrong—she was still scared of him—now more than ever.

He clawed at her wrist and reached out with his other hand to grab at her clothes. She swung the lamp around and the met the side of his forehead with a dull clunk, splitting the skin just above his eye. He looked up, stunned. Blood trickled down his face, dripping over the ridge of his brow and mixing with the sweat on his shirt. An unnatural rage filled his face as though a pressure was building up within him—and Mary knew if she stayed about, she would literally see him explode.

"You bitch!" he screamed into her face, spitting saliva at her with every word. "I'm going to put you with your damned mother." His eyes were full of darkness. Any trace of humanity he might once have possessed was gone. What remained was a pure hatred for all things, fuelled by alcohol and disdain.

He released her wrist and grabbed for her neck with both hands. She swung the lamp, and he grabbed for her wrist again. She dropped the lamp into his lap, and he threw it aside with brute force.

The lamp flew across the room and smashed against the wall. A shower of flames spilled onto the sofa. At first, there was just the orange glow of burning lamp oil—but as the fabric took hold, a thick, black, toxic smoke started to spread out in all directions like a phantom and quickly filled the room.

For a moment, David was distracted by what he had done. His rage had taken full control, and only now did he realise he had done something extremely foolish. Then he saw a figure standing in the doorway; his face lit up by the orange glow of the fire.

David turned back to Mary and grabbed her shirt. She swung her fist around and hit him hard on the nose, feeling it break. He released his grip and she ran for Thomas, who was standing by the door.

As they rushed across the hall, Mary looked back and saw the open cellar door. Thick black smoke filled the air and the door disappeared from view.

They rushed out the front door and across the street…away from the house, the insanity, and the flames that were spreading at an alarming rate and would very soon ravish the whole building.

Five years later

Mary felt a deep sense of melancholy as the train stopped and she stepped onto the platform. It had been almost five years since she had left the town behind, but she had been having dreams. At twenty-one, she had graduated from Oxford with a first in history, and she felt that if she did not finally lay her ghosts to rest, she would never be able to move on.

The walk to the house took ten minutes. The last time she had seen the old building, all that remained of the windows were jagged glass teeth clinging to the charred wooden frames. The black shiny front door had been battered down by the firemen and replaced with an ugly rectangle of plywood soon covered with gaudy pink and blue graffiti.

Uncle David had turned out to be nothing of the sort. Her mother had first met him when she was a teenager, and a DNA test confirmed that he was her father, but he had not been Thomas.'

The façade had been scarred, but the interior had survived and been gutted and rebuilt. Attached to the wall to the left of the front door, now blue, was a board that read "To Let."

After the story had appeared on the national news, an elderly great aunt had recognized a photo of Mary's mother and contacted the police. She had taken Mary in and given her a home for the two years before she went to university. She never married or had children of her own, and when she had passed away a couple of weeks after graduation, she had left Mary a house and a tidy sum in shares and savings.

The deep sense of depression Mary had battled over the past five years, and which the doctors thought she had overcome, returned—and the dreams followed. She became forgetful, her memories like drifting fog, and there were times when she could not discern one day from the last. The pull towards the house where she had lost all that was important to her became ever stronger.

The house had been unfurnished since the previous occupants had left. The estate agent had been showing people around the property, and she entered as they had been leaving preferring to show herself around the house. She preferred solitude. She closed the door and looked down at the floor. When the door had been knocked down they had found the man that had made her life such hell dead from smoke inhalation.

She walked across the hall paying little attention to the finely polished oak floor or the crisp Laura Ashley wallpaper, and focused on the cellar door. The door was new and painted blue to match the front door, and when she pulled it open she saw that the stairs leading down had somehow managed to survive the fire. She supposed the solid oak door that had once stood watch over the cellar had kept the heat and the flames out.

She found a light switch. The light was dim, and it appeared to be the only improvement made to the cellar. She walked down the steps and saw that, while the house above was fresh and new, a phoenix reborn from the ashes, the cellar had remained relatively untouched.

She heard a child giggle and she turned. Sitting cross-legged on the floor in the corner was her mother holding a large storybook. Her head turned and she smiled.

Kneeling on the floor in front of her was Thomas. He looked just as she had remembered him when she had last seen him at the top of the stairs on the day the house had burned. He looked up at her, confusion forming a frown across his brow and then, as recognition arrived, he smiled and the anguish and sadness that had been nibbling away at her mind since she had been taken away from the house were finally banished.

When the embers had died and the house had been searched, the firemen had found the mummified remains of her mother. As they had removed the boards to lift her out, they had discovered her brother lying next to her. The police had said that they had died together four to five years before the fire. The woman had died from a head wound. His temper was known to the police, and they theorized that he had simply gone too far one day and killed her, and Thomas had witnessed the death and been silenced by a similar blow to the head. The shared blood between Mary and her biological father was all that had kept Mary from joining her mother and brother beneath the cellar.

She walked across the room and sat down on the floor next to Thomas. She knew she had finally found a place she could call home...a place of solitude and peace...a home she could share with her family.

She held out her hands and her mother passed her the book. She recognized the colourful illustrations of Long John Silver—*Treasure Island* had been Thomas' favorite story. It had also once been hers. She began to read.

The estate agent peered down the stairs into the cellar. When he had returned to lock up, he found the door open and the light switched on.

"Is anyone down there?" he called. "This is private property."

He thought he heard someone whisper. He walked halfway down the stairs and shivered. The temperature in the cellar never warmed—even at the height of summer—and, although they had never said as much, he got the impression that it was what turned most prospective tenants away. He looked about and found the cellar empty.

Fifteen men on a dead man's chest... The words inexplicably drifted through his mind. He heard a child laugh, and turned to run back up the stairs. The story about the bodies in the cellar had been revisited by news stations following the recent death of the tragedy's only survivor, Mary. He thought perhaps he would pass the property onto another agent.

Winter Wheel-line by Rose Blackthorn

The Man Who Loved His Luscious Ladies
By Tina Rath

Vernon Applethwaite finished his solitary supper, washed and dried the dishes, tidied his little kitchen, swept and mopped the floor and made himself a cup of tea. Only then did he permit himself to sit down and switch on his computer. The little trill it played as it sprang into life never failed to give him a slight tremor of excitement, but, always a believer in delayed gratification, he first checked his emails, and viewed various news items which had caught his attention. But *then,* oh *then* he ran his cursor down his list of favourite websites: *Big, Bare and Beautiful, Bouncing Boobies, Fit and Fat...*he visited every one of them and finished by calling up his favoured, most luscious ladies in all their glorious amplitude. But tonight it was only a courtesy call: he looked, he smiled, he murmured to the images of Kim, and Tracey, Maggie and Orianne—and passed on.

He passed on to a dating site for men wishing to meet larger ladies. His fingers trembled on the mouse. Would he be disappointed? Would he find, ever again a lady with skin as wonderful as the roses and lilies of the gorgeous Maggie, or a figure like the cool, blonde, *mountainous* Orianne, anyone with the soft melting curves, the adorable, massive, glowing *pinkness* of Kim contrasting so delightfully with the warm chocolate of Tracey...would it be better to remain in a world of memory? But no. It was time to try again, to look for a partner of flesh and blood.

Vernon would have been rather cross if anyone had described him as a chubby chaser. It sounded so—*undignified.* He preferred to think of himself as a connoisseur, someone with a true appreciation of beauty, an artist even (think of Reubens—think of those Victorian painters and their wonderfully pneumatic models) born out of his time perhaps, or he would have said, *before* his time because he was sure that soon everyone would come to admire large ladies as he did, but he did not *chase* anything—or *anybody,* come to that. He admired. He very nearly—worshipped. Upon his desk, next to his keyboard stood a reproduction of one of those primitive goddess figures that seem to be made up of rolls of clay. His Venus. His object of desire. But was a dating site the best place to find her? He had had his disappointments before. Although there had been his glorious successes too—and this site *was* one he had never tried.

He took a deep breath, squared his shoulders and opened the site. He sifted slowly through the photographs and profiles on offer. He was a little disappointed to recognise some of those pictures. He doubted, oh he really doubted that the lovely Tamara from *Fit and Fat* was really exhibiting her truly startling figure and looking for "freindshipp, and who knows with a solvent mail gsh important because she likes a larf..." under the name of Sadie from Southend. And others, though he did not recognise the models, were clearly the work of professional photographers. In this context the trappings of glamour which he had admired on other sites—the feather boas, the long strings of pearls gripped playfully between square white teeth, the wet-look basques in pvc were tawdry. They reeked of desperation.

He began to think he might be making a mistake. He would not find a soul-mate here and he risked spoiling his vision of his luscious ladies by straying too far into these dubious by-ways... no! His mouse-finger twitched involuntarily, almost losing the picture which had caught his attention, but steadied, and pressed "Enlarge" instead of "Next." "Enlarge" indeed! This lady needed very little enlargement.

He studied her carefully. This was no professional photograph, just what had once been called "a snap", probably taken on a friend's phone. She was wearing a modest scoop-necked sweater, which permitted only a promise of cleavage, (but oh what a promise it was!) She was gazing out of the screen with the look traditionally associated with rabbits and headlights. Her dark hair was arranged in timid waves, possibly by the friend who took the photograph. It was probably the friend's hand too that had applied the pale pink lipstick and the chalky blue eye shadow...No, no...this lady should have her hair drawn back into a simple knot—or perhaps plaited into a coronet. And her lips should be painted scarlet to blaze against that dusky-pale skin...well, well such things could be changed... nervously he turned to her profile. "Doreen, late thirties" *or more likely early forties*, he thought, but none the worse for that, "likes to dance" *yesss! surely the tango, with those looks...* "wltm single male for friendship/marriage...looks not important but must be kind..."

Vernon sat back, nibbled at a hangnail on his thumb until a tiny bead of blood burst on his tongue, trying to compose the kind of email that would appeal to this timid—but so deliciously buxom—fawn. He imagined her scanning replies anxiously, probably with the friend who had persuaded her to put up her profile in the first place, rejecting this one as "too creepy", that one as "too old"...for a brief, and he acknowledged to himself, unworthy moment, he wondered what the friend looked like. A threesome now...but no. It was an insult to Doreen even to think of such a thing. And sadly, large ladies often had skinny friends. It was one of those laws of nature, like the one which in his youth had meant that the pretty girls always went to dances with plain friends, who wore glasses and couldn't be left on their own...

His email was brief and to the point. He described himself as a businessman, currently without a partner (he hesitated there, wondering if he should play the sympathy card and hint at a bereavement, and rejected it as an unnecessary complication) non-smoker, fond of dancing, a Londoner, a Londoner who happened to have been given tickets for a Tea Dance at the Cremorna Hotel near Piccadilly. How delightful if Doreen could meet him there to dance and enjoy one of the Cremorna's famous cream teas.

(He had chosen his proposed meeting place and time with great care—a lady would feel more comfortable meeting in the afternoon, in the presence of quite a number of people. She would feel less awkward about not paying her way if she thought the tickets were a gift. And if things were going awry they could always dance with other people.)

He went on—No obligation on either side. If they enjoyed the afternoon, they might exchange mobile numbers. Then again, they might not...but even so he remained, hers truly, Vernon. He hesitated, wavered, almost decided against it. And then he pressed the "Send" button.

It was three days before her reply arrived. Her spelling was faultless, her grammar only a little rocky, she did not use text-speak and she gave him her personal email. And she said yes.

YES!

He hastened to purchase tickets for earliest possible date, and to email her details of when and where to meet, with a neat little map, showing routes from the nearest tube stations. Then he prepared to wait, warning himself not to get too excited. There had been disappointments before when he met a lady in the flesh. Not quite the worst had been those occasions when she had patently used a photograph of her much younger self—or even of a more glamorous friend. *Then* he had simply vanished from the scene—he usually had a planned escape route, he was agile, and still able, in an emergency, to scramble out of a window in the gentleman's lavatories if it was absolutely necessary. It had been so much worse when she had lived up to her picture—physically—but her personality had proved sadly lacking...when she had been loud, blowsy, even not quite clean... he shuddered at the remembrance of the ring of grime he had detected round the otherwise delightful neck of Ruby from Portsmouth, or the way that Stella, so dainty at the beginning of their date, had become so quickly and loudly drunk...But he felt sure, somehow, that Doreen would not be one of these. She was much more likely to be too shy, to need too much wooing. Patient as Vernon was there sometimes came a moment when he had to cut his losses and give up.

So it was with a nicely moderated excitement that he arrived in the lobby of the Cremorna Hotel to find that Doreen was already waiting for him. M'm. His first impression was not good. It is hard to decide what to wear for a tea-dance, but Doreen's dress was almost unforgivably wrong. It was a cheap, stiff, shiny tube of mauve satin that destroyed her curves completely. A large ribbon corsage in a subtly clashing shade of pink pinned to the shoulder did nothing—well, nothing good—

for her complexion. But—the mid-length skirt allowed the observer to see that she had the small feet and dainty ankles which can be the peculiar grace of the larger lady. And the delicate silk of her throat put that tacky satin to shame. He made his decision, and stepped forward to introduce himself.

She appeared rather gratifyingly pleased to see him. He knew he was a reassuring sight, small, slight, whippet thin, wearing a nice, if old fashioned suit, a clean shirt, and having all his own hair and teeth, both of them clean and well brushed, but he was by no means handsome, and he was not expecting her shy but gratified response to his appearance. He was suddenly prepared to overlook the dress.

At first the afternoon went even better than he had expected. Doreen was a good dancer. Those neat little feet fairly twinkled round the floor. She did become a little breathless after a particularly strenuous quick-step, and while they were sitting down to allow her to recover she was approached by several would-be partners. But Doreen, as he was learning, was a lady. She did not desert the fellow she'd come in with...

Over tea he watched her eat jam and cream scones as daintily as she danced. And pour tea just as she should—correct use of strainer, and adding the milk last—even asking him if would prefer lemon! She was certainly shy, but as she gradually thawed under the influence of the best scones in London, he coaxed her life story from her. It was simple enough. She had been an only child. The last fifteen years of her life had been spent as a carer for her mother who had died a year ago. Reading between the lines he decided the mother had been the Witch Queen from Hell and it had taken Doreen twelve months to recover not so much from her bereavement as those years of care-giving. But now she was re-making her life. She had found a part time job in a charity shop (Vernon wondered, and suppressed the thought instantly, if that was where she had also found that dreadful dress), and she had started to go out with old friends...old *girl* friends, she had emphasised shyly.

He confined his part in the conversation to nodding and murmuring encouragement, and discreetly signing to the waiter to bring another supply of scones. Meanwhile he amused himself by mentally re-dressing Doreen in something more becoming. Black lace? No. Too hard, too much, let's be frank, of a cliché. But lace would certainly display that superb skin to its best advantage—well, what he could see was superb. She might run to freckles or even wrinkles lower down...still, assuming that she did not, then lace—cream?—no, and not white either, but a pale, silvery grey. With long sleeves and just the suggestion of a scoop neck...and perhaps just a subtle scatter of transparent sequins...with a full taffeta skirt. And of course, a properly constructed corset, although there he might meet a problem. Ladies, even the most refined of them, tended to favour what he thought of as the *burlesque* look, which involved satin in violent colours, and black lace, while he cherished a nostalgic fondness for what he thought of as the *real* corset, sleek, and all-encompassing, buttressed with large amounts of webbing, with broad shoulder straps, in a shade of pink he privately thought of as *elastoplast pink*. He was just dwelling on the thought of the intriguing striations such a garment could leave on a lady's skin when Doreen dropped her little bomb-shell.

"...so then I suppose I began to comfort-eat," she said in her small, apologetic voice.

Vernon very nearly dropped the half scone he had been nibbling.

"Never say that! Eating is not a comfort! It is an Art! It is an Experience..." He realised he had spoken too loudly. People were looking at them. Doreen was staring frozen, a piece of scone bleeding jam onto her plate. He lowered his voice deliberately and added a small, rueful smile.

"I'm so sorry. It's just—well—there is only one phrase worse than comfort-eating, to my mind, and I was afraid you were about to use it," he dropped his voice still further and breathed,

"I thought you might say you must start to diet. And you are perfect. Just. Perfect."

He was going too far and too fast. First he had embarrassed, and now he had frightened her. He half expected her to get up, to run away from the table and out of his life. Instead she looked across the scones at him, tears welling from those beautiful dark eyes.

"No one has ever said that to me before," she said. "And I could almost believe you mean it."

"I mean it," Vernon breathed. And he really, *really* did. To prove it he ordered a third plate of scones.

When the dance was over they walked through Green Park hand in hand and there was no need for any more elaborately arranged dates or anxious wooing. Vernon and Doreen slipped into the easiest relationship he had ever known. Doreen was far more adventurous than he had initially given her credit for. She squealed with delight when he outlined his suggestions for a re-vamp of her wardrobe, not even protesting at the corset (and it was all that he had hoped and more—especially those striations on Doreen's luminous flesh, which had not a wrinkle or a freckle upon it) and positively reveling in a game involving jam-filled doughnuts that even the peerless Kim had once vetoed as "messy"...

But as is so often the case, there was an unpleasant fly in the delicious ointment of their relationship. She had the improbable name of Krystal, and she was Doreen's best friend. She was indeed the one who had taken that photograph of Doreen, and urged her to join the dating site. Perhaps now she regretted it.

Perhaps she was jealous of Doreen's luck. Perhaps she was genuinely concerned for her. Doreen, typically, as he was beginning to learn, blamed herself.

"It could be," she said unhappily, "that I *told* her too much. About us. I *shocked* her."

"Nonsense!" Vernon said. "Nothing shocks people these days," he hesitated. "Er—what *did* you tell her?"

Doreen, it appeared, had become rather lyrical about Vernon's ways with jam doughnuts. Vernon's private reaction was that Krystal had simply been jealous. Perhaps she would have liked to join in...but no. Even Doreen would draw the line there. So, very probably, would Krystal. Although she must have chosen that exotic name, and that suggested a certain breadth of mind...no, he must stop this. Doreen was quite enough for him.

But even so. This could not go on.

He sighed and said, "I tell you what. We'll have a holiday. A short one. What they call a mini-break. No need to tell Krystal about it. Perhaps she'll have calmed down when we come back..."

"But..."

"She's upsetting you," Vernon said firmly. "I don't like to see you upset."

"But..."

"It won't cost us anything. I can borrow a holiday cottage from a friend, and I'll drive us down. We won't even need to go out to eat. We'll take a hamper full of finger food and..." he lowered his voice suggestively, "a whole heap of jam doughnuts."

Doreen giggled. She had, Vernon thought, quite the most attractive giggle he had ever heard.

"And," he added, seductively, "it's beside a lake. With a private beach. No tourists about at this time of year. We could swim. Naked..."

Doreen squealed. Her squeal, Vernon had thought several times, was definitely less attractive than her giggle. "You're so naughty," she said, "but won't it be too cold?"

"We'll build a fire," he said. "And we'll dance on the sand by the light of the moon."

"Hand in hand," Doreen agreed, "like the Owl and the Pussy Cat...at their wedding," she added after a tiny pause.

"Indeed," Vernon said comfortably. "Just like a wedding. You'll be my little fluffy owl and I'll be your big pussy-cat," and he gave such a big pussy-cat growl that Doreen giggled again and forgot to say that she'd always thought that the owl was the bridegroom and the pussy-cat was the bride...

On the Friday evening they set off as arranged with a big wicker hamper bursting with their favourite finger foods in the boot, and the minimum of luggage. Doreen found the cottage a delightful surprise. She had been expecting something rural, and, quite honestly, uncomfortable. She had thought of earwigs, and unpleasant sanitary arrangements. She was faced instead with a building constructed principally from glass and beautiful blond wood, a bathroom so modern that she wanted to pack it up and take it home with her, rooms with smooth slate floors and under floor heating which might have been—which indeed probably had been – constructed to provide a sympathetic environment for just the sort of indoor games that she and Vernon so enjoyed. There was, in particular, a central atrium which went up the full two floors to the glass roof, and opened out, through a sliding glass wall onto a tiny lakeside beach which was both playroom and theatre for them.

On the Saturday evening Doreen was lying on the warm floor, propped against a huge shell pink satin cushion. She was resting after some very enjoyable exertions and watching the whole room slowly transformed by a crimson sunset, which fired the soft steel of the lake and then blazed through the roof and the doors so that she was lying—as it were—in the heart of a fiery rose.

"What a goddess," Vernon breathed, raising his camera to record the extraordinary moment. But even as he pressed the button he heard Doreen give a faint shriek. He looked round—and saw what she had seen, the dark figure at the glass door, outlined momentarily against that beautiful, bloody sky. Then the colour ebbed, and Doreen seemed to shrink in on herself, no longer a goddess but a fat woman, naked but for a light veneer of jam and sugar, while the dark intruder became only too recognisable.

"Krystal," she moaned.

The glass doors rasped open as Krystal forced them apart and she strode into the room. Vernon stood transfixed. He had been wrong. She was larger, curvier, and altogether more majestic even than Doreen. He shuddered with excitement and—yes! — desire...

He hardly heard Doreen whimper, "How did you find us?"

"I followed you," Krystal snarled triumphantly. "I've been watching his house for days. And I watched this one until I was sure...Doreen I know what he is..."

But now Vernon most definitely was listening.

"He's what they call a Feeder," Krystal pursued venomously, "he wants you to eat and eat until you're the size of a—a walrus!

Until..."

Vernon's expensive camera clattered to the floor and both women swung round startled. They stared at Vernon. And then they both began to scream and scream. Krystal turned and blundered through the glass doors, followed, as rapidly as was reasonably possible, by Doreen, still gripping her cushion as if it might provide some protection against...against what Vernon had unmistakably become.

Because Vernon, overcome by the sight of two such perfect specimens—and the approaching rise of the full moon—was now a wolf. And though he was a small man he made a very big wolf indeed. He loped easily after the two ladies neither of whom was built for speed, especially not when running across a stony beach. Indeed, it almost appeared as if he was prolonging the chase for his own amusement. But after about ten minutes it came to its inevitable conclusion, and Vernon was enjoying the rare experience of having two splendid ladies at once. It was almost too much for him. But he managed. He was, just as Krystal had said, a Feeder...and now he fed, royally.

Next day he did the necessary tidying up. This included a bonfire (or, *bone*-fire he thought, grinning to himself) on the beach, and steering Krystal's small car from a nearby promontory into a nice deep part of the lake. And a thorough flossing and high-strength mouthwash. It was attention to those small but essential details which had allowed Vernon to carry on for as long as he had.

He returned to his little flat and added Doreen's photograph to his collection of Special Ladies, with a momentary pang of regret that he did not have a similar memorial of Krystal. For a long while they would be enough for him...until hunger for a real flesh and blood woman stirred again.

And he smiled and licked his lips at his recollection of all that delicious flesh. And that hot, sweet blood.

Brooding by John Stanton

Suburban Etiquette
By Thomas Kleaton

Allie Porter gazed through Jan's kitchen window while sipping her Folgers. She was studying something at the Wisenthals' house. Two rectangular doors made of rough-hewn boards complete with rusty Heart-style iron strap hinges covered a wedge-shaped base of similar timber butted up to the block foundation. The entire construction was weathered and gray, badly in need of re-staining. "What's that?"

"Oh, just the opening to the Wisenthal's root cellar," said Jan Ofter, pouring herself a cup of coffee. "They almost never go down there. Just old spider webs and milk crates." Allie was Jan's next-door neighbor, a tall divorcee whose luscious raven hair matched her dark eyes. Allie was the new kid on the block, having moved in only two months ago. A lot of the residents of the neighborhood had been living there since the eighties.

"Brrr." Kate Ellings, who had joined them for coffee this cold morning, shivered as she imagined spider webs drooping and clinging to her hair. "I can't wait for the Wisenthals' Halloween party Saturday night."

"You know it," Jan shot back. "I'm going to help decorate. It's been a huge hit around here for years. You could say it's become a tradition."

Allie and Jan had clicked nicely. They were very close in age, both in their early thirties. Kate was a little older, in her late forties. Jan had invited Allie for coffee and conversation as the moving van rolled off down the hot August street, its crew having unpacked Allie's few remaining possessions. The little coffee meetings had become a simple pleasure for them to indulge in, where they chatted like sisters.

Jan sat down at the kitchen table. She was a small woman with short, waxen blond hair and piercing blue eyes magnified by the large eyeglasses she wore. Crepe paper streamers embossed with bright orange pumpkins and white skeletons crackled as she unpacked them from their boxes.

"Isn't that Mrs. Pendleton?" Allie asked, distracted. Kate peered out the window, following Allie's line of sight. Brown leaves scurried by in the street, driven by puffs of cool, dry air. Theresa Pendleton was getting into her car. She wore a zigzag striped orange and black sweater and leather pants. *Just because they make it in your size doesn't mean you need to buy it,* Allie thought. "I know she's probably just a nice old lady, but I feel sorry for her. That sweater is way old-fashioned, and she's much too old to be wearing those leather pants. I'd rather be buried in a croaker sack then be seen in *that* getup. Doesn't she have any clothes?"

Kate and Jan exchanged looks, a silent message passing between them.

"I'd play it cool with Mrs. Pendleton if I were you," Kate said. Allie picked up on Kate's foreboding change of tone. "Let's just say she has a lot of *influence* with the neighborhood association."

Allie gazed at Jan, a hint of amusement in her dark eyes. She smiled. "Looks like Mrs. Pendleton could use a little influence herself. Like a few lessons from *What Not to Wear*."

Jan giggled. Kate twisted toward Jan, lips poked out, sullen.

"Just keep what I said in mind," Kate replied, looking thoughtful. A dark cloud crossed over her face as she sipped at her coffee. Her eyes fixated on the kitchen baseboard. "It helps to keep the peace around here. You don't want to go stirring up trouble."

"Oh, don't worry about me," Allie rinsed her cup and placed it in the sink, admiring the stunning tan and brown glass tile backsplash. She looked up at the Pork Chop Pig clock on the wall. The hands rested on eight-fifteen a.m. "Catch you girls later. Time to go to work. Jan, what're you going to the party dressed as?"

"A dwarf," she said, a prim smile on her face.

By the time eight p.m. rolled around Allie had donned her dress and makeup and started up the street toward the Wisenthals' house, her heels clicking on the sidewalk. The sun had long since disappeared behind the sprawling oak trees surrounding her. Gnarled twigs reached for her in the darkness as a chilly gust of wind jiggled the boughs. Candlelit jack o' lanterns watched her from porches and stood sentinel over cracked walkways as she strolled along, some grinning and others scowling at her as she passed. Trick-or-treating children, chattering with excitement as they scrambled from house to house in their bright costumes, had long since vacated the street. The pavement stood desolate and empty, lit only by a solitary street lamp and the waning gibbous moon.

Allie smiled as the strains of AC/DC's "Highway to Hell" drifted to her ears. *Sounds like a few of them have already been into the gin and tonic,* she thought, amused. Something to her left grabbed her attention. A moment of apprehension brushed her as she realized candlelight was flickering through the lopsided cracks between the boards of the Wisenthals' root cellar doors. Regaining her composure, she stepped onto the brick footpath and strolled onto the porch with an air of confidence.

A stuffed crow peeped up at her from its perch on the step, and ghostly white-painted gourds embellished with inky eyes and mouths hung from the porch roof, eerie against the backdrop of a single naked light bulb. An ebony twig wreath beckoned all visitors. She reached out and pressed the doorbell. A tinny chime resonated through the house, scarcely audible over the throbbing bass of the stereo. The door creaked open, noisy on its hinges. The music changed to Blue Oyster Cult's "Don't Fear the Reaper". Kate stood there in a black cloth dress, complete with pointed hat. She held a broom in one hand, a gin fizz in the other.

"Well, if it isn't Snow White," Kate teased. "Come on in! I've got a poison apple for you. Or maybe a Tom Collins."

Allie stepped inside. An ornate menu chalkboard hung on the wall by the beverage center to her right with the words *Pick Your Poison* written on it. Bottles of Tanqueray gin and tonic water sat on a small wooden table, along with bowls of lemon and lime slices, and a small container of simple syrup. A mummy hand made from a disposable glove stuffed with cotton balls and wrapped with gauze lay on the table, a champagne flute in its grasp. Allie mixed herself a drink, tossed it back, and poured herself another.

"Whoa, slow down on the gin," Kate warned. "You don't want to get *too* tipsy."

"I'm sorry, it's been a rough day. Too many memories. Where's Jan?"

"In the kitchen."

Allie thought back to Halloween three years ago, when Brian, her ex-husband, had sat on the porch in a rocking chair, a giant carved jack o' lantern over his head, dressed in overalls and a red-checkered shirt. Oh, how the trick-or-treaters had reacted when Brian stood up just as Allie filled their plastic bags and pillowcases with M&Ms and other goodies! One little boy had tossed his bag of candy onto the roof and took off running across the yard, braying at the top of his lungs. Those were the good times, before the miscarriage and Brian's binge-drinking episodes.

Allie followed close behind Kate, sipping her gin. Jan was standing at the window over the sink, mesmerized by the light seeping through the cellar doors. Jan really was dressed as a dwarf. She wore baggy tan pants and a white pullover shirt that was two sizes too large for her. A blue and white-striped cotton sleeping cap adorned her head. Jan turned as Lillian Wisenthal scurried over to Allie.

"Hello, Allie," she boomed. Pretty auburn hair clung to Lillian's shoulders. She wore a Sock Hop costume, white blouse and a black dress bedecked with white polka dots and matching scarf. She was in her late fifties, and pleasantly plump. "I'm so glad you came to the party. I was wondering when we'd get the chance to chit-chat."

"Hi, Mrs. Wisenthal," said Allie. "I really like the way your house is decorated. Where's Mr. Wisenthal?"

"Oh, he'll be in a little later," she paused, distracted, looking toward the root cellar. "He has to work late. Besides, this is mostly a hen party for the girls. Come on into the den and meet some of your neighbors."

Lillian started for the den while Allie went to the makeshift bar to mix herself another gin and tonic. Jan shuffled toward her, touching her arm in a timid gesture.

"Jan!" said Allie. "How are you?"

"I'm not feeling too well," she said, casting an eye over the yard again. "I think I'm going to head home."

"What's wrong with you, are you sick?" Allie put a hand on each of Jan's shoulders, peering into her eyes with concern. "And why is that light coming from the root cellar? What's going on down there?"

"Some of the neighbors are planning a Halloween surprise for later on," said Jan. "I don't think I'm going to stick around for it, though. My stomach's upset."

"Do you need me to walk home with you?"

"No, I don't think so. I'll be okay. It's just my nerves." Jan started for the door, then paused, turning. "Do me a favor. Please try not to mention Mrs. Pendleton tonight."

"Where is she, anyhow?" Allie whispered, leaning in close to Jan's ear. "Is she in the den?"

"Oh, I'm sure she's slinking around here somewhere." Jan slipped through the living room door and was gone.

Allie sipped at her drink, mulling over Jan's comment. The song changed to the Eagles' "Witchy Woman". She floated over the hardwood floor of the kitchen, twirling, making her way into the den. She could hear tinkling laughter over the music. Lillian motioned for Allie to come sit by her on the mocha loveseat. Two women sat across from her on a matching leather couch.

"Allie, this is Mrs. Jameson and Mrs. Albright," said Lillian. "We've been neighbors for the better part of two decades." Martha Jameson was a petite woman, long hot toffee hair hanging in two braids over her breasts, each accented by a red bow. She wore a cowgirl costume, frilly brown dress with red piping resting just above her knees, the upper portion a dotted crimson blouse. White ruffles lined the sleeves and neckline. A brown cowboy hat and boots finished the look.

Tammy Albright was dressed in a manner Allie imagined would be the norm in a goth lifestyle. She wore a sleek sable

Catwoman costume, and her hair was stark black like Allie's own, with bold, geometric bangs. Her lipstick was pure red. Both of them were about Lillian's age. The CD went to the next track, Credence Clearwater Revival's "Bad Moon Rising".

"How are you, Mrs. Jameson, Mrs. Albright?" Allie asked, holding her glass out as if she were toasting them.

"How are you, Allie?" the women chimed. "So you're new to the neighborhood. We love welcoming new neighbors!" Allie sank back into the leather, hesitant to join in the conversation. The way Mrs. Albright remained focused on her, never taking her eyes away, gave Allie the creeps. She was like a snake staring down a rat.

"Eleven-thirty! Almost time for the surprise!" Lillian shouted. Tammy and Martha nodded in anticipation. Allie had gone into the foyer to get another drink. The next song came up was Johnny Cash's "Ghost Riders in the Sky". Tammy and Lillian were standing around gabbing about chocolate cake recipes when Allie staggered down the carpeted steps into the den and sloshed half her drink onto Martha's dress.

"I am so sorry about that, Mrs. Jameson," Allie wobbled.

"Intolerable," Martha scowled. "Allie, don't you know when you've had enough?"

Allie was trembling, short, hitching sobs betraying the fact she was on the verge of crying.

"I'm s-s-sorry. I—I don't know what came over me," Allie, eyes blurring with hot tears. "I j-just miss Bill so m-m-much. Didn't he understand how much I loved him? Why did he have to g-g-go and th-throw it all away…?" Allie felt used up, emotionally spent, exhausted.

Kate had come in and sat on the couch. Now she stood up and turned the stereo off. Silence pervaded the room.

"Okay, everyone," said Kate, leading Allie toward the kitchen. "It goes without saying that Allie's had a little too much to drink, but we're not going to hold that against her, are we?" Kate smiled into Allie's face. "After all, it would spoil the Halloween surprise. Right, ladies?"

"Right!" said Lillian, squinting upwards at the clock. A wooden black cat sat atop it, paw perpetually extended to claw at the goldfish pivoting from the minute hand like a Ferris wheel gondola. It was eleven-forty p.m. "Allie's *gotta* stick around. After all, it's *her* surprise!"

"See," said Kate, dabbing at Allie's face with a soothing wet cloth.

"I'm sorry," said Allie, beaming through her tears. "What's this surprise everyone keeps talking about?"

"You'll see," said Kate.

The revelers stood on the dewy grass of the lawn, gathered around the root cellar opening. Silvery shafts of moonlight cascaded down around them, and a light breeze sighed in the treetops. Allie saw the cellar doors were now splayed open. Candlelight danced within, casting eerie shadows on the cinder block walls. Lillian spoke first: "I'm going to blindfold you now. It's part of the surprise. It's high time you met the rest of the neighborhood association!"

Allie flinched as Lillian tied a royal blue handkerchief around her head.

"Step this way, we're going down the steps now." Lillian grasped her arm, leading her down the concrete risers. Allie felt the air getting colder. Rather than thinking about descending into the cold, damp cellar, she imagined she was ascending the windswept planks of the hangman's gallows, each tap of her heels tolling the time to the cessation of her final, lingering thoughts.

The roof protested with a groan as the wind began to gust around the eaves. She heard the footsteps of the others following her down.

"Are you ready for your surprise, dear?" Lillian removed the blindfold. Dozens of squat, thick candles lit the interior of the root cellar, sitting on numerous wooden shelves. Hundreds of Ball mason jars filled with colorful green beans, tomatoes and squash gleamed in the candlelight. The other ladies from the party were gathered in a circle around her, along with a few faces Allie didn't recognize.

An older man with gray hair wearing bib overalls stood to Allie's left. He had removed his glasses and was wiping his sweaty face with a white handkerchief. He was propped on the handle of his shovel, a pile of loose sandy soil to his left. Allie recognized him as being Mr. Wisenthal. At his feet was a deep, dark hole resembling a grave. A white porcelain table with raised edges and a round base like a barber chair sat in front of Allie.

"You're going to love this, Allie," said Tammy. "An antique embalming table for that special touch!"

Fear clutched Allie's heart with cold fingers as she looked, wide-eyed, to her right. A mural of a Sabbatic Goat over a backdrop of flames encompassed an entire wall. Mrs. Pendleton stood there, enshrouded in a black cloak, the hood pulled up over her hair. It reminded Allie of an executioner's hood. Cold stainless steel from a carving knife gleamed in her right hand. Kate stood at her side. She was grinning.

"It's not easy being a witch nowadays, Allie, nor a sorcerer," said Tammy, nodding in Mr. Wisenthal's direction. "The rituals have to be practiced in secret, and our sacrifices of dog and chicken don't really seem to be working. What we need is a *different* kind of blood sacrifice to confer magical power on us."

"And it was so *thoughtful* of Mr. Wisenthal to help us out, wasn't it, ladies?" said Lillian.

Mr. Wisenthal took a bow.

"You people are all crazy!" Allie screamed. The women began to amble around Allie in a circle. She struggled, flailing out with her fists as strong arms latched onto her and pushed her forward. The room swirled as she was pinned to the table by a dozen hands. Some of the women kneeled before the image on the wall, heads lowered, arms above their heads with palms splayed out as if feeling for warmth from the painted flames. They were gibbering in odd syllables. Others began swaying from left to right, chanting, softly at first, rising to a grating crescendo: *Kill her, kill the bitch, kill the whore, KILL HER NOW!!*

Desperation seized Allie. She glanced around the circle of her captors, skipping from face to face, each frozen in a rictus of hate. She looked for escape, rescue, *yearned* for a means out of this madness, and there was none. She felt disconnected, the essence of solitude, the comforting quiet experienced by a drowning person as they slip under the turbulent water for the very last time.

Defeated, Allie glowered at Mrs. Pendleton, who was striding toward the table. Mrs. Pendleton removed the hood from her head in a casual gesture. Her long, gray hair lay limp on her shoulders. Her cornflower-blue eyes were blazing. She looked at Allie, reaching down to stroke Allie's hair, almost tenderly.

"Tsk, tsk, Allie," said Mrs. Pendleton, a smirk on her face. "I wouldn't be caught *dead* in that dress." She held the knife high in one hand, ready to plunge, and two baggy burlap sacks in the other.

"Here. Take your choice of outfits."

Ephemeral Sovereignty by Shawna L. Bernard

Fiona

By Justin Hunter

Lenore rubbed her face, sighed and smiled. The ice in the glass tinkled as she put the tumbler of Gin and Tonic down on the coffee table. The house was full of tranquility. Lenore felt a rare peace. Christmas Eve was over. Her daughter, a mild-looking blonde girl named Fiona, was put to bed. Lenore's gaze drifted to the stairs leading down to the basement where her child slept. There had been no trouble that night in putting her to bed. It was a blessing. It was another reason to be thankful for Christmas. God seemed to be giving her a break this evening.

Presents that were chosen with care and bought with great personal sacrifice were piled under the tree. There was nothing left to do but wait for but the morning. Lenore smiled as she thought of the joy Christmas morning would bring. Fiona would run up from the basement, squealing at the top of her voice. She would tear into the wrapping paper of her presents and reveal every delight that Lenore prepared for her.

Lenore picked up her drink and drained half of the gin in one long gulp. She swished the ice around in the glass a couple times, and then drained the rest of the drink. She smacked her lips to the quinine of the tonic and piney taste of the cheap gin. She couldn't usually afford alcohol. The bottle was her Christmas present to herself. She intended to enjoy her luxury thoroughly; until she couldn't remember who she was anymore. She wanted to obliviate everything for a while. Maybe it would be okay for her this time. Maybe she wouldn't be punished for it this time.

Lenore had her dirty blonde hair tied back in a messy pony tail. The look exposed her cigarette accelerated sagging and lined skin. She was barefoot. She wore faded red sweat pants and a Depeche Mode t-shirt and old boyfriend bought her at a concert a half-lifetime ago. She looked a lot older than she really was. Living an underemployed life of poverty had taken its toll. There was no husband...Fiona's father had left shortly after Fiona was born. There were no child-support payments, or even any contact whatsoever. Lenore had no idea where he was. She didn't know whether he remembered her or his daughter at all, not that that fact would have made much of a difference in her life anyway.

Lenore snapped out of her reverie when she thought she heard a noise from the basement. She looked down into the blackness of the stairwell and waited. Fiona might be awake. Lenore could feel her heart pounding in her chest. Her ears strained to penetrate into the basement, listening for any sound that would tell her that Fiona had stirred. All was quiet.

Lenore got up from the couch and went to the kitchen to make another drink. When she returned to the living room, he was there. The glass dropped from her hand and thumped on the carpet, spilling its contents. The breath caught in her throat. Lenore was petrified as she stared into the yellow mottled red eyes of Fiona's father. Her fear was less from his appearance and more from the heavy thump of the solid tumbler on the floor.

"She isn't awake," Fiona's father said. His voice resonated deeply from his wet, densely hairy and muscular torso. Spindly arms with pointed shoulders sprouted from the vast chest. Two hook-like hands bearing two fingers apiece flexed open and closed on his lap. Thick thighs with reverse bent knees extended to thin calves, also full of coarse hair. Chapped and cracked Hooves completed the legs. A goat shaped head with man like face peered behind long strands of white facial hair. Two long horns stood straight up from the crown of his forehead. Thick sweat beaded from his brow and dripped down its naked and wiry frame.

"What are you doing here?" Lenore said. Her feet felt frozen in place. Her drink lay forgotten on the carpet. Her head cleared instantly from the blessing of the alcohol rich gin.

"It's Christmas Eve," Fiona's father said. "I guess you could call me Krampus." He laughed. There was no joy in it. "I've come for her."

"Really?" Lenore asked. Her voice was almost a plea. She took a step, almost compelled. She marveled at the relief she felt when faced with such a horror before her. She wanted to touch him again. She wanted to feel his embrace. She remembered the intensity of his passion. She remembered the night they had together. When he used her like she wasn't even a person. She was nothing but yielding flesh, giving him everything and leaving nothing of herself. She had allowed him all of her. She didn't realize how much of a void she was until he was near her again. If only he would allow her to fill some of the hollow she was by being with him again. She looked into his eyes and realized that she had nothing left to give him. There was nothing left of her to give.

She took another step toward him and reached out her hand. He took her arm by the wrist with and closed his forked hand in hers. The sharp claws of his fingers pierced her wrist and blood dripped down onto the carpet. His touch was tender. A loud thump and scrape sounded from below. A light clicked on in the living room, illuminating the cellar stairs and showing them the perfect white cellar door.

"Did you do that?" Lenore said, but she already knew the answer.

"No," he said. "It's Fiona. She's awake." The door opened inward. A small, lily-white hand reached out of the darkness and took hold of the stair railing. She was a tiny girl. She was slow in her movements and almost skeletal in form. Her white pajama's billowed around her waif body. Lenore and Fiona's father watched her make her way up to the top step. She stopped and looked at her father. A grin spread over his face at seeing his child. Thick grinding molars were half-covered by two over-large canine teeth showed clear when his lips pulled back from the smile.

"I've come for you," He said. "I've missed you so much." Her father's smiling visage was the direct opposite of Lenore's. Her face was one of abject terror. She sat hand in hand with the beast, yet her attention was full on the meek form of her yellow haired daughter.

Fiona frowned. She raised her hand and her father's head exploded in resounding crack of thick skull. Blood and brain tissue cascaded from the hole, covering Lenore and making the living room look like the floor of an abattoir. The body of her father slumped forward. Fiona dropped her hand. Lenore sat stock still but for her chest which heaved and shook from thick and gasping breaths. Blood dripped from her face and pooled in her lap. Fiona dropped her hand.

"I'm going back to sleep now mother," Fiona said. "I will see you in the morning."

"Okay baby," Lenore said. Her words came out sodden, garbled in the gore on her face. Fiona turned and walked back down the basement steps. She closed the cellar door behind her. The light shut off. Lenore listened for a while, but couldn't hear any sounds coming from the basement. She got up and made herself another drink.

Sistina by Ashley Scarlet

Pressed Flower Memories

By Rose Blackthorn

The house was old, and set off by itself, with a steep slate roof and gingerbread carving. There were neighbors, but not within sight. Liz still wasn't sure how they had ended up with it, even now.

Six months of house hunting had been exhausting and discouraging, and nothing seemed to fit both their requirements and their bank account. At one point Joe had believed they would never find a place. But that was the day they had toured this long-empty property. That was the day he had seen the light of longing in Liz's eyes, and promised himself that somehow this one would work out.

A month later, Liz took a leisurely walk around *their* yard, and felt like she'd awakened into a wonderful dream. The mature trees that separated their property from neighbors on three sides were a lovely mix of evergreen and deciduous. A hedge of some kind of flowering vine grew along a stone wall and hid the sight of the narrow two-lane road from which their cobbled driveway began. This late in the season, the flowers had withered and fallen, and the leaves were taking on the shades of copper and bronze, which made them look as though they'd been cast in metal over the wall rather than grown there.

Liz turned to look back toward the house, with its moss-covered roof and old-fashioned architecture, and hugged herself with joy.

"Our house," she whispered, "Our home."

A breeze started, whispering through the pine needles and dying maple leaves, and she shivered a little, wishing that she'd worn a jacket. Chilled, she headed back across the lush still-green lawn toward the back of the house—*our house,* she thought—and the waiting warmth inside. Because she hurried, a happy smile still curving her lips, she did not notice the little door half-hidden in the ancient folds of bark on a huge old maple. The breeze strengthened, quickening her steps, and leaves swirled down to cover her tracks. Behind her, the little carved door painted with delicate designs in burgundy and faded gold swung open.

Inside the house out of the wind it was warm, the air redolent of cinnamon and clove. Liz made sure the door latched behind her, then stepped into the half bath off the mudroom. Her strawberry blond hair was disheveled, and she smoothed it back behind her ears, smiling at her dusty reflection. She went into the kitchen to start heating water for tea and decide what to make for dinner. Joe would be home in the next couple of hours, and she wanted to have everything ready for him when he arrived. The commute from work to their new home was almost an hour longer than it had been before they moved.

She started potatoes baking in the oven, then washed, peeled and sliced fresh pears. She set them aside in a drizzle of good brandy; after dinner she would warm them in the oven and add some heavy cream for a decadent dessert. There were two steaks thawed and waiting in the refrigerator that she would cook when Joe got home. With dinner started and a hot cup of tea in hand, she went back to work unpacking boxes.

She hummed happily to herself as she started on the boxes of books. Both she and Joe were avid readers, and between them they had acquired quite a collection. One of the selling points of this house had been the floor to ceiling built-in bookshelves in what had been advertised as a sitting room. Liz and Joe immediately dubbed it the library.

When Joe walked into the house, he found half their books unpacked and placed on the shelves.

"Hey sweetheart," he said, setting his brief case on the floor in the hall. "You've been busy."

"I keep forgetting how many books we have," she said, and went to greet him with a kiss. "Hungry?"

"Starved," he said, and held her close for a moment. The longer commute was an inconvenience, but he'd learn to accept it if for no other reason than the happy smile he'd just been met with.

"There's hot water for tea if you want some," she said and walked into the kitchen. "Dinner should be ready in about half an hour."

"No tea for me. But I would take some whiskey, if you have any idea where it got to." He took off his coat and draped it over the back of a kitchen chair, then pulled a glass out of an open cardboard box.

"In the pantry," Liz said, taking the steaks out of the fridge, and putting them in a pan on the stove top.

"It's getting pretty cold out there," he said when he came back into the kitchen. He filled the glass from a half full bottle, then set it aside and took a sip. "How would you feel about a fire?"

"I wouldn't say no."

While she began cooking the steaks, he went into the living room to prepare the fire. There was wood already cut and waiting in a stand beside the hearth, so all he had to do was place the pieces he chose with a couple of sheets of old newspaper layered between them. When he was satisfied with the arrangement, he lit a long wooden hearth match and started the paper burning. He adjusted the damper to be sure smoke wouldn't fill the room, and used a wrought iron poker to rearrange the wood a bit when it seemed reluctant to catch. Something scrabbled in the flue, and he stepped back quickly, raising the poker in front of him instinctively.

A high pitched shriek echoed in the chimney, and it sounded as though something was clawing its way up the brick interior. When it was quiet once more, Joe cautiously moved closer, leaning down to look up inside the fire box. He wasn't able to get much of a view, as the fire had truly caught and the heat was too much. Slowly, he flipped the lever for the damper back and forth, waiting for something to happen; but other than a change in the draw of smoke, there was nothing.

"Everything okay?" Liz asked.

Joe flinched and whirled, lifting the poker again.

"Honey?" There was concern in her voice now, instead of the previous teasing lilt.

"Yeah, fine," he said, his voice a bit breathless, and he set the poker back down. "There must have been a bird or something in the chimney. When I lit the fire, it freaked out and took off."

"Oh," Liz said, and her expression paled as she looked at the chimney rising above the mantel.

"Whatever it was, I'm sure it got out," Joe said quickly to reassure her. "It certainly made enough noise while it was at it. If it was still in the chimney, it would still be screeching."

She nodded, and held out the heavy-bottomed glass half filled with whiskey that he'd left in the kitchen. "Dinner should be ready in a few minutes."

"Anything I can do to help?" He crossed the room to her, and took the glass with one hand, sliding his other arm around her waist. She leaned against him and rested her head on his shoulder for a moment.

"Just come in and start your salad. Baked potatoes and the steaks should be almost done."

"Sounds great." He followed her into the kitchen, looking forward to dinner and a quiet evening after his stressful day. Neither of them noticed the luminous eyes watching from the shadows at the top of the built-in bookshelves nearest the fireplace.

They brought their dinner back into the living room, sitting on pillows on the floor to eat off the low coffee table. Joe had dimmed the lights, and smiled at the way Liz relaxed in the fire's warmth. They talked a little while they ate. He told her about the current account he was working on, and how beautiful the drive had been after leaving the city behind and entering the heavily wooded area where they now lived. She told him about the small box of photos and mementos she'd found at the top of one of the book shelves, and about her walk around their yard, and the quiet broken only by natural sounds.

"I did hear something earlier," she added when she stood to take their empty plates back into the kitchen. "I'm not sure what it was. Some kind of animal moving around in the attic."

"More birds?" he asked, leaning forward to add more wood to the fire.

"No, I don't think so." She disappeared into the other room, and came back a moment later with the bottle of whiskey and another glass. "I think it might have been something bigger. Raccoon, maybe?" She sat gracefully and poured for herself before handing the bottle back to him. "It ran around up there for several minutes, but like it was trying to be quiet, you know? That was before I went outside. Haven't heard anything since I came back in." Joe sighed, adding some more whiskey to his glass.

"Damn. Guess I should have expected it, being out here where there are so few people. It might be a good idea to call an exterminator and make sure we don't have rats or something chewing up the wiring."

Liz grimaced. She would much rather imagine a raccoon in the attic than rats. "Whatever it is, I'll get it taken care of," he promised, and lifted his glass in an unofficial toast.

She raised hers as well, and met his eyes with a smile. Without saying anything, they both drank.

* * *

After dinner and dessert, Joe banked the fire and closed the glass doors across the front of the fire box so they wouldn't have to worry about an errant spark starting a blaze. Liz went up to the second floor where their room was located and prepared for bed. When she came out of the bathroom, Joe went in to take a shower. While she waited for him, she looked through the shoebox of old photos and keepsakes that had apparently been left by the previous owners.

The photos were old, most in black and white, or color that had faded to dusky greens and nicotine yellows. Most of them appeared to have been taken either in the house or the surrounding property. There were pictures of several different people, including two children—a boy and a girl. One woman was in several of the photos, her hair and eyes dark, her face always set with an expression that made Liz think she was trying to hide anger, or maybe pain. Only one photo was written on, showing the woman standing behind the two children. On the back, in faded ink, was written, "Elizabeth, Jensen, and

Sarah". They stood to one side of a large tree, and it appeared that a small painted door had been placed in the trunk.

"That looks familiar," Liz whispered, peering closely at the faded picture.

"Honey?" Joe called through the closed bathroom door, "Did you come in here while I was in the shower?"

"No, I've been out here," she called back, still studying the old photo.

The bathroom door opened, emitting a cloud of steam, and Joe stood there with a towel wrapped around his waist. "I set my ring on the sink, and now it's gone. You didn't come in and get it?"

She dropped the picture back into the box and turned to look at him, sudden pain blooming in her chest. "Why would I come in and take your ring?"

"Shit, maybe it slid down the drain," he muttered, and turned back into the bathroom.

Liz tried to remember if he'd been wearing his ring during dinner, and felt tears sting the back of her eyes. It was still less than a year ago that he'd admitted to an affair after leaving his wedding ring at the hotel where he'd met his mistress. When the hotel manager called to let Joe know his ring had been found by housekeeping, Liz had been the one to take the call. Everything had come out after that, and only her truly deep love for him and his promises to never hurt her again had kept their marriage from ending.

"I'm going to have to take the drain apart, and see if it fell in," Joe said and pulled a pair of flannel lounge pants out of a drawer. "Do you know where any of the tools are?"

"Did you really put your ring on the sink?" she asked. She didn't want to, and bit her bottom lip when she saw him flinch. But she had to ask.

Joe came to her, shirtless and barefoot, with his dark hair still damp and tangled from the shower. But his gaze was steady, if pained, and his voice was sure when he said, "I promise that I took it off and put it on the edge of the sink. The only time I take it off is to bathe. The *only* time."

She made herself meet his eyes, trying to gauge if he was telling her the truth. She couldn't tell—and that thought made the tears well—but she nodded. "Okay. The boxes with tools are still in the garage. I haven't unpacked any of that yet." He reached out to touch her face, fingertips gently grazing her cheek.

"I love you, Liz. I'll never hurt you, never again."

She nodded once more, unable to say anything. These last few days as they signed on the house and began to move in had been wonderful, almost like a honeymoon for them. But the missing ring brought back all the remembered pain.

"I'll be right back. Don't run any water in the sink," he reminded, then turned and left the room. His footsteps were muted as he went down the stairs. The garage door squeaked softly when he opened it.

Liz wiped her eyes, and set the shoebox aside, no longer in the mood to go through it. Above, in the attic, something skittered across the ceiling, then was silent.

* * *

After Joe left for work the next morning, Liz sat at the kitchen counter for a long time nursing a cup of lukewarm coffee. She hadn't slept well. Every little noise had roused her, and she didn't know how much of it was because she wasn't used to the house yet, and how much was due to remembered heartache.

Joe had taken apart the pipes beneath the sink, but hadn't found his ring. He'd checked every nook and cranny in the bathroom, thinking maybe the ring had fallen and rolled across the floor, but there was no sign of it. The ornate brass register cover for the furnace vent was set in the wall rather than the floor, so the ring couldn't have fallen into the heating duct either. By the time he gave up looking for it, it was after midnight.

Liz had said nothing, just lay in bed cuddled beneath the blankets and tried to stop wondering if he'd had his ring on when he came home from work.

Determined to stop obsessing about it, she went up and got dressed to start her own day. She noticed the shoebox on the floor beside her nightstand, and took it downstairs with her. She poured another cup of coffee, and sat down to finish going through the contents. Besides the stack of old photos, there were also a couple of small notebooks and what appeared to be a journal.

She flipped through the notebooks, which were filled with slanted, looping handwriting. When she opened the hardbound journal, she found dried flowers and autumn leaves pressed between the pages of identical handwriting. She pulled out what appeared to be a rose in a fold of waxed paper used to protect the pages of the journal. It was stiff and light, the petals faded to a rich ivory. When she lifted it to her nose, there was still a faint trace of rose scent. Eyes closed, she imagined the dark haired woman from the photos cutting this rose, and placing it between the pages of her journal like a memory.

Slowly, she flipped through the pages, reading things here and there. A lot of it was poetry, personal and private to the author, but certain strains stood out to Liz.

What did I know about bitter betrayal? What did I know about the liar's heart? But I'm a good student, and you are my teacher in an age-old tradition -- the traitor's art.

Hold on to your pain -- The only thing that's ever truly been your own.

Love is the lie that people tell their hearts.

"What happened to you?" Liz whispered, looking over at the top photo on the stack. The dark haired woman, who had shared her name, seemed to gaze back at her. The little door in the tree trunk beside her was like another riddle. "Someone broke your heart, that's for sure."

She finished her coffee and set the cup in the sink, then went upstairs to get shoes and a jacket. She left the shoebox and its contents on the counter, all but the photo with the little door in the tree. Then she went to explore.

Outside the sun was shining, but there were clouds to the west. The breeze was cool and gusty, pushing fallen leaves before it in swirls of color. Liz pulled the collar of her jacket up under her ears, glad that she'd thought to put it on, and walked toward the nearest property line. There were no songbirds today, but crows were perched in the surrounding trees, cawing and calling to each other with their harsh voices.

Liz looked at the photo she'd brought with her, searching for some landmark other than the tree that would give her an idea of where to look. She walked along the northern edge of the yard and checked any of the trees that were large enough to match the one in the photo, then turned to follow the eastern boundary. In the southeast corner there was an old metal swing set now mottled with rust and half overgrown with leafless vines. One swing had fallen, leaving only lengths of chain dangling seatless. The other was a pendulum in the breeze, creaking back to the boisterous crows as it flaked rust into the dead leaves. Liz turned away from it, saddened by the abandoned symbol of childhood happiness, and walked the southern fence line toward the road.

She gazed at the photo again, wondering if maybe the tree in question had been cut down, or the door removed from the trunk so that she would never find it. With a sigh, she tucked the picture into her pocket and walked back around the house to where she'd left the kitchen door unlocked. As she rounded the corner, she glanced at the huge old maple set in the center of the backyard with some smaller evergreens growing around it. The slant of sunlight glinted on faded gold, and she smiled as she picked out the shape of the little door set into the bark.

"No wonder I didn't see you!" she said, and hurried across the yard. "These pines weren't here when the photo was taken."

The door was maybe three feet tall with a gothic peaked top that arched down either side. At its base, it was almost two feet wide. Someone had painted designs in burgundy and deep violet, all traced in gold that had nearly faded away. A little piece of rounded metal protruded on the right side, more like a drawer pull than a door knob. It was of copper, long covered in a green patina that made it blend into the tree. Liz crouched before the door, reaching out with one hand to trace the painted designs. Almost hidden in encroaching bark, there were hinges on the left side of the door. Like the handle, they were covered in a green patina that nearly disguised them as old lichen or dried moss.

Liz hooked her fingers under the curve of the handle and tugged, but the door didn't move. She cocked her head to one side and chewed on her bottom lip for a moment. "Why bother adding hinges, if it's all just for looks?" she wondered aloud. She grasped the metal more firmly and pulled harder, but still the door didn't budge.

The wind gusted, finally pushing clouds across the sun, and suddenly the light was more like evening than mid-morning. Liz sat on her heels for a moment longer, studying the door, then shook her head and got up. She started toward the house, looking back twice as she went. The door didn't move, and didn't disappear. Just as she had thought, it was a riddle.

Inside the house, she immediately felt warmer, and took off her jacket. She set it aside, smoothing her windblown hair with her hands, and walked around the counter to get a last cup of coffee. That was when she realized the shoebox, filled with memories from the other Elizabeth, was no longer where she had left it. She checked the floor on both sides, thinking perhaps the box had fallen off, but there was no sign of it.

"I know I left it right here," she said aloud, and ran her hands over the surface as though to make sure it hadn't become invisible. Upstairs, something scampered across the floor.

* * *

Instead of drinking coffee, or fixing lunch, or unpacking boxes, Liz went hunting. She started in the garage and worked her way through the house-- first the main floor, and then the second level. She checked under furniture and behind the boxes of their unpacked belongings, and in each closet of every room. She used a stepladder to check the top shelves of every cabinet. There was no sign of the box anywhere. When she went back into the kitchen, she verified that the single snapshot was still in her jacket pocket. In the dim cloud-obscured light from the nearest window, Elizabeth's face looked back at Liz from the faded photo.

When someone knocked on the front door, she jumped and nearly threw the picture. With shaking hands, she stuffed it in her jeans pocket, and went to answer the door.

A quick glance through the mullioned sidelight revealed a uniformed man in his late twenties or early thirties. Liz opened the door, a little breathless, and noted the logo on his shirt pocket. In bright yellow stitching it said *Bug-b-Gone,* and below that, in smaller letters, *All Pest Control.*

"Mrs. Kinsey?" the man asked.

"Yes," she replied with a smile. "Can I help you?"

He glanced at the clipboard he held before him. "We got a call from Mr. Kinsey—your husband, I assume?" When she nodded, he continued, "He said you've got some kind of animal living in your attic? My name is Brady, and I'm here to check it out."

"Oh, yes. Great, thank you." She stepped back to let him inside, and closed the door behind him. "The attic access is upstairs."

"Show me the way, I'll get started."

She led him up to the second floor hallway, and pointed out the section of ceiling with a handle affixed. "I think it has a ladder, but I'm not sure. I've never been up there."

Brady reached up and tugged on the handle. The access panel swung down, and a narrow ladder unfolded to the floor allowing fairly easy ascent. "I'll go up and take a look around, and let you know what I find. Unless you want to come up?"

Liz shook her head. "No, I'm fine down here. I'll be in the kitchen when you're finished."

"Yes, ma'am," he said with a quick smile, and pulled a flashlight out of a loop on his belt. Then he climbed up the ladder and disappeared into the darkness above.

When Brady came into the kitchen more than half an hour later, he was lightly covered in dust and sported a cobweb over his right temple of which he apparently wasn't aware. He was also carrying a familiar cardboard shoebox on top of his clipboard. "Mrs. Kinsey, I checked the whole attic, but there aren't signs of any rodent activity. No tracks or nesting material, and no droppings."

"Where did you find that?" she asked, at the moment only interested in the shoebox.

"It was near the east end of the house, under the dormer. There's a good half-inch of dust over everything up there, ma'am. If anything had been running around up there, I'd have found tracks or scuff marks. The only thing up there not covered in dust was this box." He set it on the end of the counter, his expression perplexed.

"But I've heard something running around up there," she protested, looking up from the box—*how had it gotten up into the attic?* "I heard something up there this morning, as a matter of fact."

"Honestly ma'am, I don't know what to tell you. I've been doing pest control for seven years, and if there was any sign of anything up there, I'm pretty sure I would have found it." He thought for a moment, glancing down at his clipboard. "There's the possibility that there's a space between the attic floor and the second floor ceilings. Sometimes old houses were built with spaces between the walls for wiring and such. But there hasn't been anything in that attic before me today, probably not for a couple of years."

"So then, why wasn't there any dust on the box?" she asked, looking back at it. The lid was on the box, so she couldn't see if the photos and notebooks were still inside. She didn't want to look while Brady was there.

He sighed and shook his head. "I don't know, Mrs. Kinsey. It doesn't make any sense to me. Look, I'll go ahead and check the basement and garage, and do an inspection of the outside perimeter. But from what I've seen so far, everything looks clean."

"Fine, do your inspection." All Liz wanted was for him to leave the kitchen. When he did so, looking rather sheepish, she immediately took the lid off the box.

The pictures and notebooks were gone. The journal lay on the bottom of the box. Tied to it with a length of ribbon, was Joe's wedding ring.

* * *

When Joe got home from work that night, he found the house dark and quiet. Liz wasn't in the kitchen, and there was no sign that she'd started dinner. The work order from the exterminator was the only thing on the counter. Flickering light came from the living room, and when he went in there he found a fire burning in the fireplace.

"Liz, are you upstairs?"

There was no answer, so he went up to check. Master bedroom and bath were empty. So were the two smaller bedrooms, currently unfurnished and stacked with unpacked boxes.

"Liz?"

Joe went back downstairs, and checked the library and the small formal front room, then the kitchen again and the half bath. He had parked in the garage, but checked it again as well. There was no sign of her.

"What the hell?" he whispered, coming back into the living room. That was when he noticed the book. It was hardbound and open, and hung halfway out of the fire. He knelt before the hearth, wondering why his wife—a self-professed lover of books—would ever burn one. He reached in, catching hold of the corner, and pulled it out of the flames. Half the book was fully destroyed, and what was left was scorched and stained with soot. When he dropped it onto the hearth, something *clinked* on the marble. He pushed the book to one side, careful not to touch the still-hot binding. Tied to a smoldering length of ribbon was his wedding band.

Above him, from the second level or the attic, something scuttled across the floor, and odd giggling laughter echoed through the silence. Gooseflesh rippled up his arms, and Joe stumbled back from the fireplace, nearly falling over the low coffee table.

"Liz!" he yelled.

Luminous eyes gazed down from the shadows above the bookshelves, and Joe responded the way his ancient ancestors might have -- he turned and ran from the room. He tripped, slamming hard into the doorway before righting himself, and went out the open back door—*who opened the back door?*—and down the steps. Halfway across the yard, a pale light gleamed near the base of the big maple tree.

"Liz? Is that you?" he called.

Behind him, something skittered out the open door and through the autumn leaves littering the ground. It passed so closely, it brushed against his leg, and Joe jumped to the side with a yell. Full dark had fallen, and he couldn't see what it was.

"Liz?" he whispered. The dark creature was just a blur as it crossed the open ground and seemed to disappear into the base of the tree. The pale light that had shone there was suddenly blotted out.

Joe fumbled in his pocket and pulled out his cell phone. He activated the screen, then turned on the app that made his phone into a mini-flashlight. Cautiously, he approached the tree. Inset into the bark was a small door, painted with faded colors that were nondescript in the darkness. At the foot of the door, curled slightly and with edges darkened as though burned, was a dried pressed rose.

Unfinished by Jodi Abraham

Sweet Songs of the Earth

By Erik Gustafson

The candle winked out. Dirt sprinkled onto my hair and arms, unwanted tickles from the black ceiling. Muffled roars and growls drifted in the inky space. Everything around us had been vibrating, right down to the cymbal on the side of the old band organ. Wind had woken dozens of pipes in the belly of my father's beloved musical machine, stirring haunting murmurs.

As a family, we had huddled and waited for the world to end. My mom's arms tenderly enveloped me like ribbon around a precious gift. I don't know how long we hunkered away from the angry gods shouting in the clouds, but after what seemed like an eternity, everything stopped.

Silence replaced the chaos.

My dad's low, dry voice ended the quiet. "I'll go up and check."

Footsteps echoed in the stairwell as he mounted the uneven, concrete stairs. The squeal of hinges. Light exploding, assaulting the cellar with spears of sun. Squinting, I had seen the blue sky peering down at me.

* * *

I shake myself back to the present day, my hands gripping the steering wheel tightly. It was just a vivid memory from forty years ago flashing in my mind like a sudden storm. Thankfully, the tornado had only taken out a handful of apple trees, but to a boy like me they were a beloved wonderland to climb and explore. I missed those trees. I peered through the windshield of my car at the old house where I grew up.

I have returned to settle my parent's estate to sell everything.

My sister was lounging on a wicker porch swing beneath a lingering cloud of cigarette smoke. As I exited my rental car and walked across the soft lawn toward her, I glanced at the replacement trees, now grown, and sighed with melancholy. No childhood memories were attached to those trees. She waved, but didn't get up to greet me. Sunlight caught the glass in her hand, making it sparkle like a distant beacon on stormy seas.

"Hey, sis!"

The old wooden floor boards of the porch creaked in protest under my feet. As I closed the space between us, I was both happy to see her and filled with sadness. She sat her drink on a small round table, balanced her cigarette in the ashtray, and got up. We embraced and cried without speaking.

"Oh, hey, Barry!"

I pulled out of the embrace and turned toward the voice. Mark, my younger brother, was standing on the porch holding a can of beer. It'd been ten years since I last saw him. He looked fit and well groomed, but had gone bald. My eyes were burning from the tears and my face was all wet, but I smirked anyway. I still possessed a nice thick head of hair. "Looking good, brother!"

I pulled him into a hug and rubbed his shiny dome.

"Knock it off." Mark jerked his neck back, trying to avoid my teasing. He laughed.

"I can't believe dad is gone," Heather finally announced and the mood turned serious. The jokes and formalities dropped away like laundry down a chute. No one responded to what my sister said, but I fought off tears again.

"Fuck cancer," Mark shouted and slurped beer from his can.

I sniffed. "Got any more of those?"

"It's ten in the morning, Barry!" my sister protested.

"You sound like mom."

My comment shut everything down again. Our mother died a decade ago in a car accident coming home from a quilt store. Since then, our father had lived out here alone, going to work and tinkering around the house doing God knows what. We didn't visit as often as we should. You know the story. Life was busy. It was a five hundred mile trip for me. Mark was in the Army and rarely came home. I think Heather made it out here a couple times a month, at least.

Mark slapped my chest. "Let's get that beer."

I saw Heather reaching for her smoke as we walked away. It had burned to a stick of gray ash that crumbled as she grabbed the butt.

"What the hell is that?" I pointed to the old fashioned popcorn maker in the corner of the porch. It was one of those large red machines you see at carnivals, complete with oversized wheels and a red and white striped top. The word popcorn was printed in faded gold letters along the top.

"Beats me." Mark pulled the dirty screen door open and held it for me. "Guess dad liked popcorn when he sat on the porch."

It did look well-loved. The large kettle hanging in the center was black and the Plexiglas windows were stained yellow with grease. "Might have to try that thing out later."

We went inside our childhood home.

The door banged behind us, clapping closed like jaws in a large mouth.

The temperature must have dropped fifteen degrees as I stepped across the threshold. The chilly air sent tingles through my body. Long shadows frolicked in the space, creeping over every surface. Curtains barricaded the windows, letting in only slivers of light here and there.

We padded silently across the wooden floors into the kitchen. Mark pulled open the refrigerator door, revealing two cases of beer and not much else.

"Didn't dad eat?"

"Just popcorn!"

Laughing, we opened our drinks and enjoyed the refreshment.

"Have you guys been back here yet?"

It was Heather, calling from somewhere deeper into the house. I hadn't even heard her come inside. I glanced at Mark and he just shook his head. "Pretend we didn't hear her?"

I nodded and took another drink.

Several seconds later Heather appeared in the doorway, wide eyed. "What is this for?"

She was clutching a horse's leg.

My stomach twisted in disgust. I had to blink several times to absorb what I was seeing. Upon closer inspection, the leg, ghost white, was not from a real horse after all, but rather a life-sized wooden carving.

I walked up to her and ran my fingers across the grainy surface.

"What the heck was dad doing out here? A wood carver?"

"Everyone needs a hobby!"

I took the limb from her and examined it more closely. It was heavy and had nice details worked into the soft wood. The realism was uncanny.

"Two of the back rooms are full of this stuff."

I placed the leg on the counter. "What?"

We marched down the narrow hall without speaking. I was trying to make sense of what I had just seen and anticipating what I was about to see. Moving through that dark hallway made me realize how little I knew about my father.

At the end of the hall split off into four open doorways that looked like entrances to caves. Growing up, I knew three of the spaces as our bedrooms and the fourth as the family game room. Thankfully, Heather stepped inside the room with the light on, my old room.

What I saw reminded me of Geppetto's workshop in Pinocchio. Blocks of wood in various stages of carving covered a table and floor alike. An ankle and hoof jutted up from a large block in the center of the long table. Other animals parts scattered the sawdust-covered floor; legs, ears, and even wings. It looked like a massacre of wooden animals.

A bucket of dowels stood next to the doorway like a guardian.

"What the hell?"

"Was he running a business?" I asked.

The oddest thing in the room was a large red pole that came out of the floor and nearly touched the ceiling. The metal was cold to the touch. I knelt down before the circle cut into the floor, trying to see where the rod went. All I could see was black.

"Why is this pole here?" I asked whoever was willing to venture a guess. No one was.

Heather shook her head. "The room across the hall looks like some kind of painting room."

Mark grabbed a handful of shavings and let them fall through his fingers. "Dad's got wood!"

Heather frowned and rolled her eyes.

"These are pretty big horses. What was he doing with them?"

"This is weird, even for dad," Heather remarked. "Don't you think?"

He never even sent me one thing he had carved for Christmas or a birthday present. Never even mentioned it. I couldn't venture a reason for my father's apparently secret hobby. Carving tools and chisels were scattered everywhere.

Mark left the room.

"What do we do with all this stuff?" Heather asked, her sky blue eyes sparkling with emotion. "Donate it to a school?"

I shrugged. Shifting my weight from my left foot to my right, the boards under me groaned.

I wanted to know more, not just discard everything. "These are just parts. I mean, don't you think there are some finished projects around here somewhere?"

"I guess."

Mark appeared in the doorway looking pale and agitated. "Dad can paint."

We followed Mark into the room across the hall, Heather's old bedroom, and marveled at the beautiful paint job our father had done on several animal parts. A drop cloth splattered with a rainbow of colors covered the floor.

In the center of this room was a large horse, blazing eyes seemed to stare out at me. It was half painted, half raw wood. A wooden stool and table stood adjacent to the creation. The table was littered with small cans of paint and a coffee can stuffed with an assortment of brushes. Tiny brushes capable of applying the most precise of details to the wooden canvas. It took a moment, but I recognized the table as dad's nightstand. I didn't know what to make of it or of the fact that dad had turned his home into a workshop.

A huge mess left behind for us to sort and clean. It was peculiar, but mostly I was upset because I was forced to clean up his eccentric lifestyle now. That anger persisted but a minute, when Mark found the sketches in the painting room. I then became intrigued.

The crudely drawn illustrations depicted a carousel. *Design plans* for building a carousel. We also found a number of research articles from a doctor in Texas with passages highlighted in yellow that claimed the revolving circus attraction held the power to increase blood circulation and destroy tumors.

* * *

The next morning Heather noticed the cellar doors next to the side of the house as she returned from retrieving her toiletry bag from the car. But it wasn't the mere sight of the large doors snuggled in the overgrown grass like huge buck teeth that prompted her to alert us. Dad, we assume, had stacked at least twenty cinder blocks over the twin doors. The heavy weights made it daunting for anyone to get at whatever secrets might be buried under the earth.

All three of us stared at the heavy gray blocks. "What the hell are all these blocks for?"

Quivering with fear, I noticed that no weeds had sprouted in the cracks nor had any dirt collected on the rough surfaces. This suggested that Dad still went down there frequently. Another, darker thought rose in my conscious: maybe the blocks were put there to keep something *down* there. I wanted to leave well enough alone, but Mark didn't. He wanted to explore.

So we did.

One by One, Mark and I heaved the heavy blocks of concrete off the doors and placed them in the seeded-over weeds. When we were done, two white doors revealed a gateway to the underworld.

"Remember the tornado?" Heather whispered, arms crossed over her chest.

"How could I forget that?" I replied, rubbing my sore back. I was hesitant to mention that was the exact memory that had held me in a trace as I arrived yesterday.

"That was the last time I was down there."

"Yeah. Me, too."

"I was down there one more time after you both moved out." Mark interjected, still panting from the hard work. "The sirens went off, but nothing happened."

"Is anything even down there?" Heather asked.

I knelt before the doors, rubbing the surface, chips of white paint cracking off between my fingers. The wood was cold to the touch. I felt like I was at a cemetery paying respects to a lost family member. In a way, I was doing just that. "Only one way to find out, I guess."

"Mom starting canning things. Stored all that crap down there," Mark said. "At least, she did."

"Mom made the best spaghetti sauce!" Heather's eyes glazed, she was miles away in a happy memory.

"Yeah," I agreed with a smile.

I grabbed one of the metal pulls. The handle was even more frigid than the boards. I shivered. Hesitating. A sense of dread gnawed at my stomach. Feelings of bravery washed out like the tide. "Why were all these blocks piled onto the doors?"

"Come on, don't be a chicken shit." Mark nudged past Heather and jumped on the cellar doors. The thud echoed loudly. "Anybody home?" He shouted and stomped his feet. "Knock, knock."

I fell back on my butt and observed the spectacle.

"Very funny." Heather's words were shaky, obviously masking apprehension about going down there.

"Knock it off before you hurt yourself," I cautioned. "Just move."

Mark hopped down. I leaned over and yanked open one of the doors. Shadows rose from the depths like zombies crawling out of the grave as the tall door made its awkward arc back around to the grass. I let it fall the last couple of feet.

Grave robbers. That is what I thought of as I peered into the depths. I counted four or five crumbling concrete steps, nothing further was visible.

Holding onto the side, Mark tugged the other door. It squealed in protest, but opened.

Heather leaned forward rather than taking a step closer and stared into the pit. "We need a flashlight."

"Flashlight? There are lights down there, sis, remember?"

"Maybe we shouldn't go down there."

A shrill noise drifted up from the blackness. A musical instrument of some sort, maybe a trumpet or a flute. I don't know what it was, but it made us all gasp and stagger backward.

Just a few bars, then all was quiet again.

"What the hell?"

Mark was pale. "You both heard that, right?"

I turned to Heather to see if she had heard, but she was halfway back to the front door.

I took a deep breath and stared at my brother. "What was that?"

The color had returned to Mark's face. "Probably just the wind. Remember that old organ or whatever that was down there? Just wind blowing through the pipes." He turned away and shouted, "Heather!"

"Yeah, come back, Heather!"

She stopped without turning and stood there. We beckoned one more time and she slowly returned. She pointed behind us. "Um, who's more scared now?"

The bone-colored cellar doors were closed again.

* * *

It took us almost four hours to get the courage to lift the doors again. When we finally pulled the ghostly panels of wood up, we weren't greeted by the dark. Bright light illuminated the stairs. Of course, after a moment of being scared, it's easy to convince ourselves that the light had always been on.

Mark cupped his hands over his mouth and called down. No one answered.

"We doing this?" he asked us.

There was no way I was descending into that lair. I came here to sort through my parent's stuff and get back to my life. Still, against my better judgment, I nodded. "Okay."

My sister stood directly behind me, clinging to my shoulder. She was stuck to me and going wherever I decided to go.

The cellar doors embraced us. Mark entered first.

When his legs disappeared below the threshold, I started down. I only made it two steps before I wished I had thought to pile those blocks back up on the open doors so they couldn't close again. I didn't share my thought.

The steps were narrow, much more so than I remembered. Focusing on the tiny treads, I nearly cracked my forehead on the low ceiling.

"Whoa, brother, you gotta see this!" Mark called out.

I held the edge of the opening for leverage and leaned down, trying to see. Mark blocked my view. "What is it?"

"No joking around, Mark!" Heather barked quickly, but barely above a whisper.

I descended, goose flesh rising up on my arms. My mind reeled with possibilities: stacks of bodies, a storehouse of torture weapons, or even just kinky, but embarrassing, sex toys. I could see dad making the cellar into a 'play' room. Wait, no I couldn't. Gross.

Lost in thought, I collided with Mark. The momentum launched him forward. "Watch it!"

"Sor—" I didn't even get the word out of my mouth.

Before us stood a carousel.

My eyes immediately followed the red center pole up to the ceiling, where it vanished through a perfectly cut hole. At the base of the pole, in the middle of a nest of pulleys and angled poles was the band organ I remembered from my childhood.

A red platform nearly as large as the cellar floated about three inches off the ground around all of that.

There were poles impaled to the platform at even intervals all the way around. Enough to mount a dozen horses easily, but only five of them actually had animals. The horses were beautiful, painted with bright, glossy colors. Above all the horses was a giant wheel, a barn-red halo, with thick spokes connecting everything together. A network of florescent bulbs dazzled the entire frame, making them look like a string of Christmas tree lights.

The entire layout was magical. The fear in me deflated and I was filled with a child-like joy. My dad made a carousel! How cool is that? I wanted to ride it.

"Does it work?" I asked.

"How should I know? Let's check it out."

"Dad did this?" Heather asked, peeling her sweaty body away from me.

"Bro, I don't think this cellar was this big when we were growing up." Mark commented, scanning the room. "Aren't things supposed to look smaller after you've grown up?"

"How did he do this?" I marveled. I didn't have any words to describe exactly what was going through my mind. I stepped across the dirt floor and put a foot on the platform.

It wobbled as I put my weight on wooden surface.

I stared into one large blue eye. The detail was breathtaking. I shuddered and looked away from its lifelike gaze. It felt like I had made some spiritual connection with the wooden animal. I ran my hand over the smooth orange saddle and considered hopping on.

I didn't.

"Where's the start button?" Mark asked, much closer to me than I realized. "At least this explains the popcorn machine!"

"Ya think dad turned into a closet carny?" Heather asked, still standing on the ground, arms folded tightly. "It's cold down here."

"It's a cellar, sis." Mark slapped on one horses on the rump. "Let's get this beauty started."

Movement on the far side of the carousel caught my eye. There was something *on* one of the horses over there.

Black. Amorphous. Too large to be anything comforting.

Heather noticed it, too.

I slipped around the horse and stepped down into the center. Past the slanted poles that formed a red ribcage extending from the center pole. I paused at the band organ and stared at the hand painted art on the paneling.

Two little cowboys and one cowgirl riding horses across a prairie.

Smiling.

I turned my attention back to the black form mounted on the horse. It shimmered oddly. I squinted and eased closer. My heart pounded and then stopped when I realized I was staring at trash bags. Trash bags that were not empty.

I froze.

"Um, it's something in a bunch of trash bags."

"What?" I heard Heather say, but she sounded distant. I didn't turn back around.

Whatever was wrapped in that black plastic was large. My stomach churned at the possibilities my mind was conjuring. I was two feet away from the unexplained object.

"Um, Barry."

I couldn't bring myself to turn away from the mysterious package. I was too afraid that if I did, the thing inside would burst from its sick cocoon and pummel me.

"Barry," Mark persisted.

"What?" My eyes were wide and locked on the form.

"I think this painting is supposed to be us."

The bag shifted, slid forward and draped over most of the mane. "Can we look at the cute painting later?" I stuttered, my teeth were actually chattering from the fear that had taken control.

I heard the floorboards clatter as Mark jumped back on, close to me.

Reaching out, I brushed the bag with the tips of my fingers. Cold and solid.

"What is it?"

"This isn't good."

Momentum took over and the bag toppled over, catching on one of the foot petals. Black plastic tore like a wound. The carousel shook from the impact.

A lock of white hair flowed from the rip.

"Oh shit," I mumbled. Nausea washed over me, all the blood in my body constricted and my skin went pale. Numb. Mark looked worse than I felt. We both rotated our heads back toward where Heather was last standing.

She was gone.

I prayed she fled this crypt to summon the police. The hum of many bulbs adorning the carousel became louder and louder, merging with a ringing in my ears. Colors blurred. I became dizzy. The whole room felt like it was spinning.

I dropped to one knee, gasping.

Staring at the body, my stomach heaved.

I looked up, straight ahead, to avoid the gruesome scene. The afternoon sun blazed down the steps, through the open cellar doors.

I blinked and I was staring at a dirt wall.

The room wasn't spinning at all. I wasn't dizzy. The carousel was rotating.

The band organ burst to life. A haunting, old-time carnival tune screeched through the cavernous chamber. I imagined the eerie song rising up stairs and into the yard. Calling people toward its enchanting melody.

Mark was tugging my arm, urging me into motion. I was dead weight to him.

The bag had torn away more, revealing a decayed face that had collapsed, most of the skin putrefied. One step before it was a skull. A tarnished locket rested on her chest, above a rotting black dress.

A locket I recognized as the one containing photographs of me and both my siblings.

"We gotta go!" Mark screamed.

Puke launched from my stomach and splattered on the plastic bags. I was on my feet and we ran to the edge of the platform. When the carousel rotated around to the steps again, we jumped.

The music was somehow muffled, quieted. Grinding gears spinning the pulleys became the main sound. For a moment. We weren't even on the first step when my father's voice stopped us cold in our escape.

"Don't leave me, boys!"

Wearing his navy blue suit we buried him in just a month ago, my dead father stood in the center of the spinning carousel.

"Dad?"

He didn't appear to be a ghost. Or not what I would I describe as a ghost. He was a solid form. He was smiling at us, arms open.

"I knew you would come save me."

Mark and I exchanged glances. Tears were streaming down my brother's cheeks.

I was too terrified to weep. I *saw* my father being lowered into the ground. And my mother, for that matter. There was no way this was real. If it was real, we needed to get out quick.

Mark felt differently apparently; he was shuffling *toward* the spirit thing.

"Mark, no!"

He ignored me. He was already onto the platform and maneuvering around one of the horses. Mark paused, maybe he was reflecting or reconsidering, but he stood on the carousel, orbiting around my father.

I joined him.

What other option did I have? I had to save my brother.

"That's it, young men!" My father raised his arms like a priest giving a blessing. "Pick a horse!"

I looked out across the platform at my mother's corpse poking through the bags. I was shaking and the little voice in my head was screaming something was very wrong. "What did you do to mom?"

My father was suddenly standing between Mark and me, but nearly on top of me. His breath reminded me of rotten onions when he whispered in my ear, "I'm bringing her back."

I shoved at my father with both hands, but he barely budged. He moved enough for me to see that Mark had mounted on of the horses and was sitting there patiently, his eyes as vacant as those of the wooden horses.

"Mark, help me!" I sidestepped my father. "What are you doing?"

My brother didn't acknowledge me. I didn't see my father's fist, but I felt it connect with my jaw. I fell to the ground and was staring up at the underside of a horse. Pain exploded in my head.

Before I could move, dad had me by both shoulders. He drew up to his face. "We can beat death. As a family."

He lifted me into the air effortlessly and thrust me up on a horse. My tailbone screamed from the impact.

I turned to my brother, straining the cords in my neck to see him. Long thin snakes were spiraling down the pole that held Mark's horse. The snakes latched into Mark's flesh in at least a dozen places, connecting him to the carousel like the strings of a puppet. The clear snakes, or tubes, whatever they were, began to turn red.

Mark's eyes fluttered back in his head.

Father by my side, holding me fast, I glanced up at the pole on my horse. The demonic tubes were spiraling toward me.

* * *

As the pipes in the belly of the organ wound down to silence, I heard sirens wailing above. This was followed by Heather's desperate voice, leading strangers down toward us. I wanted to scream for her to just run away, but no words came out of my mouth. My dad looked up, eyes locked on the cellar doors. A hungry grin spread his lips wide and the odd shadows made his teeth appear blue. He spoke in a serious tone.

"I need so many more riders."

Regret by John Stanton

Doors Shut Tight and Arms Wide Open

By Kerry G.S. Lipp

"Your house is so much better than mine," Bailey said. "I love coming here."

Izzy said nothing, just smiled and kissed her lightly on the lips, a little anxious but trying to hide it. They stood face to face, holding each other.

"My parents suck," Bailey said, "and I think they're catching on."

Her words jolted Izzy. Catching on to what, she thought the fact that they were sexually intimate with each other? Or something else?

"What do you mean?" Izzy asked.

"They always ask why we hang out over here all the time. I think they're either pissed or hurt that we never hang out at my house anymore."

Izzy sighed. Relieved.

"We don't hang out there because they never leave us alone. And that open door policy? What's up with that? We are teenage girls. We need our privacy. I hate going to your house."

"Exactly," Bailey said. "I hate hanging out there too but maybe we should every now and then just to shut them up, try and convince them that we're just friends and nothing more. I don't want them calling your parents or something and finding out that we're always hanging out alone with the doors shut or worse with your parents gone. Especially in your bedroom."

"You're paranoid. Just relax," Izzy said and kissed her.

"It's so weird. My parents are so strict and it's like yours don't even care at all."

Anger flared across Izzy's face for a moment and she clenched a fist at her side, tempted to strike Bailey across the face. But that couldn't happen. Not quite yet. Instead she composed herself and spoke calmly.

"My parents care," Izzy said. "They just trust me enough to give me privacy. They don't need to watch me 24/7. They give me an opportunity to be myself and as long as I don't get hooked on hard drugs or pregnant, they don't care. Hell, even if I did, they'd help me through it. And you don't even see them all the time. Hardly at all actually. You don't even know how supportive and motivating they are and how much they care and everything they've taught me. They care Bailey. They just aren't crazy."

That was probably too much, too harsh, but Bailey nodded and smiled tucking a stray strand of hair behind her own ear and wiping away a single tear. Izzy thought she looked pretty right then and felt a flutter in her stomach.

"We don't do drugs," Izzy said. "And I don't think we're going to have to worry about getting pregnant," she winked and kissed Bailey on the mouth, guiding her down to the bed.

Bailey gasped and then they both giggled a little bit and for only a fraction of a second, Izzy felt anxious about what she was about to do, but she fought through the butterflies in her stomach and climbed onto the bed. Izzy lay down, and pulled Bailey on top of her and they started kissing and touching each other, running hands up and down each other's body, and slowly removing clothes.

Breathless, Bailey said, "You're sure they're not coming home tonight? We really have the whole place to ourselves?"

"Yep," Izzy said, "they're gone all weekend. We don't even need to keep the door shut."

"Yeah but let's keep it shut anyway. If it's open, it reminds me too much of my own house."

"Icky," Izzy said and they laughed, but Izzy's was forced.

Izzy started getting antsy. She was half-sick with excitement and anticipation and ready to get on with it. Bailey always did her first, but she was moving so slow tonight. Izzy craved one last orgasm from Bailey's fingers and tongue. She'd learned that it felt much better when someone else was making it happen.

After a few more minutes of Bailey teasing and playing coy, they finally started shedding each other's last layer of clothing. Bailey worked her magic, and before long, Izzy was writhing in the ecstasy of orgasm under the hypnosis of Bailey's sexual spell. She was going to miss this, but her parents assured her there would be plenty more lovers like Bailey. Some worse, but many much better. And Izzy trusted them.

Most would harshly judge Izzy's parents for the way they'd raised their girl. But by cultivating a wide-open relationship with their daughter, they could allow Izzy to live her own life with the door shut. Her parents trusted her. They knew Izzy had nothing to hide and they knew that Izzy valued her privacy and she'd always open up to them. They'd spent the formative years of Izzy's young life laying the foundation for that kind of unique relationship.

Her mother and father started by introducing her to sex at a very young age. Not molesting her, not touching her at all, but clearly and openly explaining to her all of the different aspects of sexuality from the dangers it presented to the shameless joys of free masturbation. The world was progressing into a much more liberated and open-minded place to live with recent struggles for the freedoms of homosexuals and the slow lifting of feminine shaming and oppression headlining the daily news.

Sex was changing shape, and while Izzy was in the womb, her parents talked and agreed about how exactly they would raise their daughter. They decided to gauge how she responded to their open approach to sexuality and if she was successful, happy, and showed great promise, they decided only then would they introduce their little girl to murder.

They'd told her all this as she grew into a young woman, and it all flashed through her mind in a second as she waffled one final time before deciding to kill Bailey. Her parents told her that they'd love and accept her either way. They'd be waiting behind doors shut tight with arms wide open whether Izzy decided to commit to the kill or wait until she felt a little more comfortable.

With her body still twitching with the final pangs of her fading orgasm, Izzy made choice. She felt fantastic, though a bit nervous. She felt ready to kill.

Her parents offered advice on method, but ultimately left the choice to Izzy. The only conditions were that she had to use a weapon (to avoid the risk of Bailey getting away) and it couldn't be a gun (too loud, too easy, too messy, not intimate) the rest was up to Izzy.

They told her that just like sex, murder was something that couldn't be explained, only experienced and they wanted their baby girl to have that rich experience for as many years of her life as possible. They'd coach her through not getting caught once she felt that first sweet, powerful rush.

Sweating a little and smiling a lot, Bailey slithered up Izzy's body. Bailey's face radiated equal parts happiness for satisfying her partner and desire for her own pleasure.

Izzy had a plan.

A bullet-proof plan that would bait and intrigue Bailey, ultimately leaving Bailey helpless. More importantly Izzy's strategy and thought involved would impress her parents. Izzy knew they expected her to stumble, to not quite get the job done. Not because she was unworthy, but because they were the parents and she was their child. Whether learning to catch a ball or kill a person, her parents would guide her to success. She wanted to blow them away this first time.

It would've been easy for her to grab the hammer she had placed under the bed and just start swinging, but she didn't want any unnecessary risks. Instead, with a sultry smile, Izzy told Bailey to lie back and relax.

Bailey did so with an expectant, silly grin lighting her pretty face.

"I've got something for you," Izzy said and reached into the nightstand drawer and pulled out a black blindfold with fuzzy edges like Pomeranian fur.

"Kinda kinky," Bailey smiled.

"Kinda fun," Izzy answered and seductively slipped it over Bailey's eyes.

"Be gentle," Bailey said, lying there, smiling, happy, and ready.

Izzy kissed her neck and her breasts and kissed her a final time on the lips, letting it linger for an extra few seconds. She didn't feel, sad, or sick or remorseful. She felt powerful, in control, craving the sensation the hammer would bring when she drove it down.

She reached under the bed and picked it up with one hand.

"What are you doing?" Bailey asked raising a hand to the blindfold.

"Another surprise," Izzy said. "And if you take that thing off I'm gonna kill you," she laughed.

Bailey giggled and placed her hand back behind her head.

Izzy took a deep breath. And in that breath realized that she was at a crossroads. Her parents always told her that life before orgasm was a lot different than life after orgasm. Murder similar, but worse. The sensation felt different, incredible in its own way, but unlike orgasm, it was much harder to achieve and illegal. If caught, one way or another, the penalty was probably your life. But Izzy craved this final loss of innocence and complete freedom from the taboos that life tied down on nearly everyone.

Very few people were truly free and almost none at such a young age or with the fantastic support system Izzy felt so blessed to have. She could only imagine what she could do with all of this early guidance as she continued to gain knowledge and experience throughout her life.

With Bailey unseeing but still grinning and desperate for Izzy's body, Izzy smiled at her blindfolded first-lover and with everything she had, Izzy drove the hammer down.

Bailey didn't even scream. But Izzy did. She screamed and swung and worked the hammer free and swung again like a savage fighting for her life. Her parents weren't lying. It felt incredible. Indescribable. Brutal. Beautiful.

Bailey went limp. Dead.

Izzy went limp. Exhausted. Though she'd only swung a few times, she felt completely drained, but not bad. Like an easy crash from the perfect high.

She looked at her bedroom door. Still shut tight. Then she remembered they were already in here and looked at her closed closet door.

Her mother and father started slowly clapping, getting faster and faster before they opened the door and rushed out to hug her with gigantic grins splitting both their faces.

"That was fantastic sweetie and completely without a struggle," her father said.

"I just knew my baby would pick a hammer. She's been fascinated with those ever since she was a little girl," Izzy's mother mused, kissing her daughter on both cheeks.

"I'll go get the cupcakes and the champagne," her father said thumbing a bit of blood from Izzy's brow then tasting it. "But we can only celebrate for a moment. It's a hell of a lot easier to clean up before everything dries. We're so proud of you honey," he beamed and turned to leave the room, with a noticeable spring in his step.

"We'll get the garbage bags and the cleaning supplies," her mom said. "This is so exciting. Our little girl is growing up so fast," she gushed.

They met back upstairs a few minutes later.

"And Bailey actually thought you guys didn't care what I did. If she only knew," Izzy said through a mouthful of chocolate cupcake with spots of blood drying on her face.

Then the three of them hugged and laughed and listened to Bon Jovi while they cleaned up with both her mother and father offering tips on cleanup and body disposal.

When it was done, Izzy wrote about her new experience in her diary. She concluded the entry by describing how thankful she was that she had such encouraging, helpful and supportive parents.

And motivating.

They sure as hell were motivating.

They'd opened the doors to sex. They'd opened the doors to murder.

But they were just getting started.

And Izzy hadn't seen anything yet.

Water Lily by Shawna L. Bernard

The Virtuoso

By J. Daniel Stone

Venturing into the basement that rebellious day, sixteen-years-old and your best friend is a year younger, tagging along like the brother you never had. Your best friend means everything to you, and he feels the same: two unhappy hearts living an unhappy life, but together you find a spark of light at the end of a boring tunnel.

Flasks in hand, black leather trim, and a shot of stinging Jägermeister every time you say you're scared to go in the basement…too weary of that treacherous, damp dark that could swallow you whole. Nothing stands in the way but you and the door, tall rectangle of ancient wood, knob like the golden eye of a Cyclops marking your every step. Turning back is out of the question.

"Open it," Delilah said.

"No."

Delilah had been curious as a cat since the day Alex met her, long dark haired androgyne, tough as nails and grinding her teeth to some psychotic tune. She listened to heavy metal while napping, industrial while showering; shrieking guitars and sibilant vocal melodies soothed her soul. But as much as Alex loved her, and would abide by her wishes for they always promised adventure, he just couldn't do what she said, not right now. He'd heard too many noises down there.

"It's just a basement," and Delilah swung her lengthy hair over her shoulder, smelling of licorice and apples and sweet clove smoke. "What about your flowers, your precious orchids? They need water."

Delilah just wouldn't let it go.

"They don't need that much care, you know that already."

Her sharp face pierced into his with a fascinating glow as one hand slithered out of her pocket and tugged his freshly pierced ear. It hurt. It was annoying. Alex took a step back, pressed himself against the door and shook his head, but Delilah pulled his ear again. The pain sent a hot bolt down his legs and his feet did a marvelous dance; wavy black hair spun out of control; a sketchy blur of pink and yellow converses slashed the tiled floor.

But no matter what he couldn't let her do it; he didn't want *it* to get out. But Delilah was serious; her teeth were bared now and her shoulders scrunched like a football player. She was drenched in sweat which made her Nine Inch Nails shirt stick to her skin like a wasted condom on a limp dick. Her face met his again; those sapphire eyes meant business, so innocent yet so brutal. Within them were an eon's worth of dreams and nightmares.

"*Do it,*" she hissed.

The finality in her voice was all it took. For a moment he bowed like a crane in front of the door, feeling a slight breeze, cold and ugly, and put his eyes to the brass key hole, wondering if *it* was looking back at him, wondering if some tongue would slip through to take out his eye. But nothing stared back at him, too dark to see this October afternoon. Then Alex remembered that only music called it out, and that the lone window in the basement was covered with and piles of newspapers his grandfather had left down there to save as relics, as history.

"See anything?"

"Nothing."

"Well then we've gotta go down there and see for ourselves."

"Delilah...please," lips tight over his small teeth, ghost of lipstick smeared across. "It only happens when I play the piano. Don't you remember?"

"Remember what?"

"You were here with me. You saw it!"

"I didn't see shit," Delilah snarled, evil smile like a bird. "Get to playing. I'll wait *here for it.*"

"...I don't know, my grandparents—"

"Grandparents, schmandparents. Where did you hide the skeleton key?" Delilah asked with an upturned hand, pale palm like a small monkey.

"On the key ring...by the front door."

Delilah flew out of the kitchen, leaving Alex alone for the longest two seconds of his life. *Can't do this, she's wrong. We mustn't mess around with the thing in the basement. My parents are dead, been dead, and there's no such thing as ghosts or the boogeyman.*

"Got it!"

Delilah slid the key in, clicking lock sound like the end of days, and the door creaked open. Four feet took baby steps; four hands shivered, and two hearts began to beat faster than they ever expected.

* * *

It was winter when it first happened, when fingers manipulated cold piano keys and a sweet song called out the thing from the basement. Alex and Delilah had cut class that day because they didn't like to be stuck in that prison called High School; they liked to learn by their own vices, by their own adventures. They hid away from the world inside a dumpster on the edge of the school's property they called The Hut. No one remembered where it was, and thus no garbage was ever put inside. It was the place Alex lived in before class, before the big mother fuckers decided to steal his lunch money because they had nothing better to do but fight in packs, before kids and teachers would stare Alex down wondering if he was a boy or a girl being that he wore tight girl's jeans and band t-shirts.

Alex had been born with the gift of androgyny, and it was no mistake that some days he was called a lesbian, and others days a twinky bottom. But it was no secret that he loathed being labeled boy or girl; being referred to by his first name made people think. Most people left Alex up to his flaunts, but the lunch money monkeys never gave it up. Yet the past few weeks saw a dissipation of bullies; Delilah had shown all the boys how sharp her butterfly blade was, cutting herself in front of them, her forearm marked up like a sopping blue print of flesh. Nothing more frightening than the sideshow freaks at your door.

In The Hut Alex had an electric heater, two small lava lamps and a velvet blanket for comfort. Delilah's hands formed around one of the lamps, throwing soft colored shadows in the near reflection. Today Alex was outwardly freaked out; he hated snow, hated to wear heavy clothes because he was so skinny and all they did was weigh him down. The snow was getting thicker, huge flakes came down like ice chips flying off an Edward Scissorhands sculpture. But that's what happens when you live in a patch town deep within the coal region of Pennsylvania, nothing but anthracite and the neon lights of bars to pass time, snow and cold; best to dress up warm and not let the wind skew your bones because once winter came, it never stopped. Snow in October? Thank you, global warming.

But he had also dreamed of his mother again.

She was locked in *that* closet in the basement.

"She died during childbirth, not anything terrible. Not murder or anything," Alex said.

"So then why are you scared?"

"I don't know. I just am."

"It's a classic horror tale, *The Thing in the Basement*. And we're living, breathing characters."

"I guess so."

"You look tired, Alex."

"I didn't sleep a wink last night, too worried…"

"I bet it's only a fucking rat, maybe even a bat."

"You and your damn bats. You need to just go out and get one. There are so many in these Pennsylvania forests."

Delilah lit a black votive and put it between their shivering bodies, soothing pin-point flame yellow as a dandelion, adding more heat to The Hut like blood to the brain for conversation. The snow was piling atop them and a line of water was squiggling down the inside, small glittering river.

"I've been having fucked up dreams, real fucked up dreams, Alex," Delilah said with her finger in her mouth, chipped maroon nail polish like the missing pieces to her soul.

"Still like—"

"Yes, like I leave my physical body and can walk in the land of the dead."

"Is that like a Shaman?"

"No, I don't believe in any religion, not even mystical ones."

"Black Sabbath talked about outer body experiences in *Behind the Wall of Sleep*. Did you know that?"

"You've told me a hundred times," Delilah lit a cigarette and let the smoke form around her like an embrace.

"I like when you do that trick with the smoke, it's funny."

Delilah rolled her eyes. "*Anyway*, I'm thinking we should—"

"No."

"But you can play the piano while I—"

"NO!"

Delilah's face soured in shock.

"I mean...*why*? You want to fuck with the damn dead, again? Haven't you learned your lesson—"

"Yeah spare me, I already know...since the graveyard incident. I got too drunk and fell into a ditch...couldn't get out until you and Jimmy pulled me up."

"They *pushed* you in that ditch Delilah; you didn't get drunk and fall."

"So what? I read in *The Wild Boys* that with certain drugs you can create your own near-death visions. The power of the mind is impossibly strange, but real."

Alex just nodded. What else could he do? When Delilah got into one of her famous moods, when her mind was set on something—a simple task, a mission, a fucking plate of macaroni and cheese—it had to be seen through to the end or she'd just sit and pout, dig her knife into her forearm. He hated seeing Delilah cut herself, had thought she'd stopped, but at times those suicide ghosts come back to haunt old territory.

"I'm not kidding anymore. I'm scared."

"You don't have to be scared, I'm here with you. Your parents are dead, but if they're walking around your basement like Captain fucking Howdy, we should get involved," cigarette smoke whirling now, trickle of cold coming into The Hut.

"When does it happen...your outer body experiences?" Alex asked with a trickle of curiosity.

"Like I said...when I sleep. And when did these dreams start for you?"

"I think I've had them all my life, but now, well, since puberty they've been getting worse."

"Let's start with this."

Delilah pulled a dimebag out of her back pocket, opened the seal and filled The Hut with the sharp verdant smell of an open field. She broke it up and quickly rolled two joints and passed one to Alex, masterpiece in white. Alex lit the joint and took a hit; spicy green smoke suffused his mouth, his throat. His head began to spin almost instantly; the effect smashed him like a sock full of pennies, and as Delilah was talking, the world he knew clicked out.

When Alex awoke he was in his living room with Delilah, dreaming of the grand piano, dream as cold as fever sweat as he stared down the basement door, waiting for it to open to his wicked tune. But the thing only woke at night, insomniac phantom much like Delilah and Alex. It was always better to play in the dark anyway, by candles, because not even a sliver of moonlight made it through the trees in this part of town.

Face forward before the grand piano, each key like polished slivers of bone. Alex outstretched his thin white fingers and pressed them like spider legs to the piano keys. The notes climbed free from the air, swirled above them like shooting stars, Moonlight Sonata. Delilah was all of a sudden next to him, her face vacuous, curious. Her eyes were blue diamonds in the soft dark, eyes that sensed oncoming danger.

And then Alex saw why. The basement door was slowly *moving;* pearl colored fingers wrapped around the edge, sliming their way to freedom. Suddenly Alex's vision whirled as if inside a funnel. Then Delilah was pulling him as she ran toward some kind of light at the end of the tunnel: fetus breaking free of the placenta, exiting a blood-slicked womb.

And he woke up.

* * *

"Grandpa's asleep, Alex. What's it you want to tell him?"

Grandmother in the kitchen, veined arms like small purple serpents twisting beneath thin skin. Alex saw every stress line, every bruise she endured cooking in that kitchen, every knife scar like a mark of relief. She was a marvelous cook, and a marvelous talker. Grandmother: the treasure chest of advice, of solace and care. The stove was hot and some kind of loaf was cooking. Alex smelled salty ketchup and the sizzling red juice of butcher meat. She was taller than he remembered, more gaunt and strict.

It was nighttime, and the moon was full, a huge beach ball like an omniscient god staring down into Alex. Its light slid off of the window pane, gliding across the wood island where grandmother's kitchen knife lay as if ready to spring to life and turn flesh into a red ruined mess. But grandmother came back to her cutting board and worked her magic with the knife; onion sliced in half and carrots chopped. Alex watched her, young boy not yet fifteen, but with a face so childish one could mistake him for five years younger. His hair was growing out of control and his features were so smooth one could not tell if he was a boy or a girl.

His eyes were locked onto grandmother, her long hair scaling down her crooked spine, and the twist-tie of her pink apron. She almost looked like the woman he saw the other night, the one at the foot of his bed with the deep set eyes and pin straight hair that hung over her face. But it was a dream he remembered, nothing his own mind couldn't have made up before he went to bed. He knew dreams were how the body filtered the stressors and sensory stimulation of the day out of one's mind, and he'd been thinking of her heavily.

"It's my mother. She came to visit me."

Grandmother slammed the knife down. "Don't say that, Alex."

"I wouldn't lie! She comes when I play the piano."

"Your mother was our daughter," wet hands on Alex's face now, sharp onion stench and carrot smear across his cheek. "We loved her, and you would have too, but she died giving birth to you."

Grandmother's eyes were spider web red and the palest green in lie the center, soul of a jewel: the badge of making it passed sixty years of age. She was going to cry, so Alex let the conversation go, let the woman go from his dreams. He wouldn't think of her anymore, her body shaking and cold. It was like a bad memory waiting to be let out of purgatory. For a young kid with nobody to talk to, no parents to tell him how to go about these kinds of problems, he had to suck it up, and wouldn't tell grandpa either. It was best not to wake him until passed ten at night anyway.

"Your grandfather works too hard at the Gheligg factory for you to be making up these tales. He needs his rest and his sanity. Please…for the sake of this house, speak of this never again."

"…never again, I won't. But I know from the pictures in the closet down there."

"You've been snooping?" Grandmother shook her head. "You know, sometimes, when your mother went snooping we made her stay in that closet…with all the lights out!"

"Are you serious?"

"And she would complain about a…presence in there. But you know us Pennsylvania folk, we don't believe in that kind of junk."

"Why that closet though?"

"We didn't believe in hitting, but we did believe in punishment. Now let me finish cooking," and grandmother winked as Alex stepped away. "Oh, Alex?"

"Yeah?"

"She used to love to play…that same piano."

Kitchen behind him now, bright square in the dark living room, his back to the wall so to not see the door on his way out, the formation, the chiaroscuro illusion, and Alex sat at the grand piano. Black lacquered surface, tooth-white keys ready for him to play. One finger at a time, knuckles moving in symphony with the tortured music in his head; Alex played until the house swelled with scales and notes, until they tore away from the piano and sifted into the senses fine as wine.

Then the old brass knob turned and the basement door creaked open. But Alex continued to play, moving his limbs in tempo with the brand new song he'd written last week, a blend of rock ballad and orchestra. He didn't see the warbling fingers clutching the edge of the door, the nails rimmed in black blood, and the wretched face behind the curtain of hair; not until he heard grandmother screech, dropping her knife to the floor, spill of carrot and onion slivers, and the basement door slamming shut as his fingers moved off the piano.

* * *

A few tumbling weeks went by. Alex lay wasted in his own dark thoughts, still dreaming of the woman. He and Delilah had broken into the local morgue and accessed some records, looked up names and tried to pair them with faces, but no luck. Alex couldn't remember the face too well, and Delilah had yet to admit that she'd even seen it. His grandparents were of no help; grandpa spent his days sleeping because he was on the night shift at the Gheligg Factory, and grandma spent her time cooking, doing house chores like any old lady would.

She didn't want to talk about the thing in the basement, not of her daughter, not of anything. Alex knew that old people were to be respected, so he left them alone, and stopped burdening them with the talk of his sleepless nights, of his worsening dreams.

Plus, grandmother was an academic and academics do not believe in life after death. In death there is just blackness, but trouble is that no one has risen from the dead to prove this…not yet anyhow.

So Alex cut class with Delilah more than usual. He wrote his troubles in notebooks, filled three a week, and this showed no signs of stopping. His words evolved into lyrics, ones that Delilah fine-tweaked, syntax and plural endings and proper spelling. But words never suited him well. Alex was suited best in writing out his fear in music, in the piano. So he replaced his prose notebook and began to learn the mysteries of musical scales. He drew wiry looking notes with ugly faces, C major, D harmonic minor, and raging chords.

Delilah showed him her notebooks too, words she'd scrambled together when drunk, when feeling like life was worth less than what a pig could spit, when wishing of a better life. They became more attached at the hip than ever, weaving together the strings of music like a tight piece of clothing. These songs were the demons Alex held deep inside his soul, the fright he felt living within his own home, the one place he should've felt *safe*.

The music books piled high; the sessions grew longer and their songs tighter. Delilah's voice changed too; her poetry buzzed over Alex's scales as she fused harmonics and a capella, the sultry sounds of industrial and heavy metal. Alex's fingers were strengthening too, his knowledge of chords, scales and time signatures were limitless. They were music's children—bent backs, slouched jaws and growing brains—scribbling poetry across loose leaf, musical notes on ruled paper to materialize them into songs: self-taught musicians practicing loud and hard as maestros. Even Alex's grandparents said that they were onto something good, and Delilah's conservative adopted parents approved dismally of her celestial voice, her stinging lyrics.

Their music was inspired by and dedicated to the macabre. It raged with unpolished talent as much as it was loathsome and dark. It calmed their nightmares, their hummingbird hearts, and one day they would start a band, but when that day was both of them didn't know. But their music didn't stop Delilah's need to see what Alex was so afraid of. He'd forced their practices to daylight hours because he claimed night is when it came alive and crawling for fresh air from the dirty basement.

"I want to see it!" Delilah demanded.

"No! It's a demon…a mermaid…"

"Mermaids aren't evil."

"That's like saying there aren't any *good* witches. Are you that naïve?"

Delilah snatched a handful of Alex's hair and made her butterfly blade flutter open; she traced the hollow of Alex's pale neck softly, coming around to his sharp nose and thin lips. She always had trouble controlling her anger.

"I'll gut you like a fish, Alex. Isn't that what they said in the movie?"

"I'm not scared. Go ahead. It'll stop my dreams."

"Forget it. Let's play…now!"

"It won't come."

"Because all we've done is practice...we've never really *played*. We've never really put on a show."

"A show?" Alex twirled his dark hair in his thin white fingers, wormy things in a forest of black.

"Yes, let's put one on. Now"

Nothing could stop the moment. Delilah began the song, a capella voice like ground diamonds sprinkled over a decadent cocktail, a song she wanted to entitle *My Personal Hell*. Part love story of the dream world, part mystery of her missing past. Alex put his fingers to the keys, creeping slow as death into Delilah's silvery voice. From the window yellow spirals of sunshine dripped and streaked across Delilah's face. Alex noticed there was not a cloud in sky; only a fine vapor was at the window. Some kind of watcher? A soul? But it was soon gone once the graceful twirl of music hit its crescendo. Their first show came with no audience to applaud but it felt so right, so feral. They paid attention to nothing but the sounds.

And yet the basement door opened slowly, and a hooked finger slimed the door knob.

* * *

Down the narrow hallway, cement stairs untouched in weeks, grandmother avoiding the basement now too. Delilah down first, brave girl with nothing to fear for she'd been more curious than ever. Alex behind her, hand tight around her shoulder, best buds, and Delilah squeezed him back tight. *I'm here to protect you,* he thought he heard her say.

Dropping down the last step and nothing out of the ordinary, wide square space, a single pool table scrawled with Alex's pre-pubescent poetry, stacks of newspapers, dust bunnies and landmines of mouse shit. One wall was swarmed with orchids that were growing from huge pots; long green stems stabbed the air, petals swirled white and red opened their eyes. A rare carrion species from South Africa looked like a vile head of cabbage and stunk like evil. Alex loved orchids; he'd been growing them since he was a kid and had mastered their intricate care. Orchids are some of the most fastidious flowers in the world; too much or too little water, light, and air could kill them instantly.

"I don't see what you mean," Delilah said, small joint between pursed lips colored in pale red.

"It's empty, I know. But it's down here. I'm scared out of my wits. I wanna go upstairs."

"Not yet," Delilah scowled, gritting her teeth so hard she drew blood.

"It's like a whole new world. I don't know my own home."

Alex was half right. Delilah could feel the strangeness down here, could smell it in the musty air: Hell, the devil's lounge, whatever you'd call it. A room that collected sadness like flies on a glue trap, a jar full of rage spilled from the shelf of madness. Bad room, indeed, but what made it this way? What was the secret?

They both walked further in; Delilah noticed daylight was nowhere to be found, blocked by the notorious piles of newspapers on the adjacent wall. Their hands broke by the pool table, bad luck to separate, like lovers who let go at the sight of the oncoming pole on a romantic stroll, and then break up a month later. Delilah ventured to the closet, black boots moving across the basement floor like an ice skating rink made of gravel and mist.

She thought about the only television to ever set foot in this house, that it was locked in that closet because reading is fundamental: the television only brainwashes. Alex planted himself by the orchids, sitting Indian, eyes closed, his face covered by those vampiric hands, his black nail polish like bugs crawling across his head.

"I don't want to see what you're going to do," Alex said, putting a joint in his mouth and lighting it until cinders billowed down to his lap.

Soon the basement was filled with smoke, swamp fog smell and thickness, too misty to see in front of you. Delilah cackled because she was always the tough girl. Nothing scared her; she didn't believe in ghosts.

And then she heard a faint scratching noise.

Captain Howdy wants attention.

"I'm going upstairs. I don't give a fuck anymore!"

Alex scrambled away, broomstick legs running so fast Delilah barely had enough time to scream for him to stop, to stay with her in this cavernous hole fit for an underground library, Bat Cave's evil sister. Fuck it. Delilah's hand found the doorknob and she opened the door so fast something came tumbling down toward her: dirty ragged hair, faint white hue of pissed off eyes in its face. Delilah did a pratfall as she stepped backward, but saw that it was only a mop. Simple mop, and embarrassed, Delilah kicked the floor, hurting her ankle.

Then another scritch-scritch-scritch. Flies buzzing inside her head, keys slammed to the counter.

In a fit of rage she threw her arms into the closet, pulling out the television by its chord; blankets as old as Alex's grandparents full of wasted smells and old basement air came out too, and old photographs scattered everywhere. Ancient family portraits of ancestors long dead, the women of the first settling family dressed in sober black lace, fresh as pilgrims marching off the Mayflower and running scared of the war-scarred land.

Then there are other photos, from the early '70s, tie-dye patterns, swirly bell bottoms and long hair knotted down the entire length of her back. The woman resembles her puritan ancestors; Alex too. She's in all the photos, ones taken in the very living room above Delilah at the same grand piano, same fingers as Alex, playing and smiling. Delilah knows that this is Alex's mother by the signature sharp features and long black hair delicate as rain. There are hand written piano scales, lyrics too, and notes about strange things happening when she played her music.

Scritch-scritch-scritch.

Delilah heard enough. She gripped the hang bar, pulled her legs to her chest and plowed them through the wall. An explosion of sheetrock and old spider webs blasted her, and below the pile a small rodent stirred, afraid of the big monster in front of it with the painted nails and lips pulled tight over teeth.

The mouse's eyes are black as sin, but Delilah picked it up by its scruff anyway, cradling it between her arms and couldn't help but to laugh. It was proof that Alex was wrong, that dead mothers can't rise from the grave and come back to haunt their offspring. Ghosts are not real. Reality itself is what we should be afraid of.

But then Delilah hears the piano take charge.

Notes drummed above her head; deep dark chords weeded their way through the thin floor boards as if some vicious plant. The song is well practiced, dreamy, can put a motion movie soundtrack to shame, can make the symphonies of Beethoven and Mozart sound amateur. The beat goes on and Delilah sits by the photos, smoking the last of her joint, watching the room grow smaller around her, darkening like that tunnel she seems to always walk through in the slippery void between sleep and dream. Each note is quick and haunting as chamber music in a seventeenth century play.

Then the photos next to Delilah begin to stir. Not just stir, but come together, paper and ink globs melding into one entire being. And then it happened. First it's the hair, and then it's the whispering, and then Delilah sees its eyes: careless and lost, palest green like a lucky charm, deep sea gem brought up by brash fisherman. The hand comes up from the floor first, slimed in plasma, reeking of death and confusion and brine. Delilah dropped the rodent and bolted for the top of the stairs, just in time to see Alex waiting for her with his foot stamping the floorboards.

She was a believer now.

What Grows In Between

By Sally Bosco

The house stood like a piece of modern artwork, its angular form a sharp contrast to the soft oaks, pine trees and lilacs that filled the northern Massachusetts landscape. Rectangular sections jutted from its center core like a hand of outstretched fingers.

Daniel watched Emily climb out of the car and stretch from the long trip then drink in the fresh alpine air. "Look at it—poetry in architecture. I can't believe this place is ours." She took a few steps toward the geometric wonder that was all wrapped in smooth white skin with rounded edges. This house reflected all of her dreams.

He followed behind carrying the suitcases. "It's a marvel, no doubt about that." Though Daniel didn't have the same enthusiasm she had for the place, he acknowledged the fact that it was an architectural wonder. He'd give her that.

"It's been my dream to live in a real Givornay house and now it's happening. A bit better than Manhattan, right?" She took small steps toward the front of the house like a devotee approaching an altar.

"God, yes, and it's a hell of a lot better than St. Simon's." Anything was better than that hellhole. Though it had lush lawns and tennis courts, it had still been a prison to him.

"Don't think about that now, sweetheart. It's all behind you." She held the key out in front of her. "Ready to go inside?"

"Sure."

Emily inserted the key into the plain, white monolithic door and twisted. When she looked inside her breath stuck in her throat, and she made a gasping sound. "It's so beautiful."

Daniel stepped uneasily into the front hall and glanced at the cavernous room with its angular stairway. Just like the outside, it was white with rounded edges like a 1950's refrigerator. *This place gives me the creeps,* he thought. Emily was so enthusiastic about the house; he didn't want to spoil her moment. It would

Machiko (Finding Truth) by Beth Murphy

probably be fine. He'd get used to it. If it made her happy, that was enough for him.

She twirled around with her arms extended gazing up at the high ceiling. "I love this place." She stopped, still swaying from side-to-side. "Thank God we didn't get one of those old farmhouses."

Like the one I wanted. Go ahead and say it. At least those houses were real, not molded plastic monstrosities. Okay, he knew the house wasn't actually plastic, but it looked like plastic and felt synthetic.

"I love the fact that this place is brand new. There are no weird, creepy attics, no basements with ghosts, no antiques that other people have handled. Those give me a weird vibration, but this house is all new and clean with no clutter. That's the way we like it, right?"

"I suppose." Daniel placed the luggage onto the immaculate white tile floor.

"You don't sound very enthusiastic."

"I'm sorry. The house is amazing, no question about it." He needed to try to like the place—for Emily's sake.

They brought in groceries from the car and made dinner in the chrome and white kitchen. Chicken stir-fry seemed like an easy-prep meal, so they both got to work chopping vegetables. Emily made rice and Daniel prepped the pan. When Daniel went to turn on the burner he couldn't figure out how to operate it. The multiple dials and buttons irritated him. "Do they make this stuff purposely confusing?"

Emily glanced at the stove. "Here." She punched some buttons and the burner glowed. "All ready." She gave him a sweet smile.

All of the furniture was designed to fit the house. The dining room had a long white Plexiglas table with angular white chairs shaped like the letter "S." They couldn't be more uncomfortable. Daniel shifted in his seat, unable to find a position that didn't press on his tailbone.

They'd made a pact to get rid of or store all of their furniture, keeping only minimal personal effects. Daniel was sorry he agreed to that. He missed his comfortable old recliner and the beat-up oak desk he had since he was a student. *Relax, Daniel. Just relax. Stop thinking.*

When it was time to clean up, Emily opened the door beneath the kitchen sink. She scowled.

"Daniel, come in here and look at this."

As Daniel squatted down in front of the sink one of his knees popped and he winced at the sensation. "I'll be damned." The plumbing under the sink was worn and rusted, like it was fifty years old. Water dripped out of a joint that had been patched with some kind of sealer.

"What's with the old plumbing?" she asked in an uncertain tone.

"I have no idea, but we'll call someone tomorrow and get it all fixed up."

"Thanks, honey." She hugged him.

After dinner they settled into the master bedroom, a room that extended out over the landscape. Structures that jutted out with no support made him nervous. He had a hard time stepping out onto cantilevered apartment and theater balconies; the observation deck over the Grand Canyon had given him a panic attack; and now he had to face living in a house like this?

And the bed jutted out from the wall like a granite slab. Sitting on the suspended object gave Daniel an unsettled feeling, like it might come loose from the wall and crash down to the floor in the middle of the night. The cantilevered room combined with the hovering bed gave him double anxiety.

"Do you miss it?" Emily asked.

Daniel knew exactly what she meant—the hustle and push of work in the financial district. He thought about her question intently—did he miss it?

"Yes and no. I miss the people I used to work with, I miss the excitement, but I don't miss the soul-crushing stress." He turned to face Emily, and took her in his arms. "This is going to be a good life for us. I can paint like I've always wanted to, and you can continue with your freelance architecture projects."

But he worried. Emily was considerably younger than he was. Would she get bored out in the sticks? No way. This house was her personal wet dream. She was in heaven. They'd make this the honeymoon he'd been too busy to take six months ago when they'd wed.

Still, sleep eluded him. He kept having dreams of the bed breaking away from the wall and smashing to the ground in the middle of the night, at which point he'd jolt awake and lie there with his eyes wide open.

In the morning, after a quick breakfast (now he knew how to turn on the burners, thank you) Daniel decided that while Emily was working on a freelance project he'd go up to his studio to paint.

As he hauled his easel and paints up to his third-floor garret, he thought about his years at Stemmons-Whitley. He'd been a partner in a hedge fund that made an obscene amount of money in a short period of time. It had been a heady experience coming into all that cash so quickly. But they had to fly high to maintain their position, and soon his daily job turned into a nightmare. He gave it all he had, and that took a vast amount of drive. First it was gallons of black coffee and energy drinks all day, then after work he needed to wind down with some Macallan scotch. But soon the coffee wasn't enough and he turned to coke, and the scotch turned to Nembutals. Hell, he could afford it. But it all came crashing down the night Emily, his grown son and three of their best friends staged an intervention.

Emily had an ultimatum for him. Rehab or she'd walk.

"Listen, Daniel," she said. "You've made enough to never have to work again. After rehab, let's check out of life in the fast lane, call it quits and get a place in the country before that life ruins you."

How could he say no to that? No reasonable man would. Still, it left him feeling neutered somehow.

His studio was a pie-shaped wedge that jutted out across the forest. Again, the cantilevered room gave him an uncomfortable feeling.

Daniel positioned his easel next to the window. The view of the countryside was breathtaking. He unwrapped a new canvas and got to work mixing colors. The scent of the oil paints brought him back to his youth when he loved to paint the trees at his grandparents' farm.

As he painted he thought about Emily. They'd met about one year ago—two years after his nasty divorce from his first wife—and it had been love at first sight, cliché though that might be. He gave her a new outlook on life, and her youth invigorated him. He liked her even-keel temperament, her ability to handle every situation. Her work as an architect never made her have to escape into using. But suddenly he resented her. It was easy for her. Little miss perfect. What hardship had she ever had in her life? It dawned on him, that's why she loved this house—everything in it was perfect. But he shouldn't feel that way; she'd saved him from his hamster wheel life of uppers and downers.

Daniel brought his focus back to the beautiful view. He tried to capture a pine tree with a few strokes, but it looked all wrong to him. The sterile white of the room left his creativity drained. He longed for a beat up couch on which to lounge, a wall that had dings and nicks from previous tenants, a room that stunk of cigarettes. There was not a speck of dirt or an article out of place anywhere. The house was so freakin' perfect.

He loaded up his brush and tried to capture the soft shape of the rolling hills in the distance. It all looked like crap to him. Face it; he had no talent. Blaming the house was only an excuse.

In the afternoon he supervised the plumber.

The man pushed his baseball cap back on his head. "Well, I'll be damned. The old plumbing only goes as far back as the sink. Everything that extends outside of that is brand, spankin' new."

"I have no idea why that would be, but go ahead and fix it."

It took the plumber about two hours to make it all fresh.

That night Daniel made a simple dinner of salad, salmon, broccoli, and quinoa with mushrooms. It was part of their pact to eat healthier out here…and that he'd cook. That was fine; he could handle that.

"This is wonderful, Daniel," Emily said savoring her herb-roasted salmon. "Thank you so much."

"Thank *you*. I thought that after dinner we could go out to look at the stars."

"Honey, that sounds wonderful, but I have to finish up this project. It's my own..." she made air quotes, "...modern art house. Just a little more in OUWIE, and I'll be done."

"What's OUWIE?"

"That's my 3-D rendering program. You didn't think we still drew out blue prints, did you?"

"Oh, no." He vaguely thought she did but realized that was silly.

She finished her dinner and got up and kissed him before she made a move to head back toward her office.

"When do you think you'll be done?"

"I have a deadline, so I'll be working most of the night." On her way out the door she turned to him. "After this my schedule will be clear for a while, so we'll be able to do stuff together, okay?"

"Yeah, sure." He loaded the dishes into the dishwasher and decided to go out to look at the stars by himself. That was just great. They moved out here to spend some quality time together and now all she could think of was work.

He walked around to the far side of the house. That's when he saw it.

"What the hell?"

Tucked into the side of the house was a cellar door. It had gray double doors set slanted into the ground on a metal frame set in cement—the kind of cellar door people used to access storm basements. In fact, it reminded him of the one his grandparents had years ago. That cellar held canned peaches, homemade jams and jellies, and the makings for strawberry rhubarb pie. He could practically smell his grandmother's homemade peach pies.

Could this have been there all along and they didn't notice it? Was he dreaming? He pinched himself. *Ouch!* No. In the bright moonlight he could see rust on the handles, which meant it hadn't sprung up yesterday.

He wanted to run in and grab Emily to tell her about it, but he had an unreasoning fear that if he went in to get her, when she came out it'd be gone. Was he losing his mind? He remembered hearing something about how if you were under a great deal of stress that suddenly went away, you could experience hallucinations, like post-traumatic stress syndrome.

He took out his phone and snapped a photo then checked it. Yeah, it was a photo of an old-fashioned cellar door after all. He texted the picture to Emily. There. That was proof positive. What if the photo was blank? No harm done. He didn't actually say, "Look at this cellar door growing out of our house." While he waited for Emily's response, he tried the doors. They were stuck, and he was kind of glad, because he wasn't sure he wanted to see what was down there.

His phone beeped. It was a text from Emily. *Where are you?*

He answered, *Outside the house.*

Very funny, she responded. *What great Photoshop skills you have.*

No, it's real. Come outside.

He'd have to go in and get her. She was so wrapped up in her work she'd never come out on her own.

But he didn't have to go in and get her. She came rushing around the side of the house with a sweater thrown over her to ward off the chilly night air. "Will you quit goofing around with me. I have work to..." At the sight of the cellar door, she stopped, dumbfounded, and gaped at Daniel.

She squeezed his arm to the point of bruising. "What the fuck have you done? Did you get this on eBay and stick it to the side of the house?" She went over to it and pushed it with her foot. "How the hell did you do that?" She kicked it "Ouuwww," and held her foot with tears in her eyes. "What did you do, cement it? You defaced this incredible magical house because you can't take living in something that's new and modern. I don't know how you did this, but I don't think it's funny. Get rid of it now."

"I did not put the cellar door there. It just appeared."

"How dumb do you think I am? Things don't just appear."

"Well then someone put it there. But it wasn't me."

"You promise. You swear to God?"

"I do."

Emily, who was not inclined to believe in anything she couldn't prove scientifically said, "Let's go to bed and we'll deal with it in the morning."

Daniel slept on the couch that night—the unyielding white plastic couch.

He hoped they'd wake up in the morning and the thing would be gone.

But in the morning the cellar door wasn't gone. They examined it in the light of day. "Daniel, this is the north side of the house, and there's moss growing on the cement around the door. This has been her for a while. It had to be here the whole time and we just didn't see it."

"Are you kidding me? As many times as we drove out here to look at this house, you think we missed a nineteenth century cellar door stuck on the side of a Givornay house for Christ sake? One of the most visionary architects of the twenty-first century would do that? You have the plans. Check it out."

They went upstairs and Emily brought the plans up on her over-sized monitor. "No cellar door. You're right. I can only think that some vandals stuck it there as a joke."

"How does that explain the moss?"

"They faked it," she said as though stating the most obvious thing in the world.

"Okay. What do you suggest we do?"

Emily shrugged. "Report it to the police, of course."

They did, and the officer who came out looked at them as though they had unicorn horns growing out of their heads, but when he saw the cellar door he whistled. "This is a serious prank, defacing a building like this. We'll put out a bulletin to find the culprits. Probably some of those art students making one of their installations. You know, when they put on some kind of public demonstration or show they hope will get them noticed?"

"Yeah." Emily sighed and put her hand to her chest. "That makes me feel better…that we're not going out of our minds."

"No, I assure you. It's a prank, and we'll catch the offenders."

They tried not to think too much about the cellar door. It stood there like a stage prop. It wouldn't open, and seemed to be mainly decorative. That was fine. They accepted that explanation.

Until the front porch appeared.

They woke in a light-hearted mood. Things weren't so bad. So what if art students had punked their house? Daniel inhaled the reassuring sent of their morning coffee. Emily poured herself a cup and headed toward the front of the house. "I think some flowers might look nice out front. Break up the severity of the house, you know? I'm going to check."

After about five seconds he heard a blood-churning scream. "Aaaeeiiiahhh." *Crash.* "Daniel!" she shrieked.

He rushed outside to find her face ashen, her coffee cup shattered into a million pieces and coffee spilled out over the wooden floor. Wooden floor? "What?" He looked out to see wooden posts and a wrap-around front porch like you'd see on an old farmhouse. "Holy shit."

"Is this the work of art students, too?" Emily grabbed onto him and scanned the forest.

"No. No, it can't be." Daniel felt reality shift on him, like a section of flooring had crumbled under his feet. He sat down, and not until he was seated did he realize he'd parked his butt into a wooden rocking chair. Again, he did a quick reality check—he pinched the skin on his forearm hard. No dream. *Damn!*

After Daniel got his bearings, they both stepped away from the house, far enough to see the whole thing in perspective. Someone had removed the clean, white lines of the modern facade and replaced it with a wooden front porch with a railing around it. You half expected to see ladies in pastel dresses, sitting in rocking chairs, drinking mint juleps and fanning themselves. Emily sobbed hysterically.

"All that we paid for this house, and somebody's ruining it. The local police force sucks." He put his arm around her.

"Think about it. It would be impossible for someone to have replaced the front of this house in one night without us hearing it."

Nonetheless, Emily called the local police and reported it. Again, an officer drove out and surmised it was a prank perpetrated by art students.

That was the night weird things started happening *inside* the house.

"It's your fault," Emily pulled off her clothes and donned her white terrycloth robe. "This house knows you don't like it."

"That's crazy. How can my feelings affect a house?"

"I don't know, but that's what's happening." She went to the bathroom to take her nightly shower, shut the door as usual and ran the water to steam up the room.

Daniel tried to read a book, but he couldn't concentrate. *She has some nerve blaming me for whatever's going on with this house. She was the one who wanted to move to this Godforsaken place, and I went along with it. Stupid idiot me.* It was time to break open his secret stash, so he went downstairs to the dining room, opened one of the thousands of identical white cabinets and pulled out a bottle. Macallan scotch. He poured himself a stiff one and chugged it. The nectar of the gods. There was nothing like a good Macallan. Why had he waited so long to lose himself in its peaty goodness?

That's when he heard the screams.

"Daniel, Daniel, help!" Emily sounded like she was a million miles away.

He plunked his scotch down on the dining room table and rushed up the stairs two at a time. "Emily." When he reached the bathroom, the door opened easily. "Emily, where are you?"

"I'm here in the bathroom. I think we had a power failure, because it's dark. I can't see anything. I feel like I'm in a coffin. Help me!"

"Where are you?"

"For Christ sakes! Do you even listen to what I say? I'm in the bathroom." She sounded muffled like she was in a closet.

He rushed around to all of the closets and opened them.

"What's taking you so long? This isn't funny. I'm scared." Her voice sounded like it was coming from inside the wall.

"Emily, I'm *in* the bathroom. The lights are all on, and you're not here."

"Are you in the ensuite off our bedroom?"

"Yeah, that's where I am."

"Stop being mean." She broke into a torrent of sobs.

"I'm not being mean. Keep talking."

"I'm trying to touch things around me, and I can feel a wall, but it's rough; it's definitely not smooth tile like our bathroom. I'm pretty sure it's wood." He heard her take a quick deep inhale. "I turned around and I can touch the other wall. I'm in a small space like I'm buried."

He tried to gauge her location from her voice. "Are you standing up or lying down?"

"Standing up. Oh, hurry. The oxygen is running out in here."

"Keep calm. I'll find you. I promise. Keep talking."

"Do you remember when we first met?" Her voice was broken up by intermittent sobs. "I was so taken with you. You had such self-confidence."

Then he realized that the walk-in shower was sealed over. He wasn't familiar with the house so he didn't see it immediately. The area was so smooth he couldn't tell that there had ever been a shower there. It was as though the spot had healed over like scar tissue walling off an injury. "Emily, sit tight. I have to go get some tools."

"Don't leave me."

"I have to, but I'll be right back." He ran so fast he gasped for air as he searched around the garage, not sure what he was looking for. Certainly the gardeners had left some tools in there. But he'd never used a tool in his life. He found a sledgehammer and a chain saw. He'd never used either one, but he'd watched those home improvement shows where they did demolitions of kitchens or bathrooms. Well, he was about to demo a multi-million dollar piece of art.

After he bolted up the stairs, Daniel was so short of breath he thought he'd have a heart attack.

"Emily, are you still there?"

"Yes." Her voice sounded weak this time. "I'm here, but I'm having trouble breathing."

"As much as you can, stand back from the wall—the side where you can hear my voice, okay?"

"All right. What are you going to do?"

"I'm going to get you out. Just stand back." He aimed for the area to the right of the linen closet, picked up his sledgehammer and gave the wall a mighty whack. It barely dented the surface.

"Oh, my God, I'm going to faint." Her voice sounded weak and small.

"Hang on." He whacked the wall again for all he was worth. The outer coating shattered like glass, and he saw that he'd bashed a tiny hole all the way through.

"I can see light!" Emily said.

"Awesome. Stand back now. Cover your eyes." He made the hole a little bigger by pounding the hell out of it then got in there with his chain saw—an electric one, thank goodness—and opened up the hole. There she was, crouched on the floor naked looking small and terrified. He demolished the rest of the wall and lifted her out.

"What happened?" she asked.

He pulled a terry robe from a hook on the wall and wrapped it around her shivering frame. "If I didn't know how crazy this sounds, I'd say that the house swallowed you up."

She dusted the plaster chips off her legs, "I'm not staying here."

"I'm inclined to agree."

They each packed a small bag—Emily brought her laptop—and they headed for a motel in town.

In the morning they went to a café and had breakfast. After that Daniel dropped Emily off to work in the reassuring atmosphere of the local library. While she worked he went to the clerk of the county court to look up records on the house. It took a considerable amount of time and effort locating the history of the house, but when he did, it all started to make sense. He made copies and brought them over to Emily at the library.

Emily still looked pale and scared sitting at a wooden table in the library by herself.

"I went to the county to look up records on the house."

"But I did all of that before."

"You didn't look up the history of the land before the present structure was built. Here's the original house." He took a photocopy out of this briefcase and showed it to her.

She scowled. "This house was here before our house was?"

"Yes. See? The house was wooden. There's the front porch, the same one that grew on our house. And here's the interesting thing—our current house was built on the footprint of this older house. It's dated 1884."

"How did I not know this? How did my research on the house not turn this up?"

"No idea, but if you look at the plans for the house," he tossed her a photocopy of the plans, "you'll see that the current house exactly overlays the old one."

"What does that mean?"

"I'm not sure." He sat down next to her at the wooden table.

"What do we do?"

"I say we stay in the house."

"Easy for you to say. You weren't just swallowed up. I'm not going back there."

"I think if you stay with me you'll be all right." As they sat next to each other, he pressed his shoulder up against hers.

"Why would that be?"

"I don't know. I think I'm in harmony with the vibe of the old house."

"You're so weird."

When they returned to the house they were relieved to see that nothing more had changed. The gentle light of dusk made lacy patterns on the house, softening it. The vintage porch was still attached to the front, and the cellar door was still glued to the back.

It seemed less scary now, more livable.

"Do you think you could sleep here tonight?" Daniel asked.

"No."

"Try. It'll be okay."

She said nothing, just turned away from him and crossed her arms in front of her chest.

He rubbed her shoulders. "Listen, tomorrow I'll find a contractor who will remove the front porch and the cellar door and restore our beautiful modern house to its full glory, the way Givornay intended."

"You really will? You're not just saying that?"

"I promise you."

Reluctantly she agreed to stay.

In the middle of the night, Daniel woke up feeling claustrophobic; like it was so hot and stuffy he couldn't breathe. And it was so freakin' dark. They really should get a night-light. When he put his hand out in front of his face, he hit something solid.

He realized he was enclosed in a box of some kind, perhaps under the floorboards. "Help! help! Get me out of here!" he screamed until he thought his lungs would bleed. Then he pounded and scraped at the wood enclosing him until his arms gave out, and he felt splinters under his nails. "Help! Emily, are you there?" He thought he heard her muffled reply.

* * *

William Shatner fixed his hair and stood on the wooden front porch, making sure that his good side faced the camera. An assistant snapped a clapboard in front of him. "Take one."

Shatner assumed a serious squinty-eyed expression. "This may be an ordinary wooden house, but its benign exterior holds a tale of terror and madness. This house was at one time a super modern structure designed by the internationally renowned

French architect, Paul Givornay. We'll have an interview with him later. This modern artwork house slowly transformed itself into its former shape—a farmhouse that was originally built in 1884. If that isn't hair raising enough, its new owners disappeared mysteriously without a trace. Is tonight's story *Weird or What?* Is it the tale of some bizarre inter-dimensional architect, or is it merely a hoax? Only you can decide."

"That's a wrap. Eerie music and fade to commercial," a young woman with a clipboard said.

Shatner turned to the producer and camera crew. "Let's get out of here guys. This place gives me the creeps."

Doorway by Rose Blackthorn

Night Flowing Down

By Melissa Osburn

Lila's heart soared as she and Jordan rode up the long dirt path. A Dutch Colonial emerged into view, nestled into a large meadow surrounded by pines and maples. Her fingers sought her camera bag next to her. Jordan chuckled, sounding pleased. The car halted before the house, and Lila craned her neck, dipping her head to stare through the windshield, mouth agape at the edifice. She drew her camera bag onto her lap, unpacking the device without looking.

The white paint was peeling and the boards underneath weathered to a fine gray, skin shedding to reveal the bones below. On one side, wild grapevines had conquered the wall, their questing, creeping tendrils finding the smallest nook to take hold. Young fruit had begun to form, and pale green clusters dangled, winking into view when the breeze lifted the leaves. Some of the windows were cracked; one had a perfect circle with jagged lines radiating outward, a starburst caught in glass. It winked in the bright sunshine.

"Where did you find this?" Lila asked, her voice a harmony of awed excitement. She opened the car door and unfolded gracefully from the seat. Holding the camera in her hands, she started snapping pictures. The device making soft whirring and snickering sounds.

"Greg lost it in a hand," Jordan said.

"Remind me never to play poker with you," Lila said with a twist of her lips.

"Don't worry, I'd only let you lose your shirt and maybe your pants."

"Ha-ha," she said dryly but smiled, her eyes dancing.

The lawn was overgrown; graceful sweeping blades of grass tickled Lila's thighs as she waded through the sea of green to the door. Perhaps shorts hadn't been such a good idea. Ticks and snakes could be lurking, waiting for their next victim. Her steps became careful, measured, her eyes on the ground. She peered into the window, her hand cupped before her eyes to prevent glare from obstructing her view. Lila could see only shadowy forms inside. Jordan appeared beside her.

"Do you want me to check you for ticks?" Jordan asked, unlocking the door.

"Maybe later, Romeo." Lila laughed and followed him inside.

Weak streams of sunlight poured in through grimy windows, dappling the carpet and the sofa in shades of gold. Lila wrinkled her nose. Dust and mildew crept into her lungs and she coughed. Jordan strode to the nearest window and opened it with a brief, groaning struggle, flooding the room with fresh mid-summer air and sending dust motes leaping and twirling in the breeze. Lila held the camera to her eye and snapped a picture of Jordan standing in the sunlight surrounded by darkness and dancing specks of golden dust.

"Did Greg tell you anything about the house?" Lila wandered over to the bookcase tucked in an alcove to the right of the door. A narrow stairwell, carpeted in green the shade of forest moss, twisted upward to the topmost floor of the house. Curious, Lila stood at the side of the stairs, trying to discern what lay beyond the sun-mottled gloom of the second floor. She could see nothing but the stained ceiling framed by the winding banister. Glancing over her shoulder, she spied the crooked line of books in the case. They called to her and she concentrated on perusing the works, hoping she'd have the chance to later explore the loftier half of the house.

The shelves were laden with tomes of every size. Cracked, leather-bound volumes crowded slender books with golden lettered titles. As Lila watched, a pale sepia-colored spider skittered along the ghostly silken web. It tempted her, and she seized her chance, catching the arachnid's stroll with her camera.

"Only that it belonged to his great aunt. She was a spinster."

"Spinster, really, Jordan? In this day and age?"

"I'm using his word. I'm all for women being independent," Jordan said, laughing. "She was unmarried. Better?"

"Yes, thank you," Lila said, amused. She floated along the bookcase.

"She was put into a nursing home about six years ago and then passed away. Greg was her only living relative, so the house came to him."

"Does Greg have a gambling problem?" Lila paused, frowning. There were books on various hobbies such as crocheting, cooking, and decoupage, as well as children's books. Winnie the Pooh sat next to *Taxidermy for Fun and Profit*. She shivered but took a picture of the juxtaposition of genres and turned away.

"Why did auntie have picture books if she was childless?" Lila ventured back around the corner, finding the living room empty. She stood alone amidst the petite sofa, lilac chairs, and dusty knick-knacks. A shadowbox with a mirrored back reflected her own bemused expression, fractured and doubled. It was the only thing on the bare walls. "Jordan?"

"Back here."

Lila followed the sound of his voice through the living room and into the dining room. A rosewood table stood before a pair of large windows covered in moth-eaten lace. Lila wove around and fingered the delicate material, fascinated with the pattern. Roses capered in the fabric, and the leaves were vacant staring eyes veined with thread. Beyond the grubby window, the wild lawn, home to drowsing wild carrot, chicory, daisies, and spreading lilies, stretched out to meet the edge of a lake. Lila stepped back and framed the shot.

"Beautiful." She sighed, lowering the camera. Jordan drew her to his side and kissed her cheek.

"You are an odd one, Li."

"You just don't appreciate beauty. I do."

"There's one beauty I do appreciate," Jordan said, his hands roaming along her back. Lila giggled and danced out of his grasp.

"Don't distract me. I want to work."

"I didn't bring you here so you could work."

"I'm not having sex with you in a dead woman's house, Jordan." Lila crossed the faded carpet, drawn to the china cabinet against one wall.

"I didn't bring you here for sex." He sounded irritated. Lila shot him a look of disbelief and opened the cabinet.

"Uh-huh." The shelves of the cabinet were lined in doilies, a pattern of pineapples draped over the edge in cobweb curtains. Neat rows of dolls perched in the murky gloom of the hutch. Glass eyes bored into her, and delicate faces smiled secretive smirks, unable or unwilling to divulge their confidences.

"What did you bring me here then?" Lila captured the cluster of dolls on film. She grinned, thrilled with the material she had gathered, and turned away from the sea of empty eyes. Lila sighed, smile melting. Jordan had disappeared.

"Jordan?" She shut the cabinet door with slightly more force than was required, rattling the contents. The dolls lurched drunkenly; several tumbled sideways. Faint laughter floated from another room and prickling goose flesh erupted along her skin. She ignored her collecting dread, focusing it into annoyance.

Lila swore under her breath, slung the strap of the camera over her head, and walked to the door. Warily, she swung the portal open.

"Jordan?" Lila found herself in a cramped kitchen. Cupboard doors hung open, displaying boxes of cereal with frayed corners, and tins of hot chocolate mix, dust covered spices and canisters of pasta. A small table sat against a pair of windows, two empty coffee cups resting on its grayed surface. The mugs' interiors were stained dark, as if the coffee had been left in them and slowly evaporated. A white door stood opposite her in the midst of a narrow strait formed by the chipped counters. Outside, the sky was turning shades of gold and saffron, gilding the swaying grass and trees. All around her silence fell. She could hear the sounds of wind chimes somewhere in the distance. Lila grew uneasy. The breeze flowing in through the cracks of the window carried the sound of childish laughter. Lila stalked forward, her anger and fear urging her on. She grasped the doorknob and turned it roughly.

"Jordan, stop being such a—"

She fell, tripping on the edge of a rug and scraping her knee on the rough wooden planked floor. Cursing, Lila drew her knees up to her chest and examined the wound. It was a mere scratch. Only the top layer of skin had been torn and seeped blood. She touched it gingerly, hissing at the sting her gentle probe had wrought.

"Jordan!" Lila waited in silence for her call to be answered. "Dammit."

She sat in a bedroom. The pale pink walls were edged in a yellow rose pattern. Everywhere she looked, dolls of every size could be found. They graced the top of the bureau, sat lounging in a floral chair, and posed prettily in white wicker shadowboxes. Two sat on the bed, propped by lacy pillows. Their heads leaned together, while their eyes stared at her, appearing to conspire. A silver framed photograph stood on the bedside table. A girl of five or six posed before a flower garden, gowned in a white and blue dress. Lila studied the face of the child, finding the cherubic visage familiar.

Wanting to investigate, Lila braced herself to stand but stopped. A line with the thickness of a pencil, grooved through the floor. Lila moved the rest of the carpet, raising clouds of dust and dirt which plumed into the air. Before her was a trapdoor. The photograph of the girl fled her mind as intrigue blazed within her. Lila leaned forward. Her fingers skittered around the edge, questing for enough room to lift the door open.

A yawning maw of darkness awaited her as she swung the door open. Lila dug into her pocket for her penlight. The slender beam provided little illumination, but it was enough for her to discern that another room lay below. Grunting, Lila slipped over the edge and fell, landing on her feet. A brief, bone-numbing ache rippled through her legs, leaving her muscles stinging.

In the weak beam of her penlight, Lila began to explore. A table with several chairs and a desk covered in papers cluttered a small area, making her progress slow. The light revealed newspaper clippings with photographs, articles of missing girls. There were gaps in the dates, the first from May 21st of 1990 and the most recent, just a few years ago, occurring on November

16th of 2008. Lila read names: Mary Frens, April Kestrel, Molly Wester, and Catherine Vickers among eight others. Each article was neatly clipped, preserved in a photo album. Holding her penlight in one hand, Lila took pictures of the collection, her skin crawling.

"Ma always wanted a girl," Jordan said above her. Lila started and spun around to face him, her heart lodging in her throat, almost choking her. He crouched near the edge of the opening. "I think it broke something inside her when I was born. The doctors told her that she wouldn't be able to have any more children."

"What?" Lila asked. She stared up at him. "Your mother?"

Jordan lifted a flashlight, a heavy duty, plastic monstrosity, and clicked on the switch. Lila raised a hand to shield her eyes, the beam blinding her. She heard him land, a soft but substantial thud as his feet met the concrete floor.

"It ruined her marriage to my father. He left us shortly after my fourth birthday, so I don't remember him much. Come on, I'll show you." Jordan gripped her arm in his hand. Lila hissed, struggling as her feet slid along the floor.

"If this is some sort of sick joke, Jordan, I'll fucking kill you," Lila said. Her stomach knotted, twisting tightly with icy fear.

The beam of the flashlight bounced, skittering off the walls. Flashes of the curling floral wallpaper sharpened, briefly visible before succumbing to darkness. Jordan tossed Lila in front of him. She stumbled and halted, spotting a doorway ahead of her. She shook her head, glancing back at Jordan. Lila did not want to know what was hidden. Jordan was nothing more than a silhouette; the light he held obscured him from her view.

"This is why I brought you here," he said. The beam of the flashlight focused on something in the room beyond. Lila looked in spite of herself, her head drawn inexorably to the enigma exposed.

Here was another table surrounded by chairs. Lila gasped, and her shaking hands fluttered to her mouth. Twelve dolls the size of children dressed in frilly party gowns abundant with lace and crinoline. Cobweb encrusted silk bows graced their hair. Lila stepped forward, recognizing the faces, remembering the stories captured in print. Nearest her sat Mary Frens, only nine when she disappeared from Wilkinson's Bakery. She smiled at Lila, eyes empty, a chipped teacup on the table before her. To Lila's right was Catherine Vickers, ten when she was discovered missing. She had been walking home from the library. The police had found her waterlogged books in the ditch along her route.

"I wanted you to meet my sisters," Jordan said. Lila felt him behind her. His flashlight jerked to the head of the table as his breath lifted the tendrils of hair along her neck. Lila screamed. The matriarch sat there, reigning, almost perfectly preserved. She grinned widely, if somewhat lopsidedly, frozen in time. "And my mother."

Lila backed into Jordan, pushing against him. She fought to escape but his hands were quick, biting snakes that would not let her go. She swore, struggling as he enveloped her in an embrace. Her fists struck his chest, and she lashed out with her legs, kicking furiously. Lila bit down on his hand as he tried to subdue her. She tasted blood and felt a thrill of triumph when Jordan cried out in pain. His grasp loosened, and Lila rushed ahead, flying toward the open door. She streaked down the wide, short hall. Papers fluttered in her wake. Lila bumped against the edges of the table and the chair as she waded through the furniture, reaching the trapdoor.

"Shit!" Lila stood freedom several feet above her. She heard Jordan swearing, the sound drawing nearer. Lila grabbed the nearest chair, scraping it across the floor, and placed it under the opening. She stepped onto the seat; it teetered dangerously under her.

Springing forward, she sent the chair flying. Her fingers scrabbled for purchase, nails digging into the gaps between the boards. She screamed as Jordan seized her legs. He yanked and her nails broke as she fought to keep her handhold. Lila kicked, her skin crawling as Jordan's hands slid down her calves to capture her ankles. Slowly she was losing ground. Lila sobbed as she watched her own fingers betray her. They uncurled as Jordan drew her down.

Lila fell, toppling down to land heavily on the floor. Her teeth clicked together, and a sharp, burning pain radiated through her torso, up along her jaw into her neck. She groaned, dazed, her chest aching from the wind that was knocked so violently from her lungs, her camera beneath her. Stars burst before her eyes, dancing orbs in the cellar night. Lila fought the urge to follow the will-o'-the-wisps into oblivion.

"I thought you were different," Jordan said. Lila crawled along the floor, discovering new injuries as she progressed. Pain shot through her, frolicking along muscles and reverberating through bone. Lila feared something might be broken, and she coughed, tasting copper. Roughly, she was jerked onto her back.

"When I met you, I thought I could finally share my secret. We could do it together, make a family." Jordan's face was shrouded in shadows, his hair gilded from behind by the light spilling from the open trapdoor, creating a dark angel.

"It's a damn shame." He shook his head ruefully, crouching beside her.

"Let me go, Jordan, please," Lila said, her voice hoarse as she drew in ragged breaths. She could barely move on her own. Beseeching him for her freedom was her only option. The pleading didn't sit well in her, coiling bitterly in her stomach.

Jordan gathered her into his arms, cradling her to his chest. Lila pushed against him but she was weak, her muscles rubbery. "You are so beautiful, even like this," Jordan said. His fingers traced the curve of her cheek as Lila wept. "I hope I can do you justice. My skills are a little rusty."

Jordan lowered his head to kiss her softly; one hand caressed her chin while the other slipped to the base of her skull. With deft hands, he swiftly broke her neck, then held her in his arms as the life fled from her, leaving them empty as those of a doll.

Demesne by Shawna L. Bernard

Silhouettes in Soil and Prose

By Jeff C. Carter

October 8, 1956

My name is Orrin Kirk. I live at 378 Chester Hill Road. I am twelve years old. I am writing this so that people will know what really happened. Does anybody use English anymore? Did the Reds blow up New York? How bad was the fallout? Well, if you have found this time capsule and can read these words, then none of that stuff ever happened.
Even if the world does go on, it is too late for me and my family. I don't have much time to explain, so here are some pages from my Honors English journal.

December 22

Georgie M. and I were making snowballs for a fight with the Morris boys, and I bet him five dollars that the Bears would cream the Giants.
Frankie Morris went home with a bloody nose, so I guess we won the snowball fight.

December 23

Big trouble! I don't have five dollars, so Georgie threatened to tell everyone that I had welched on the bet.
I don't want him sore with me because he's my only friend on the block. I haven't made any new friends since I skipped ahead two grades in school.

All the older kids in my grade think I'm a real crumb, even the ones in the Poetry Club and the school paper. Thank gosh I have a class with Esther and I can play with Georgie after school. I have to forfeit something, but the only thing he wants is the Black Diamond baseball glove I'm getting for Christmas. If Father finds out, I'm a goner.

January 9

What a day! We had a new bomb drill at school. Instead of crawling under our desks, Mrs. Ryerson had us all line up in the main hallway. It was boy-girl-boy-girl, so I made sure I was next to Esther. We all kneeled facing the wall, with our hands over our heads and our heads between our knees.

I was close enough to smell the shampoo in Esther's curly black hair. I usually get nervous around her, but since we weren't facing each other, it wasn't so bad. I snuck a glimpse of the gold necklace that had slipped free from her dress. It had a charm on the end that was a little star.

I asked her if she was scared and she said not really. I asked her what she got for Christmas and she told me that her family didn't celebrate Christmas. I did not know that she was Jewish. She said that she got a record player and we talked some about who was better, Little Richard or Elvis.

January 12

Terrible news! Tonight at the dinner table, Father told us that he had been to Esther's house!

Her parents had hired him to put in central air conditioning. While he was up in their attic, he peeked through their stuff. He said that he found a goat horn. Worse, he found an old family tree full of Russian names! He said that they were not Christians, and that they might even be commie spies. He ordered me to stay away from them, even Esther.

Father showed us a pamphlet he got in the mail from the Church of Star Spangled Wisdom. On the front there was an American flag wrapped in tentacles of orange and yellow flames. In the street below, a mob of leering Russian and yellow skinned soldiers were strangling women and children. Big letters shouted 'IS THIS TOMORROW?'

He waved the pamphlet about and said that, "the world was sliding into chaos." He said the Reds had the H-bomb, and when they dropped it on New York, the fallout would hit the whole East Coast.

I could tell that Mother was upset, because she took an extra pill after dinner. I was upset too, but I tried to hide it. Father doesn't know that I have a class with Esther.

February 2

This is my ticket from the Yale Peabody Museum in New Haven.

We took a field trip with our whole class and had a swell time. There were exhibits of dinosaur bones and meteorites, but the best part was easily the mummy exhibit.

It's a drag that Georgie wasn't there because he loves mummies. I wasn't too sorry though, because I got to spend the whole day with Esther.

One wall of the exhibit had a mural of a giant pyramid. Underneath the pyramid, there was a secret room, full of mummies and gold. That same stuff was displayed in the museum!

There were real honest to gosh mummies, wrapped up and wearing golden masks. Mrs. Ryerson said that the big sarcophagus belonged to a pharaoh named Nephren-Ka. The other mummies were servants and slaves. They had been buried to serve him in the afterlife.

At lunch, Esther and I sat together and talked about the exhibits. I thought all the Egypt stuff was neat, but she didn't. She said that her ancestors were the pharaoh's slaves, and they had been forced to build the pyramids. I remember seeing something about that in my beginner's Bible.

I got to talking and accidentally spilled the beans about my father and the stuff in her attic. I thought Esther would be mad, but she was just embarrassed. She told me that the ram horn was like an old trumpet that had belonged to her grandma. She made me swear not to tell anyone that she had relatives from Russia. I promised, and she looked mighty relieved.

We went back to the museum and saw the rest of the exhibit. At the end, there were some mummies from other countries. These were all bog mummies that had been buried in swamps. The swamp water preserved their skin and organs but dissolved their bones, so the bodies looked like melted tar.

One of them had a crooked hand with curled fingers and long brown nails. I couldn't believe we were looking at rotten corpses. The Egyptian mummies had seemed so peaceful that they just looked like they were sleeping. The bog mummies had wide open eyes and screaming faces.

Esther squeezed my arm the whole time, so I pretended like I wasn't creeped out. Still, I wouldn't go into a swamp for a thousand bucks.

February 4

Dinner was on hold because Father was working late again, so I finished my homework with time to watch The Vitacco Action Hour with Rocket Sampson. After that was The Adventures of Doctor Fu Manchu. I really like Fu Manchu's brunette assistant, Karamaneh. She reminds me of Esther.

The show had just started with its famous intro, "It is said that the Devil plays for men's souls. So does Dr. Fu Manchu, Satan himself, evil incarnate." That was when Father came home. He stumbled in and glared at the television set.

He said that he would "put a bullet in that gook's skull." Father never talked about Koreans unless he was really mad, so I should have known to keep my big mouth shut. Instead, I blurted out that Fu Manchu was from China.

Father stomped across the living room and kicked his boot through the screen of the television set. I froze up, unable to speak or move a muscle. Mother ran in from the kitchen and yelled at me, telling me that I should "never disagree with Father." She was shouting like she was angry, but I could tell that she was as scared as I was.

Father went down into the cellar and slammed the door so hard that the family portrait fell off the wall and broke.

Later, Mother and I sat at the dinner table. Father normally serves the food while we wait and talk about our day, but not tonight. Instead of eating or talking, Mother and I sat and listened to the angry sounds coming from the cellar. It sounded like Father was pounding on the floor.

I said I wasn't hungry, which was true, and asked to be excused. After Mother let me go, I heard her shake out a bunch of extra pills.

I fell asleep to the distant beat of hammering. I had a dream that I was still in the living room with the television set. I was watching Alan Worth: Space Explorer until a row of flickering shadows marched along the wall.

I turned and saw a chain gang of slaves in dusty turbans walking through the kitchen. A girl in front carried a torch that shined in her long black hair and gold star necklace. I wanted to go after her but I was frozen to the floor, so I watched them shuffle through the cellar door and out of sight.

Behind them came Father. He was dressed in robes, with the golden headdress and tall crown of a pharaoh. In one hand he carried a long hooked staff with a shovel blade on the bottom, in the other he held a blazing torch. The torch had a black mushroom cloud of smoke floating over it. Father marched blindly towards the cellar as he stared into the chaotic flame, trailing a long black shadow behind him.

I thought it was his shadow, because it had the shape of a pharaoh, and it followed in his steps. Then the walls and floor around the faceless shape turned black with rot, and I realized that it was a living, creeping corrosion. I could not tell if Father was leading it inside our home or if it was pushing him forward. They descended together with a terrible scraping sound all the way down the stairs.

I woke up and Father was standing over me with a shovel. We went down to the cellar. The concrete was all busted up. The chill of the frozen ground crept up my legs, and my fingers turned pale and numb. He said we were going to build a secret bomb shelter deep under the house and yard. He handed me my winter gloves and the shovel.

I tried to break the surface of the exposed black dirt, but it was like a block of solid ice. Father drank a beer and watched me fumble with the shovel. He called me a sissy, and said I had to learn how to do a real man's work. The more he talked, the harder I dug. Eventually I pretended that the brittle soil was his face, and the blade of the shovel sank deep.

I don't know how long I spent digging. I remember the cramps knotting up my hands, and the burning in my back. I remember sweat stinging my eyes, and hacking up wet clots of dust. The worst part was the sound, the scrape of metal against stone. It seemed to get into my bones.

Father kept drinking until he got real sad. He said that the commies were going to drop the bomb on New York any day now. All the people and buildings would burn into a radioactive cloud that would poison our food and water. He said that he was sorry for calling me a sissy, but he needed me to grow up strong, because we wouldn't just be fighting the Russians, but all the secret commies in our neighborhood.

I don't remember falling asleep. Father's voice and the cellar just faded to black until the only thing left was that scrape-scrape-scraping in my bones.

February 5

Mother shook me awake and told me to get washed up and ready for school. Before I could look her in the eyes or ask her any questions she zipped out of the room to start breakfast.

My whole body felt as stiff as a rusty bicycle. I was able to scrub the dirt from my skin and nails, but the dark circles under my eyes were there to stay. I got dressed and crept down the stairs.

Mother and Father were sitting at the table, just like any other morning. Mother piled steaming eggs onto my plate next to a towering stack of waffles and bright yellow glass of O.J. Father was hidden behind the Arkham Gazette as usual.

I ate quietly, afraid some noise would cause the wall of newspaper to crumble and reveal the faceless black pharaoh from my nightmare.

I cleaned my plate and Mother handed me my lunch box and coat. I was almost out the door and into the sunshine when I heard Father call out. He reminded me that the cellar project was our special secret.

I never knew how good school could be. I felt protected by the walls, teachers and books. Being around other kids, even the older kids that didn't like me, made me feel safe and normal.

Esther was away on vacation, and part of me wanted to talk to her. The other part was glad though, because I wanted to pretend that last night never happened.

I wished that the day would never end, but it flew by faster than ever. Georgie wanted to ride bikes over to the skating pond and throw rocks at the ice, but I told him I had chores.

When I got home Mother took my school books. She said that she would do my homework so that I could help Father on his project. I tried to talk to her but she shook me off and pushed me to the cellar door.

I reluctantly opened it. I heard scraping sounds echo down below. The scraping stopped and everything was real quiet. I lowered myself one step at a time on numb and shaking legs.

The hole was deeper now, and so black that it swallowed the light that trickled down from the kitchen. I stood at the lip of it and trembled. It was like standing at my own grave.

A mud black arm reached out of the pit, followed by a pitch black face. Father was covered in an oily sheen of dirt and sweat. His eyes were sunken and hollow. He waved me closer with a sloshing beer can and when I didn't budge, he grabbed my wrist. His flesh was cold and gritty, but his grip was strong.

He pulled me down and I yelped as I fell. The bottom was deeper than I had imagined. How long had he been digging? I was about to ask when he pressed a shovel against my chest.

My fingers curled back around the handle. It fit perfectly into the blistered grooves of my hands. The digging had left its mark on me. The damp chill and smell of mildew was now familiar. I put my foot on the top of the spade and began to scrape.

Father stacked cinderblocks along the rough walls of the underground chamber. He explained that even if the house got destroyed, we would be safe from radiation. He showed me the stacks of steel and aluminum ducts that he had taken from his job. These would filter the fallout from the air coming in from outside.

We worked for hours, skipping dinner and stopping only to go to the bathroom in the corner of the cellar. When we finished, we had a small concrete walled cell. I noticed trickles of dark water seeping out between the cinderblocks of the walls and floor, but I didn't dare point it out. Father said we still needed shelves for supplies and a reinforced door to keep out commies.

I started to head upstairs to a well-earned dinner and shower when Father stopped me. He hollered up the stairs for Mother to bring down our camping bags. From now on, he said, we would sleep in the shelter, "in case the Reds dropped the bomb in the middle of the night." I was super hungry, but that sleeping bag looked better than any meal I'd ever seen. We all settled in on the damp floor and lay in uneasy silence.

I had another weird dream. I want to write it down before I forget.

I was standing alone in a field. I don't know if it was day or night, I couldn't see the sun. It must have been winter, because everything was cold and gray. It was our town, but the houses and trees were all gone. There was just a field of ashes that went on forever.

It started to rain, and the rain was black and hot. Soon the whole field was flooded, like a shallow bog. The muck started to bubble and millions of maggots began oozing out of the mud. I realized that the swamp rising around my feet was full of dead and rotting things.

I wasn't scared of the maggots. I was scared because they were trying to get away from something that was right underneath me. I tried to run and rough leathery hands wrapped around my ankles – that was when I woke up, to the sound of Mother crying.

My folks are now having bad dreams too. Mother is grabbing her stomach and moaning something about a girl. Father's hands are balled into fists. He says, "They won't take us alive."

February 6

Another sunny day. I washed the smell of mold off my skin, but I couldn't get the grime out of the corners of my ears and the little folds of my neck and eyelids. I didn't even bother cleaning my mud stained nails.

The kitchen cupboards and refrigerator shelves are all empty. Mother flitted about, humming as she emptied jars of rancid pickles and stale crackers onto our plates. She smiled at me, as if the food was fresh and homemade with love.

Some of the food was rubbery and some was brick hard, but I tore into it with my thick nails and scarfed it down.

Father sipped a beer and studied his pamphlets from the Church of Star Spangled Wisdom. He flipped through a book called 'ARE YOU READY?' On its cover, a wall of marching boots cast long shadows that stretched out to form the word 'CHAOS' in lumpy black letters. I saw that his hands were shaking.

At the bus stop, Georgie tried to give me back my mitt. I told him to keep it.

At school, I drifted through the halls like a ghost. The older kids were giddy about upcoming basketball games and spring dances. They were laughing like the world was going to go on forever.

When I got to first period, I stared out the window at the bare trees and gray sky. I watched flurries melt against the glass until I nodded off to sleep.

In my dream, the view outside the window was mostly the same, even though the calendar said MAY. A blizzard of fallout blew across the school grounds and buried the burnt and twisted trees in radioactive drifts.

The only light was a flame high up on the school flag pole. The flag sizzled and curled into a heap of black slag. Its smoking husk dropped off and hissed as it died in the poison snow.

Everything went black. I felt the walls close in on me. They were cold and wet, and when I opened my mouth to scream I tasted dirt. I was buried alive!

I clawed at the dirt, fighting against the walls of black that had swallowed me whole. I felt the scrape, scrape, scrape of my nails against chunks of stone. I didn't want to be trapped in the earth. I didn't want to die!

I woke up surrounded by shreds of white lined paper and torn up school books. Esther was screaming my name. I looked down and saw my fingers, hooked into gouges that I had scraped into my desk. My fingernails were broken and leaking blood.

Esther grabbed my arm and I pulled away. I screamed at her to, "Get her commie Jew hands off of me."

The entire class was silent. Esther buried her face in her arms and cried.

Mrs. Ryerson sent me to the nurse's office. I left class and went home instead.

Father was working in the yard, putting in the air pipes for the bomb shelter.

I couldn't remember the last time I had seen him in daylight. His baggy, mud stained clothing hung from his bony frame. His skin was encrusted with dirt. His hair and beard grew wild in greasy tangles. His fingers and spine were twisted, like they were crooked and broken. Against the glare of the white snow, he was just a faceless black shape. I could have sworn that he was a bog mummy that had escaped from the museum and followed me home.

A flicker of curtains snagged the corner of my eye. Mother peered out the window and then ducked out of sight. I caught a glimpse of pale skin and scared glassy eyes.

Father didn't ask why I was home early, or notice my bloody nails. He just told me to get to work. The house was full of canned food, water and supplies. I hauled the stuff down to the cellar while he put the big latch onto the shelter.
On my last trip, I noticed a box of rat poison. I don't remember even seeing a mouse around our place. I do remember Father talking in his sleep. He said they'd never take us alive.

* * *

There isn't much time. I have to go. A man came to our door looking for me. I think he was a truancy officer. Father says he was a spy. He says we need to get into the shelter immediately, so I only have a minute to get this down and bury it in the yard.

Father finally has his shelter in the cellar. He has plenty of supplies, and soon he will have me and Mother. I don't think he really wants to fight the commies, or to rebuild after the bomb. I think he wants to keep his family together, and this is the only way he knows how.

If you find this letter one day and decide to open the shelter, I pray that you find us perfectly preserved, like the Egyptians under a pyramid. I am afraid that won't happen, though. I'm afraid that you will find three twisted black husks, and they will look like they are screaming.

Dragonfly Girl by Ashley Scarlet

Moving Past the Ashes

By T. Fox Dunham

"I am a good man."

The Sturmbannführer laughed. "Emil Goldberg was a Jew."

"I am Emil Goldberg. My mother was Zofia Goldberg. I was born in Krakow on December 1st 1900. My father was . . ."

"Ashes. We burned them up. Your family. Your cousins. Your friends."

Emil thrashed in his bed clothes, pulling the sheet off the mattress. He reached his arm over to the empty side of the bed, searching for his wife. She'd always been there, to rub his arm, run her fingers through his silvery-blond hair and comfort him. *He's not real. Put those days behind you.* Three days ago, she collapsed at the market, and an ambulance took her to Philadelphia Mercy. Her doctors told him it was a stroke, and she'd yet to regain consciousness. Finally, they insisted that he go home and get some sleep. He refused to leave her side. He knew what waited for him.

Just a phantom. All in your mind. Let go the ghost.

"You are dust, butcher!" He reached for his cane, searching for the ivory elephant's head and found it in the dark by the bed. "I am alive. You rot." Sturmbannführer Kurt Goldschmidt cackled, standing in the faint light of the Philly street lamps shining through the lacy curtains. He stood in the semblance of death, wearing his full SS uniform—black fabric, leather jackboots, dark tunic styled with cording, and a sharp black cap bearing the death's head skull, the symbol of their power. When the SS marched, goose-stepping, it marched to murder.

"You are the ghost," the Sturmbannführer said. He laughed, his mouth wide exposing his pristine white teeth. Shadows consumed his face, mixing and twirling, hiding the eyes that had tormented him those years at the camp.

"Enough with your lies."

"On my honor as an officer in the SS. Meine Ehre heißt Treue."

"My honor is life," Emil said, translating aloud, responding by reflex. The motto of the SS was written onto the blade of every member, and a soldier in the Schutzstaffel kept the dagger for life. Nazi war criminals hunted down years later and brought to trial often kept the dagger, even though it incriminated them.

"You only need to step downstairs and open the cellar door to know the truth."

"The door is broken."

"Now you lie!"

Emil slashed at the air with his cane, hitting the curtains and knocking over the colored bottles his wife collected. The bottles crashed to the hardwood floor, broke into shards. He looked down to survey the damage, and when he returned his gaze, the Sturmbannführer faded back to the dark pit in his chest where he'd held him so close all these years, keeping him alive like a lover who can't let go of a shattered romance.

"The door is broken!" Emil yelled at the darkness. "It broke the day we moved here when we came to America."

Emil sweated through his pajamas, and he took off his drenched shirt. He ran his fingers down his furry chest and played in the raised scar tissue along his side—another reminder of his stay at Treblinka. He tried to sleep, but he sweated along with the city in the hot dry night. Finally, he picked up the receiver and dialed the hospital. He hadn't gone a night in twenty years without hearing her voice, her sweet words. She drove the butcher back into the pit.

A nurse answered. "There is no change in your wife's condition. We will call you immediately."

He sighed and hung up the phone then dried the sweat off his wrinkled forehead. He lay there for at least an hour, rolling from side to side. Wasps buzzed in his head.

"The cellar door is broken!" he yelled again into the darkness.

He rolled out of bed and hit the hardwood with his elephant cane. His leg still smarted from the work injury three years ago, though he managed once he was moving. He pushed out of bed, angling his long slender limbs. They had to buy special beds to accommodate his height, and he got to his feet. Even though he could not see the butcher, he knew he still lingered—always just beyond sight, inchoate in the night, always tormenting him at the edge of his thoughts. Other survivors from the camps often complained of the same mental malady, but they only spoke of it among themselves, keeping it away from the outsiders. The world spun on, but for them, time had frozen. The floor boards groaned beneath his girth. The old house moaned—the house of memories, of fondness and love, of twenty years lived in defiance. He had survived.

Emil descended the steps, carefully supporting his damaged leg and turned around the bottom. The house had been built in the 1800s, though it had been rebuilt twice, so most of the wood work was new. He stepped with care so as not to bump into the piano—his wife's instrument. He'd placed it in front of the old cellar door—not having any use for the leaky chamber. The previous owner complained that mildew grew wild with impunity, so they'd decided to just use the attic for storage and ignore the subterranean room. The old key hung on the wall above the piano, and he grabbed the key from the wall then unlocked the piano cover. He played an old German song—"Lilli Marlene"—and remembered the passion he'd felt when Marelene Deitrich sang it on the silver screen.

He finished the song then shut the piano. "I will show you the door is broken, butcher." He leaned over, using the piano to support his bad leg and slid the instrument to the side. He fumbled in the darkness for the doorknob. It had never been replaced when the previous owners renovated the row house on Walnut Street and still used an antiquated oval knob. The cold metal bit his skin. He gripped the knob but hesitated. Strength drained from his muscles, and he sighed, blowing out a long breath.

"Coward," the Sturmbannführer said. "Open the cellar door."

"I do not take orders from you anymore!"

Faces pushed through the black ink pouring into the dark parlor—white glowing visages rising from the ocean bottom and pressing to the light, to be seen, witnessed. The skin stretched over their skulls, hanging off the bones. Their emaciated bodies collapsed and broke to dust. They spoke sans words. They worked their mouths, yet no sound emitted. He didn't need to hear. He knew their accusations, saw it in their pale eyes—always staring, never blinking. He worked on the Sonderkommando crews—selected inmates to do the dirty work of the SS and allowed to survive longer. They carried the bodies in wheelbarrows and pushed them into the stoves. Each body collapsed like a forgotten child's doll, without regard, lost to time and then erased.

"Turn the knob," Goldschmidt said. "Be fast. I'm waiting." His hand trembled on the knob.

"It is broken and will not turn."

"You cannot imprison me forever! I will be free!" Tears smeared Emil's vision. "Do it now." Emil began to turn the knob. The knob freely spun, and he paused halfway through then released it. He grabbed his cane and ran back upstairs, nearly collapsing. When he reached his bedroom, Emil opened the dresser drawer, found his wife's sleeping pills and swallowed two. Then he hid his head in bed like a frightened child and waited for the soporifics to assuage his turbulent thoughts.

"Sleep now, coward." said the Sturmbannführer. "I will be waiting. We will try this again tomorrow and the next day. Never leaving. You killed them all. It was you, no matter how much you deny it, justify it. Then they burned to ashes."

"I only burned them. And that filth is on my hands."

The Sturmbannführer laughed and kept giggling far beyond the point when Emil fell mercifully into drugged sleep.

* * *

The next day, Emil woke to the sound of wailing in Walnut Avenue. An old black woman sat on the sidewalk and buried her face into her skirts. The keening echoed down the empty avenue—a Philly artery and the silence made it seem as if the city had choked and died. He got up, leaning on his cane, maneuvered his long body down the stairs and turned on the radio to hear the news, to learn of this sudden city syndrome.

The news from Dallas. President Kennedy has died at . . .

"Terrible shame, he thought. Such a nice young man."

He set the tea kettle on the stove and tried phoning the hospital. There was still no change in his wife's condition, and he poured tea, set out biscuits and placed his lunch on the end table by his threadbare chair. He put on his robe and checked the mail. A note stuck to his front door fluttered in the light breeze. He already knew whom it was from, and his hand shook, thinking the man had been to his house.

Mr. Goldman. I remember you from the camp. I was only there a short time before they closed the camp. I must see you. I must know if you remember my wife. We were friendly there. You have avoided my phone calls, so I feel no other recourse but to pay you a visit. Please expect me tonight at five. I apologize for this rude action. –Ezra.

Emil tore up the note and tossed the scraps into his tea. They floated, soaked up the liquid and expanded in the cup.

"You'll have to kill him," the Sturmbannführer said.

"I am not a butcher like you!" Emil said, yet still he listened, considering the Nazi's council.

"He will know the truth. He'll tell everyone in your community. You will be driven out. Your wife will leave you."

"Perhaps he will not remember what I did at the camp."

The Sturmbannführer cackled and quoted Emil: "Some places you never leave."

The tea burned in Emil's stomach. "I am not you!" he yelled. The Sturmbannführer laughed.

Emil lumbered upstairs, found his wife's sleeping pills and brought the bottle downstairs. He sucked three into his mouth and swallowed them down with tea sipped from the globs of paper floating in his cup. Then he eased back in his chair and let the apparition fade away. Narcotic fog suffused through his mind, and his memories turned to waking dreams.

"Work faster, Jew!" Sturmbannführer Goldschmidt yelled into the crematorium. The heat choked. Sweat poured down their faces, soaking their striped uniforms. The bodies kept coming—pale white. Their eyes hung open, watching, accusing—Jews brought in from Poland as the SS cleared the ghetto then transported them to Treblinka to be erased from the world.

Emil paused to close the eyes of each victim, to send them to peaceful sleep before they burned away to wind and ash. It slowed the process, and the Sturmbannführer saw it. He raised his arm, holding his pistol, and beat Emil. Emil didn't raise his arm to shield himself. He took the blows. His nose burst with blood. His cheek cracked.

Then his perspective shifted. He switched places. Emil became his attacker, and he looked down on the poor little Jew cowering in the ash and bodies and felt disgusted. He drew his dagger and sliced him down the side, just enough to hurt him so he'll suffer as he works.

* * *

As the evening set, someone shattered his front window, disturbing Emil from sleep. He yelled in German and reached for a pistol at his waist—an old instinct, one he'd buried. He found his cane and rubbed the ivory elephant top, ready to strike the burglar. A stubby hand reached through the broken window and unlocked the front door.

"Herr Goldman," said a humble voice. The man wore a raincoat, even though he was so small that he was probably the last to feel the rain drops. A few gray threads still clung to his bald head, growing out from under a yarmulke. "It is Ezra. I left you a note. I am sorry to take these measures. But I must speak with you."

Emil kept behind the chair, hiding his face. "You have no right."

"I only need to speak to you for a few minutes. I must know about my wife."

"Go away. I'm going to call the police!" Emil heard the man tap the floor as he walked. He lifted his head over the back of the chair and spotted his intruder. He tapped a slender cane on the ground, helping him to see. Sunglasses shielded his eyes, and he tapped the bench under the piano, the back of the couch, finding a route through the parlor. Emil sighed, easing back into the chair. The blind man couldn't recognize him; he wouldn't know his guilty past.

"You are the only one living who can help me," Ezra said. "I must know about my wife."

"I cannot help you. I cannot help anyone. I did what I had to do to survive."

His visitor sighed. "I have forgotten her face, but I have a picture. I know what you did."

Emil gripped his cane and raised it into the air, ready to strike. He prayed it wouldn't be necessary, hoping that the man would just leave him to his peace. Everyone deserved peace at the end of their lives. "And I forgive you as I long to be forgiven."

"Why so?"

"Do you not remember me? We slaved at the ovens together. I was Sonderkommando too. We were friends. We survived together. You told me about your family in Krakow. You told me everything of your life, trying to hold onto it. We helped each other guard our souls."

"Ja. Of course." Emil lied.

Then Ezra wept from beneath his sunglasses, letting go his cane. "And I betrayed you. I seek your forgiveness. That monster. Sturmbannführer Goldschmidt. He made me tell him everything you told me. That night. He kept me awake, and I so longed to sleep, to see my wife in the women's barracks. The butchers cleared her barracks that night. You must tell me. I must know. Did you see this face? Did you burn her?" He slipped out a grainy monochromatic photo and held it into the air, facing the wrong direction. Emil paused, pretending to study the visage.

"There were so many faces. They melted together. I cannot remember." His visitor hunched his shoulders. His soul drained out of him. "I wish I could help you," Emil said.

"Your voice is . . . different."

"I have gotten older."

"Your accent, too. It is mostly American now, but you sound like you're from Hamburg. I studied architecture there."

"I was born in Krakow."

Ezra rubbed his chin and considered. Emil's heart raced, and his stomach pulsed, trying to throw back the tea. His arm shook, and he brought the cane down on Ezra's head, cracking his skull. Ezra yelped, mostly out of surprise and collapsed to the hardwood floor. Emil beat him, hammering his skull with the elephant's head until the pulped mass drained blood on the round carpet. All the while in the background, the butcher laughed.

* * *

Emil washed the blood from his face, scrubbing it off his forehead and cheeks, tasting a little of the salty fluid. Then he returned to the parlor, picked up his dishes then carried them to the sink. He set them with the other dirty plates and cups, planning to leave it for his cleaning woman. She'd be in the next morning, and he had to do something about Ezra's body.

His spirit had numbed. The world ran like a movie, unreal, sans consequence. No one had died in his mind. He'd dreamed it. He wasn't even Emil any longer, and at times his perspective left his body entirely, floating above it all. Time collapsed and spilled, merging together, and he moved from the parlor to the oven rooms of Treblinka then to the kitchen, passing between the divisions of present and past. To calm his mind, he took two more sleeping pills, but the soporific effect failed and churned his stomach with nausea. He slipped the bottle into his robe pocket.

"This can all end," the Sturmbannführer said, standing over Emil as he stood over the body.

"I have to hide this before tomorrow."

"There is loose dirt in the cellar. Easily dug. No one will miss the old Jew."

"Nein! I cannot."

"All this will end. Your heart beats in the cellar. You buried it in the dark, your old secrets. Don't you remember? Just a few steps and you'll have peace."

Emil wrapped the body in the rug, kneeling down on his bad leg so he wouldn't fall. The cellar was the only place he could hide the body in time. He had no choice. So Emil got up, went to the cellar door and turned the knob. Stale air floated up from the tomb, and he choked on the mildew stench. The mold had brewed down here for years, growing into the foundations, poisoning the ground and the house of his marriage.

"Just a few more steps," the Sturmbannführer said. "I am here to bring you home. Do you remember how I killed the Jew?"

"It is coming back to me," Emil said. "The Red Army poured into the country. Himmler closed the camps and marched the prisoners, the survivors, those who had held on. You took him to the side of the road and recited everything about his life. His eyes glared with fear. You knew everything."

"And then I tried to shoot him, but my pistol jammed."

He stepped into the darkness. Faint light bled in from filthy windows, seeping in from the sallow lamps lining Walnut Street. He broke through viscous cobwebs and filth, running his fingers down the dirt coating on the wall.

"There," the Sturmbannführer said. "Dig there."

He found loose dirt and dug with his hands, pulling out chunks of cement, wood, brick and soil. His fingers ached and bled from scratches, and he dug nearly a foot, piling the dirt in his lap. His head ached, and he swallowed down the rest of his wife's sleeping pills, not noticing how many landed in his mouth. They stuck in his dry throat, and he choked. His fingers continued and hit a box. He yanked it out of the soil. Electrical current surged through his hands into his chest. His head spun.

"I buried this on the day we moved in?"

The Sturmbannführer nodded. "And forgot. It was the best way to hide. You murdered with this then stole his soul." He opened the box and pulled out his SS ceremonial dagger and scabbard wrapped in a cloth. He pulled it from the scabbard and released the blade. Pleasure poured through his chest as he held his dagger, his honor found again and restored. He found the memories—faint and distant like the recollections of early childhood that adults often doubted, attributing to some dream. He remembered escaping, taking Emil Goldman's identity, even having the tattoo of the SS blood group burned off his body, leaving the scar. He'd found a wife soon after and married, a Jewish woman from the Ukraine. And he worked to forget, making a new life, burying it all, but he could never bury this. He saved it for the day when the world realized its mistake, when the SS would be honored again in history.

The pills set fast to work, and he laid his head on the loose soil to sleep and slept peaceful.

About the Authors and Artists

Jodi Abraham is an artist and therapist. She is called a healer and is heavy handed. She enjoys avant-garde art, old book, and her exquisite journey. She currently resides in New England with her family and menagerie of animals.

Shawna L. Bernard is a freelance writer, photographer, graphic artist, former English teacher, editor, and native of the North Shore. Her poetry, prose, and photography has been featured in *Merrimack Valley Magazine, Sex, Drugs & Horror, Barnyard Horror,* local art exhibits, and on bar napkins across the country. She is currently editing the anthology *Ugly Babies* along with the second volume of *Cellar Door*. Shawna's darkest fiction and horror is written under the guise of her literary double, Sydney Leigh. Sydney's stories and poetry have appeared in *Daily Bites of Flesh 2011: 365 Days of Horrifying Flash Fiction, Dark Idol, Sex, Drugs & Horror,* and *Serial Killers Tres Tria*. Her poem "The Undertaker's Melancholy" will appear in Villipede Publication's October *Darkness ad Infinitum* anthology. Other work is scheduled for publication later this year in *Splatterpunk Saints, Bones,* and *Delicious Malicious*.

Aaron Besson is a writer of horror and dark fantasy from Seattle. His writing has been published in the *Weird Fiction Review* from Centipede Press and *Spinetinglers*.

Rose Blackthorn lives in the high mountain desert of Eastern Utah with her boyfriend and two dogs. She spends her time writing, reading, beading and doing wire-work, and photographing the surrounding wilderness. An only child, she was lucky enough to have a mother who loved books, and has been surrounded by them her entire life. Thus instead of squabbling with siblings, she learned to be friends with her imagination and the voices in her head are still very much present. She is a member of the HWA and has published genre fiction online and in print with Necon E-Books, Stupefying Stories, Cast of Wonders, Dark Moon Digest, Buzzy Mag and the anthologies *The Ghost IS the Machine, A Quick Bite of Flesh, Fear the Abyss, From Beyond the Grave, Horrific History, Barnyard Horror, Eulogies II: Tales from the Cellar, Shifters and Another 100 Horrors,* among others.

Larissa Blaze loves to write poetry. Her poem "A Father's Plea" is in the *Serial Killer Tres Tria* anthology. She loves to dissect the psychology and dynamics behind human depravity, lust and violence. Her other interests are photography and travelling. She has visited the Philippines several times, and recently explored some remarkable cities in Europe—Rome, Florence, Venice and Paris. She is busy juggling her life as a wife, mother of three, and as a full time registered nurse working the grave yard shift. She currently lives in Saint Augustine, Florida.

Max Booth III is the editor-in-chief of Perpetual Motion Machine Publishing, the assistant editor of *Dark Moon Digest,* and the fiction editor of Kraken Press. His two story collections, *True Stories Told By a Liar* and *They Might Be Demons,* are currently available, and his debut novel, *Toxicity,* will be released by Post Mortem Press in Spring 2014. You can follow him on Twitter @GiveMeYourTeeth and visit him at www.TalesFromTheBooth.com.

Sally Bosco (SallyBosco.com) writes dark fiction. She is inexplicably drawn to the Uncanny, the shades of gray between the light and dark, the area where your mind hovers as you're falling off to sleep. Her published novels include *Death Divided, Death Undone* (written with Lynn Hansen), *The Werecat Chronicles,* and *Shadow Cat* (written as Zoe LaPage). She contributed a chapter on writers' craft to *Many Genres, One Craft.* She's had short stories published in literary magazines and anthologies, including the *Small Bites* and *Hazard Yet Forward* anthologies, and she has an MFA degree in Writing Popular

Fiction from Seton Hill University. Sally lives in Florida with two of the most spoiled cats on the planet, Shadow and Hazel.

Guy Burtenshaw lives in a small town in southern England and has been writing horror stories for many years. He has self-published several horror novels and has had short stories published in various magazines and anthologies. He also writes murder mystery novels under the pseudonym G D Shaw.

Tracy L. Carbone resides in Massachusetts with her daughter and a house full of pets. She writes fiction in her spare time, setting most of her work in the fictional New England town of Bradfield. She's published four novels and one collection of horror short stories. Her short stories have also been published in the U.S. and Canada in various anthologies and magazines. Please visit her Amazon author page or her personal site at www.tracylcarbone.com.

Jeff C. Carter lives in Venice, CA with two cats, a dog, and a human. His short stories appear in the anthologies TALES FROM THE BELL CLUB, SHORT SIPS 2, SCIENCE GONE MAD, AVENIR ECLECTIA VOL 1, FRIGHTMARES and SONG STORIES: BLAZE OF GLORY as well as issues of Trembles, Calliope and eFantasy magazine. He is currently developing MECHAWEST, a steam punk RPG for Heroic Journey Publishing. Visit him at Jeffccarter.wordpress.com.

Originally from just south of the Thames in London, **Simon Critchell's** life journey has taken him through Europe, deepest darkest Africa, and all the way across the globe to Australia. Along the way, he has experienced a broad spectrum of what life has to offer—the grit, diversity and culture of London, the beauty and brutality of the Congo, the paradise of the South Pacific, and the wonder that is Australia. There have been brushes with murder, suicide, mobs and the darker side of human nature. Throughout the journey he has developed a morbid curiosity about some of the bad people that walk on this planet. Having had a strong creative side since a very young age, Simon developed skills in graphic design and has worked in that field for many years. He is also a professional photographer and combines these disciplines to create artwork for corporate clients, rock stars and writers. In more recent times Simon has discovered a love for writing, and in particular writing horror. The combination of the morbid curiosity, a very visual mind and a well-developed imagination has resulted in a number of very dark and twisted short stories being published. Simon is also the co-author of *21:24*, a brutal horror novel to be published soon.

Residing in North-Western Ontario with his wonderful wife and four kids, **Dave Dormer** spends most of his time outdoors either fishing, camping, or hunting. In one form or another, he's been a horror/ fantasy enthusiast since grade school.

T. Fox Dunham resides outside of Philadelphia PA—author and historian. He's published in nearly 200 international journals and anthologies. His first novel, The Street Martyr will be published by Out of the Gutter Books, followed up by Searching for Andy Kaufman from PMMP in 2014. He's a cancer survivor. His friends call him fox, being his totem animal, and his motto is: Wrecking civilization one story at a time.
Site: www.tfoxdunham.com.
Blog:http://tfoxdunham.blogspot.com/. http://www.facebook.co m/tfoxdunham & Twitter: @TFoxDunham

The art and poetry of **Morgan Griffith** saw publication during the '80s and early '90s in such magazines as *Eldritch Tales, Fantasy Macabre*, and *Grue*. She is revisiting the dark fantasy genre with fiction and currently lives in central Florida with three pet rats.

Aaron Gudmunson lives and writes in the Chicagoland area. He has worked as a contributing writer and columnist for local and regional media. His work has been published in numerous markets. *From the Dusklands,* Aaron's first collection of dark fiction, was released on May 7, 2013 and his debut novel *Snow*

Globe is due out February 2014. Visit Aaron on the web at http://www.aarongudmunson.com/.

Erik Gustafson holds master's degree in psychology and is a veteran of the United States Air Force. He is the author of two novels and many short stories. His first novel "Fall Leaves and the Black Dragon" is self-published and his second novel is out seeking a publisher. His has also been previously published in *The Horror Zine, Death Throes Ezone* and by Visionary Press, The Horror Society, and other anthologies. He is currently working on his third novel "The Carousel in the Sky." To learn more, please visit his blog at www.erikgustafson.wordpress.com

C.L. Hesser studied at the University of West Georgia with a major in English and a minor in Psychology.

Justin Hunter is an emerging author and freelance writer. He writes primarily on the human condition, wrestling with idealism and dignity in poverty. Sometimes he writes a bit of horror, but it keeps him up at night. He is an early childhood educator, husband and adoptive father of two beautiful boys.

Mathias Jansson is a Swedish art critic and poet. He has been published in *The Horror Zine Magazine, Dark Eclipse, Schlock, The Sirens Call* and *The Poetry Box*. He has also contributed to several anthologies from Horrified Press and James Ward Kirk Fiction such as *Suffer Eternal Anthology Volume 1-3, Hell Whore Anthology Volume 1-3, Barnyard Horror* and *Serial Killers Tres Tria*. Homepage: http://mathiasjansson72.blogspot.se/

Tom Johnstone lives in Brighton and Hove, where he works as a gardener for the local council. This experience sometimes appears in his fiction, such as in his contribution to the award-winning Wild Wolf Publications anthology *Holiday of the Dead*. Other stories have nothing to do with it, such as his tale that appeared in the *9th Black Book of Horror* (Mortbury Press), and his mock EC comics parody script for *Brighton - The Graphic Novel,* published this October by Queen Spark Books The author would like to thank his eleven year old daughter Katya for inspiring this tale when she mentioned the macabre Aztec musical instruments she heard about on the BBC TV show *Horrible Histories*.

K. Trap Jones is a writer of horror novels and short stories that appear in numerous anthologies. With a sadistic inspiration from Dante Alighieri and Edgar Allan Poe, his temptation towards folklore, classic literary works and obscure segments within society lead to his demented writing style of "filling in the gaps" and walking the jagged line between reality and fiction. His novel THE SINNER (Blood Bound Books, 2012) won the Royal Palm Literary Award. He is also a member of the Horror Writer's Association.

Vada Katherine lives in Indiana with her dog, Teddy. She has multiple short story publications. She is looking for peace.

Colleen Keough is a Transmedia artist working in video, performance, sound, installation, mixed media, and hybrid art forms. Her work explores the intersection of pop culture, identity, myth and technology through narratives and anti-narratives which deconstruct traditional modes of storytelling and performance. She earned an MFA in Electronic Integrated Arts from NYSCC Alfred University and is currently a Visiting Assistant Professor of Trans-Disciplinary Art at Ohio University in Athens, OH. Her works have been exhibited throughout North America, Europe and Asia.

Thomas Kleaton grew up in Crescent City, California, and is of German and English descent. His stories have appeared in *Death Throes Webzine, SNM Horror Magazine, Sirens Call Magazine,* and the anthology *Serial Killers Tres Tria*. He is married and currently lives near Auburn University, Alabama. Find him on Facebook as Thomas Kleaton Author.

Lisamarie Lamb loves to write horror but dabbles in various genres, including mystery and children's stories. She's written and published a horror novel called *Mother's Helper* as well as *Some Body's At The Door*, a collection of short stories. She also recently completed her second novel, *At Peace With All Things*, and is writing the second draft of her third, *Perfect Murder*. Dark Hall Press has published another collection of her short stories, entitled *Over the Bridge*. Her work can be found online at http://www.themoonlitdoor.blogspot.com and within many anthologies, including books from Angelic Knight Press, Cruentus Libri Press, and Sirens Call Publications. Lisamarie has also edited a collection of short stories called *A Roof Over Their Heads* set on and around the Isle of Sheppey, Kent, where she resides in the United Kingdom.

Lisa Landreth lives in Fayetteville, North Carolina where she works as a school librarian. When she's not shuffling among the bookshelves or glued to her computer screen, she spends her time exercising, playing the violin, or taking care of her cat, Morris. This is her first publication but she looks forward to publishing many more stories of mind-bending horror.

Esther Leiper-Estabrooks has been selling fiction, poetry, and other prose since college—many years back! —and each piece is a challenge and an adventure. She feels compelled to wow herself before an editor sees a piece, (and succeeded in doing that with this one). She wrote a regular column for Writers' Journal for thirty years and now is writing a column for the e-magazine, *Extra Innings*.

Kerry G.S. Lipp teaches English at a community college by evening and writes horrible things by night. He hates the sun. His parents started reading his stories and now he's out of the will. Kerry's work appears in several anthologies, including *DOA2* from Blood Bound Books and *The Best of Cruentus Libri Press* from CLP. He has stories in several more forthcoming anthologies. His story "Smoke" was adapted for podcast via The Wicked Library episode 213, and pioneered TWL's inaugural explicit content warning. KGSL blogs weekly at www.HorrorTree.com and will launch his own website www.newworldhorror.com sometime in 2013. Say hi on Twitter @kerrylipp or on his Facebook page, New World Horror – Kerry G.S. Lipp.

Ken MacGregor's work has appeared in anthologies from Siren's Call Publications, Hazardous Press, Bloodbound Books, and others. Ken is a member in good standing of The Great Lakes Association of Horror Writers. Ken will reread something he wrote and shudder in revulsion and/or glee. He lives in Michigan.

Greg McWhorter is a pop-culture historian and teacher who resides in Southern California. Since the 1980s, he has worked for newspapers, radio, television, and film. He has been a guest speaker at several universities and the San Diego Comic-Con. Today, McWhorter owns a highly acclaimed record label that specializes in vintage punk rock. He is also the host of a cable TV show titled Rock 'n' Roll High School 101. Since 1985, McWhorter has been writing nonfiction music-related articles for print and has recently turned to writing crime and horror fiction. McWhorter's stories have appeared in several anthologies and magazines. Follow him at http://gregmcwhorter.blogspot.com.

Beth Murphy is the editor's imaginary roommate and paints to get the twisted things out of her head. She is always searching for new adventures (when they're not finding her, that is) and packs way too many shoes for her road trips. You can find her burying bodies in her garden or looking for more dogs to adopt...and when she wins the lottery, she'll adopt them all.

Theresa C. Newbill is an avid reader and lover of poetry. She is also a psychic medium and can be found giving tarot card readings along with other forms of divination. She has been published by Hedge-Witchery Books and has appeared in a number of various publications.

Todd Nelsen's literary and film interests include horror, fantasy, and science fiction. He cites Stephen King, Robert E. Howard, and Hermann Hesse as influences. He is an avid fan of metal music and currently resides in Denver, Colorado, where he writes, reads, and is constantly fantasizing. His short fiction has been featured in numerous publications, including the anthologies *Schlock! The Pulpateers* and *Just One More Step*.

Gregory L. Norris is a full-time professional writer, with work published in numerous fiction anthologies and national magazines. He once worked as a screenwriter on two episodes of Paramount's modern classic STAR TREK: VOYAGER and is a former feature writer and columnist at Sci Fi, the official magazine of the Sci Fi Channel (before all those ridiculous Ys invaded). He is the author of the handbook to all-things-Sunnydale, THE Q GUIDE TO BUFFY THE VAMPIRE SLAYER, the recent THE FIERCE AND UNFORGIVING MUSE: TWENTY-SIX TALES FROM THE TERRIFYING MIND OF GREGORY L. NORRIS (Evil Jester Press), and many paranormal romance novels, two of which were republished as special editions by Home Shopping Network in late 2009 as part of their 'Escape with Romance' line -- the first time HSN has offered novels to their global customer base. Norris judged the 2012 Lambda Awards in the Science Fiction/Fantasy/Horror category. Visit him on Facebook and online at www.gregorylnorris.blogspot.com.

David North-Martino's stories have appeared in numerous fiction venues, including *Epitaphs: The Journal of the New England Horror Writers*, *From Beyond the Grave*, *Daughters of Icarus*, and *Dark Recesses Press*. He is also hard at work on his first novel. A graduate of the University of Massachusetts, he holds a BLA in English and Psychology. When he's not writing, David enjoys studying and teaching martial arts. He lives with his very supportive wife in a small town in Massachusetts.

Melissa Osburn lives in Michigan where she spends her time writing, reading, and crocheting. She also blogs, where she writes about inspiration, discusses fairytales and folklore, and whatever else interests her or pops into her head. Her blog, Dreaming Blithely can be found at http://melissasosburn.wordpress.com.

David S. Pointer has recent acceptances for *Ugly Babies, Bones, Twist of Fate* (a charity anthology), and *The Southern Poetry Series Anthologies* for the states of Georgia and Tennessee.

Michael Randolph is a horror author and poet currently residing in San Antonio Texas. When not crafting new horrific stories and poetry, he works in aviation and facets gemstones. His work has appeared in the *Barnyard Horror* and *Sex, Drugs & Horror* anthologies by James Ward Kirk Fiction, as well as Burial Day Books and *Dark Eclipse Magazine*. His poetry collection, *Missives in Red,* was published by Dark Moon Press and is slated to be released in the near future.

Tina Rath lives in London with her husband and several cats. She has been writing dark fantasy for many years and has a number of stories published in both genre and mainstream press. Her collection *A Chimaera in My Wardrobe* is available from Amazon and other sites in both digital and print versions. She works – when she can – as an actress and model, and she is also a vampire expert and can be seen in a variety of documentaries talking about the fanged folk. For further information see: www.academicvampire.com.uk.

Robert J. Santa has been writing speculative fiction for almost thirty years. His short works have appeared in numerous print and online markets. He lives in Rhode Island, USA, with his beautiful wife and two equally beautiful daughters. Robert is the editor-in-chief of Ricasso Press.

Never judge a book by its cover. **Ashley Scarlet** likes to keep things dark and mysterious, yet the other side of her feels compelled to bring out the naive child-like beauty in her art. Growing up in the Midwest, Scarlet broke the rules of Society and hides inside a house made of candy, painting to her macabre delight.

J. T. Seate writes everything from humor to erotic to the macabre, and is especially keen on transcending genre pigeonholing. Over two hundred stories appear in magazines, anthologies and webzines. See longer works at www.melange-books.com and www.museituppublishing.com for those who like tales intertwined with the paranormal. Homepage: www.troyseateauthor.webs.com. You can also find him on Amazon and B&N books.

Natalie Sirois is a North Andover native who just happens to take magnificent photographs. Hers were the first official submissions for Cellar Door, and are featured on the anthology's official Facebook page. She's also a little crazy... just like the rest of us.

John Stanton is a writer/photographic artist living in Indianapolis, Indiana. For the past eight years, John has provided hundreds of images to the small press, electronic and print editions as well as book covers, earning Top Ten Finisher in the annual Predator and Editor polls, as well as three mentions in Ellen Datlow's "Best of" collections. His "Subtractive Illusion" is featured on Corel.com, along with an interview. Currently, his artwork can be seen in *Not One of Us Issue #49*, the *Indiana Horror 2012* and *Indiana Crime 2013* anthologies, as well as www.3AMBlue.com and http://johndstanton.blogspot.com/.

26-year-old **J. Daniel Stone** writes from New York City where he was born and raised. It is a place that has yet to cease to inspire him. He does not eat meat, absorbs as much art and science as he can and has been a reader way before he was ever a writer. He sold his first short story when he was twenty-two and since then has sold stories to some cool places like Prime Books, Blood Bound Books, Grey Matter Press, Icarus: The Magazine of Gay Speculative Fiction and more. His first novel, *The Absence of Light,* was published by Villipede Publications. His story "The Virtuoso" was originally titled Basement Story and appeared in Monster Notes© 2012)

Tais Teng works as a writer, cover artist, illustrator and sculptor. He also paints murals and decors for theater.

Tony Thorne MBE is an Englishman, born and technically educated in London, England, as a Chartered Design Engineer. He lives in Austria in summer and the Canary Island of Tenerife in winter. Earlier in life he wrote science-fiction and humorous stories, was an active SF Fan, and a spare time lecturer for the British Interplanetary Society. For developments in the field of low temperature (cryo)surgery instruments, and very high temperature processing furnaces for carbon fibre, the Queen awarded him an MBE. He is now an author of quirky speculative fiction, mostly tall Science Fiction and Macabre tales, with over 100 short stories published in many magazines, various collections, and anthologies. His first novel, POINTS OF VIEW, was published in 2012 by Eternal Press, Santa Rosa, CA. Much more information is listed on his website: www.tonythorne.com. A Spanish language version of "Natural Selection" appears in the short collection TENERIFFA CUENTOS ESPECULATAVOS and in English in TENERIFE TALL TALES Volume 1.

Carmen Tudor writes from Melbourne, Australia. Her interests include the lives and works of Chopin and Liszt, children's literacy, and animal rights. Info on her short story publications can be found at carmentudor.net. Recent speculative fiction credits include *Nightfall Magazine, Lissette's Tales of the Imagination*, and *Spirited: 13 Haunting Tales* anthology.

Matthew Wilson, 30, is a UK resident who has been writing since he was small. Recently his stories have appeared in The *Horror Zine, Star*Line,* and *Sorcerers Signal*. He is currently editing his first novel and can be contacted on twitter @matthew94544267.

Stephanie M. Wytovich is an Alum of Seton Hill University where she was a double major in English Literature and Art History. Wytovich is published in over 40 literary magazines and HYSTERIA is her first collection. She is currently attending graduate school to pursue her MFA in Writing Popular Fiction, and is working on a novel. She is the Poetry Editor for Raw Dog Screaming Press and a book reviewer for S.T. Joshi, Jason V. Brock and William F. Nolan's *Nameless Magazine*. She plans to continue in academia to get her doctorate in Gothic Literature.

Made in the USA
San Bernardino, CA
02 February 2014